SECRETS OF THE DEAD

SECRETS OF THE DEAD

Tom Harper

WINDSOR
PARAGON

First published 2011
by Arrow Books
This Large Print edition published 2012
by AudioGO Ltd
by arrangement with
The Random House Group Ltd

Hardcover   ISBN: 978 1 445 87818 8
Softcover   ISBN: 978 1 445 87819 5

British Library Cataloguing in Publication Data available

Printed and bound in Great Britain by
MPG Books Group Limited

Every man seeks peace by waging war,
but no man seeks war by making peace.

– St Augustine, *City of God*

The dead keep their secrets, and in a little
while we shall be as wise as they.

– Alexander Smith

I

Pristina, Kosovo—Present Day

Escaping work on a Friday afternoon was still a luxury Abby hadn't got used to.

For ten years, work had been long days in the dark places of the Earth, listening to shattered people relive brutality on an unimaginable scale. Then evenings at a laptop in rooms converted from shipping containers, freezing or baking with the seasons, wringing all the blood and tears out of the stories until they became dry pieces of paper that would make presentable evidence for the International Court in The Hague. She never escaped. She'd lost count of the nightmares, the times she'd found herself kneeling over the chemical toilet deep in the night, desperate to purge the things she'd seen. Among the casualties over the years had been several promising relationships, a marriage, and finally her ability to care. But always, next morning, straight back to work.

Now all that was history. She'd transferred to the EU mission in Kosovo—EULEX—teaching the Kosovars how to be model European citizens. There had been war crimes in Kosovo, true, but they were someone else's problem. She worked with the civil courts, trying to unwind the tangled questions of who owned what after the war. *The Lost Property Office*, Michael called it. She didn't mind being teased. She could sleep at night.

She folded up her files and locked them away. She cleared her desk for the cleaners to come in over the weekend. *Shut down, turn off, leave behind.* Just before she killed her computer, she noticed a new e-mail had come in from the Director. She ignored it—another luxury. She could deal with it on Monday. It was 2 p.m. on Friday and her week was over.

Michael's car was waiting for her outside the office. A red Porsche convertible, vintage 1968, probably the only one in the Balkans. Top off, despite the thunder clouds massing over the city. Michael revved the engine as she stepped out the door, a full-throated roar that would have made her wince with embarrassment if she wasn't so happy. Typical Michael. She slipped into the passenger seat and kissed him, feeling his salt-and-pepper stubble graze her cheek. A couple of people coming out of the office stopped to stare, and she wondered if they were looking at the car or at her. Michael was twenty years her senior and looked it, though age suited him. There were lines on his face, but they only accentuated what was good about it: the ready smile, the devil-may-care gleam in his eye, the confidence and strength. When his hair started greying he didn't cut it, just added a gold earring. So as not to look too respectable, he said. Abby teased him that it made him look like a pirate.

He cupped her chin and turned her head so he could see her throat. 'You're wearing the necklace.'

He sounded pleased. He'd given it to her a week ago, an intricate golden labyrinth studded with five red glass beads. In the centre was a monogram, a form of the early Christian X-P symbol though she'd never known Michael be religious. The necklace itself felt ancient. The gold was dark and

2

glossy like honey, the red glass misted with time. When she asked Michael where he got it, he just gave a crooked smile and told her a Gypsy gave it to him.

From the corner of her eye, she noticed her black overnight bag lying on the Porsche's back seat, next to his briefcase.

'Are we going somewhere?'

'Kotor Bay. Montenegro.'

She made a face. 'That's six hours away.'

'Not if I can help it.' He pulled out of the parking lot, past the security guard in his blue blazer and baseball cap. The man gave the car an admiring stare and threw them a salute. Among the drab rows of EU-issue sedans, the Porsche stood out like some kind of endangered species.

Driving one-handed, Michael reached down and pulled a hipflask from beside the handbrake. His hand brushed her thigh where her sundress had ridden up. He took a swig, then handed it to her.

'I promise it'll be worth it.'

*　　　*　　　*

And maybe he was right. That was the thing with Michael: however wild his idea, you always wanted to believe him. As soon as they'd escaped Pristina's gridlock, weaving in and out of the traffic in ways even the locals—comfortably the worst drivers in Europe—wouldn't have dared, he punched the accelerator and gave the car its head. Abby snuggled into her seat and watched the miles fly by. Roof down, they raced ahead of the wind, outrunning the storm that always threatened but never touched them. Across the Kosovo plain and up into the foothills, towards the mountains that squeezed the setting sun against the sky until it bled crimson. At the Montenegrin border a few words from Michael sped them past the customs officials.

Now they were deep in the mountains. Cold air eddied around them; above, even August hadn't dislodged snow from the peaks. Michael kept the roof down, but turned the heat on full blast. Abby found a blanket in the footwell and pulled it over her.

And suddenly there it was. The road bent around through a rocky defile and emerged high above the bay, sunk in shadows between the mountains. All Abby could see were the lights of pleasure yachts and motorcruisers, clustered around the coves and beaches that fringed it like luminous algae.

Michael slowed, then veered left. Abby gasped: it looked as if he was driving off the edge of the cliff. But there was a track, unpaved, that ended at an iron gate in a stucco wall. Michael rummaged in the glove compartment for a remote control. The gate slid open.

Abby raised her eyebrows. 'Do you come here often?'

'First time.'

Through the open gate, Abby could see the flat roof of a house, ghostly white in the gathering darkness. It stood on a promontory halfway down the slope—about the only place you could put a house on this side of the bay. Across the water, Abby could see the bright glow of a town, and its outer suburbs strung all across the opposite hill. On this side, there was nothing.

Michael stopped the car on a strip of gravel outside the house. He pulled an unfamiliar key out

4

of his pocket and unlocked the fat oak door.

'After you.'

Nothing in the villa's plain exterior had prepared her for what was inside. Working in Pristina on an expat EU salary, Abby was used to living comfortably, but this was luxury on a whole other level. The floors were marble: green and pink slabs forming intricate geometric patterns. Everything seemed to have been built for a race of giants: chairs and sofas deep enough to lose yourself in, a mahogany dining table that could have seated twenty people, and the biggest television she'd ever seen hanging on the wall. Opposite, almost as big, three Orthodox saints stared out of the gold of a triple-panelled icon.

'How much did this cost you?'

'Not a penny. It belongs to an Italian judge, a friend. He's letting me borrow it for the weekend.'

'Are we expecting anyone else?'

Michael grinned. 'Got it all to ourselves.'

She pointed to the briefcase he'd carried in. 'I hope you weren't planning on getting any work done.'

'Wait until you see the pool.'

He pulled open the glass door. Abby stepped through and gasped. Behind the villa, the pool terrace stretched right to the cliff edge. A mock-classical colonnade framed three sides: fluted columns and Corinthian capitals that didn't really fit with the rest of the modern architecture. The fourth side was the cliff, with the bay far below. In the twilight, the pool seemed to flow straight into the sea. There was no rail.

Abby heard a soft click behind her as Michael touched a switch. Recessed lights in the pool made the water glow. When Abby peered in, she saw an undersea world of nymphs and dolphins, mermaids and starfish, a seaweed-haired god in a chariot drawn by four sea horses—all picked out in a dappled black-and-white mosaic. Fine traces of light shimmered across it, so that the monochrome figures seemed to dance underwater.

More lights had come on behind the colonnade. Each alcove held a marble statue on a marble plinth: Hercules, draped in a lionskin and leaning on his club; a bare-breasted Aphrodite clutching a robe that had somehow slipped below her hips; Medea, a coil of serpents fizzing from her hair. They looked solid, but when Abby touched one she felt it tremble on its base as if a gust of wind could blow it off. She flinched.

'Careful,' said Michael. 'They're not making any more of those.'

Abby laughed. 'They can't be original.'

'Every one, so I'm told.'

Dazed, Abby wandered on past the silent figures. She came to the end of the terrace and looked down. The cliff was so steep that even there she couldn't see its base: only a froth of silver foam on the water drifting off the rocks. She shivered. The flimsy sundress wasn't nearly enough this late in August.

She heard a bang behind her; something flew past her face, almost touching her cheek. For that instant, she was back in Freetown, or Mogadishu or Kinshasa. She gave a low scream and spun around, almost losing her balance on the unprotected cliff edge. She grabbed on to the nearest column, hugging it for dear life.

'Are you OK?'

Michael was standing beside the pool with two champagne flutes in one hand, an uncorked bottle of Pol Roger in the other.

'Didn't mean to scare you. I thought we could celebrate.'

Celebrate what? Abby leaned back against the column and clung on, her heart still pounding. The night breeze blew the gold necklace against her throat and a mad thought struck her. *Was he going to propose?*

Michael poured the champagne and pressed a glass into her trembling hand. It slopped over the rim and dribbled down her fingers. He put his arm around her shoulders and drew her to him. Abby sipped her drink; Michael stared out to sea as if looking for something. The last crack of sunlight made a rim on the horizon, then vanished.

'I'm hungry.'

*   *   *

Michael fetched a cool-bag from the car, and soon the house was filled with the smells of frying garlic, prawns and herbs. Abby drank and watched him cook. The champagne didn't last long. A bottle of Sancerre appeared from the cool-bag, and that quickly went down, too. Abby found a switch to turn on the terrace heaters, and they ate outside by the pool. She dangled her bare legs in the water, while light rippled off the colonnades and stars pricked the sky.

The food and drink began to unwind her. When the evening cooled, Michael lit the fire in the living room, and they sat on the sofa watching the stars over the bay. Abby curled up like a kitten with her head on his lap, eyes half-closed as he stroked her hair. *You're thirty-two*, a small voice chided her, *not seventeen*. She didn't care; she liked it. With Michael, she had no responsibilities. He made life easy.

Much later—after the second bottle of wine had emptied, after the town across the bay had gone dark and the fire had died to embers—Abby pulled herself off the sofa. She swayed; Michael rose and held her, surprisingly steady considering how much he'd drunk.

She wrapped her arms around him and kissed his neck.

'Shall we go to bed?' She was drunk, she knew, and it felt good. She wanted him. She began fumbling with the buttons on his shirt, but he ducked out from under her embrace and spun her around.

'You're insatiable,' he scolded her.

He steered her to the bedroom and unclasped the necklace, then eased her down on to the bed. Abby tried to pull him on top of her, but he stepped back.

'Where are you going?'

'I'm not tired.'

'I'm not tired either,' she protested. But it was a lie. By the time he'd kissed her goodnight and closed the door, she was asleep.

*   *   *

The cold woke her. Lying on top of the sheets, still in her sundress, she could feel an air-conditioned chill blowing across her skin. She rolled over, looking for Michael's warmth, but didn't feel him.

8

She groped her way across the wide bed until she touched the far bedside table.

The bed was empty.

She lay there a moment, trying to get her bearings in the unfamiliar room. She looked for light, but saw nothing. All she could hear was the hum of the air conditioner and the tick of the bedside clock. Its luminous hands showed 3.45 a.m.

And then something else—a murmuring voice. She listened, trying to grasp the sounds of a strange house. Was it two voices—some kind of conversation? Or maybe it was just the waves breaking on the rocks.

It's the television. Michael must have fallen asleep watching it. Now that her eyes had adjusted, she could see a dim blue light flickering in from the hallway.

Still sluggish from sleep and alcohol, she wondered what to do. Part of her said she should leave him there, let him wake up stiff and alone. But the bed was cold.

She got up. Barefoot, she padded down the hall to the living room. The enormous television played on the wall, filling the room with its diode-blue glow; half a dozen cigarette butts lay stubbed out in a silver ashtray. The leather sofa bore a deep impression where Michael must have been lying.

He wasn't there now. And the television was muted.

So what did I hear?

A gust of air blew in the smell of the night: jasmine and fig and chlorine. Out in the courtyard, the lights were still on. The door stood open. Through it, she could see Michael standing by the pool smoking another cigarette. The briefcase that

9

had been in the car sat on a metal table beside him, the lid raised. A man in a white shirt and black trousers was examining the contents.

Abby stepped out into the courtyard, still unsteady from the alcohol in her system. Just over the threshold, her bare foot kicked against something unseen in the shadows. She yelped with pain and surprise. The empty champagne bottle rolled across the paving and dropped in the pool with a splash.

Two heads snapped up and stared at her.

'Am I interrupting something?'

'Go back inside!' Michael shouted.

He sounded desperate, but she still didn't get it. She took two steps forward, into the glow of the pool light. Offering herself up. The man in the white shirt reached behind his back. When his hand reappeared, a black pistol gleamed in his grip.

That was the last thing she remembered clearly. Everything afterwards was blurred and fragmented. Michael knocking the man backwards, so that the shot went wild; the table toppling over; the briefcase spilling its contents across the tiles. If she saw what was inside, it didn't register. She sprang away, slipped on the smooth tiles and fell.

The water hit her hard. She flailed and went under; she tasted chlorine at the back of her throat and gagged. The sundress wrapped her like a shroud.

She broke the surface and kicked to the side. From the floor of the pool, soft-lit sea nymphs beckoned her to join them. She put her bare arms on the side and hauled herself out.

Sprawled on the poolside, she saw it all from ground level. The scattered briefcase and overturned table; the marble gods looking down on her. And at the far end of the terrace, two men locked in a struggle over the abyss. Michael threw a punch that didn't connect; his opponent grabbed his arm and jerked it back, spinning him around to face the cliff. They stood there for a second like two lovers staring at a sunset. Then, with a brusque motion, the man kicked out Michael's feet and pushed him forward. Michael flailed and stumbled. He tried to regain his balance and almost succeeded, teetering on the edge like a broken-winged bird. His impatient assailant moved in for the kill, but it wasn't necessary. Without a sound, as if the life had already left him, Michael flopped over the edge and vanished.

Abby screamed; she couldn't help it. The man heard her and turned. All his movements were precise, unhurried. He'd dropped the gun in his struggle with Michael—now he picked it up. He checked the slide and the magazine. He ejected the cartridge in the chamber and reloaded.

Abby pulled herself off the ground The wet dress clung to her body, dragging her down. She had to escape—but where? To the car? She didn't know where Michael had left the keys. She didn't even have time to get back to the house. The intruder was walking along the side of the pool, gun raised. She hurled herself into the colonnade as the next shot went off. Stone cracked; something shattered.

She crouched low and ran down the back of the colonnade, ducking between the columns and the statue plinths. It was like being in a shooting gallery—except the man wasn't shooting. Had he run out of bullets?

She reached the end of the colonnade and

paused. A marble Jupiter towered over her, a lightning bolt clenched in his fist. Measured footsteps approached.

With a sickening shock, she realised why he hadn't bothered shooting. She was trapped in a corner with nowhere to go. She cowered behind the base of the statue. The footsteps stopped.

The silence was worst of all.

'What do you want?' she called.

No answer. Water dripped off her sodden dress and pooled around her feet. *What was he waiting for?*

She had thought she knew what it was like to face death. She'd heard the stories a thousand times and recorded them diligently. But the people who'd lived to bear witness had been survivors. Some had run when the killers came; others lay rigid in the killing fields and played dead, sometimes for hours, while their families and neighbours died around them. They never gave up.

She had one chance. She pushed off on the plinth, jack-knifed up and spun around, throwing her entire weight against the statue. It wobbled, tottered and fell. The god crashed down and smashed into pieces. The gunman leapt back, losing his balance.

Abby was already running. She crossed the last few yards of the terrace and dived back inside the house. On the wall, the giant TV screen played its rote images of war and revenge, oblivious to the real horror in front of it.

Where now?

But the gunman had recovered too fast. The first bullet shattered the window behind her. The second tore into her shoulder, spinning her around.

12

She saw him stepping through the broken window, gun raised.

'*Please*,' she begged. She wanted to run, but her body had failed her. 'Why are you doing this?'

The man shrugged. He had a black moustache and a mole on his right cheek, sprouting hairs. His eyes were dark and hard.

Her last thought was of a witness she'd interviewed years ago, a grey-haired Hutu woman grinding meal in a jungle camp somewhere between Congo and Rwanda. 'You never gave up,' Abby had told her in admiration, and the woman had shaken her head.

'I was lucky. The others were not. That was the only difference.'

The man raised the gun and fired.

II

Roman Province of Moesia—August 337

It's still August, but autumn has already arrived. Like every old man, I fear this season. Shadows fall, nights lengthen and the knives come out. On evenings like these, when the chill in the air makes my old wounds squirm, I retire to the bathhouse and order my slaves to stoke the fire. The pool's empty, but I sit on the rim and tip water over the scalding stones. The steam goes up my nose and softens my flesh. Perhaps that will make it easier for my murderers, when they come.

I'm ready to die—it holds no terrors for me. I've lived longer than I deserved. I've been a soldier, a courtier and a politician: none of them professions noted for their longevity. When my murderers come—and they are coming—I know they won't linger. They're busy men these days. I'm not the last person they have to kill. They won't torture me: they don't know the questions to ask.

They've no idea what I could tell them.

A shiver goes down my back. I haven't undressed—I'm not going to die naked—and my clothes are sodden. I throw more water into the pool and lean forward into the steam, peering through the mist at the black-and-white sea gods picked out in the floor tiles. They stare back and reproach me. Dying gods from a dying world. Do they know the part I've played in their oblivion?

Another shiver. I'm ready to die: it's death that terrifies me. The afterwards. Gods who die in springtime occasionally come back to life; old men murdered in autumn never do. But where they go . . .

The steam thickens.

All my life I've contended with gods—a god who became a man, and a man who became a god. Now, at the end of it, peering into the steaming abyss, I have no more idea what the gods intend for me than I did when I first peered over the edge of my cradle all those years ago. Or even four months ago, on a dusty April afternoon in Constantinople, hearing about a dead man who would change my life. As much as remains of it.

Memories cloud about me and bead on my skin. The mind is a strange land with many walls but no distance. I'm no longer in the bathhouse, but another place and time, and my oldest friend is saying . . .

14

*　　　*　　　*

'. . . I need you.'

We're in an audience hall at the palace, though there's no audience. None except me. We're both old men with the years scored into us, but it's been this way since I can remember. He performs, I applaud.

Except now I'm not applauding. I'm listening to him tell me about a death and wondering if I look right. After so many years at court, I can pull out my emotions like masks from a well-oiled drawer, but I'm not sure what the occasion demands. I want to seem respectful to the dead man. But not too much—I won't invest in his death, as I'm being invited to do. Does that make me callous?

'They found him two hours ago in the library by the Academy. As soon as they realised who he was, they sent straight to the palace.'

He's trying to draw me in to the story, pique my curiosity. I stay silent. There aren't many men alive who can stay silent when he wants them to speak—I might be the only one left. We grew up like brothers, inseparable sons of officers in the same legion. His mother was an innkeeper, mine a laundress. Now titles adorn him like the gems sewn into his heavy robe. Flavius Valerius Constantine— Emperor, Caesar and Augustus, Consul and Proconsul, High Priest. Constantine the Pious, the Faithful, the Blessed and Benevolent. Constantine the Victorious, Triumphant and Unconquered. Constantine—succinctly—the Great.

And even now, a grandfather in his declining years, the greatness radiates from him. I still feel it. His round face, puppyish and seductive when

15

he was young, may have fattened out and sagged; the muscles that wrestled together an empire may have gone soft. But the greatness remains. The artists who paint him with a golden nimbus are only colouring in what every man knows. Power inhabits his body—the unconquerable confidence that only the gods can give.

'The dead man's name was Alexander. He was a bishop—important in the Christian community. He also tutored one of my sons, apparently.'

One of my sons, apparently. Something wraps around me like a cold current in the sea, though I don't flinch. My face betrays nothing. Neither does his.

Without warning, he tosses me something. My body's grown slow and cumbersome, but I still have my reflexes. I catch it one-handed, then open my fist.

'They found this near the body.'

It's a necklace, about the size of my palm. An intricate web surrounding Constantine's X-P monogram, the bright new gold studded with red glass beads. A broken chain shows where it was ripped off someone's neck.

'Did it belong to the Bishop?'

'His servant says not.'

'The man who killed him, then?'

'Or it was left there deliberately.' He breathes an impatient sigh. 'These are the questions I need you to answer, Gaius.'

The necklace is cold in my hand, an unwanted token of the dead man I'm being forced to carry. But I still resist. 'I don't know anything about the Christians.'

'Not true.' Constantine reaches out and touches

16

my shoulder. Once, it would have been a natural and intimate gesture. Now his arm is rigid, holding me back. 'You know enough to know that they feud like cats in a sack. If I send in one of their own, half his colleagues will immediately come to me condemning him as a schismatic and a heretic. Then the second half will arrive and denounce the first half for the same crimes.'

He shakes his head. God though he is, even he can't fathom the mysteries of the church.

'Do you think a Christian killed him?'

His shock is so natural I almost believe it's real. 'God forbid. They spit and scratch, but they don't bite.'

I don't disagree. I don't know anything about the Christians.

'But people will speculate. Others will say the murder of Alexander was an attack on all Christians by those who hate them. These wounds are raw, Gaius. We fought fifteen years of civil war to unite the empire and restore peace. It can't fall apart now.'

He's right to worry. He built his city in a hurry. The cement is hardly dry, and already cracks are appearing.

'In two weeks, I'll leave on campaign. In two months, I'll be a thousand miles away in Persia. I can't leave this problem behind. I need someone I can trust to do it quickly. Please, Gaius. For our friendship.'

Does he really think that's something to sway me? There are things I've done for our friendship that even the god Christ, notoriously lenient, wouldn't forgive me.

'I was going to go home to Moesia next week.

17

Everything's arranged.'

Something like nostalgia enters his expression. His eyes take on a far-off look.

'Do you remember those days, Gaius? Playing in the fields outside Niš? Climbing into the hen coops to steal eggs? They never caught us, did they?'

They never caught us because your father was the Tribune. I don't say it. You meddle with an old man's memories at your peril.

'I should go back there—feel native soil under my feet again. When I come back from Persia.'

'You'll always be welcome at my house.'

'I'll be there. And you'll be there sooner. As soon as you've solved this problem for me.'

And there it is. A god doesn't have time for protracted wrangling. We could have debated it for hours, days, but he's condensed all his arguments into a single sentence. And all my resistance and evasions, my determination not to get involved, collapse to an instant decision.

'Do you want a culprit? Or do you want me to find out who actually did it?'

It's a crucial question. In this city, not all murders are crimes. And not all criminals are guilty. Constantine, more than anyone, understands that.

'I need you to find out who did it. Discreetly.'

He wants the truth. Then he'll decide what to do with it.

'If I go knocking on the Christians' doors, will they open for me?'

'They'll know you're there for me.'

I'm there for you. All my life, I've been there for you. Your counsellor and friend; your right arm, when action was required and you had to sit still. Your

18

audience. You perform, I applaud. And obey.

He claps his hands and a slave appears out of air and shadow. I'd forgotten: in this city, there's always another audience. The slave carries an ivory diptych, two panels hinged together with leather bands. The front is carved with a cameo of the Emperor, his eyes turned skyward and a solar crown on his head. Next to it, the familiar X-P monogram, the same as on the necklace. A few lines of text inside derogate Constantine's authority on me.

'Thank you for doing this, Gaius.' He embraces me, and this time something like warmth passes between our two old bodies. He whispers in my ear: 'I need someone I trust. Someone who knows where the bodies are buried.'

I laugh; it's the only thing to do. Of course I know where the bodies are buried. I dug most of the graves myself.

III

Present Day
The wall was grey and pocked. The roof was white. The door was wood, with a smudged glass window and a crucifix above it. A static hum filled the air, and also an irregular beeping sound, like the random firings of an antique video game. She hurt like hell.

She lay on her back, concentrating on the details to fight off the pain. The wall wasn't pocked: that was an illusion caused by paint peeling off the concrete. Grey paint. She wondered who on earth

19

bothered to paint concrete grey. The beeping wasn't irregular: it came from two sources, subtly out of rhythm with each other. One started behind the other, closed in on it until—for a few merciful seconds—they ran almost in synchrony, then overtook it and pulled away.

The roof wasn't all white. Dark patches stained the tiles like spilled wine.

The smudge on the window moved. It wasn't on the window: it was outside, someone standing with his back to the door. She waited for him to go away, but he didn't.

Where am I? she thought. And then, a second later and infinitely more terrifying, *Who am I?*

Panic seized her. She tried to get up and found she couldn't move. The panic redoubled; she couldn't breathe. Her heart raced out of control so fast she thought it would explode. The room began to go dark. She writhed and fought; she screamed.

The door flew open. A man in a tight-fitting suit burst through, shouting words she couldn't understand. His jacket flapped open. A gun bulged from a brown leather holster under his arm.

She passed out.

*　　　*　　　*

'Abigail? Can you hear me?'

The panic was still there, but now it was dormant, a slow fuse burning a hole in her gut. Her breaths came shallow and unfulfilling. She tried to move her arm and couldn't. The breaths came faster. *Keep calm.*

She located the beeping noise and listened,

20

forcing herself to fix on one rhythm among the syncopation. She tried to breathe in time with it. She felt herself relax a fraction—enough that she dared to open her eyes.

A face stared down at her. Brown hair, brown eyes, brown beard. Was he real? Or had her imagination formed him from the brown stains on the roof?

The face moved. The roof didn't.

'Abigail Cormac?' he said again.

'I don't know . . .'

'Don't you remember . . . ?'

The panic quickened. *Should I remember? What should I remember? Is it important?* Her mind felt as helpless as her body, pushing against bonds it couldn't see.

'I don't.'

'*Nothing?*' Incredulous. That only made the desperation worse.

The face drew away. She heard the scrape of a chair. When the face reappeared, it was lower and further back, a sun on the horizon of her flat world.

'Your name is Abigail Cormac. You work for the Foreign Office on secondment to the EULEX mission in Kosovo. You were on holiday here and things went wrong.'

That sounded mostly right. Like seeing the film of a book you'd read. Some things skipped or not quite right, others changed for no apparent reason. She peered at him.

'Who are you?'

'Norris, from the embassy here. Podgorica. It's . . .'

'. . . the capital of Montenegro.' It came out of nowhere, surprising her as much as him. *How did I know that?*

The brown eyes narrowed. 'So you do remember.'

'Yes. No. I don't . . .' She struggled, trying to articulate it. 'I *know* some things. When you say words like "British Embassy" or "Kosovo" or "holiday", it makes sense. I understand you. But if you ask me a question, there's nothing.'

'Nothing?'

She struggled to think. The effort exhausted her.

'There was a man with a gun,' she said carefully. Trying on the words like a dress she didn't think would fit.

'Do you remember him?'

She closed her eyes, trying to squeeze the image back into them. 'A blue suit. He came through the door.'

'At the villa?'

'Here. In this room.'

Norris sat back with a sigh. 'That was this morning. They've put a police guard on your door. He heard you screaming and came to make sure you were OK.'

A police guard? 'Am I in trouble?'

'You really don't remember?'

She wished he'd stop saying that. She let her head slump back on the stiff pillow. 'Just tell me.'

He glanced towards the door, as if looking for confirmation of something. Abby felt a new stab of panic. *Is there someone else here?* She tried to lift her head, but couldn't see.

'You were shot. All we know is that when the police turned up, you were lying there half-dead. Blood everywhere, a bullet inside you. They found your passport and called us. As for your husband . . .'

Something tightened inside her. 'What about him?'

'Do you remember?'

She shook her head. Norris shot another sidling glance into the corner.

'There's no easy way to say this. I'm sorry to inform you that your husband is dead.'

'Hector?'

Now it was Norris's turn to look baffled. 'Who's Hector?'

I don't know, she wanted to scream. The name had come to her like a ghost, unbidden and unexpected. 'Isn't he my husband?'

But even as she said it, she knew that wasn't right. *I'm not married*, she thought. And then, with the ghost of a smile, *I'm pretty sure I'd remember that*.

Norris was looking at a piece of paper. 'According to his passport, his name was Michael Lascaris.'

And that did mean something. The smile left her; she slumped back in the bed. The monitor raced away at a million miles an hour. *Beep*. A red sports car gunning through mountains. *Beep*. A dark bay and a bright pool and dead faces watching from their plinths. *Beep beep*. Waking up in the middle of the night. A man with a gun. A struggle. The scream as Michael fell over the cliff—her scream. *Beep beep beep beep beep . . .*

Someone banged through the door—not a man with a gun, but a woman in green overalls with a syringe in her hand. 'Wait,' she heard Norris say. 'Give her a chance.'

But they wouldn't give her a chance. Strong

hands clamped around her arm and a sharp point slid into her flesh. The monitor slowed its runaway pace.

Then there was silence.

*　　　*　　　*

'So you remember Michael Lascaris?'

The metronome beat of the monitor was stable now, a gentle andante. They'd sat Abby up in her bed, though she couldn't move much more. A plaster cast covered her right arm and shoulder, entombing her chest and most of her stomach. Somewhere underneath, she'd been told, was the bullet wound.

You were shot. It still didn't seem like her. Being shot happened to other people—victims. Abby had seen enough wounds in her old job to know they weren't just things that happened on TV or in the cinema, but there'd still been the distance. *You suffer, I pity*.

'Do you remember Michael?'

'He drove a Porsche.'

Norris's piece of paper had grown into a folder. He flicked through the pages.

'A 1968 Porsche Targa, red, UK registration?'

Abby shrugged her one good shoulder. 'It was red.'

She wasn't trying to be flippant—not much—but Norris took it badly. He stood, flapping his folder at her.

'I know you're in a bad way—Christ, you're lucky to be alive—but you have to understand how serious this is. Someone bursts into a house and attacks two European diplomats. It doesn't look

24

good.'

He didn't burst in, Abby thought. *He was already there, out by the pool with Michael.*

'The Montenegrins are running around like it's the end of the world. They're terrified it's going to cause a storm in Brussels, derail their EU application, put them on a terrorist blacklist or whatever. Frankly, they're overreacting.' A stern glare, as if it was her fault. 'You're not that important.'

'Thanks.'

'But we're still trying to keep it quiet. It doesn't look too good for us either. Pretty embarrassing, to be honest.'

The monitor accelerated a fraction. 'I'm sorry if I embarrassed you.'

'We'll cope.' The sarcasm missed him completely. 'But we need to know what happened.'

'I wish I knew.'

But she was stalling. There were pieces there, waiting to be turned over and examined. She didn't quite know what they'd show, but she knew they frightened her.

'Let's start with Michael Lascaris.'

A fragment of their earlier conversation came back to her. 'He's not my husband.'

'We know that now. Your file in London said you were married; you and Michael were found together; we made an assumption. Turns out we were wrong.'

'Am I divorced?' Again, she knew she'd got it even before Norris confirmed it. The word tasted sour and true.

'Michael Lascaris fell off a cliff,' Norris continued. 'The police fished his body out of Kotor

25

Bay three days later.'

Abby forced herself to sit up straighter. Pain shot through her ribs, making her wince, but she held herself steady. 'He didn't fall off the cliff. He was thrown off it.'

'So you *do* remember.'

'It's starting to come back.'

Norris took out a pen. 'Let's take it from the beginning. Was going there your idea?'

'I don't think so.'

'Michael's?'

'The villa belonged to a friend of his.'

'Did he say who this friend was?'

The memories were coming more easily now. 'An Italian judge.'

The pen moved across the paper. 'Was he there? The judge?'

'Just us.'

'A romantic getaway.' There was a tone in his voice that Abby didn't like. She slumped back.

'It didn't end up very romantic.'

As quickly as she could, she fed him the scraps that had come back to her. Waking up in the night; hearing a noise; going out to the pool terrace.

'Michael was fighting with the other man.' She paused. All she had were fragments, glimpses and moments. Norris wanted a coherent story. 'The house was full of antiques. I suppose he was a burglar. Michael must have heard him and surprised him. I tried to help. He—' She broke off. With everything she was desperate to remember, that was one image she wished she could forget. 'He pushed Michael over the cliff. Then he came after me.'

'Did you get a look at him?'

She tried to think, but it was like a dream. The harder she interrogated it, the more it receded. She peered into faces and saw only blurry blanks.

'I'm sorry.'

'And you're sure no one else was there?'

'I don't remember anyone.' She read the disbelief on his face. 'Should I?'

'Somebody rang the police.'

'Maybe it was a neighbour.' But she knew that wasn't right. She could remember the darkness—no lights for miles around. And Norris was shaking his head.

'The call came from the villa. That's how they knew where you were.' Norris put down his pen. 'You must have done it. You were too weak to talk: you didn't say anything. Just left the phone off the hook and crawled away.'

The effort of remembering was giving her a headache. She squeezed her eyes shut and rubbed her temples. 'I don't remember that at all.'

She opened her eyes, hoping Norris might have disappeared. Instead, he'd turned to a vinyl pocket at the back of his folder and was pulling something out, a sealed plastic bag, with gold in it. He held it up for her to see the necklace inside: an intricate labyrinth woven around a monogram, the shape of a P with the loop continued back left across the stroke. It looked old.

'Do you recognise this?'

'It's mine,' she said. 'I was wearing it that night.'

'What's the design?'

Was he testing her—a trap? *What would that prove? I barely remember my own name.* Her eyes darted around the room: the monitor that looked like an ancient wireless set; the drip feeding

27

her veins; the peeling paint; the crucifix over the door . . .

. . . and something connected. A spark leapt between the necklace and the crucifix, bridging the gaps in her mind with a bolt of understanding so sharp it hurt.

'Michael gave it to me. It's an old Christian symbol.'

She tried to stretch out, as if the old metal might still retain some memory of Michael that she could touch. The bandages and strappings held her down.

Norris dropped the necklace into the folder. Abby felt an ache of loss, her last fragment of Michael slipping out of reach again. *Was this how it would be for the rest of her life?* Longing for something she could never have back.

'The police found it in the pool at the villa. They thought it might be connected to your attacker.'

He snapped the folder shut and stood. 'I think that covers it. Unless there's anything else you can remember?' He moved towards the door.

'Wait,' Abby called. She could feel the panic returning. 'What's going to happen to me now?'

Norris paused in the doorway.

'You're going home.'

IV

Constantinople—April 337

Every time I open a door in this city it's like entering a forgotten storeroom in a vast mansion. Everything's covered in dust. Every footstep leaves a print, every touch leaves a smear. You'd think the city had been lost for centuries. But this isn't the hallowed dust of antiquity—it's the dust of a craftsman's workshop, the dust of creation. And it's still settling. Every day it casts a haze over the city. I can taste it on my tongue as I walk to the library: the brittle flavour of cut stone, the sweetness of sawn timber, the tartness of the quicklime they mix into the cement. Much longer and I'll become a connoisseur, able to recognise every note of Athenian marble or Egyptian porphyry or Italian granite in the atmosphere.

But dust never settles on memories. The longer I live, the cleaner they become: each one buffed and scraped and chiselled into glossy, hard perfection. Extraneous details are ground out and smoothed over. All that remains is my story.

*   *   *

I know the library by the Academy, though I've never been inside. Two black sphinxes crouch either side of the door, riddling passers-by: people call it the Egyptian Library. The sphinxes aren't new, even Constantine can't manufacture his new city from whole cloth. When you're in a hurry, you have to work with what you've got. He's ransacked the empire to fill his city with antique treasures: statues, columns, stones, even roof tiles.

And books. As I push through the door, past the crowd who've gathered on the stairs, I can see hundreds if not thousands of manuscripts, neat scrolls tied and stacked in their criss-crossed shelving like bones in an ossuary. The unfamiliar smell hits me a second later: the must of old parchment and the rotting-grass scent of papyrus,

29

distilled by the heat into something so ripe it makes me gag.

The room is round and wide, with overhanging balconies under a domed ceiling painted with cyclamen and roses. It was designed to be a garden of knowledge, ordered architecture to grow cultivated thoughts. But already, the shelves around the rotunda have grown wild like thorns, tangled and dark, sometimes even spilling their fruit on the ground. All the windows are glazed shut, trapping the smell in the room and magnifying the sun's heat. The whole room seems to sweat out its poisons.

A dozen anxious conversations fall silent as I step through the door. I can tell the men who recognise me by the way their faces fall. I don't take it personally. In my pomp, I used to enjoy it.

A man's waiting for me. He looks older than me, though he's probably younger. He squints, leaning his head forward like a quail pecking grain. He's wearing a calf-length tunic in grey cloth, and unlike the others he doesn't have ink splashed on his hands or sleeves. I guess he makes his living carrying books, not copying them.

'Are you the librarian?'

He just about manages a nod. His face looks crushed, like a balled-up scrap of cloth. He's lived his life among his scrolls, neatly rolled and stored. He didn't expect this in his library.

'Is the body still here?'

He looks horrified. 'The undertakers came an hour ago.'

A murder with no body. 'Can you show me where you found him?'

He leads me down a narrow aisle between

shelves, twisting and turning until suddenly we come out by a wall and a window. Yellow light leaches in and falls on the desk below, which is littered with papers and scrolls. The stool's pushed back—it's easy to imagine the reader has just gone to relieve himself, might come back any moment to find us leafing through his things.

'Do you know who did it?'

It's an obvious question, but it has to be asked. The librarian shakes his head vigorously, affronted. He gestures at the walls of manuscripts hemming us in.

'No one saw anything.'

'Who found him?'

'His assistant—a deacon called Simeon. The Bishop was lying face down on the table. The deacon thought he was asleep.'

'Is the deacon here?'

Without answering—or perhaps by way of an answer—the librarian scuttles away. He holds out his arm like a stunted wing, trailing it along the shelves as he moves. A lifetime staring at books must have left him almost blind. No use as a witness.

And what can I see? An inkpot and a reed pen on the table, with an ivory-handled knife and a small jar beside them. Thin shavings litter the table where the Bishop sharpened his pen.

Why didn't you use the knife to defend yourself? I wonder.

I uncork the jar and sniff the white paste inside. It smells like glue. I put it back down and examine the pile of papers beside it. Bishop Alexander was a voracious reader: half the table is filled with scrolls, some untouched, others left open half-read. A few seem to have shaken off the spindles that held them down and rolled themselves up, perhaps when the dead man hit the table.

In the centre sits a different sort of volume. A codex, individual vellum pages bound together to make a book. It seems an awkward and fragmented way of reading, but I know the Christians like it. I peer down to see what he was reading when he died.

It's impossible to tell. His broken face fell straight on to the book, drowning the words in blood. The left page is illegible, the right unwritten. His past obliterated, the future empty. I try to wipe off the written page, but the blood's congealed. All I do is smear it. Shadows of words swim beneath the stain like fish under ice—unreachable.

'Do you think you'll find answers in there?'

I look up. The librarian's returned with a young man—tall, with a handsome face and tousled black hair. He's dressed in a plain black robe and sandals, his hands are stained so dark at first I think he must be wearing gloves. Then I realise it's ink. Then I wonder if there's anything else with it.

I gesture to the empty desk. 'You found the body?'

The youth nods. I scan his face for guilt, but it's such a mess of emotions I can't tell. There's sadness, but also anger; anxiety, but touched with defiance. If he didn't know who I was before, the librarian's probably told him. He's determined not to let my reputation cow him.

'Your name's Simeon?'

'I'm—I was—Bishop Alexander's secretary.'

His dark eyes watch me, wondering what I'm thinking. Does he really want to know? *You'll do.* If

Constantine needs a quick answer, then the young servant with ink or blood on his hands—who found the body, who had who-knows-what grudge against his master—he'll do. If he's a priest, Constantine won't torture him or execute him. He'll pack him off to some rock in the sea and justice will be done.

But that's not what Constantine wants. Not yet.

'How did he die?'

'His face was smashed in.' The deacon says it viciously: he wants to shock me. He'll have to try harder than that.

'How?'

He doesn't understand. 'Smashed in,' he repeats. 'He had blood all over him.'

'On his face.'

Simeon touches his forehead. 'The wound was here.'

'A clean wound, like a knife would make?'

He thinks I'm being obtuse. 'I told you it was smashed in. Broken open.'

It doesn't make sense. If the Bishop was sitting facing the window, back to the room, the back of his head would have been the obvious target. But the blood on the book supports the deacon's story.

I pull out the monogrammed necklace Constantine gave me.

'You found this?'

'On the floor, next to the body.'

'Did you recognise it?'

'It wasn't Alexander's.'

'And do you know who killed him?'

The question surprises him. It's so obvious, he thinks it must be a trick. He stares at me, looking for the trap, then realises that silence doesn't make him look good either.

33

'He was dead when I found him.'

I let my impatience show, playing on his nerves. 'I know he was dead. But whoever did this didn't walk away spotless. He must have had blood on his clothes, or his hands.' I let my gaze drop to Simeon's ink-stained hands. He clenches his fists.

'I didn't see anyone.'

'Did you hear anything?' This as much to the librarian—perhaps his ears compensate for his struggling eyes. But he's already shaking his head.

'They're building a new church next door. Every day, all we hear is noise and workmen. It's almost too loud to read. "*Eripient somnum Druso vitulisque marinis*," as Juvenal says.'

I'm not interested in his erudition. Constantine once said that men show off their learning when they have nothing else to say for themselves. My eyes drift away.

And catch something. A spray of blood on the shelved scrolls, well away from where the body was. I push past the librarian, almost knocking him into his beloved manuscripts.

My foot kicks against something in the shadows on the floor. It rolls away, deeper into shadow. Simeon moves to pick it up, but I wave him back and kneel down myself. The floor's dusty, littered with broken fragments of wax and fine threads of papyrus. As my hand searches the darkness, I feel something cool and smooth under my fingers. When I pick it up, I see a small bust carved in black marble, about the size of a man's fist. The face has wise features and sightless eyes, though both are obscured by the blood matted onto it. I guess this was the last face Alexander saw before it smashed his brains in.

'Who is this?'

'The name is inscribed on the base,' says the librarian. He can't bring himself to look.

I turn it over. 'Hierocles.'

I don't recognise the name—or perhaps I've heard it and paid no notice. But the others know him. Simeon especially.

'Hierocles was a great hater of the Christians,' he says, though I can see he's thinking much more.

'Do you know where it came from?'

'From the library,' says the librarian. 'We have dozens of them.'

And as soon as I look, I see. Midway up each shelf, about shoulder height, stone heads sit on wooden plinths guarding the manuscripts. Except on the shelf where blood has spattered the books. There, the plinth is empty.

The story unravels like a scroll.

Item: Alexander was standing by the shelf, looking for a document.

Item: The killer arrived. Did Alexander suspect what he was going to do? Probably not—he would have made a noise, and even with the building works next door someone would have heard it. Perhaps they even talked for a few moments.

Item: The killer snatched the bust off the shelf and killed Alexander by smashing in his forehead.

And as my mind reads all this, the final line emerges.

Item: He dragged the corpse to the table and propped it up, so that anyone who glimpsed it would think the man was sleeping. Then he escaped.

Or went to announce that he'd found the body. I look back at Simeon. He can tell what I'm thinking.

His face is hard and blank, the anger drawn inside. He's waiting for me to accuse him.

Casually, I turn back to the librarian.

'How many men were here this afternoon?'

'Perhaps twenty.'

'Can you give me their names?'

'The porter on the door will have seen them.'

'Have him make a list.'

'Aurelius Symmachus was here.'

Simeon blurts it out so fast I hardly catch the name. Simeon's lost his battle with his anger: his eyes are fixed on me in defiance. Perhaps he thinks it's the only chance he'll get to speak.

'Aurelius Symmachus is one of the most eminent men in the city,' I point out. Aurelius Symmachus is old Rome, patrician to the core, still a man to be reckoned with, though he's out of date in this city of new buildings and new men. Not that I'm one to talk.

'He was here,' Simeon insists. 'I saw him talking to Bishop Alexander earlier this afternoon. He left just before I found the body.'

I check the librarian for confirmation. He's fiddling with the stylus he wears on a chain around his wrist and won't meet my eye.

Simeon points to the bust, still in my hand. 'Hierocles was a philosopher known for his hatred of Christians. So is Symmachus.'

An old Roman with the old gods—it doesn't surprise me. But it doesn't make him a murderer.

'Perhaps he wanted to send a message,' Simeon persists.

Perhaps he did. I remember what Constantine said: *Others will say the murder of Alexander was an attack on all Christians by those who hate them.*

36

'I'll look into it.' I turn to go, but there's still something else Simeon wants to say.

'When we came here this morning, Alexander had a document case. A leather box with brass bindings. He wouldn't let me see it—wouldn't even let me carry it.'

'And?'

'It's missing.'

V

London—Present Day

You could always tell England from the air. Other countries looked messy: fields and houses littered across the landscape without logic, isolated squares of cultivation in ragged, contested lands. In England, all the lines joined up. She watched the tessellated fields and estates drag by under the wing as they descended to Gatwick. Everything was as grey and damp as a dungeon.

They'd flown her back as soon as they dared. She sat on the flight wearing a shapeless smock and a skirt they must have found in a maternity shop. Underneath, she was trussed up like a corpse. At least she could walk, more or less. The airport had a wheelchair waiting for her, but she waved it away. Every step sent bolts of pain through her shoulder; her lungs ached as if she'd run a marathon, but she forced herself to walk to the exit unaided.

Lost in the effort, she didn't see the sign with her name on it. It was only when she felt a tug on her sleeve that she looked up from the floor. A young man in a suit and an open-necked shirt was waiting for her, a mobile phone in one hand and a printed sign saying CORMAC in the other.

'Mark,' he introduced himself with an apologetic grin. 'The office sent me to pick you up. Said it was the least they could do.'

'Thanks.' She didn't mean it. Everything about him screamed youth: the golden hair, tousled without affectation; the soft fat around his cheeks; the energetic confidence, newly minted from Cambridge or the LSE or wherever the civil service got them these days. She hadn't felt this old since her divorce.

'Have you got a suitcase?'

She hefted the black overnight bag she'd somehow managed to carry from the plane. 'Just this. I didn't pack for a long trip.'

'Right.' And then, as if she'd said something else. 'Golly.'

Did I step through a time warp? Do people really say 'golly' any more?

It was a stupid thought, but it didn't take much these days. Just the least hint of uncertainty. She began to tremble: the panic swelled inside her. She saw Mark watching, his blue eyes concerned and uncomprehending. He put a hand on her arm.

'Are you OK?'

'Dizzy.' She found a row of plastic seats and sat down. 'Just the flight.'

'I'll fetch the car.'

As soon as his back was turned, she popped the cap on the yellow beaker they'd given her at the hospital and shook out two pills. The airline had confiscated her water bottle: she swallowed them dry and hurt her throat.

Get a grip, she told herself. *Don't let them start to*

pity you.

Mark reappeared. She hadn't realised how long he'd been gone. Perhaps the pills were doing something.

'Where to?'

*   *   *

Abby owned a flat in Clapham, on the north side of the common. When the divorce proceedings began, the lawyers had said it would have to go, but Abby had doubled down on the mortgage to buy out Hector's share. It was a silly thing to do—she probably hadn't spent more than three months there in the last two years. It held some good memories of her marriage, but more bad ones, and anyway she was supposed to forget them all. But her moorings in the world were tenuous enough: the thought of being without a permanent home frightened her too much. She'd rented it out when she left for Kosovo, to a pair of Pakistani doctors working at St Thomas's. The estate agent had assured her they'd be excellent tenants, and probably they had been, but they'd had visa issues and left in a hurry. Since then, the flat had sat empty.

It was like revisiting somewhere from her childhood. The outlines were there, but the detail wasn't right. The tenants had moved some furniture around and not put it back; there were things in the kitchen cupboards that weren't hers, and tacked to the wall was a Magritte poster that she didn't think had been there before. It made her uneasy, as if someone had tried to piece her life together from photographs and made some clumsy mistakes.

Or are they my mistakes? Most of her memory

had come back, but there were still weak spots. Like a warped old record that might stutter or skip without warning.

'Great view.'

Mark stood by the full-length window looking down on the Queenstown road, the row-houses and chip shops huddled in the valley, Battersea Park and the spires of the Thames bridges beyond. He'd insisted on walking her up. With the pills in her system she found she couldn't say no.

'I've spoken to work,' he continued, cheerful as ever. 'They told me to tell you not to worry about rushing back. You've been signed off for as long as you need.'

Abby stood in the kitchen area and looked down on him. The flat's top floor was open plan, three rooms squeezed into the space of one, with the kitchen raised above the living area by a couple of steps. She felt as if she was floating above him.

Don't make me stay here, she thought.

He reached inside his jacket and gave her a card embossed with the Foreign Office crest. *Mark Wilson, Office of Balkan Liaison*.

'If you need anything at all, just call me.'

*   *   *

She barely survived the weekend.

On Friday, she forced herself as far as Clapham High Street to buy some clothes. The day was grey and overcast, but not cold, and the effort of walking with her bandages brought on a suffocating sweat. She had thought that getting out of the flat might do her good, but being among the crowds on the high street only made her feel lonely. So many people, nothing in common with her. She tried her phone when she got home but there was no dial tone. BT must have cut it off. At least she still had her television—though judging by the increasingly aggressive letters from the TV licensing authority piled up on her mat, they'd have cut that off, too, if there'd been a way.

On Saturday, she endured the bus to Sloane Square to buy a cheap laptop and a prepay mobile phone. The crowds were thicker than the day before, but she found she could tune them out more. She walked among them like a ghost, unnoticed. That evening, she flipped through the stack of takeaway leaflets that had piled up in the hall until she found one that didn't look too toxic, and watched a succession of bad films until they bored her to sleep.

On Sunday, she spent three hours fiddling with the phone and the computer, and felt an absurd sense of triumph when the phone finally delivered the primary-colour letters of a search-engine logo on to the laptop's screen. She tried to log in to her e-mail, and couldn't remember the password. She read the news and forgot most of it straight away. She searched for stories about the attack at the villa and was surprised how few there were. Of those, only one gave more than the briefest facts, an article from the Montenegrin magazine *Monitor*. One line in particular stood out.

Police have categorically refuted the hypothesis that a prominent criminal organisation may have been involved.

Hypothesis? Whose hypothesis? Try as she might, it was the only reference she could find to it.

That night, nightmares took her back to the

villa. She was running down the colonnade, statues smashing and shattering around her. The gunman stood over her, pistol raised. She stared up into his cruel face—only suddenly it was Michael's face, mouthing words she couldn't hear.

The gun went off. She woke in a cold sweat, the skin under her bandages itching so badly she wanted to tear them off, even if it meant she'd bleed to death. She snatched her new phone off the bedside table and stared at the clock, willing the minutes to pass.

First thing Monday morning, she dialled the number on the card.

'Hi, Mark, it's Abby. From Kosovo.'

'Right. How are you?'

'Fine. Really well.' *Never let them pity you.* Then, rushing it out: 'Can I come and see you? At the office?'

A pause. *He doesn't want to see me,* Abby thought. *All that concern, it's just diplomacy. What he's paid for.*

'Of course.'

'When?'

He must have heard the desperate edge sharpening her voice. 'Come by this afternoon.'

* * *

The sepulchral walls of the palace of Whitehall loomed large over King Charles Street. Modern buildings might rise many times higher, but they lacked the scale, the knack the Stuart architects had of dwarfing a visitor. Abby walked through the vast triple gate to the Foreign Office, submitted her bag for a search and gave her name at reception. A

42

camera on the wall swivelled round and took her picture. A machine spat out a temporary pass. She locked her phone in a small locker and sat with the other supplicants and plaintiffs, waiting for Mark to come down and rescue her.

'Sorry.' He was always apologising, though he never seemed contrite. He led her up to the third floor, and left her in a glassed-in meeting room while he fetched tea. When he closed the door behind him, she heard the click of a latch; a red light came on on the panel next to it.

She peered out between the frosted bars etched on the window. Her department had moved since she was last in London, and the new layout had no desk for her. One more thing taken away. She felt as if her whole life was a jigsaw, that someone was dismantling it piece by piece and throwing it in a box. She looked for her boss, but couldn't find her.

'Where's Francesca?' she asked Mark, when he returned with two cups of civil service-issue tea.

'She's at a conference in Bucharest. She told me to tell you whatever you need to know.'

'When can I come back to work?'

He pulled out his teabag and tossed it in the bin. 'Sorry. Above my paygrade.'

And what is your paygrade? His card said Office of Balkan Liaison, but she'd never heard of that.

'I *want* to come back,' she insisted. 'The doctors said it'll help my recovery.'

He looked as if he believed her—or at least as if he wanted her to think so. 'You've been on secondment for eighteen months. And before that, you didn't have a London job for five years. They'll find you something to do soon enough.'

He gave a reassuring smile, which, eight years

43

her junior, couldn't help but patronise her. Abby gave a glassy smile of her own.

'Is there any news from Montenegro? The police—any progress?'

'They're keeping us informed.'

'Do they know who attacked me?'

'They haven't arrested anyone.'

'Any leads?'

'Probably.' Mark stretched his legs, pointing out the toes of his shoes, as if to admire them. 'Look, you know how it is. There are a lot of sensibilities here. The Montenegrins have only been independent five minutes and they're pretty touchy about it. We're putting pressure on them, discreetly of course, and they'll tell us when they've got something.'

'I read something online—that there's a rumour organised crime might have been involved.'

'You know as well as I do that the Balkans is one big rumour mill. Put it together with the Internet and you'll probably hear that Father Christmas was involved.' He blushed as he saw her face. 'I'm sorry. I didn't mean to be flip. I know this is pretty dire for you.'

Pretty dire. Abby closed her eyes. She could feel a headache coming on, and the throb in her shoulder that said she needed another pill.

She opened her eyes again. Mark looked up from checking his watch and rearranged his face in concern.

'Is there anything else?'

'Do you know what happened to Michael?'

He looked surprised. 'I thought you knew. They say he fell—'

'I know. I mean . . .' She could hardly say it. 'The

body.'

'There's a sister who lives in York. Apparently, she flew out to Montenegro and brought it—him—home for burial.'

'Do you have an address for her? I'd like to write.'

'Human Resources are the ones who'd know. They must have had something on file to track her down.'

Mark stood and gave her a lukewarm smile. He looked as if he might try to pat her on the shoulder, but thought better of it.

'I know how hard it must be for you, coming to terms with this. The best thing for you is to stay at home and get some rest.'

Please, she wanted to say. Don't make me go back there. But she let him open the door, and steer her out of the office. She thought he'd leave her at the lift, but once again he insisted on accompanying her all the way to the street.

'Good luck,' he said. 'If there's any news, we'll call straight away.'

'My phone's been disconnected.' She dug the new mobile out of her bag and gave him the number. 'This is how to find me.'

But she knew he wouldn't use it.

*   *   *

She picked up a curry on the way home and ate it curled up on the sofa. She was already putting on weight, though she'd lost so much in the hospital she thought it didn't matter. She stared out of the windows at the suburbs below. She imagined a glass canopy covering the whole city, cocooning its inhabitants in their daily lives, and herself above it hammering to be let in.

An hour on the web turned up no one called Lascaris in York. She tried to look up some friends, panning through online profiles to dredge up their contacts. But the numbers she could find were out of date or not answering; most of her friends, she supposed, weren't even in the country. It occurred to her she hadn't really had that many friends, not for a long time. She even thought about calling Hector—was seriously tempted—but drew the line at that.

And how long's that going to hold?

Somehow, she survived three more days. She forced herself to take walks on Clapham Common, morning and afternoon, setting herself little goals each time: the bandstand, the fishing lake, the Tube station. She binned the takeaway leaflets and bought a stack of supermarket ready meals, which she told herself was progress. She searched the Internet for news of her case, though there was nothing. She took her pills.

And then the letter came.

She almost threw it out. The address and the postage were both printed on the envelope: it looked like another reminder from TV Licensing. But it had her name on it, and she was grateful for anything that proved she still existed to the outside world.

How pathetic am I? she wondered as she tore it open.

It wasn't a demand from TV Licensing. It was a single sheet of paper, with three lines of text typed in the centre.

Jenny Roche
36 Bartle Garth
York

VI

Constantinople—April 337

A lifetime with Constantine has allowed me to form certain opinions. One is this: that the secret of greatness is escaping the past. The past is a fog, always trying to smother you, a chorus of cavilling voices counselling caution, restraint, moderation. A reproachful 'No' with the full weight of history.

A great man is dissatisfied with the world and impatient to improve it. The past's a messy impediment. A great man wants to rationalise the world, to remake it in the image of his own clarity.

That's why Constantine never liked Rome. Too much history. Too much mess. Temples built of mud and reeds, palaces overshadowed by tenements. In our youth, when we were taught how Julius Caesar grew up among plebeians in the Subura, I could see this jumbling of the natural order appalled Constantine. Grandeur and disease, divinity and squalor all tangled together. Too much history, too many ghosts.

I don't like Rome either.

Constantinople gave Constantine a blank canvas to start afresh (not literally—there had been a town here for a thousand years, Byzantium—but another aspect of greatness is the ability to see only what suits you). And so the new city, Constantine's city, fits his vision of how the world should be. It

47

stands on a promontory, not a marshy river basin. It progresses in orderly grades along the peninsula: plebeians out by the land walls; then the middling sort, merchants and *curiales*, as you head east towards the Philadelphion; then the grades of Senators, the *spectabiles* and the *clarissimi*, their grand houses queuing towards the hippodrome like fans on race day; and, finally, the imperial palace at the tip of the point. Beyond that, the only neighbour is the sea.

Or that's the theory. In practice, the city's only five years old and already it's beginning to deviate from Constantine's plan. Weeds have sprouted in the tiered garden he laid out: a tenement block somehow growing in the space between two villas; a grand house sold and converted into apartments; jumped-up merchants muscling in on an upscale neighbourhood. I imagine it causes Constantine more grief than barbarians or usurpers ever have.

*   *   *

I walk up the Via Mesi towards the palace. In my hand I clutch a paper scroll, a list of the men who were in the library that afternoon, as much as the porter could remember them. I've spent the last two hours interrogating the men who were still there and not learned a thing. Nothing seen, nothing heard. No one recognises the monogram necklace. A part of me whispers this might all be some elaborate hoax.

But the blood on the desk was real enough, and there are names on my list I haven't yet seen. Starting with that notorious hater of the Christians, Aurelius Symmachus.

Aurelius Symmachus was here. He left not long before I found the body.

Aurelius Symmachus lives suitably close to the palace, as befits his impeccable status. His doorman looks at me in disbelief when I announce myself: he can't believe I've come alone. He cranes his head out so far looking for my retainers he almost falls into the street. Of course, he's too well schooled to say anything. He admits me through to a peristyle garden surrounded by colonnades. White carp sit motionless in an oblong pool, watched over by a quartet of stone nymphs. In the shadows under the colonnades, I glimpse painted scenes of reclining gods. Dark heads watch me from the alcoves. Everything's exquisite and strangely dead.

Aurelius Symmachus emerges from a door, glancing over his shoulder as if midway through a conversation. He's a short, stout man who walks with a stick. He's almost bald, though white hair sticks out in tufts from behind his ears. He's wearing a toga: he must be getting ready to go somewhere, though for the moment it just enhances the impression that he's an anachronism. But his jaw is firm, and the eyes that watch me are as clear as diamonds.

We exchange pleasantries and size each other up. I suspect he dismisses me as a jumped-up soldier who's risen beyond all reason on a great man's coat-tails. He probably thinks I see him as a fossil of an order that passed a hundred years ago. Neither of us is entirely wrong. But neither of us has lived as long as we have without keeping an open mind.

'Were you at the Egyptian Library this afternoon?' I ask.

His stick scratches the ground, leaving a snake trail in the dust. 'I was.'

'Why?'

'To read.' He cocks a bushy white eyebrow, as if to say *I expected more of you*.

'Who were you reading? Hierocles, maybe?'

'Not today. Seneca, I always go back to, and Marcus Aurelius. They speak to our age.'

The mask on his face hasn't moved. Neither has mine. His stick still draws patterns in the dust.

'What do they say?' I ask.

'How ridiculous it is to be surprised at anything that happens.' The stick pauses. 'Imagine what I've seen in my life. Civil wars and peace. Sometimes one emperor, sometimes many, sometimes none. A bizarre cult condemned by one emperor, and that same cult now triumphant. Everything changes— even the gods.'

Does he think I'm seventeen? I know all this. But I'm not going to let him distract me playing the rambling old man.

'A man died in the library today.'

His face doesn't change. 'Alexander of Cyrene.'

'You knew him?'

'He was the Emperor's friend. That alone made him worth knowing.'

I admire the old philosopher's ambiguous phrasing. *That alone*—or—*that only*? We both know he might be talking about me.

'Did you see him there?'

'It's not a bathhouse. I don't go there for company.'

'When did you leave the library?'

'When the sun had moved round off my desk.' He brushes his hand over his eyes. 'My sight's not as strong as it was.'

'Did you know Alexander was dead when you left?'

'Of course not. Otherwise, I'd have stayed.'

'To see what happened?'

'So as not to look guilty.'

A pause. I look at the fish in the pool, as still as the reflections on the water. The house is close to the Via Mesi, Constantinople's great thoroughfare, but the walls do a good job keeping out the sound. I can hear servants in the rooms inside, filling lamps and fetching crockery. It's late in the day. The sun's come so low it's prised its way under the lip of the portico, washing the paintings and the statues in gold. My gaze wanders over them—and stops.

'Who's that?'

I take two steps towards the bust that's caught my eye, but Symmachus's voice outpaces me.

'Hierocles.'

Does he sound surprised? Was he expecting me to notice?

'Do you read him?' he asks. 'You should. He was no friend of new religions. Nor are you, I hear.'

I murmur Constantine's old platitude, 'Every man should be free to worship in the way that seems best to him.'

'Perhaps that's why you fell out with the Emperor,' he taunts me. I don't rise to the provocation. He must know it's not true, but he carries on regardless. 'They say you're not seen at the palace as often as you were.'

I turn politely. 'There was a bust of Hierocles in the library. Someone used it to smash Bishop Alexander's skull.'

Another pause. Our eyes lock.

'Has Constantine made you his *stationarius* now? A thief-taker dragging good men into the gutter?' His tone is even, but his craggy face is alight with rage. 'The penalty for bringing unsubstantiated charges is steep, Gaius Valerius. Even with the Emperor behind you, I doubt you could afford it.'

'Everyone knows your attitude to the Christians.' At the far end of the garden, beside the door, I can see the small shrine of the *lararium*, where he venerates his household gods. They're not so fashionable these days, I hear. Lots of families have moved them out of sight, into a back room where they can be safely ignored.

'Every man should be free to worship in the way that seems best.' He spits the words back at me, bobbing up and down. I watch him carefully. The anger's too real to be manufactured—at my age, I can tell the difference—but that doesn't mean he can't control it.

'Free to worship—as long as it's for the public good.'

He bangs his stick on the ground. 'If you want to accuse me of murder, say so. Say it, or get out of my house.'

But at that moment, a new actor enters our drama through the door by the *lararium*. He must be even older than me, but he has an air—a boyish grace, a carelessness—which makes him seem younger. His face is still handsome, his hair still dark, his smile still easy. He's munching on a fig, and he throws the peel into the fishpond as he passes. It's the first time I've seen the fish move.

Symmachus forces himself to swallow his anger.

'Gaius Valerius,' he introduces me. 'This is my friend Publilius Optatianus Porfyrius.'

The name catches me by surprise: it's not the first time I've heard it today. It's on my scroll of paper.

'Were you in the Egyptian Library today?'

I try to phrase it blandly, but he's attuned enough to catch the undertone of suspicion. He gives me a curious look. 'Is it a crime?'

'A man was murdered there,' says Symmachus. Is there weight in the glance that accompanies the words, a warning? Porfyrius doesn't seem to notice. He laughs, as if the old man's made a joke.

He sees that neither of us has joined in and his laugh trails off. He looks between us.

'But I was there myself,' he exclaims, redundantly. 'I didn't hear anything.'

'What were you doing?'

'I'd gone to meet Alexander of Cyrene.'

I wait for him to notice the look I'm giving him. I wait for the penny to drop. It doesn't take long.

'No.'

Porfyrius looks stunned. He recoils, as if he's felt the blow himself; he throws up his hands. Every movement's overdone, like an actor on the stage. Though, like an actor, it seems natural when he does it.

'Clubbed over the head,' Symmachus adds.

All the life's gone out of Porfyrius. He sits on the edge of the pond, his head in his hands. 'He was alive and well when I left him.'

'Why were you there?'

'The Augustus had commissioned him to write some sort of history. I served twice as Prefect of Rome—perhaps you remember?—and he wanted to check some facts about my tenure.'

'What sort of facts?'

53

'The monuments Constantine erected. The arch the Senate dedicated to him. Small details.'

'Did he seem frightened? Any hint of something worrying him?'

'Of course not.'

'Alexander's secretary said he had a document case. Do you remember it?'

'Yes . . . no . . .' Porfyrius drops his head. 'I don't remember.'

I pull out the necklace Constantine gave me.

'Do either of you recognise this?'

That forces them to look towards me, though they give nothing away. Both these men are so well schooled in the ways of court I could pull out their own mothers' heads and neither one would flinch.

Porfyrius stands, and moves closer to examine it.

'It reminds me of the Emperor's monogram. But not quite.'

He's right. Constantine's monogram is an X superimposed on a P, thus: ☧. The version in the necklace is subtly different, the two characters melded into one: ⳨. I ought to have noticed straight away.

'You didn't see anyone at the library wearing this?'

Porfyrius shakes his head. Symmachus just scowls.

'There were no women at the library,' Porfyrius says.

'But plenty of Christians.' Symmachus is standing on the line where sun gives way to shadow. Half his face is bright as gold, the other half sunk in darkness. 'Eusebius of Nicomedia. Asterius the Sophist. Any number of priests and hangers-on.'

'Could a Christian have killed one of their own?'

It's the first time I've heard Symmachus laugh. It's not a pretty sound—like a quarry-saw cutting marble. When he's finished, and hacked the phlegm from his throat, he says, 'Can an owl catch mice? Porphyry the philosopher said it best: "The Christians are a confused and vicious sect." Thirty years ago we were about to exterminate them. If I'd wanted to murder Alexander I could have done it then and been hailed a hero. Now the wheel has turned. They murdered their own god—what wouldn't they do to keep their privileges?'

Another serrated burst of laughter. 'They're only Roman.'

VII

York—Present Day

The city stood on a hill at the junction of two rivers, with the square towers of the Minster looming from its highest point. High walls hemmed it in— walls which had repelled Picts, Vikings, Norsemen and Scots in their time, but which couldn't resist the columns of traffic that now queued through the gates. On the facing bank, executive flats and smart chain restaurants occupied what had once been thriving wharves and warehouses.

The moment she got off the train from King's Cross, Abby could feel the difference. London had been close and warm, the friction of ten million people rubbing together. Here, the cold made her blush. A fine mist left dew on her cheek, while clouds overhead promised heavier rain to come.

She left the station and entered the city

where a roundabout breached the wall. A few gravestones from a long-lost churchyard waited outside, marooned by time and the ring road. A bridge and a hill brought her up to the great medieval cathedral, the Minster. It had been built to be bigger than the mind of man and was now, if anything, stranger, looming over the city like a visitor from an alien civilisation.

It was late in the season, but a few sightseers still clustered in front of it. A busker played ragtime on an open-faced piano; a man dressed as a Roman legionary tried to get tourists to photograph themselves with him. Behind them, mostly unnoticed, a green-bronze emperor lazed on a throne and contemplated the pommel of his broken sword.

The rain was getting harder. She wiped a drop from her forehead, and was surprised to feel how wet her hair was. Her body seemed to be drinking up the damp in the air.

Behind the Minster, the open spaces gave way to a warren of cobbled lanes, blind passages and narrow houses bunched together. The buildings were brown brick and squat, probably built in the last forty years, but somehow the ancient pattern of the streets still asserted itself on them. Some of the houses had pointed door frames, with strange leaded hoods hanging over them. She squeezed under the porch of Number 36 and rang the bell.

The door opened a few inches—as far as the chain would allow. A petite woman in a pink sweatshirt and jeans peered out at her. Her face was lined, her dark hair streaked with grey and pulled into a loose bun.

'Are you Jenny Roche?' A deep breath. 'Are you

56

Michael Lascaris's sister?'

She didn't need an answer. She could see it in the eyes: the same bright, inquisitive eyes as Michael, though dulled by age and pain.

'My name's Abby Cormac. I was Michael's . . .' *What?* 'I knew him in Kosovo. I was with him, when . . . I'm sorry I came without calling, but I didn't . . .'

The woman wasn't listening—wasn't even looking at Abby. She peered over Abby's shoulder at the empty street and the rain.

'Did you come alone?'

'Yes, but—'

'You'd better come in.'

*   *   *

It was hard to imagine Jenny as Michael's sister. Everything about Michael had been bold, extrovert, light-hearted; by contrast, Jenny seemed frail and deadly serious. Where Michael had been incurably chaotic, Jenny kept her house immaculate. Abby perched on a rose-patterned sofa covered in plastic and sipped tea from a fine-bone cup. Framed photographs covered every surface, a silent congregation watching them. Faded children on summer holidays in short shorts and floral dresses; teenagers with big hair and awkward smiles; proud adults cuddling babies. Abby wondered who they all were. There was no evidence of children in this pristine house, and Michael had never talked much about his family. He'd always given the impression they might be rather grand, though it was hard to square with this small, compressed house.

Several of the frames were empty, blank windows where photographs had recently been removed.

57

History unwritten.

'The police told me you were there,' Jenny said. 'I wanted to get in touch, but I didn't know how. They wouldn't let me in to the hospital.' She saw Abby's confusion. 'In Montenegro. I was there for the body.'

'Of course. They said.'

'They made me identify him.' Jenny shuddered. Tea slopped in her cup, but didn't escape over the rim. 'Don't ever let them make you do that. He'd been in the water three days when they pulled him out. Horrible. I felt like if I didn't look properly, they wouldn't think I'd done it right. I almost sicked up my lunch on him.'

'Did they say anything? Any clue who might have done it?'

Jenny put a hand to her throat. Slim fingers fiddled with a golden heart on a chain. 'Nothing. I thought you might know.'

'Not really.' Abby bit into her biscuit and tried not to spill crumbs. 'I've heard a rumour—not even that, just an idea—that organised crime might have been involved. I don't know how much you know about Kosovo—the Balkans generally—but it's like the Wild West. Weak governments that are no match for the organised criminals they're up against, if they're not completely owned by them. Michael worked in the customs service. It's possible he made some enemies, maybe without even realising it.'

'He didn't say anything to you? Before . . .'

'You know what Michael was like. Nothing was ever a problem.'

That drew a rueful smile that threatened to spill into tears. 'Always up to something. I was the big sister getting talked into his adventures—and then Mum blaming me for not stopping him when it went wrong.' A grimace. 'It usually went wrong.'

Jenny poured a fresh cup of tea from the pot. The spout rattled against the cup.

'I wasn't surprised he ended up out there. He was never one of those save-the-world people, but he loved adventure.'

'It's not that adventurous,' said Abby. 'And we're not saving the world. Michael used to say we were just trying to make Kosovo as dull as everywhere else. He said we were leading by example.'

'He couldn't have been dull if he tried.'

'No.'

A silence. A look passed between them: two strangers finding common ground in their grief. To Abby, it felt like nothing more than shared helplessness, but it seemed to decide something in Jenny. She stood abruptly and crossed to a mahogany cabinet in the corner.

'He did know something might happen.'

She unlocked a drawer. From inside, she pulled out a thick yellow envelope and passed it to Abby. Abby's heart quickened. It was postmarked Germany and addressed in Michael's handwriting. A neat scissor-cut had already opened it.

'Go on,' said Jenny.

Abby fished inside. Out came a postcard folded within a sheet of official-looking paper. There was a crest with a cross and a lion, and the heading *Rheinisches Landesmuseum Trier—Institut für Papyrologie*. Below it, a brief letter written in German, signed at the bottom by a Dr Theodor Gruber.

'Do you know what it says?' Abby asked.

Jenny shook her head. 'There's a man at church who speaks German, but I didn't like to take it to him. It's too personal, isn't it? Like a sort of message from beyond the grave.'

Abby looked at the front of the postcard, divided into three pictures. One showed a huge ancient gateway in the middle of a roundabout, blackened by fire; the second, a formal red-brick building on a tree-lined avenue; the third, a bearded man in a frock coat and a scowl. *Karl Marx*, said the legend at the bottom.

On the back, Michael had written two simple words.

My Love—

Nothing else. *Was that meant for me?* Abby wondered. She slid it back into the envelope with the paper and passed it to Jenny.

'What are you going to do?'

'What can I?'

'There's a phone number on the letterhead. You could call it.'

'I couldn't.' Jenny seemed to shrink into her sofa. She pushed the envelope back in Abby's hand. 'You have it. If there's any good can come of it, you'll do better than me.'

Jenny's strength seemed to be fading. Her face looked drawn. Abby sensed she didn't have much time.

'Where's Michael now?'

It was unfortunate phrasing. Jenny's anguished look made Abby wish she could melt onto the plastic-covered sofa. 'I meant . . . I just . . . I'd like to visit his grave, while I'm here.'

Jenny took Abby's teacup and stacked it on a brass tray. Her shaky hands threatened to smash the china.

'He was cremated. We scattered his ashes on the sea at Robin Hood's Bay. He didn't want a memorial. He always said: when you're gone, you're gone.'

And that seemed to be the signal for Abby to go. Jenny murmured something about having to collect her niece from Brownies; Abby said she ought to catch her train. The intimacy that had briefly united them had passed, but on the threshold, Jenny surprised her by sticking out her arms and giving Abby a hug. It was an awkward gesture, as if she wasn't used to such things. *As if she's as desperate for contact as I am*, thought Abby. *Clinging on.*

'Tell me if you find anything.'

Out on the street, the rain was unrelenting. Abby found a snicket between two houses, sheltered from the rain, and pulled out Michael's letter. She checked her watch. It was just past five o'clock—six in Germany—they'd probably have gone home. But she couldn't wait. She took out her phone and dialled the number, hoping she had enough credit.

A voice answered in German.

'Doctor Gruber, please?'

'A moment. I put you on hold.'

The voice gave way to a soft digital pulse that reminded her of the hospital in Montenegro. She shivered. At the far end of the street, a shadow detached itself from one of the houses and started to come towards her. A man in a long black raincoat and an old-fashioned trilby hat. The day was dark and the rain blurred her vision: the shapeless coat made him seem little more than a pocket of darkness.

'Hello?' A man's voice down the phone, thin and

61

accented.

'Doctor Gruber?'

'*Ja.*'

The shadow moved down the street. He could have been going anywhere, but there was something about his movement that seemed aimed straight at her. She looked around for reassurance, but the rest of the street was empty. Even the houses had turned their backs. White curtains blanked out the windows, like the sightless eyes of Jenny's empty photo frames.

Did you come alone? Why did Jenny ask that?

'*Hello?*' The phone—impatient—perhaps a little irritated. Abby turned and began to walk briskly, stumbling out her words.

'Doctor Gruber? Do you speak English? My name's Abby Cormac—I'm a friend of Michael Lascaris. Did you know him?'

A cautious pause. 'I know Mr Lascaris.'

'He's—' She glanced over her shoulder. The man in the raincoat was still following. 'He died. I was going through some papers he left and I found a letter you wrote to him. I wondered . . .'

If you know why he never mentioned you to me? If you know why he was in Trier? If you could tell me who killed him?

'. . . if you remembered him,' she finished lamely.

She came round a corner on to a street lined with shops. A car drove past, splashing through the puddles. She quickened her pace.

'I remember him,' said Doctor Gruber. 'I am sorry he is dead. He came to visit me not so long ago.'

'What did he want?'

The sound of the rain made it hard to hear, but

she thought she caught a new edge in his voice. 'I am the Director of the Institute for Papyrologie. You know this word, *papyrologie*? The study of papyrus. Ancient documents.'

'OK.' Another pause. 'I didn't know he was interested in ancient documents.'

'No?'

Another glance. The shadow was still there. He must have closed the gap—she could see a dim slice of his face between the brim of the hat and the coat collar, though it was too rushed and wet to make out any detail.

'Are you there? Is this a good time that you are able to talk?'

'Yes. It's fine. I—'

She swung around another corner and came face to face, unexpectedly, with the Minster. Rain had driven away the busker and the tourists; she thought she glimpsed the Roman legionary sheltering in a doorway, but he was so faint he might have been a ghost. Behind her, quick footsteps slapped on the cobbles.

'Where are you, Frau Cormac?'

'England.'

'Is it possible you come to visit us?'

'In Germany?'

'The Landesmuseum in Trier. I think face to face it will be easier to explain some things.'

She was running now, praying the church was still open. Weren't they supposed to be places of refuge? Under the bandages, her chest throbbed as if it would tear open. 'Please can't you tell me—?'

'In person is better.'

'Anything at all—'

'Herr Lascaris left instructions. Total

confidentiality. I cannot—'

The shadow had melted back into the rain, but she knew he had to be there. She ran up the steps and pushed through the heavy door into the Minster. 'I'll come. Thank you. Goodbye.'

And here at last there were people. Ushers in red cloaks and tourists in wet anoraks, heads tipped back to stare at the ceiling bosses. In the distance she could hear the pure high line of choristers singing a psalm. She shut off her phone and stood still, letting the immensity of the building embrace her.

One of the ushers approached. 'Are you here for the service? Evensong's just started.'

She looked at him dumbly and nodded. He led her into the quire, the wood-panelled area that was a virtual church within a church, and seated her on the end of a row of high-backed seats. More people, more warmth. Candles glowed on the pews, while hidden spotlights created soft pools of light and shadow in the high hollows of the church.

The congregation stood as the choir began to sing the Nunc Dimittis. *Lord, now lettest thou thy servant depart in peace.* Abby stood and closed her eyes. Tears and rain ran down her face; she wondered if the people around her could tell. She didn't care. In her mind she was in a small whitewashed church in Ealing, and a serious man was standing in the pulpit in his long white robe and golden stole. Her father.

Blessed are the peacemakers, for they shall have peace. Blessed are the merciful, for they shall have mercy.

'What would you have made of me now?' she whispered.

The song had finished. She heard a fluttering like birds around her as the congregation sat back down in the pews. She opened her eyes. She looked back to the door of the quire, a great wooden gateway underneath the stockade of organ pipes, to see if the shadow-man had followed her here.

The gates were shut and no one could come in. Beyond it, all was darkness.

VIII

Constantinople—April 337

I'm weary. I've been tramping around town for hours, breathing in the heat and the dust and finding that no one knows anything about the murder at the library. There was a time when I could walk forty miles in a day, but those days are a memory. I find a fountain and splash water over my face. I ease myself down on the wall and sit. The children playing in the street don't see me; their mothers, hurrying to finish their errands before nightfall, ignore me. They don't know who I was.

There's one final place I need to go today. It isn't far, but I almost miss the turn. I'm looking out for a statue on the corner, a nice bronze of a sea god riding in a chariot. It's only when I've gone fifty paces past it that I realise I've gone too far. I retrace my steps—and almost overshoot again. The statue's gone.

Constantinople's like that: a city of moving statues. They watch you from their plinths and pedestals, tucked in niches or on the tops of buildings. They become your companions, friends and guides. Then you wake up one morning and discover they've disappeared. Only the plinths remain, the inscriptions chiselled blank, waiting for their next occupants to move in. Of course, nobody mentions it.

Ten years ago there were a lot of empty plinths. Most of them are reoccupied now, but I still miss the old, familiar faces.

*   *   *

Alexander lived in a humble block of apartments above a tavern. A staircase to the left of the front door leads to the upper floors. I climb it and come to a landing.

It isn't hard to guess which is Alexander's door: it's the one with the painted chi-rho monogram and the heavy lock. The lock didn't work. The door's wide open, as if blown in by a breeze. But it's a still day, and it would have to have been a storm worthy of Jupiter to have splintered the jamb and ripped off the lock like that. I can hear movements inside.

A voice inside me says I shouldn't be here. I don't have much life left, but I don't want to lose it yet. Alexander's nothing to me except a ticket out of the city. I can come back in the morning and no one will know.

But I'm stubborn—and I've never run away in my life. I stand with my back to the wall and peer around the open door. The room's dim and utterly ruined. Hangings have been torn off the walls and ripped up; a shelf has been pulled over and its crockery smashed. In the midst of it all, a lone figure stands at a table strewn with papers, slowly leafing through them.

66

'Simeon?'

His head jerks up in surprise as I step into view. I stand in the doorway—close enough to make sure there's no one else, far enough to run if he pulls a knife.

He doesn't look like he's going to attack me. He looks more frightened than I do.

'What have you done?' I demand. 'Why—?'

'No.' He looks horrified. 'It was like this when I got here.'

'When?'

'Not long ago. I wanted to bring Alexander's books home. From the library.' His eyes are puckered trying to hold back tears. 'He wouldn't have wanted them left abandoned. Books were like children to him.'

I sweep my arm around the destruction in the room. 'And this?'

'When I got here,' he repeats. And then— gratuitously, given the shattered lock hanging off the door: 'Someone must have broken in.'

'You had a key?' But I can answer my own question: it's hanging on a string around his neck. I take it and try it in the lock. It fits.

'Was the lock new?'

'He had it fitted a month ago.'

'And is anything gone?'

A slack-jawed look. 'I don't know. Some papers, maybe. He had nothing worth taking.'

'What about the document case missing from the library? What was in that?'

'He never let me see.'

He gave you the key to his house, but he wouldn't show you what was in the case? I lean over the writing desk and look at the scattered papers.

Prominent among them is the codex that Simeon has brought from the library. Blood has oozed out from between the pages, as if some part of Alexander has been pressed inside it.

I remember what Porfyrius told me.

'I heard Alexander was writing a history—that the Emperor commissioned it.'

Simeon's face brightens. 'The *Chronicon*. A history of everything that's ever happened.'

He opens to a page at random. Again, it takes me by surprise. It doesn't look like the histories of Pliny or Tacitus that we studied in school. It looks like a ledger. Parallel columns line the page, haphazardly filled with short paragraphs. Greek and Roman numerals weave through the margins and run into the text.

I lean over, struggling to decipher it. I've never been good with Greek—and this is filled with barbarous names and exotic places.

'Alexander designed it to reconcile the histories of the Jews, the Greeks, the Romans and the Persians from the beginning of the world,' Simeon explains. 'The whole unfolding of God's creation. A map of time, laid out to reveal its mysteries.'

But I don't hear him. It's a book of time, and every page is a door. To read it is to step through.

In the sixteenth year of his reign, the Emperor Constantius died in Britain, at York.

*　　　*　　　*

York—July 306—Thirty-one years ago . . .
There's blood in the air when we ride into York. It's accompanied us every step of our journey, a thousand miles across the empire. Blood in the

stables the night we left, our long knives wet from the horses we'd lamed. Blood on our knees, our thighs and our hands where the saddles chafed us raw. Thirty-seven days' hard riding, always peering over our shoulders. It wasn't until we caught sight of Britain's dirty-white cliffs that I believed we'd make it.

Constantine's been living on borrowed time for a year now. The politics are complicated but reduce to this: he's after another man's job. Two emperors share the empire at the moment. Galerius rules the eastern half, while Constantius, Constantine's father, rules the west. Constantine stays at Galerius's court in Sirmium as a hostage to their bargain. Galerius knows there's nothing more dangerous than an imperial heir at a loose end, but he can't kill Constantine while Constantius reigns as his colleague. Instead, he encourages Constantine to occupy himself hunting dangerous animals in remote places, or picking fights with barbarian tribes noted for their savagery.

But now Constantius is dying. The news arrived at dinner-time thirty-eight days ago. If it had come in the morning we'd be dead by now. But Galerius is an insensible drunkard: anything that happens after noon might as well not happen until next morning. By then, we were already a hundred miles away, leaving behind only a stable full of hamstrung horses.

And now we're here in York. The fortress stands on a hill between two rivers, with the square tower of the Principia, the headquarters, crowning its highest point. On the far bank, the civilian town sprawls up the slope from the jetties and warehouses where sea cargoes are unloaded.

The guards at the gate stiffen as they see us approach, then go ramrod straight when they hear Constantine's name. That's a good sign.

'Is my father alive?' he demands. 'Are we in time?'

The guard nods. Constantine lifts his eyes to the sun and touches his forehead, giving thanks.

The moment we reach the Principia, ready hands pluck Constantine away from me to some inner chamber. I loiter in a corridor and watch. Guards are moving heavy strongboxes towards the portico at the front of the parade ground, while officials keep count on wax tablets. Everyone seems to know exactly what they're doing.

The heavy tramp of footsteps rises above the noise as Constantine comes around the corner. A knot of generals and aides in full uniform surround him: somewhere in the last hour he's found time to scrub his face and put on a gilded cuirass. It's jarring to see him like this, reclaimed by his old life. We've lived in each other's pockets for months now, first in the palace and then on the road. I wasn't prepared for how suddenly it would change.

As he comes level with me, I call out, 'How's your father? Will he—?'

'He died two days ago.' Constantine doesn't look at me, doesn't break stride. His entourage brush past, walling him off. 'The Praetorian Prefect kept it secret until I got here.'

The Praetorian Prefect is marching beside him, a horsehair crest as stiff as a corpse. Constantine's face is blank: it's impossible to tell if he resents what they did or if he approves. Does he have a choice?

I fall in behind them as they march through

70

a pair of double doors on to the parade ground. The whole assembled army roars when they see Constantine. He holds up his hands for silence, but they're in no mood to obey. They keep on shouting, chanting his name and stamping their boots, while Constantine stands there with arms stretched wide apart. It's impossible to tell who's controlling whom.

I don't remember exactly what Constantine says when they eventually fall silent. He tells them his father passed away half an hour ago and they bellow out their grief. He tells them that he, Constantine, has no standing in the empire and that Galerius will appoint a successor to Constantius in due course.

They don't like that. An angry murmur swells within the crowd—and suddenly it's not the noise but the crowd itself surging forward. The bodyguards at the front make an effort to hold them back, but it's curiously ineffective. A dozen legionaries clamber on to the dais and start shouting at Constantine: it's an extraordinary violation, but he doesn't move, not even when they grab his arms and drag him down into the crowd. The clamour is deafening. The Praetorian Prefect fingers the hilt of his sword, but doesn't dare move.

And then a curious thing happens. No one can see Constantine, but somehow the mood changes. Faces brighten; the menace in the air evaporates. The shouts no longer sound angry, but triumphant.

Constantine's head appears, rising out of the crowd as if he's being drawn to heaven. The noise redoubles. Somewhere in the scrum, someone's managed to tie a purple cloak on to him. They hoist him on to a shield and hold him aloft. The shield sways and tilts as they pass it from man to man, but Constantine keeps his balance: shaking the upraised hands, smiling, shouting unheard replies to the acclamations of his men.

For some reason, the image that comes to mind is Neptune, his seaborne chariot skimming across the waves. Constantine looks magnificent—a god defying the elements.

But his footing is precarious. And if he falls, he'll drown.

*   *   *

Constantinople—April 337
'Count Valerius?'

I'm not in York. I'm standing in a ransacked apartment surveying the wreckage of a dead man's life. And Simeon the deacon is waiting for me.

I'm embarrassed by my lapse into memory. To cover it, I ask, 'Do you know a man called Publilius Porfyrius, a former Prefect of Rome?'

'He was a friend of Alexander's.'

'He was in the library today—he said Alexander asked to meet him there. You didn't see them together?'

'Alexander had me running errands most of the day. I was barely in the library.'

'What sort of errands?'

'Fetching more paper and ink from the stationers. Picking up some books he'd had copied, and some documents from the imperial archives for his history. Delivering messages. That was why I was away when he died.'

'Where had you gone?'

'Alexander sent me to fetch Bishop Eusebius of Nicomedia.'

It's the second time today I've heard Eusebius's name. 'Why didn't you mention him before?'

The question surprises him. 'He never arrived.'

'Symmachus said he was there.'

Simeon's face tells me what he thinks of that. 'Eusebius is a bishop.'

I can't tell if he's trying to be provocative, or just naïve. I remember Symmachus's words. *The Christians are a confused and vicious sect.*

Which are you? I wonder. *Confused or vicious?*

IX

Trier—Present Day

The passport made her feel like someone else. The embassy had issued it to get her home from Montenegro, after her old one vanished somewhere between the villa and the hospital. It wasn't the photograph, though that was pretty horrific: it was the emptiness. Her last passport was eight years old and had visa stamps from half the countries in the world, barely a page unfilled. 'Your life in bureaucracy,' Michael had teased her. And now it was gone.

But the new passport was valid, and that was enough for the bored man at St Pancras Station who waved her through the checkpoint. Six hours and three trains later she was in Trier, wondering if she was mad to have travelled halfway across Europe on a whim. Her shoulder hurt from being squashed on trains all day; she felt as though she'd run a marathon.

She checked into the Römische Kaiser Hotel, across the road from the Porta Nigra, the Black Gate featured on Michael's postcard. She couldn't stop staring at it.

Did you see it? she asked Michael, carrying on a dialogue she'd been having all the way from London. *Did you stay in this very same hotel? When were you here?*

At least she could guess that. The letter from the museum was dated late July, a month before Michael died. Michael had been unexpectedly away around then, at a conference of EU border agencies in Saarbrücken. She thought she could remember a conversation about it: a sudden change of plan, a colleague who'd dropped out at the last minute, forcing Michael to go. He'd brought her back a sausage and a bottle of Riesling—the only good thing to come out of the conference, he'd said.

He hadn't mentioned going to Trier.

*   *   *

Most towns, Abby supposed, stood on the foundations of the past. In Trier, past and present stood side by side. It seemed everything in the last thousand years was just a threadbare carpet laid down over the Roman town, whose remains poked through the holes at every turn. The Black Gate, four stories high and completely intact. The modern road bridge across the Moselle, supported on piers originally sunk by Roman engineers. The high brick walls of the Roman basilica, dwarfing the pink gingerbread mansion beside it. And beyond it, across a green lawn and a lake, the museum.

She had an appointment, but the receptionist said Dr Gruber was in a meeting that had run over. Abby bought a ticket and wandered through the museum while she waited. In a long, semi-circular gallery, she found huge pieces of sculpture lined up in rows. When she read the descriptions, they all seemed to be tomb monuments.

'To reach the living, it is necessary first to navigate the dead.'

She turned. A thin man in a blue suit had come up behind her. His hair had receded, revealing a bulging, glossy forehead. He had a bony face, and a bristling moustache that ought to have gone out of fashion seventy years earlier.

'Mrs Cormac?'

That caught her out. Even when she was married, she'd never felt like a *Mrs*. She shook his hand. 'Dr Gruber?'

'The Romans believed that the dead contaminated the living. They buried them outside the city walls. You could not enter a Roman city without walking past the tombs, sometimes for many kilometres. That is what we try to replicate here.'

He led her out through an unmarked door and up a flight of stairs to his office. A beige machine stood on a table against the wall. Behind the desk, tall windows overlooked the park and the high brick building across the lake.

'You know what that is?' Gruber asked.

'Constantine's basilica.' She'd read it in a leaflet in the hotel.

'It was the throne room of Constantine's palace, when he ruled the empire from here in Trier. *Der*

75

Kaiser Constantine.' He fiddled with a pen on his desk. 'Of course, today you ask most people, they say Beckenbauer is *Der Kaiser.*'

Abby smiled as if she knew what he meant. 'What's the building next to it?'

'The local government.'

'Not quite the same as a Roman emperor.'

'But functionally it is the same, no?' He scratched at his moustache. 'There are certain places where power abides. One thousand and seven hundred years ago, Constantine built his palace there. Since then it has been used by Frankish counts, medieval archbishops, Renaissance prince-electors, Prussian kings and now our local government. Every generation of power comes to this place. Do they think that the history gives them legitimacy? Or is there some animal response inside us, which these places subconsciously provoke? That attracts.'

Abby had heard men talk about animal responses before. Usually, they only had one particular thing in mind. She pulled her cardigan closer across her chest and forced herself to look him in the eye.

'You said that Michael came to visit you here.'

The pen in his hand stopped moving. 'This is correct.'

'You said you could tell me what he wanted.'

'I said I could not tell you on the telephone.'

'He brought you something—a piece of papyrus he wanted you to analyse. I've read the letter you gave him.'

She'd picked up some basic German on the mission in Kosovo: that, together with an online translation tool and a dictionary had allowed her to piece together most of the meaning. She hadn't wanted anyone else to see it.

This is to confirm receipt of a late antique papyrus, unknown provenance, for micro-CT scanning. All results will be kept highly confidential and informed to the owner solely.

'If you have read the letter, you know this is confidential. The results of the tests, I can give only to Mr Lascaris himself.'

'Michael's dead.'

'And you are his executor? His heir? You have papers that prove it?'

'I was his partner.'

'I am sorry. He did not mention you.'

Abby leaned forward. 'Dr Gruber, Michael was murdered in some pretty extreme circumstances. I was there. I don't know how much he told you about himself . . .'

Gruber pulled a pack of cigarettes out of his desk and lit one. 'He was economical with his biography.'

'Michael worked for the European Union, and his murder was an international incident. The police are still investigating. I'm sure they'll be keen to retrace his movements in the weeks before his death—and find out what was in his possession.'

'But you are talking as if we are some sort of criminal enterprise here.' He frowned, to show he wasn't insulted, simply expected better. 'We are a government-funded institution with an impeccable academic reputation. The most advanced in the field. If the police come here with questions, naturally we will cooperate.'

But she'd sat at tables opposite infinitely more difficult men than Gruber—and learned how to play them. The cigarette had burned down quickly. She could see the thought rattled him.

Provenance unknown, the letter said. In other

words: *if no one claims it he gets to keep it. And he definitely wants to keep it.*

'I only want to see it. And the papyrus wasn't the only artefact. There was something else that Michael left me—perhaps you could advise me on it, after I've seen the manuscript.'

I'll show you mine if you show me yours.

The cigarette had burned down to the filter. Gruber stubbed it out in a copper ashtray, then stood. He took a fat bunch of keys from his pocket and unlocked a deep drawer in the filing cabinet behind his desk. Out came a steel briefcase with a combination lock. Gruber's finger hovered over the dial.

'I appreciate if you keep this in confidence. The analysis is incomplete. It would be unfortunate if misinformed speculation created confusion— before we can publish in the correct channels.'

'Of course.'

He snapped open the case. A soft bed of tissue paper and raw cotton filled it: in the centre lay a dark brown, tusk-shaped lump that reminded Abby of some petrified wood she'd seen in a museum. Gruber pulled on a pair of white cotton gloves and lifted it carefully into a white mould that looked like a plaster cast.

'You are familiar with our work here in the institute?'

'I read a bit on your website.'

'Micro-CT. The CT stands for Computed Tomography. It is a multiple X-ray scan which builds a fully three-dimensional digital model of an object to a resolution of twenty-five microns.' He saw the look on her face. 'Very precise.'

'OK.'

He slid the mould into a perspex cannister and carried it across the room to the machine that Abby had noticed when she came in. It looked like a cross between a microwave oven and an early Eighties computer—a small compartment with a glass door, between two angular blocks of beige metal. A yellow sticker in one corner warned of radioactivity.

'Is that it?'

'Michael Lascaris was unusual in bringing the papyrus to us—most manuscripts must be scanned in the libraries which hold them. We make the machine portable enough to travel.'

He put the papyrus upright in the chamber and closed the glass door. He pressed a button. A white light came on, spotlighting the canister, which slowly rotated in place.

'Forgive me, but what's the point of all this? You're trying to read the scroll with X-rays?'

'Eventually. To begin, we must first unravel it. The papyrus is a scroll that has been rolled up for centuries. Over that time, the paper has become damp and fused together. To physically unroll it would destroy it. What we are doing is using X-rays to build a 3-D model of the entire roll on a microscopic level. Then, with powerful algorithms, the computer can virtually unroll this into a single sheet as it would have appeared to the man who wrote it.'

'And then you can read it?'

'Perhaps. Before about AD 300, the ink is carbon-based. They use soot to make the ink black. After that, they start to write with iron-gall ink. This uses a chemical reaction between acid and iron sulphites to make an ink that lasts much longer. Because there are actually tiny particles of iron in the ink, it absorbs light differently, and so it is possible to register it on the scan.

A picture appeared on the wide screen mounted on the wall above the scanner—a monochrome image of the scroll spinning in virtual space. In black and white it looked like a lump of coal. When Gruber touched it, the image seemed to fly towards them until it filled the screen. It turned end-on, revealing tiny concentric whorls.

'Those are the spirals of the scroll,' said Gruber.

'Can you read it?'

Gruber touched the corner of the screen and it went blank. 'Scanning is easy. Unravelling . . .' He sighed. 'Imagine cutting an onion into the smallest possible pieces. Then imagine you have to put back the pieces to reassemble the original onion. The analytical power required is immense. And this is not an official project. If I run the analysis, I must do it when the computer cluster is not in use.'

Hope withered inside her. *And what was Michael doing with an ancient papyrus scroll?* 'Did he say where he found it?'

Gruber sat down and lit another cigarette, offering Abby one as an afterthought. She took it gratefully.

'Mr Lascaris was—I think it is the right word—reticent, yes? He did not tell me where he found this thing. He did not tell me how he happened to possess it. He did not even say his occupation, though it was obvious he was not a researcher. I was hoping if you came here, you might give me some answers.' He tapped some ash into the ashtray. 'At least now I know he was a diplomat.'

Abby took a drag of the cigarette. The nicotine was like a gift. 'I wish I could help you.'

His eyes narrowed. 'You said you had something you would show in return.'

'I do.' She took the gold necklace out of her bag and passed it across. Still wearing his white gloves, he held it up between finger and thumb and squinted at it through the magnifier he kept on his desk. His eye went as big as a tennis ball.

'Did he find this with the manuscript?'

Abby blew out a long stream of smoke. She hadn't smoked in years—she was already feeling dizzy. 'I didn't know he even had the manuscript until you told me.'

'Do you know what it is?'

'An old Christian symbol.'

'It's a variant on the Christogram—the monogram of the Emperor Constantine. You know this story? He had a vision the night before a battle, an angel came and showed him the sign. It's like the Greek letters X and P, which are the first two letters of *Christos*—Christ—in Greek. He made a jewelled model of this sign, the *labarum*, and carried it into the battle as his standard. He won the battle—and ever since we are all Christians in Europe.'

'Could it relate to the manuscript?'

'The Christogram has been in use ever since Constantine. You can go into any church here in Trier and find it today, probably. The most I can say is that the necklace looks like late antique workmanship.'

'What about the ink? You said if it contained iron it would be after AD 300.'

'Preliminary analysis suggests the ink is the gall-iron variety. And there is the language. Most papyrus scrolls that have survived are written in

81

Greek. This one is in Latin, which suggests it dates to the fourth century after Christ. The Roman Empire was changing in this period.' He waved out the window to the high basilica. 'Regrettably, Trier did not keep the Emperor Constantine's affection. He built a new capital—Constantinople, now Istanbul—a new Rome for a new Christian empire.'

But Abby wasn't interested in Gruber's history lecture. She could feel her heart throbbing against the bandages.

'How do you know it's Latin?'

'Excuse me?'

'You said this manuscript's in Latin. But you also told me you haven't managed to analyse the scan yet. So how do you know what the language is?'

Gruber stood. 'Thank you for your interest, Frau Cormac, but I think you must be leaving. I am a busy man; I have given you already too much time.' He moved around the desk to open the office door, but Abby stepped in his way, blocking him in next to the machine. She put her hand on the glass hatch.

'If you send me away now, I'm taking this with me.'

Gruber's moustache twitched. 'That is theft.'

'You're welcome to call the police.'

'But you cannot read the manuscript. If you even try, you will destroy it.'

'There are other machines like this in the world. I'll try them.'

Leverage, they'd called it on her Foreign Office-approved training courses. Out on the field they'd just called it squeezing the bastards.

Gruber sank back and sat on the edge of his desk. 'You think someone else will help you?

An unknown woman with a manuscript that has probably been stolen. Maybe you try to take it to an American university. The Americans will confiscate it. They will lock it away in a warehouse without temperature or humidity controls, and in ten or twenty years, if anyone thinks to look, they will find nothing but dust.'

Abby picked up Gruber's pack of cigarettes and offered him one. He took it with a rueful sigh and let her light it.

'*Danke.*'

She took a drag on her own cigarette and wondered if two made it a habit. 'Why don't we start with the truth?'

'What I said was the truth.' He saw her anger coming and waved it back. 'The computational power necessary is immense—possibly weeks of machine time. Even when we have the image, it is not like just reading a book. Every letter must be deciphered, checked, corrected.'

He looked down and blew smoke at his shoes.

'But, I admit, I was curious about this document with no past and no owner. I have analysed a few lines.'

He leaned back over his desk and reached in the drawer. Out came a sheet of notepaper covered in what looked like childish scribbles. Only when Abby leaned closer could she see it was writing—fragments of text written and crossed out, rewritten and recrossed out, until the words ran out of room and escaped further down the page, only to be caught up and savaged again. It looked like the ravings of a madman.

'On the back.'

This was neater. Three paragraphs, four lines

each. One in Latin, one in German and the third in English.

> To reach the living, navigate the dead,
> Beyond the shadow burns the sun,
> The saving sign that lights the path ahead,
> Unconquered brilliance of a life begun.

A chill passed through her as she read it. She thought she could feel the blood pressing on the bandages. She remembered what Jenny had said: *It's too personal, isn't it? Like a sort of message from beyond the grave.*

'Do you know what it is?'

'The language fits with a date somewhere around the fourth century. The imagery is Neoplatonic, and this word "unconquered"—*invictus*—is a standard epithet for Roman emperors of this period.'

'But do you know who wrote it?'

Gruber scratched his throat, where his collar had chafed it.

'The first two lines match an inscription on a gravestone which was once in the Imperial Forum Museum in Rome. The other two lines do not appear anywhere in the classical corpus. So far as I can establish, it is an entirely new discovery.'

No wonder you wanted to keep your hands on it. She folded the paper and put it in her bag, then cast about for something to say, but couldn't think of anything.

'Did you do the translation yourself?'

'Herr Lascaris wanted his money's worth from me.' He saw her confusion and laughed. 'Perhaps I should have said. For this work, he promised he would pay me one hundred thousand euros.'

A hopeful look.

'Perhaps you will honour his agreement?'

X

Constantinople—April 337

I'm distracted. I should be thinking about the task at hand, but every time I try to concentrate my mind slips the leash and is back in the past. I'm lying on a couch in the *triclinium* of my house, poring over Alexander's papers by the light of a bronze lamp. Even the slaves have gone to bed.

Alexander's *Chronicon* lies open, walking me through my own history. What strikes me most, in the years after Constantine's acclamation, is the great profusion of names. *Maxentius named Augustus . . . Severus Caesar killed . . . Licinius named emperor by Galerius.* Names which once carried so much power. Now their statues have been pulled down and their names are never spoken. Not unless someone whispers them off a page in the deep darkness of the night.

*   *   *

Trier—March 307—Thirty years ago . . .

When the army acclaimed Constantine emperor, Galerius responded as he always did: with bad grace and a play for time. He accepted Constantine's accession—he didn't have the strength to oppose him—but gave him the junior rank of Caesar, rather than the senior rank of Augustus, which Constantine should have inherited from his father. If Galerius hoped to provoke Constantine into an

85

act of treachery, he was disappointed. Constantine accepted the slight without demur, and sent his credentials to Galerius to show he would willingly serve under him.

But emperors aren't what they used to be. For more than two hundred years after the first Caesar Augustus, one man ruled the empire as sole proprietor. In the last thirty years, it's become a joint enterprise. I still wonder why. Did the empire become so bloated that no one man could manage it? Or did men somehow shrink in stature, unable to fill the purple shoes of the giants who made Rome? Whichever it is, the ramifications are obvious. Emperors are like rabbits: either there is one, or there are many. Diocletian split his empire into two, then expanded it to four. Some of those four had sons who needed an inheritance; others abdicated, then thought better of it. At last count, there were six men claiming the title of *Imperator Invictus*—unconquered emperor.

Six men, each jealous of the others, can't all stay unconquered for long.

Two of those men are a father and son called Maximian and Maxentius. Old Maximian was persuaded to abdicate five years ago, but retirement didn't agree with him. Young Maxentius was overlooked for promotion, like Constantine, but found an obliging corps of praetorian guards in Rome who, for a consideration, were willing to drape him in purple. They're an impossible family, each as bad as the other. Both have dainty flushes on their cheeks that make them look permanently embarrassed, and wide, feminine eyes that have seen every wickedness imaginable.

But today they're on their best behaviour.

86

They've come to Constantine's capital at Trier to celebrate the marriage of Maxentius's sister Fausta to Constantine. It's actually Constantine's second marriage, but his first needn't detain us. It certainly didn't detain him, when a quick divorce offered the opportunity for a more advantageous match.

Everyone's pretending it's a completely normal occasion. No one's so crass as to mention the fact that this happy day is also a calculated act of treachery. By allying himself with the pair of father-and-son usurpers, Constantine is leaving Galerius no choice but to move against him.

'Maximian and Maxentius could have made peace with Galerius and combined to crush me,' Constantine explained, when I warned him against the match. 'If Galerius wants to come after me now, he'll have to attack my new brother- and father-in-law first.'

'You'll be obliged to defend them,' I pointed out.

Constantine smiled. 'Perhaps.'

For now, harmony reigns. We're gathered in the throne room of Constantine's palace, which is decked with garlands and the light of a hundred torches. The marital bed stands in the centre of the room draped with a purple cloth, embroidered in gold with scenes of hunts and battles. It's only symbolic. The real action will happen elsewhere, later.

I hear singing as the bride approaches, the glow of torches from the chamber beyond. Slaves throw open the doors and there she stands. A veil spun from russet silk covers her face, and her dress is belted under her breasts with a cord tied in the intricate knot of Hercules. The bridegroom's supposed to unpick it, though knowing Constantine, he'll probably just cut it.

Her attendants lift her over the threshold—carefully. You don't want to drop an emperor's bride in front of him. Everyone's watching. I've seen brides shrink under the attention, but Fausta seems to be enjoying it. She's only fifteen, but there's nothing of the virgin in her pose. Under her dress, one leg's cocked slightly forward, thrusting out her hips and arching her back. As if she's daring us to imagine what's going to happen that night.

Constantine steps forward, a torch in his hand and his *auspex* beside him. The auspex is supposed to read the entrails, though there'll be no blood sacrifice at Constantine's wedding. Constantine takes Fausta's hand and asks her name in the ritual fashion.

'Wherever you are Gaius, I am Gaia,' she replies, the words so ancient no one knows what they mean.

When Constantine married the first time, I stood beside him as *auspex*. Now that he's an emperor, only a fellow emperor will do. I try not to let it bother me.

Constantine hands her the torch. His brother-in-law-to-be Maxentius passes him a gold ewer filled with water, and Constantine gives that to Fausta, too. Then he pulls back her veil.

Whatever the political merits of the marriage, there's no denying its physical compensations. The family resemblance comes out well in Fausta: the long-lashed eyes and buttery skin, so effeminate on her father and brother, give her a voluptuous beauty. She's at an age where her body's plumped up like ripe fruit, breasts and hips and thighs swelling under her gown, while her face still keeps its childish innocence. A dangerous age.

Constantine leads her to the marriage bed. They recline there in a stylised embrace, while the guests queue to congratulate them. There are three emperors here and precedence is a nightmare, but there's no question who should go first. Constantine's mother, the Dowager Empress Helena. She's sixty, but still the most commanding woman in the room: high cheekbones and a stern mouth, blue eyes that miss nothing, no hint of a stoop in those bony shoulders. Rumour says she was the daughter of a brothel keeper, but I've known her all my life and never dared ask. Underneath the applications of white powders and Tyrian vermilion it's impossible to tell what she's thinking. Perhaps she's wishing this was a Christian ceremony. Perhaps she's thinking she's seen this scene played out before: when Constantine's father divorced her to make a more expedient marriage.

In fact, the parallel's even more excruciatingly exact. Constantine's father divorced Helena to marry one of old Maximian's daughters; now Constantine has shrugged off his first wife to marry another of the fecund old man's children. His uncle-in-law will become his brother-in-law. Even the women of that family are serial usurpers.

A small boy barges into the line behind Helena and grabs the skirts of her dress. No one else would dare touch her, but Crispus is her only grandson and can tap a seam of indulgence that even Constantine can't access. Perhaps he reminds her of Constantine as a boy: even if you'd only ever seen Constantine's profile on coins, you'd know Crispus was his son. He has the same round face, the same brilliant light in his eyes. Helena lifts him up on to the bed. Constantine hugs him and ruffles his hair;

Fausta lets him give her a kiss on the cheek. She smiles, though it doesn't reach her eyes. The look she gives him makes me think of a cuckoo sizing up another bird's eggs.

Crispus's tutor, a skinny man with a long beard, runs up and pulls him back off the bed. The crowd laugh.

'What will become of him, do you think? The boy, Crispus.'

A courtier, I can't remember his name, has sidled up behind me. He tips his cup towards the marriage bed, as if toasting the happy couple's health.

'Will the Emperor push him aside, do you think?'

I hate these guessing games. 'He's still Constantine's firstborn son,' I say firmly. 'Constantine, of all men, won't abandon him.'

Constantine knows what it's like to see your mother jilted for a younger, better-connected woman. Not that it's stopped him doing exactly the same thing.

Too many wives and too many emperors, and too many sons repeating their fathers' mistakes. No wonder the empire's always at war with itself.

XI

Thalys Train, Near Rheims—Present Day
What was Michael doing with a seventeen-hundred-year-old scroll?

Why was he willing to pay a hundred thousand euros to read it, when he didn't even know what it would say?

Where did he get that kind of money?

The questions chased themselves around her head as she sat in her seat and stared out of the rain-spattered windows. An illuminated readout above the carriage door registered their speed. *287 kmh*. Hurtling along—going where?

Michael had always had money. If she was honest, it had been part of his appeal. Not the money itself, but his way with it, the easy extravagances. Growing up as the daughter of a minister, indulgence wasn't just a practical impossibility: it was a moral outrage. Being with someone who spent his money without doubts or regrets had been a gush of freedom. His ridiculous car, which even the gangsters in Pristina wouldn't touch; the champagne and fine wines that flowed every time he entered a restaurant; the hotel suites whenever they went away. Each time Abby thought she'd got used to it and couldn't be shocked, he'd find some new way of spending money that appalled and thrilled her all over again. And if she said anything, he'd shrug and give her a kiss on the forehead.

You can't take it with you.

A phone started to trill. She didn't recognise the sound: it was only when other passengers started staring at her that she realised it was hers. It was the first time she'd heard it ring. She jabbed the button.

'Abby? It's Mark.' She needed a moment to place the name. 'From the Foreign Office. Are you out of the country?'

She hesitated. *How does he know?* The ringtone must have sounded different.

'There wasn't much to do in London,' she said. 'I thought a change of scene might help.'

'Right. Gosh. No stopping you. Are you going to come back?'

'I'm on my way home now.'

'Wonderful. Give me a bell when you're back and we'll arrange for you to come in.'

'Have you got a job for me?'

'We'll have a chat.'

*　　　*　　　*

London

Mark met her and brought her up to the office. Once again, the vast and empty corridors overwhelmed her. Statues of Victorian statesmen dressed as Roman generals lurked in the shadows, one empire to another. Classical Graces peered down from a ceiling frieze. Trust, Fortitude, Justice . . . Everything she'd once believed in.

Mark led her back to the third-floor meeting room. It overlooked a vast marbled atrium, where a hundred years ago an imperial monarch had taken homage from her far-flung subjects. Now it was mostly used for seminars and cocktail parties.

'How was the trip? Somewhere nice?'

'I went to Paris.'

'Mmm, lovely. Gorgeous this time of year. Did you make it to the Matisse exhibition? How long were you there? Stay somewhere nice? Sugar?'

It was all small talk as he pottered about making coffee, but she had the feeling he was paying close attention to her answers.

'When can I come back to work?'

'Champing at the bit, eh?' His pomposity was breathtaking.

I was ducking bullets in war zones while you were

still round the back of the bike shed playing with dirty magazines, Abby told him silently.

'HR are worried about your "well-being".' He held up his fingers in quotation marks. 'They're insisting on a full assessment—medical, psychiatric, the works—before they'll bring you off the bench.'

She put on her best sane face. 'Psychiatric assessment?'

'You've suffered severe physical trauma, stress, and bereavement. Your file says there was also some memory loss.'

'Short-term. Haven't they ever heard of getting back on the bike?'

'We're just watching out for you.' He took off his glasses and gave her a nothing-shall-come-between us look. It made her want to punch him.

'So why did you want to see me?'

'I didn't.' A self-deprecating grin. 'I'm just the go-between, really. Chai-wallah. Hello.'

A man had appeared at the door. He came in and locked it behind him. He had iron-grey hair chopped short and awkward, a hard face and an economical precision in his movements that reminded Abby of soldiers she'd known.

'Mrs Cormac, my name is Jessop.'

'Jessop's from Vauxhall,' Mark explained.

He means SIS, Abby thought. *Often known as MI6*, as their incongruous job adverts put it.

Jessop seated himself across the table from her and unzipped his bag. Out came a small, pen-shaped piece of plastic.

'Does that squirt poison ink or something?' Nerves made her flippant.

'Voice recorder.' Jessop pushed a button on the end of the device. A red light went on.

'This interview is taking place under the terms of the Official Secrets Act. Please state your name and confirm you're aware this conversation is being recorded.'

Interview? 'What's this got to do with the Official Secrets Act?'

'Just bureaucracy,' Mark assured her. 'Dotting the i's and t's. It's as much for your protection as anything.'

It's good to know I'm protected. 'What do you want?'

'We don't believe that Michael Lascaris's death was an accident.'

Abby almost threw her coffee over him. 'Of course it wasn't an accident. They broke in and murdered him.'

'People can still be murdered accidentally,' Mark said. Trying to smooth the waters. 'The wrong place at the wrong time, that sort of thing. What Mr Jessop's saying is that he doesn't think this was one of those scenarios.'

'We think Michael Lascaris was targeted,' Jessop confirmed.

Abby tried to control her breathing. 'And?'

'In an earlier statement, you said you believed the villa in Montenegro belonged to an Italian judge.'

'That's what Michael told me.'

'In fact, it's registered to a charter yacht outfit in Venice, which is a wholly owned subsidiary of a shipping company based in Zagreb. The ultimate beneficial owner is believed to be Zoltán Dragović.'

'Should I know him?'

'You worked in the Balkans and you never heard of Zoltán Dragović?' said Jessop.

94

Mark looked up from his pad. 'She suffered some memory loss,' he offered. *Always happy to help.*

But the memories were coming back. Abby put her hands on the table and looked at Jessop.

'He's a gangster.'

Jessop gave a dry laugh. 'That's one way of putting it.'

'You can see it doesn't look good,' Mark put in. 'A senior EU customs official staying in a house that belongs to one of the most wanted men in Europe.'

'Michael didn't know,' Abby insisted.

'Did you ever hear him mention Dragović?'

'Never.'

'Have you been in touch with any of Michael's associates since you returned to England?'

'Associates?' She stared at him in disbelief. 'You're making him sound like some kind of criminal.'

'Colleagues? Friends? Family?'

'I visited his sister in York. I wanted to offer my condolences.'

'How did you get her address?'

'Someone sent it to me.' She glanced desperately at Mark, but he was writing something and didn't look up. 'Wasn't it you?'

'Don't know what you're talking about.'

Come on, she told herself. *You've been through worse than this.* Sitting in a shack in some godforsaken corner of the earth, the only unarmed person in the room. The awful smell of sweat, blood and rifle grease. Men—some of them just boys—jabbing guns at her, their nostrils flaring from the cocaine that gave them their courage. Her only protection then had been a piece of paper from a court five thousand miles away.

But that was there—*the outer darkness*, as some of the old Foreign Office hands still called it. This was home. All those years, all those hellholes, what kept her alive hadn't been her pieces of paper or her diplomatic accreditation. It had been faith—unwavering belief that whatever fatuous, bureaucratic mistakes her government might make, it was a force for good in the world. And now that same government had her locked in a room, twisting her words with unspoken allegations and lies.

'What made you decide to go to Paris?' Jessop asked.

'I fancied a break.'

'Less than two months ago, you suffered a horrendous attack. You're barely back in the country a fortnight and you're already racing off on overseas adventures.'

'Mark says I'm supposed to be acting erratically. He thinks I'm cracking up.'

Jessop raised his eyebrows and gave her a sceptical look. She supposed that was a compliment, of sorts. Mark picked up a file and leafed through it.

'According to our man in Podgorica, they found a gold necklace at the crime scene. You said it was yours?'

'That's right.'

'A present from Michael?'

'Yes.'

'Can I see it?' Mark saw that she was about to say something and cut her off. 'I'll save you some embarrassment. The security people who searched your bag when you came in, they said they'd seen it in there. Couldn't help noticing it, actually.' He held out his hand. 'Please?'

She wanted to wipe the patronising sincerity off his face once and for all, but didn't know how. She wanted to run, but the red light next to the door didn't blink. She wanted to scream, but she wouldn't give them the satisfaction.

She fumbled in her bag and brought out the necklace. Mark gave her a smile that made her want to knock his teeth out.

'I think we'll just keep this for a little while.'

Of course, she thought dully. She could see them waiting for a reaction and refused to give it to them. It was the one thing she could withhold.

She picked up her bag and stood. 'I'd like to go now.'

Mark was still eyeing the gold necklace. Jessop escorted her to the door.

'Be careful,' he warned her.

'In case my government locks me up and robs me again?'

'Someone targeted Michael. It's entirely possible they'll come back for you.'

He swiped his card and the light went green. Abby pushed past without a word. No one tried to stop her.

*   *   *

She didn't know where to go. She felt as if she were dangling on the end of a rope, strung up to the sky for all to see and jeer at. Every face that glanced at her, every footstep behind her, every arm that jostled her in the crowds around Trafalgar

Square seemed to accuse her of something terrible, unsayable. *This is what we were supposed to stop*, she thought. Guilt without evidence, accusations without charge. And walking out of a room without the things you brought in.

That was what hurt most. The necklace had been her last relic of Michael. To have surrendered it felt like the worst sort of betrayal.

Why do you need to know? a weary voice inside her asked. And another, firm and insistent, answered as it always had: *To do him justice.*

She wandered, aimless at first, but gradually gaining purpose as an idea took root in her mind. Her stride lengthened, and she noticed with small pleasure that the scar in her side didn't hurt so much. She walked up Southampton Row, past Russell Square and the British Museum, and then worked her way north-east until she came out on the Euston Road. Across from her loomed the British Library, a vast, red-brick piazza in the shadow of St Pancras Station. In the courtyard, a bronze giant sat hunched over a pair of compasses, inscribing the laws of the world. A pair of leafless iron trees guarded the door, where a rubber-gloved guard rifled through her bag.

There's nothing in it, she wanted to shout.

She'd left the Foreign Office without the necklace, but she hadn't come away empty-handed. They'd given her a name. And names, she'd learned through ten years of beating against locked doors, were what got you through the labyrinth.

She went into the reading room, settled down in front of a computer terminal and started searching. Answers appeared almost at once.

Zoltán Dragović. War criminal, sex trafficker,

drug baron, spy—the Balkan full house. Definitely a millionaire—probably billionaire. Place of birth unknown, possibly circa 1963. Rumoured to be the child of an Albanian father and a Serbian mother, though no one who would admit to being his parent had ever been found. Believed to be active in the Rome underworld from the mid-eighties, first as an employee and then rival to the notorious *Banda della Magliana* criminal gang. Took on the Italians at their own game and, by all accounts, won bloodily. Returned to Yugoslavia in 1991, just in time to see the country disintegrate and profit from it.

She read on. In the years 1991 to 1995 Dragović had operated like a state within a state. NATO might have tried, belatedly, to bomb the country back to the dark ages: on the ground, Dragović had already got there. He'd set himself up like a barbarian chieftain of old, running a military kingdom based on plunder, rape and permanent war. *The reaper*, they called him. His paramilitary army was second only to the Yugoslav National Army in size, and in brutal efficiency second to none. But while others killed for politics or religion, Dragović focused on cash. When sanctions bit the Serb people hard, prices sky-rocketed and so did his profits. Oil, gold, cigarettes, shoes—if there was a market for it, Dragović owned it. He took looted artworks from the Sarajevo Museum and fenced them to private collections across Europe.

After the Dayton Accords ended the war, Dragović went to ground. While his fellow gangster-paramilitaries spent their war gains in an orgy of alcohol and drugs and murder in Belgrade, he disappeared. There'd been speculation he feared

99

reprisals from a state apparatus that wanted his silence—DOES THE REAPER FEAR DEATH? one contemporary headline in the Serbian magazine *Vreme* asked—but later reports suggested he'd actually used the time to travel Europe's cities. London, Paris, Amsterdam, Frankfurt, Rome, Istanbul—all the places where the heroin trade flourished. One story said he'd even visited the International Criminal Tribunal in the Hague as a tourist. He'd walked right past the security guards and sat in the public gallery for fifteen minutes. No one noticed.

In 1999 his patron Slobodan Milošević had attempted a comeback tour reprising his greatest hits: the brief but bloody attempt to do to Kosovo what he'd done to Bosnia. This time, an impatient NATO gave him three months and then launched the bombers. Everyone thought Dragović would pile in with the rest of the Serbian paramilitaries for one last tilt at the golden goose, but instead he stayed out. Some claimed he'd actually supplied the Albanian-nationalist UÇK with weapons he'd bought in the IRA's going-out-of-business sale. Perhaps it was a quixotic gesture to his Albanian heritage; perhaps he'd seen that Milošević was doomed and had been buying credit with his enemies. A year later, he was rumoured to have been helping Albanian-nationalist terrorists trying to foment the civil war that almost erupted in neighbouring Macedonia.

For once, Dragović failed. NATO moved in to Kosovo and Macedonia and showed the gangsters what real military power meant. Dragović stopped trying to overthrow governments and, by all reports, concentrated on making money. While justice slowly caught up with his contemporaries— either the fastidious, time-consuming justice of the Hague, or the summary version doled out on the streets of Belgrade—Dragović stayed in the shadows. The last of the old-time gunslingers who still hadn't hung up his guns. There were warrants outstanding from the International Criminal Tribunal on war crimes charges, and Interpol on drug- and people-trafficking charges, but as the years went by the urgency faded. They'd almost got lucky in 2008, when the Turkish authorities had arrested him in Istanbul, but he'd escaped before extradition proceedings could begin. Allegations that the Russian security services had facilitated his escape as reward for services rendered were vigorously denied.

Abby sat back feeling slightly ill. It wasn't just the crimes: it was the queasy feeling of rifling through her own memories as much as Dragović's past. She'd never met him, but she'd filed paperwork at the International Tribunal on his case; once, she'd ridden along with a squad of NATO peacekeepers as they turned over an abandoned farmhouse in a remote corner of Bosnia where he might have been seen. All they'd found was a pile of rubbish where the locals had been tipping, and a dead crow.

She looked at the photograph staring out of the screen. There weren't many pictures of Dragović on file: this one was small and out of focus, as if it had been cropped from the background of something else. All she could see was a narrow face, an angular jaw and two jet-black eyes staring at the camera, as if he'd just noticed the photographer.

And what did Michael have to do with you? she wondered. Dragović ran one of the biggest smuggling rings in Europe, and Kosovo was its crossroads. Michael must have come up against him in the course of his work.

So why did you take me to stay at his house?

She pressed the mouse button so hard she thought she'd break it. The window closed, the face vanished.

The reading room was stifling. She needed air. She pushed through the doors, past the stacks of ancient books entombed in glass that made the core of the building, and down the steps to the piazza. She was craving a pill, but settled for a cigarette.

As she rummaged in her bag, she saw her phone glowing in its depths. She'd kept it on silent for the reading room, but someone must have sent a message. Her heart sank. The only person who'd ever called her on that phone was Mark.

What do they want from me now?

Trembling in the cool evening air, she took out the phone and opened the text message. Strangely, the sender's number wasn't displayed.

ARCUMTRIUMPHISINSIGNEMDICAVIT. Friday 17h. I can help.

XII

Constantinople—April 337
I wake with the dawn, my hand clenched on the knife under my pillow. Somewhere in the night someone's removed the oil lamp. Panic strikes me—what else did he take?—but when I paw the bed around me, I feel Alexander's book and the necklace, still there. It must have been one of my

slaves, keeping watch while I slept. He didn't risk covering me with a blanket. They know never to touch me when I'm sleeping.

I wash and dress and make my obeisances to my ancestral gods. The house was a gift from Constantine and typically extravagant: far too big for a lonely old man. Most of the rooms are kept shut up, like old memories.

My steward brings me bread and honey and news of the morning's visitors. It seems the ghost of my reputation still wanders the streets of this city, tempting a few misguided souls into thinking I can secure the Emperor's favour. Mostly, I send them away without a hearing. At this stage of my life, I don't have time to waste on them.

The steward runs down his list. 'And there's a priest. A Christian.'

I groan. Until yesterday, I thought I'd never have anything to do with Christians again. Now, they're interrupting my breakfast.

'He says his name is Simeon.'

I chew my bread and reveal nothing. It's good practice for being at court. Slaves know you better than courtiers; they're much harder to fool.

'I'll start with the priest.'

The steward nods, as if it's exactly what he expected. He's mastered the game better than I have.

'Show him to the reception room.'

I find Simeon waiting there quarter of an hour later. It's a shabby room: plain plaster on the walls that I never had painted, monochrome floor tiles. On the rare occasions I receive my petitioners, I bring them here to impress on them how humble my fortunes are. I enjoy watching their faces fall.

But it doesn't faze Simeon. He's standing in the middle of the room, hands behind his back, staring at a damp spot on the ceiling with a smile on his face. Christians are devious that way: ostentatious in their humility.

'I haven't learned who killed Alexander, if that's what you came for,' I tell him.

That breaks his composure. His cheeks flush; a look of anger crosses his face. I watch and judge. I've met him twice, now: once with Alexander's body, once in his ransacked apartment. Either Simeon's got an unfortunate knack for being in the wrong place at the wrong time, or he's as guilty as Romulus.

'I thought you might go and visit Bishop Eusebius today.'

'I might.' Why is he saying this? To deflect suspicion on to someone else? 'You said a bishop couldn't possibly have done this.'

'I can help you with him.'

'Do I need help?'

'Do you know where to look for him?'

I have to laugh, though it makes Simeon squirm with anger. He's so blunt: Constantinople hasn't yet honed his manners into the polite, sharp-edged weapons we wield. It'll be a shame if I have to accuse him of murder.

*　　　*　　　*

In fact, the hardest thing about finding Bishop Eusebius is glimpsing him through the crowds that surround him. He's at the church that Constantine's built adjoining his palace, at the far tip of the peninsula. In a fit of optimism, or perhaps wishful thinking, Constantine dedicated it to Holy Peace.

It isn't far from my house, but the heat's already building. I'm sweating by the time I get there, my face grimy from the dust. Banners draped from buildings flutter as a desultory breeze stirs off the water. Constantinople exists as two cities: the city that is, and the city yet to come. The city of the living is filled with shopkeepers and bath attendants touting for business, lawyers and their clients filing into the courts, women and children queuing for their grain ration. The city yet to come is silhouettes on the horizon and pounding tools, portents of an army coming over the hill. Even as we live in the city that *is*, the city to come takes shape around us.

It's early, but the crowds at the church are so thick they've spilled outside on to the square. The high doors have been thrown open. Inside, a figure in golden robes stands on a marble pulpit and addresses them. I won't cross the threshold, but I nudge my way through the crowd close enough to hear what he's saying. The sun pours through a glazed round window, bathing him in yellow light and branding the ☧ monogram straight onto his forehead. Behind him, an ornate wall screens off the sanctuary within the church. The Christians will give anyone a taste of their mysteries, but only true initiates get to watch them unfold.

Eusebius is talking about the god Christ. I struggle to understand: something about his nature and his substance, the difference between the eternal and the infinite. 'Christ is the head of the church and the saviour of its body, just as a husband is the head of the wife. So it must be an affront to God that our church here in Constantinople still lacks a head. I urge you, brothers and sisters, to resolve this situation with speed and justice.'

I glance at Simeon, who's listening intently. 'What's he talking about?'

'You know the Patriarch of Constantinople died three months ago?'

I do now. 'Was there anything suspicious about it?'

'He was an old man who'd lived a hard life. Nothing unusual. Eusebius is one of the obvious men to replace him.'

'Is that why Alexander wanted to talk to Eusebius in the library yesterday?'

'He didn't say.'

'Was Alexander a candidate? A rival?'

'He said he was too old.'

But there's something defensive in the way he says it. I stare him down. 'It's your master's murder we're talking about,' I remind him. *And you're the most obvious suspect.*

'Alexander opposed Eusebius's election.'

'So with Alexander gone, Eusebius has a clear run at the top job in the church.'

Eusebius has finished speaking. The crowd start shuffling in to the sanctuary for the distribution of the sacrifice—those who are allowed. The rest begin to drift away. But a few linger on, staring into the dark church like dogs at a kitchen door. Most of them are young men, intoxicated by their own intensity; one stands out, an old man with straggling hair and a pointed chin. He squats on the steps of the colonnade, head cupped in his hands, contemplating the church with ravenous eyes.

There's something so arresting about him that I point him out to Simeon. 'Do you know who he is?'

Simeon's so surprised he has to look twice. First

at the man, then at me. He can't believe I could be so ignorant.

'Asterius the Sophist.'

He sees my reaction to the name and nods, pleased to think his world view has been vindicated. But it isn't what he thinks.

'Symmachus said that Asterius was at the library yesterday.' He's on my list.

'I didn't see him there.'

'Symmachus said that Asterius was a Christian. Why doesn't he go into the church?'

A solemn look comes over Simeon. 'During the persecutions, Asterius was arrested. The persecutors gave him a choice: betray the church, or die and become a martyr for Christ.'

'He's still alive.'

Simeon spits in the dust. 'There were a dozen Christians—families, with children—hiding in the cistern below his house. He betrayed them to the Emperor Diocletian, who crucified them all. That's why they call him the Sophist—he'll say he believes anything. He's forbidden from ever setting foot in a church again.'

'But he still comes here.' I look at the face again. The eyes narrowed, the lips slightly parted. His body is tense with a longing that's almost ecstatic.

'Do you think he knew Symmachus during the persecutions? Or Alexander?'

'Ask him. I wasn't born then.'

I push across the square and step in front of the old man, cutting off his contemplation of the church. He waits for me to move by. When I don't, he's forced to look up.

Seen from above, hunched up like a dwarf, he's a scrawny, diminished figure. His face is grey and mottled with liver spots; his hands are folded around his knees, hidden in his sleeves.

I sit down beside him on the step. 'It must be hard for you. Like watching your first love at home with her husband and children.'

He keeps his gaze on the church and doesn't respond.

'Perhaps I should introduce myself. I'm—'

'Gaius Valerius Maximus.' He spits out the words like a centurion summoning men to be flogged. 'Your notoriety precedes you.'

'So does yours.'

'I repented my sins. Can you say the same?'

'I sleep easily enough.'

He looks at me then, and though age clouds his eyes they seem to go right through me. 'Have you come to ask me about the Bishop?'

'Do you have anything to tell me?'

'I was there in the library. I assume someone told you. I'm sure Aurelius Symmachus was eager to help.'

'You know him?'

'He and I are old friends.' He crunches down on the last word as if biting a nut. 'We were in prison together during the persecutions. Did you know that? Only one of us was in chains, mind, not a relationship of equals. He had the whip hand.'

'Did you see Bishop Alexander at the library?'

He raises his eyebrows, stretching the skin around his eyes so that they widen alarmingly. 'I struggle to see what's a foot in front of me.'

I remember his nickname. The *Sophist*—the man who can twist any argument. 'Did you encounter him?'

'No.'

I point to the church. 'What about Bishop Eusebius?'

'What about him?'

'He was there too.'

'Then I'm sure he avoided me. He doesn't like to be seen with me. Churchmen don't—like your little friend here.' A nod to Simeon, who's fidgeting as if he has ants crawling up his legs. 'They worry I'll drag them to Hell with me.'

Simeon tugs my arm and murmurs that the ritual in the church is ending. I stand and look down on the withered old man.

'Do you know who killed Bishop Alexander?'

His face is clear and innocent as rain. 'Only God knows.'

'Did you kill him?'

Asterius lifts up his arms like a beggar, so that the sleeves of his robe fall back to the elbow. Simeon gasps and turns away. I have fewer qualms; I study them with professional interest.

He has no hands. All that protrude are withered stumps.

*   *   *

'A half-blind man with no hands probably didn't smash Alexander's head in.'

We're walking across the square, against the crowds streaming out of the church. Simeon's angry.

'Why do you always ask these people who killed Alexander? Do you expect them to tell you?'

I slow down, so that Simeon comes level. 'When I was a young army officer, one of my men was stabbed in a tavern brawl. Three men had been with him. I asked them who was guilty and two gave the same answer. The third named one of the others.'

'He was lying?'

'He was telling the truth. The other two had agreed to frame him.'

As Simeon digests my homily, the crowd's momentum changes. They stop, drawing apart to open a channel in their midst. Simeon and I are pushed back. A golden litter seems to float past in the air—you can barely see the eight Sarmatian slaves sweating under its weight. The purple curtains are embroidered with the imperial monogram, and beside it the peacock emblem of Princess Constantiana, Constantine's sister.

'Eusebius attracts quite a congregation,' I observe.

The litter passes and disappears through the palace gate. The crowd starts to move again. Simeon and I make our way around the side of the church and let ourselves in a small door in an octagonal annexe. Simeon looks anxious: I can't tell if it's Eusebius he's worried about, or my presence in the church. But, in fact, barely anyone notices us. The room's filled with men undressing themselves and gossiping freely: for a moment, I think we've stepped into a bathhouse. This must be where the priests disrobe after the service.

Eusebius is a heavy-set man with drooping cheeks, a thin scraping of hair and fat lips that are a strange purple colour, as if he's eaten too many berries. He's standing in the middle of the room, surrounded by attendants who are unwinding a long golden cloth from around his shoulders. I can see he recognises me; I wait and watch, while he tries to place me. We've crossed paths before, though I

110

doubt either of us cares to remember it.

'Gaius Valerius,' I remind him.

'Gaius Valerius *Maximus*,' he reproves me, as if I'd forgotten my own name. He rolls the Maximus around his mouth like a punchline. 'You were at Nicaea. Standing in the shadows, listening to what we said with one hand on your sword. We used to call you Brutus. Did you know that? We worried there'd be a knife in our backs if we said something you disliked.'

I didn't know that.

'Perhaps we can go somewhere more private to talk.'

A stern look. 'I have no secrets from my flock.'

Very well. 'Alexander of Cyrene died yesterday at the Egyptian Library. The *Emperor*. . .' I weight the word, arrogating its power. 'The *Emperor* asked me to investigate.'

'And?'

The reaction shocks me. First, for its utter lack of sympathy; second, for the fact he doesn't care who sees it. Every man in the room is watching our conversation, like gladiators sparring. And not one of them—Christians all—seems troubled by the death of their bishop.

'One of the last things Alexander did was ask to see you. Soon afterwards, he was dead. They found a necklace with a Christian monogram near his body.'

I show him the gold necklace Constantine gave me. 'Do you recognise this?'

Eusebius turns like a plump scarecrow, arms aloft so that his acolyte can remove his robe. 'No. And I never went to the library yesterday.'

'Aurelius Symmachus saw you there.'

'Aurelius Symmachus.' He says it with a lisp, distorting the name into nonsense. 'You know his history? In Diocletian's time he was one of the chief architects of the persecutions. He made so many martyrs that heaven could hardly hold them. He almost killed Alexander thirty years ago. He probably decided to finish the job.'

If I'd wanted to murder Alexander, I could have done it then and been hailed a hero.

'Symmachus said he saw you at the library,' I persist. 'Is he lying?'

Eusebius turns back to face me. With his surplice gone, there's less to smooth the rolls of fat bulging under his tunic.

'By the time I got to the library, Alexander was already dead.'

'Did you see the body?'

'I arrived and heard he was dead. There was no need for me to stay.'

'You didn't want to help?'

'Christ said: *Leave the dead to bury the dead.* It's no secret that Alexander and I had differences. If I'd stayed there crying crocodile tears, who would have believed me?' And then, in case a quick show of contrition will make me go away, he adds, 'I preferred to grieve in private.'

He's telling the truth about one thing. If this is the best simulation of grief he can give, it wouldn't have fooled anyone.

XIII

London—Present Day
ARCUMTRIUMPHISINSIGNEMDICAVIT. Friday 17h. I can help.

She ran back into the reading room, barely stopping to show the guard her pass. She sat down at the computer and copied the words into a search engine.

Your search—**arcumtriumphisinsignemdicavit** —did not match any documents

She couldn't believe it. *The whole Internet, and this doesn't appear once.* And yet, in a perverse way, it gave her hope. *Whoever sent it, they didn't want it to be easy to understand. They knew it might be read by someone else.*

It looked like Latin. She wrote it out in block capitals on a request form, then accosted the librarian at the Reference Enquiries desk.

'Do you know what this means?'

The librarian, a tall black woman in an extravagantly patterned dress, pulled on her glasses.

'"He dedicated the arch as a sign of triumph."'

'Do you know where it comes from?'

The glasses came off. 'At a guess? From a triumphal arch.'

'Is it possible to find out which one?'

'You could try the *Corpus Inscriptionum Latinarum*. It's a catalogue of all the Latin inscriptions which survive from the Roman Empire. If it is Roman, of course. It could be a Second World War memorial.' She saw Abby's blank look and sighed. 'People still wrote them in Latin.'

She scribbled a shelfmark number below the Latin and pointed Abby across the reading room. It wasn't hard to find: the Corpus volumes took up most of a shelf, and probably weighed more than a human body. But they were well organised. In five minutes Abby found what she wanted. The full text of the inscription that ended with the line, 'He dedicated this arch as a sign of his trumph.' And underneath, the location.

Rome. Arch of Constantine.

*　　　*　　　*

Rome, Italy—Present Day

Once, voyagers bound for Rome landed at Ostia, the thriving port at the mouth of the Tiber river. But the harbour had silted up centuries ago, first burying the ancient city and then preserving it for future generations of tourists and archaeologists. Now, visitors landed three miles away on the other side of the river, at Fiumicino Airport. Abby took the train in to Rome and checked in to a small hotel in the Trastavere quarter. She could barely sit still.

It was only mid-afternoon. She had hours to kill before the meeting. She bought herself a guidebook and took a cab to the forum. On her right, across a bare excavation, a huge brick building rose up the hill in expanding concentric curves. *Trajan's Market*, the guidebook called it, and when she went inside it was breathtakingly easy to imagine it as a shopping mall. She'd thought that most Roman ruins were either two-dimensional foundations, or hollowed-out shells like the Colosseum. But this seemed to be perfectly preserved: an open atrium overlooked by three full stories of galleries above.

She was disappointed to learn that they'd probably housed government offices, rather than shops.

She wandered through galleries of sculpture and fragments recovered from the ruins of the Roman forum until she found the hall she wanted. Funerary Architecture. The exhibits were displayed in mock-stone cabinets that had been erected around the room to mimic tombs. You had to stoop to see inside.

Fragment of a grave plaque, 4th century AD said the placard. Her breath came faster as she read the inscription printed underneath. UT VIVENTES ADTIGATIS MORTUOS NAVIGATE. *To reach the living, navigate the dead.* She took Gruber's piece of paper out of her pocket and compared it. Exactly the same.

But the tomb was empty—nothing but a blank, black wall. A forlorn card taped to the backing offered a meek apology in three languages: *This item is temporarily unavailable.*

A young security guard sat on a stool in the corner. Abby went over and forced a smile. 'Do you speak English?'

A nod, and a warm smile in return.

'Do you know what happened to this piece?'

A solemn look came over him. 'It has been stolen. One night two months ago, a gang broke in and took it.'

Something tightened inside her. 'That's terrible.' She looked around the room. Red lights blinked at her from the dark corners. 'Aren't there alarms?'

'They were professional. The hill behind here is very steep—it is simple to come on the roof. They climbed through a ventilation shaft, cut the alarm and—*ciao.*'

115

'Did they take much?'

'Only this one thing. We think they must be working for a collector who knows *exactamente* what he likes.' He shook his head. 'Is strange. The museum was open for them, and we have many more valuable things. Why they do not take them?'

'Did the police trace anything?'

'Nothing.'

His radio crackled, summoning him. He stood. 'Enjoy your visit, *signorina*.'

*   *   *

She still had time to kill. There was a modern road which Mussolini had bulldozed through the ancient heart of Rome, but she took the old route, the Via Sacra through the forum. She wandered among the broken temples and shattered columns, trying to imagine it filled with life. Past the Senate, where Brutus stabbed Julius Caesar; past the church of San Lorenzo, a baroque church caged within the columns that had once been the pagan temple of Antoninus and Fausta.

Clouds began to mass over the gaudy heights of the Victor Emmanuel monument. The vast hollow arches of the Basilica of Maxentius loomed on her left, a scale of architecture not seen again until nineteenth-century railway stations. And ahead, the biggest relic of all: the breached caldera of the Colosseum. Even this late in the season, tourists were still queueing to get in, as they had almost two thousand years ago. Abby ignored them, and wandered across the surrounding square to a dirty white arch standing like an afterthought in a corner of the great plaza. Behind her, traffic roared around the ancient arena. She looked at her watch: 4.58.

The Arch of Constantine. Built to commemorate Constantine's victory over Maxentius at the battle of the Milvian Bridge, which made him undisputed master of the Western Roman Empire, the guidebook said.

Constantine the Great. She knew the name, but not much more than what Gruber had told her. Roman emperor, converted the empire to Christianity, and thereby Europe and afterwards wherever Europe's tentacles spread. The guidebook gave a thumbnail sketch that didn't add much, except the trivia that he'd been born in modern-day Serbia, and his mother had been a brothel-keeper's daughter.

But there had to be more. Ever since she'd woken in hospital, Constantine had been a strange, flickering companion, greeting her at every turn, then melting into shadow. The gold necklace with his monogram. The fourth-century manuscript left in the shadow of Constantine's palace at Trier. The text message quoting the inscription. *Is it a coincidence? A joke? Am I going mad?* She felt as if she were trapped in a dream, running through a labyrinth where every turn brought her up against the same wall.

She looked up at the arch. Stern men, bearded and cloaked, gazed down on her as if trying to tell her something.

And what does it have to do with Michael?

She heard footsteps behind her and turned. A guide was leading a group of tourists across from the Colosseum, a severe-faced woman holding up a furled umbrella like a military standard. Abby

117

scanned the faces and wondered what she was looking for. No one noticed her—they were too busy staring at the arch on the screens of their cameras, while the guide lectured them with facts they didn't really want to know. She was speaking English. Abby drifted close enough to hear, waiting for someone to jostle her arm or meet her eye.

'In fact, modern scholars think the arch was originally built by Constantine's enemy, Maxentius. When Constantine defeated him in the battle, he adapted it for himself.'

The tourists who were bothering to listen looked surprised.

'Everybody assumes that the Romans built everything from scratch, right?' the guide said. 'But no. The marble carvings were taken from other monuments. The big relief panels come from, we think, an arch dedicated originally to Marcus Aurelius. The frieze is from the forum of the Emperor Trajan, also in the second century. The round *tondi* come from a monument of Hadrian—like the wall, you know? In each case, the faces have been recut or replaced to look like Constantine.'

The tourists peered dutifully at the carvings, the stone men jumbled up in battle and hunts, the stone emperor bareheaded in their midst. They finished taking their photographs and ambled off for their next serving of history. Abby stood there like the last girl at the dance, waiting for someone to swoop down and rescue her. No one turned back; no one came.

She circled the monument to check she hadn't missed anyone. She checked her phone for messages. She reread the text message for the hundredth time, wondering if she'd missed something.

ARCUM TRIUMPHIS INSIGNEM DICAVIT. Friday 17h. I can help.

She'd got it right. The pixelated words on the screen were identical to the ones chiselled in marble above her, over the central arch. She read the rest of it, comparing it with the translation she'd copied from the British Library.

She checked her watch for the umpteenth time. 5.19.

He's not coming, she thought bleakly. The sheer futility of it hit her like a brick. The ruins of the past lowered over her and rebuked her. What had she been thinking, coming here on the basis of an anonymous text message? She reached out and leaned on one of the bollards that protected the arch from motorists. She felt if she didn't touch something real, she might float free of the world for ever.

More footsteps approached—another tour group, coming around like clockwork. This time the guide was an elderly man, a white moustache and a tweed suit and the regulation umbrella. Again, Abby scanned the following faces—but these were teenagers on a school trip, and she was invisible to them.

'The Arch of Constantine,' the guide pronounced. 'Built in the year 312 as a memorial of Constantine's victory at the battle of Milvian Bridge. Constantine was a Christian and Maxentius was a pagan. When Constantine won, Europe became Christian.'

The pupils played with their phones and their music players. A few snapped pictures. But Abby was transfixed. A crazy thought had occurred to her.

'Excuse me,' she asked. 'Where is the Milvian Bridge? I mean, does it still exist?'

The guide looked grateful for the interest. 'The Ponte Milvio. It is here in Rome, at the end of the Via Flaminia, past the Villa Borghese. Popular with lovers,' he added, for the benefit of the teenagers.

'Thanks.'

Abby found a taxi opposite the Colosseo metro station. At half-past five on a Friday evening, the Roman traffic was locked tight. It took twenty minutes just to get into the Via Flaminia. She sat on the back seat, gripping the door handle and staring straight ahead. Rain began to bead on the windscreen.

He dedicated this arch as a sign of his victory. The inscription pointed to the arch, but the arch itself was just a symbol, a sign pointing to the battle it commemorated. It was a dim hope, even she could see that—a mad detour on a fool's errand. But she had to try.

*   *   *

The bridge stood on the northern edge of Rome, just where the Tiber's concrete embankments took over from nature. She paid off the taxi and advanced on to the bridge. Thick trees crowded the riverbank; ripples gouged the surface of the river where it ran fast over shoals. If you tuned out the apartment blocks and market stalls beyond, you could almost imagine it as it must have been in Constantine's day, a wild place beyond the city.

The ancient Romans had built it as a road

bridge, but modern Romans preferred not to trust their traffic to its 2,100-year-old arches. She had it almost to herself, except for a few businessmen walking back from work, and a pair of teenagers giggling in front of her. As she watched, they knelt together in front of a rail at the edge of the bridge. The boy took a padlock from his pocket and locked it on to the rail. He said something, and the girl kissed him. Then they both stood, and with one arm around the girl the boy threw the key over his shoulder into the river.

Curious, Abby went over and looked at where they'd been. Locked on to the rail was a gleaming, shaggy coat of literally hundreds of padlocks. Some had hearts and words scrawled on them in black marker pen: messages of love, passion, perpetual devotion. None of them, so far as she could see, was for her.

A tide of loneliness washed through her. She stared at the steel wall the padlocks made, a barrier locking her out. All those people tight together in their loves, and a lonely woman standing there because an anonymous text message might have told her to.

Mark's right, she thought sourly. *I do need a psychiatric evaluation*.

She walked back across the river. Halfway along, she caught herself dawdling, clinging to the hope that someone might yet tap her on the arm, sweep her up like a lost teenager and give her the key she needed. *Idiot*. The bridge was empty. Even the teenagers had gone home. She redoubled her pace and wondered where she could catch a tram back into the city.

As she stepped off the bridge, she noticed a black

Alfa Romeo sedan parked on the kerb, engine running. A man jumped out of the passenger seat.

'Abigail Cormac?' He had an accent, probably not Italian. Something more guttural. He was wearing a black rollneck jumper and black jeans, with a long black leather coat and black leather gloves. 'I need to speak to you about Michael Lascaris.'

Michael. The name was a narcotic, overriding all caution. As if hypnotised, she carried on walking towards the car. The man smiled, baring teeth that glinted with gold. He was nodding, encouraging her forward like a cat into a cage. The black butt of a pistol bulged against his stomach where it stuck out of his waistband.

And suddenly she saw how stupid she'd been. *I can help*, the message had said, and she'd believed it because she was desperate. But people who wanted to help didn't send you cryptic messages you couldn't reply to, or drag you halfway across Europe on an obscure treasure hunt.

She turned to run, but she was too close and too slow. The man was beside her in a single step. A black arm wrapped around her, pinning her arms; a second locked itself around her throat and forced her down into the car.

A voice in her ear said, 'If you struggle, we will kill you.'

XIV

Italy—Summer and Autumn 312—Twenty-five years earlier . . .

And then there were four.

Galerius died last year, an embarrassing death, which Constantine went to great lengths to publicise. His bowels rotted from the inside out; a tumour grew inside his genitals until (they said) he looked like a man in a permanent state of arousal. Worms infected his body, so that his attendants could lay a piece of fresh meat against his wound and pull it away crawling with maggots. The Christians were delighted.

But Constantine still has battles to fight. The marriage alliance with Fausta has borne neither children nor peace with her usurping family. Last year, old Maximian tried to turn Constantine's army against him. Constantine forgave his father-in-law; Maximian showed his gratitude by trying to stab him while he slept, but the plan was betrayed. At that point, Constantine lost patience and suggested Maximian drink poison.

But the son, Maxentius, Constantine's brother-in-law, still occupies Rome and all of Italy, unrecognised and unrepentant. With Galerius dead, Constantine can afford to turn his attention south.

*　　　*　　　*

The priests say we shouldn't go. They went through all the correct procedures: killed the animals in the

123

prescribed manner, dissected the organs, tested the evidence. The guts said it was a bad time for a campaign. Constantine said: what do dead animals know about war? Maxentius has the bulk of his army in Verona, on the north-eastern frontier, expecting an attack from the Balkans. An attack from the north-west will catch him where he's unprepared. 'Show me where it says that in the entrails,' says Constantine.

'My brother always does what the soothsayers recommend,' Fausta observes. It's hard to tell if it's a rebuke—or a suggestion. Five years on from the wedding, the ripeness of adolescence has started to go hard, like a date left in the sun. When her father tried to have Constantine murdered, it was she who came to the bedchamber and warned her husband. Now we're tilting at her brother, and those long-lashed eyes are as blank and innocent as ever.

It's a miracle you were able to kill the old man with poison, I think. *That whole family have it running through their veins.*

And so we cross the Alps, like Hannibal six centuries earlier. Constantine proves a better augur than his priests. At Segusio, the gateway to Italy, we set the town on fire with the garrison inside it. The lesson's not lost on the garrison at Turin: they don't wait to be surrounded, but sally out to meet us on the battlefield. Constantine reads their plan, squeezes their flanks, then smashes their centre back against the walls with his cavalry so hard that the press of corpses knocks down the gate.

How do you beat Constantine? The citizens of Milan don't know—they just open the gates and surrender. At Verona they fight harder and almost break our line. Constantine has to throw himself into the fray, stabbing and hacking and punching with his men as if he's going to cut his own way to Rome one body at a time. A spear flies within an inch of his face: for a second, all history hangs in the balance.

The spear misses. We win the battle. The road to Rome lies open.

*   *   *

These are blessed times. September proceeds to October and the sun shines, golden light on golden leaves. The skies above our march are blue, the air crisp. We see the world clearly. Away from the ritual flattery of court, Constantine's a real man again: when I think of him now, this is how I like to remember him. Joking with sentries with mud on his boots; leaning over a map by lamplight, firing questions at his generals; riding his white horse at the front of the column, while the army's sure stamp shakes the road. The world may be dying around us, but we know we're marching to make it new.

'Rome is nothing,' Constantine says one night, lounging on the couch in his tent after dinner. He gets thinner, sharper on campaign. The soft flesh around his cheeks and chin melts away. 'Name me one emperor in the last fifty years who stayed there more than a month.'

I sip my wine and smile. We both know that what he says is true—and not. Rome is too far from the frontiers to make a usable capital, which is why we've spent our lives eyeballing barbarians from Nicomedia and Trier and York. The tides of history have gone out and left the city of Rome

125

stranded like a whale: bloated, flailing, with only its own self-regard to sustain it. And yet she remains the queen of cities, the heart of our civilisation, the wellspring of the empire's dreams. To possess her conveys a power that has nothing to do with supply lines and garrison forts.

'Are you having second thoughts?' I tease him.

'We'll take Rome.' He's so certain. Ever since I've known him, Constantine's had an aura about him that makes you believe things that ought not to be possible. But on this campaign, it burns brighter than ever. It's like cutting into a cocoon and seeing the butterfly, still liquefied. Some days, I look at him and think I hardly know him.

He bites into an apple. 'Do you remember the road to Autun? When we were campaigning against the Franks, three years ago?'

It takes me a moment, but then it's there. Marching at noon, a blue sky with a high haze. Suddenly we looked up, and saw a perfect circle of light. In its centre, the teardrop sun glowed molten gold, and from its burning heart four rays burst out, forming a cross.

As a man, the army dropped to its knees and gave thanks to the god of the Unconquered Sun, Constantine's patron. For a whole day after, a wild-eyed mood overtook the army, as if we had been touched by the hand of the god. But we slept, we ate, we marched and gradually the impact faded. Just another of those occasional wonders, like blood-red moons and lightning storms, by which the gods remind us of their grandeur.

'I remember we still had a hard fight against the Franks,' I say.

Constantine laughs at me. 'Always looking ahead

126

to the next battle.'

'It's never far off.'

He props himself up on his elbow, spinning the apple core in his fingers. 'But what if we could make a different world? A world where summer meant playing with your children and drinking wine, not strapping on your boots and going to war?'

'Then you'd be a god.'

He considers that. 'You know what the Christians say? They say their god, Christ, came into the world to redeem it. To bring peace instead of war.'

If that's so, he conspicuously failed. I don't say it. It would damage something between us.

'All the empire wants is peace. From the humblest peasant in the field to the proudest Senator on the Palatine—peace. Do you know what made a small city on the Tiber into the greatest power in history? A longing for peace. To be able to walk on a road without being afraid of what might come over the hill. We pushed back the frontiers of civilisation until they stretched to bursting.'

Through a gap in the curtains, I can see his son, Crispus, poring over his Greek homework with his tutor. Constantine speaks Greek, but he can't write it: he's determined his son will do better.

'The cross in the sky that day was a message, Gaius. God stretched out his hand and called me to glory. To be his instrument bringing peace to the world.'

He swings his legs off the couch and stands. I follow.

'We're going to win the battle against Maxentius, and we'll win it in a way that no one can doubt

127

where it came from. Please God, it'll be the last battle we have to fight.'

'Please God,' I agree obediently. And that night, when the camp is asleep, my brothers and I meet in a cave and pour bull's blood into the earth to make sure of it.

*   *   *

On a chill morning, at the very end of October, our army arrays for its last battle. Ahead of us stand an army, a river and a city. The order's important. Rather than sheltering in the safety of Rome's invincible walls, Maxentius has brought his legions out and crossed the Tiber. Apparently he consulted the augurs who told him that if he took the field for battle, Rome would be liberated from a tyrant. And no man is a tyrant in his own mind.

An hour before dawn, Constantine parades the army. Tombs line the road: he climbs up on a brick mausoleum, its marble long since stripped away, and addresses the men. Even I don't know what he's going to say. Standing there, with dew seeping into my boots and the moon waning, drawing warmth from the men pressed around me, it feels like the dawn of all things.

'The supreme God on high sent me a dream,' Constantine announces. His armour gleams like a star against the deep blue sky. Beyond the fields, dawn cracks open the horizon. 'God's messenger came to me with a sign. He told me that if we fought under His sign today, and in His name, we would surely conquer the tyrant and win a victory for the ages.'

Some movement at the base of the tomb. A

soldier climbs a ladder and passes up what looks like a long spear draped in white cloth. Constantine takes it, and, as he lifts it, the cloth comes away revealing a new standard. A tall pole plated in gold, with the imperial banner hanging from a golden crosspiece. A wreath spun from gems and gold wire crowns the top, and set within it, silhouetted against the dawn, the superimposed letters X-P.

'This is God's sign.'

He times it perfectly. The sun comes over the top of the tomb and wraps him in its radiance. Glittering shafts of light shoot from the jewels in the standard and play over the faces of the watching army. In that moment, even I might believe.

*　　*　　*

Maxentius's soldiers don't survive the first charge. Normally, you wouldn't send cavalry at well-formed infantry, but Constantine guesses that these men—levies and auxiliaries, mostly—don't have the stomach for a fight. We charge down the slope and the human wall crumbles. Maxentius tries to flee across his pontoon bridge, but in the chaos of the rout the ropes break and he's pitched into the water. We fish him out half a mile downstream, when the corpse washes against the pilings of the Milvian Bridge. I cut off his head myself for Constantine to show the citizens of Rome.

*　　*　　*

Constantinople—April 337
I sit on the bench in the courtyard of my house. My fingers pluck at my belt, twisting it so that the

brass lion on the buckle catches the sun. I slide my thumbnail into the cuts and scratches in the metal. This was my *cingulum*, the sword belt I wore that day and ever since. But is it the same belt? The leather's worn out three or four times and been changed, made longer; several of the plates have fallen off and had to be replaced. Just as Constantine and I are the same men we were on that campaign, and yet strangers to ourselves. The old lion's brass skin is scuffed and dull.

There's a commotion at the door. I wait for my steward to tell me who it is, but he doesn't come. Instead, four soldiers in blood-red tunics and burnished armour burst in from my dreams and a scarred centurion says, 'Come with us.'

XV

Rome—Present Day

'If you struggle, we will kill you.'

The man forced her into the car and pushed her down on the back seat. A cloth went over her head: a smell attacked her, and she wondered if it was chloroform. She tried to hold her breath, but her heart was beating too fast.

It was only aftershave, she realised, sickly sweet and drenching the blindfold with the smell of lilies. The car started to move. A hand on the back of her head kept her face pressed against the leather seat.

This is how it happens, she thought numbly. They come in the night and take you. Maybe they kill you, maybe they're satisfied just to rummage around and break a few bits. But you're never the

130

same. She'd heard the story a thousand times in the field: brown eyes, blue eyes, always the same dead tears.

The car drove. All Abby could do was focus on the sounds around her: the rattle of a loose seatbelt; the revolutions of the engine; the occasional tick of the indicator. If she'd been a spy in a film, she might have counted off seconds and turns to work out their route. But she was frightened and far from help: it was all she could do to keep the panic from overwhelming her.

She heard a siren in the distance. Hope gripped her. Had someone seen her? Called the police? Arranged a rescue? The siren grew louder until it must have been right behind them. She felt their car slow down, then drift towards the kerb. She wanted to rip off the blindfold, leap up in her seat and shout for help. The hand on her head pushed down harder.

And then it passed. The Doppler wail stretched into the distance and faded away. She was alone again.

She vomited on the leather seat.

*   *   *

The car stopped in darkness. The hand pulled Abby up and dragged her out. She was still blindfolded, but she knew they must have turned a light on when she heard them swearing about the mess she'd made of their seat.

I can understand what they're saying, she thought. It took her another moment to realise they were speaking Serbo-Croat. She closed her eyes, though under the blindfold it made no difference.

They led her up a flight of stairs, handling her carelessly, knocking her shins and stubbing her toes on obstacles she couldn't see. Then the floor levelled off. She heard the sweep and thump of doors opening and closing. At last she stopped. The hand pulled the blindfold off her head.

She thought they must have brought her to a museum. She was standing in the middle of a black, windowless room. Silver spotlights in the ceiling picked out exhibits on the walls: slabs of white stone carved into friezes of gods and beasts, tendrilled plants or simply stern inscriptions. Most had rough edges, as if they'd been hastily chiselled away from some larger structure. A desk stood in the middle of the room, steel legs and a black marble top with nothing on it. Behind it, in a leather chair that dwarfed him, sat a slight man with greying hair. He was wearing a black suit and a white, open-necked shirt. He looked as if he was getting ready to go out for the evening. In his lap, he cradled a chrome-handled pistol.

He pointed the gun at her, smiling as he saw her flinch away.

'Abigail Cormac. Have you ever wondered why you're not dead?'

She just stared at him. 'Who are you?'

He waved the gun towards the pieces on the walls. 'A collector. A dealer. I buy and sell.'

She looked at his face: the sharp cheekbones and angular jaw, the eyes sunk so deep no light reached them. It was infinitely more real than the snatched, blurry photograph she'd seen in the British Library; also some years older. The skin had toughened, the hair retreated. He'd grown a small beard that had flecked grey. But there remained some quality,

132

the same ferocious intensity, that even the camera couldn't blur.

'You're Zoltán Dragović.'

The eyes narrowed. His bloodless lips stretched tight. He trained the gun back at her and flipped a catch on the side. She heard the guard behind her take a step sideways.

'Are you going to shoot me?' *Get on with it!* she wanted to scream. *End this now!* 'Why did you bring me here?'

'To answer my questions,' he snapped. The gun didn't move. The chrome barrel threw starbursts of reflected light on the walls. 'Like, for example, why you aren't dead already?'

'I don't—'

'You should have died in Kotor Bay. I sent a man—his name was Sloba. I want to know why didn't he kill you?'

'I don't remember.' It came out as a croak. She was desperate for water, desperate to sit down before she fainted. 'He shot me.'

'He never came back.'

'I don't know what happened to him.'

'No one does. You will say, perhaps he ran away.' He held up the gun, as if he were addressing it and not her. 'Impossibility. My men do not run away. If they try, I always find them. And him I cannot find.'

Abby rubbed her eyes, hoping she'd wake up and find this was all a nightmare. 'He killed Michael. I saw him.'

'If I cannot find Sloba, it means he is dead.' Dragović swung lazily in his chair, like a boat swaying on its anchor. 'Let me give you some facts, Miss Cormac. Sloba came to the villa in a car. When the police arrived, this car was still there.'

133

Look at the man, not at the gun. That's what they'd taught in her Hostile Environment training, years ago. *Looking at the gun makes it more likely he'll use it.* That didn't make it any easier.

'You were lying on the floor with Sloba's bullets in you. In your shoulder, but not in your heart or brain. Why? Sloba was not a careless or a sentimental man. If he let you live, it means he was dead.'

Look at the man. 'I didn't kill him, if that's what you want to know.'

'Who else was there?'

'No one. Just Michael and me.'

But was that true? She thought back to something they'd said in hospital. *Somebody rang the police.* Her memories were so scrambled it was hard to be sure of anything, but she didn't think it had been her. It rang false.

So who else was there?

Dragović rolled back on his chair and stood. He sauntered over to the wall and examined one of the stone plaques. This one was painted, not carved, the colours washed out but still clear. A mummified man, wrapped in bandages, stretched out a hand from a stone sarcophagus, while a bearded Christ reached to stand him up. A dog played at his feet.

'Here is another fact. Sloba died and Lascaris died. But I have seen the police reports. They found only one body.'

He spun around and fixed his gaze on Abby. She took a half-step backwards, though immediately a hand pressed against her back to stop her getting any ideas.

'Did your man have an accomplice?'

'Sloba worked alone.' Dragović moved on to a

134

marble statue, a female nude with upturned breasts and no arms. He stroked a finger across her throat. 'Two deaths, one body. How do you explain this?'

'I don't know.'

And suddenly Dragović was right in front of her, crossing the room so fast she barely saw him move. The guard behind her pinned her arms and almost lifted her off the floor. Cold metal pressed on her jaw as Dragović jammed the pistol against her face. The dead smell of lilies stifled her.

'Understand this, Miss Cormac. You are already dead. If I decide someone will die, they die. If I keep you living a little longer, it is only because I need you to tell me some things. But I can kill you now and throw you in the Tiber, and no one will care. They will not even recognise you, when I am finished.'

His face was so close to hers his bristles scraped her cheek. Tears ran down her face and soaked into his beard. The intimacy felt like a violation.

'I don't know,' she pleaded. She heard herself repeating it again and again, caught in a stuttering loop she couldn't escape. Dragović stepped away in disgust. The guard behind her loosened his grip, so she sagged limply into him. She felt him move against her, rubbing himself on her like a dog.

'Enough.' Dragović snapped his fingers; the guard let go. Abby fell forward on the floor, crouched on all fours.

'Your lover Lascaris was meant to give me something. That is why he came to my house.'

'A briefcase,' Abby mumbled—too clumsy for them to understand. The guard stepped forward, grabbed her hair and pulled her head back so she was looking up at Dragović. The mouth of the gun yawned open above her, and this time there was nothing she could do but look at it.

'Michael had a briefcase. I saw it.'

'It was not there when the police arrived. What happened to it?'

'I don't know.'

Another yank on her hair pulled her to her feet. The guard dragged her after Dragović, across the room to a spotlit stone on the wall. There were no carvings or paintings, just two lines of text in sharp capital letters, and a ☧ monogram above. Abby stared.

Dragović waved the gun at it. 'You recognise this?'

There was no point lying. He'd read it in her face. 'I've seen the symbol before. At the villa— there was a gold necklace.'

'What happened to it?'

'The police gave it to me. I took it back to London. My Government found out and confiscated it.'

Dragović pointed back to the stone tablet. 'And the text? You recognise that?'

'I don't know Latin.'

Her jaw went numb as the butt of his pistol smashed into it. She spun away, but the guard held her hair tight and dragged her back. She dropped to her knees. Dragović stood over her, his breath fast and excited.

'You went to the Forum Museum this afternoon. You looked where this tablet came from. *Why?*'

She spat out a gob of blood on the floor. *He doesn't know about the scroll, about Trier and Gruber*, she thought. With horror, she realised she still had Gruber's translation in her jeans pocket.

136

She stared at the tablet, the sign like the cross above the words she couldn't read, and prayed to the God she didn't really believe in to help her.

'The symbol,' she mumbled. She flapped an arm towards the plaque. 'The tablet had the same symbol as the necklace. I wanted to see it.'

'Is that why you have come to Rome?'

Now her surprise was genuine. 'The message.'

'What message? Who told you to come here?'

She looked at him blankly. Blood dribbled down her chin—she didn't know if it came from inside her mouth or out. 'Didn't you?'

He almost hit her again. She saw his arm tense, felt the grip on her head tighten in anticipation. She saw the fury in his face, and knew that if he hit her again, he'd keep going until there was nothing of her left to hurt.

The blow didn't come. 'Tell me why you came to Rome,' he repeated, his voice tight with the strain of self-control.

'The text message. I don't know who sent it. He quoted the inscription on Constantine's arch. He said he could help.'

Dragović said something over her head. The hand let go; she slumped on to the floor again. Footsteps went and came back. When she opened her eyes, Dragović was rifling through her handbag. They must have got it from the car. He pulled out her phone and read off the screen. He looked surprised, Abby thought.

'You see?' she mumbled. 'Wasn't that you?'

The guard lifted her up and a cloth went over her head. The last thing she remembered was the choking smell of lilies closing in around her.

XVI

Constantinople—April 337

The soldiers aren't palace guards. The badges on their cloaks show twin men wrestling each other. The fourteenth, the Gemini. By rights, they should be a thousand miles away on the Rhine frontier, watching for barbarians trying to creep across the river.

The centurion salutes. 'General Valerius. Please come with us.'

It's a long time since anyone called me General. 'Who wants to see me?'

'An old friend.'

It must be a lie. All my friends are long gone, one way or another. But there's no point resisting. I pull on a cloak and a wide-brimmed hat and let them take me. We avoid the obvious destinations—the palace, the Schola barracks, the Blacherna Prison—and instead plunge down the steep-stepped hill towards the Golden Horn. Early afternoon on a Sunday, the city dozes like a dog: the market halls are empty, the shops shuttered, the ovens cold. Even the picks and hammers have gone quiet. The whole world's stopped, because Constantine commanded it. Who'd reject a god who gives you a day off once a week?

A skiff's waiting for us, bobbing among the litter and debris that clog the harbour. Twelve strong slaves bend over their oars. I'm expecting them to take us across the Horn; instead, they turn out into the open water of the Bosphorus. I glance down into the bilge. A length of chain makes an iron nest near the bow, and the anchor fastened to it looks heavy enough to sink an old man. With the wind up, blowing spray off the whitecaps, you wouldn't even see the splash.

I pull the cloak closer to keep off the wind, and fix my attention on the city on the Asian shore—Chrysopolis, the city of gold. It's lost some lustre in recent years—the magnificence of Constantinople casts a long shadow across the strait—but a certain class of person still values its amenities. The houses are spacious, the air's clear, and the jealous eyes that watch every inch of Constantinople can't reach quite this far.

The boat steers clear of the town harbour, and pulls along the coast to a private stone landing. Long gardens stretch away from the water towards a handsome villa at the top of the slope. Almond trees are in bloom; bees buzz among the cyclamen and roses. Halfway to the house, two men wait on a terrace. One hurries down the steps to greet me.

'General Valerius. After all these years.'

It takes me a moment to place him—not because I don't recognise him, but because to see him here is almost the last thing I expect. It's Flavius Ursus, Marshal of the Army, the most powerful soldier in the empire after Constantine. I knew him when he was Tribune of the Eighth. Flavius the Bear, we called him. In the field he wore a bearskin cape and a necklace of claws and teeth. He's short, broad-shouldered and barrel-chested, with a full beard that hides most of the scars on his face. His father was a barbarian who crossed the Danube in the chaos before Diocletian's reign, and then joined the Roman army to stop his countrymen from following him. The son, I think, is similarly flexible.

139

He shows me up to the terrace.

'My men coming to get you—I hope you didn't mind. I'm sure you understand.' We climb the final step and come out on a broad terrace. 'And here's another face from the old days.'

The man waiting there is younger than both of us, probably half my age, with short dark hair cut straight across the forehead, and a smug patrician face. He looks pleased to see me, though I can't think why.

'Sir.'

He clasps my hand, but doesn't introduce himself. He's waiting, hoping I remember him.

'Marcus Severus?' It's half-guesswork, but his smile says I've got it right. 'I haven't seen you since . . .'

'The Chrysopolis campaign.' Now I've recognised him, he's happy to remind me. 'I was on your staff.'

'And now the Gemini?' I guess. 'You must be a tribune by now, at least.'

His face flushes. 'I'm Chief of Staff to the Caesar Claudius Constantinus.'

'Of course.' It's been fully twelve years since our last campaign, when he was a hot-headed young officer buzzing around my staff, angling for any command that might give a whiff of glory. I flap my hand, an apology for my age. 'An old man's memory . . . I knew and I forgot. Congratulations, richly deserved.'

An awkward silence descends between the three of us. *Why is Severus here?* He should be a thousand miles away in Trier. And why is Ursus harbouring him?

A slave brings us cups of spiced wine on a silver tray. I sip mine, and stare across the water. A brown

140

haze of dust and smoke smears the sky over the city.

'Is this your house?' I ask Ursus.

'It belongs to a merchant, a contractor for the army. He lets me use it from time to time, when I need somewhere private.'

Obviously, the merchant's done well out of supplying the army. 'And did you row an old man across the water just to reminisce about the old days?'

'In the old days, General, you always had your finger on the pulse,' says Severus.

'I retired. I have a villa in the mountains of Moesia, and in a month I'll be there for good. As soon as the Emperor lets me go.'

Ursus gives a short, barking laugh. 'Nothing changes. Every campaign I fought with you, you said it would be your last. And I hear the Emperor has you doing yet another last job for him. Still his trusted right hand.'

Of all the things I expected when the soldiers arrived at my door, this must be the least likely. What did this bishop have that makes everyone from an old pagan to Constantine's field marshal so sensitive to his fate?

'It's trivial,' I assure him. 'I don't know why the Augustus bothered himself with it.'

A fringe benefit of my reputation is that people always assume I know something when I plead ignorance. Severus gives me a conniving smile. 'There are rumours, General. You must have heard them.'

'Imagine I haven't.'

'They say that when your dead bishop was found, a document case was missing.'

When did he become *my* dead bishop? 'Bishop Alexander was writing a book for Constantine—a compendium of the events of his reign. Whatever papers he had were just for that.'

Severus leans in closer. 'We're not interested in the past.'

I believe him. Constantine's raised a new generation in his image, and the past is simply embarrassing. The ancestral gods get lodged in the attic, and old books make good kindling.

I glance at Ursus, looking for a hint.

'You know there are factions at court.'

'That's why they call it a court. People choose sides and play games.'

Neither of them smiles. 'They say that Constantine's sister, Constantiana, has a secret will he's written,' says Severus.

'Benefitting whom?'

'No one knows.'

'Then who's spreading the rumours?'

Ursus grunts. 'You know how it goes. Whispers and glances and shadows in the smoke.'

I know how it goes. 'There is no secret will,' I say flatly. 'Even if there were, why would Alexander have it? When was the succession ever decided by a priest? The army's loyal.' I fix on Ursus's brown eyes. 'Isn't it?'

'To Constantine.'

'But after Constantine . . .' The red wine has stained Severus's lips purple. 'It's important that all the sons inherit equally.'

'The army wants an orderly succession,' Ursus confirms.

I know what he means. The army wants Constantine's three sons to divide the empire.

Three emperors means three armies, three times as many generals, three times the profits for the contractors in their palatial villas on the Bosphorus shore.

'One heir would be more orderly.'

'Only if he was undisputed.'

'That time has passed,' says Severus. 'This is a new age.'

'Every age thinks so.'

'And old men think nothing changes.'

I study him more closely. He's wearing a leather thong around his neck: it dips under his tunic, but when he tips his head back I glimpse a curved, scaly fish-back rendered in bronze.

'I remember when you were the crow, and I was the scorpion,' I say. Severus looks at me as if I'm spouting gibberish, as if the phrase genuinely means nothing and he never heard it while squashed together with his comrades in a damp basement with frontier earth oozing through the stones. As if he never knelt in front of me so I could sign the blood of Mithra on his forehead and induct him into the mysteries he was so desperate to know.

'There is only one God, Jesus Christ,' he says blandly. Ursus, who stood beside us in those caves, says nothing.

There's no point arguing. I could accuse Severus of treachery, of abandoning the old gods, but he wouldn't care. He's not interested in the past, not even his own.

'Why is he here?' I ask Ursus. 'Does Constantine know?'

Their faces tell me he doesn't.

'The Caesar Claudius is worried for his father's health,' says Severus.

Translation: *Constantine's an old man. If anything happens, Claudius wants his man in place to guard his inheritance.* No wonder Severus is holed up here, watching the palace from across the water. If Constantine found out, he'd have Severus counting gulls on some rock in the Aegean for the rest of his life.

An aide sidles up and presents a scroll to Ursus. He withdraws a little distance to study it, leaving me and Severus alone.

'I saw the Augustus two days ago,' I tell him. 'You can go back to Trier and report that he was in rude health.'

Severus nods, as if my news is helpful. We both know he's not going anywhere. 'I need to know about the will, Valerius.' He's dropped the 'General'. 'There are factions at court, and who knows what they might do to deny Claudius his inheritance.'

'Constantine knows his own mind—more than any man who ever lived.'

'He can still be swayed by gossip. As you know.'

Again, that twist of the knife in my heart. I want to hurl him into the water, hold him under the waves until the fish nibble the privilege off his face for good.

'You're still the crow, Severus, even if you don't remember those days. Sitting in your tree, waiting for the wind to bring you the smell of death.'

It's my last attack, and it doesn't touch him. I never had a family of my own; I've been spared the experience of seeing my offspring start treating their parents like their own children. Now I know how it feels.

Ursus, who's been waiting at a safe remove,

interposes himself again.

'My boat will take you back.'

He doesn't escort me. But as I step on to the landing stage, a final question follows me down to the shore.

'Have you wondered why Constantine asked someone who knows nothing about the Christians to investigate the death of a bishop?'

XVII

Rome—Present Day

Until the very last minute, she didn't guess what they'd do to her. Blindfolded, she was dragged back downstairs to the car, then driven for what seemed an eternity. The hand on her back never relaxed. She lay curled in a ball, face down in her stale vomit, reliving her nightmares. The villa on the coast and the black museum and all the evil places on earth she'd been. Different voices spoke inside her, overlapping ghosts. Hector: *You spend too long chasing dead people, you need to come up for air.* Michael, on a beach somewhere on holiday: *Never get involved.* Reports she'd written, dispassionate and correct. *Witnesses saw the victim being bundled into a car by unknown men; she was found dead in a forest eight hours later.*

Except when they came for me, there weren't even any witnesses.

The car stopped. A door opened. She felt a shove against her back, and then a shuddering blow as she fell and landed on her shoulder. Above her head, the door slammed shut. She heard the roar of an engine and the squeal of tyres; she choked as a blast of exhaust fumes blew in her face. Then there was silence.

She pulled the blindfold off her face, and emerged, gasping, into the sodium glow of the city at night. Far in the distance, a pair of brake lights veered around a corner and vanished.

She was alone. Plane trees rustled overhead; a fine rain wet her cheeks and washed down her tears. She pulled herself to her feet and staggered to the stone wall a few feet away. Below, hemmed in by concrete, the Tiber flowed eternally by. A hundred yards downstream she could see a bridge, and on its far side the bulk of the Trastevere Prison, next to her hotel.

They've almost brought me home. It felt like one final twist of the knife.

She staggered over the bridge, and hammered on the door of her hotel until they let her in. In her room, she pulled every spare blanket she could find out of the cupboard and heaped them up on the bed, then crawled under them.

It was almost dawn before she fell asleep, and when she did, the dreams were savage.

*   *   *

She slept until noon, until a chambermaid barging through the door made her scream so loud the desk receptionist heard it and came running. She showered and dressed. She went to the little café on the corner and drank three espressos sitting on a tall stool at the counter. She caught a couple of the men staring, though they weren't likely to proposition her. In the mirror behind the bar, she could see a fat bruise where Dragović's gun had left its mark on her swollen chin. She touched it and winced.

She picked over her memories of the night before, still sharp and raw. She had to handle them carefully, like a rubber-gloved pathologist. A cigarette would have helped, but a sign above the counter said NO SMOKING and she didn't want a confrontation.

Have you ever wondered why you're not dead?

Dragović doesn't know either, she thought. Something happened at the villa that even he doesn't understand.

It still felt incredible. Two days ago, Dragović had been headlines and rumours, a bogeyman on the shadows of the world stage. Now, he was as real as a beard scraping against her skin. Her coffee cup trembled on its saucer.

Two deaths, but only one body.

There had to be someone else. Someone who'd stopped the killer and called the police. Who'd sent her the letter with Michael's sister's address, and then the text message at the British Library. *I can help.*

Was that true? Nothing had helped so far. She remembered the figure in York chasing her through the rain. In Rome, the only person who showed up was Dragović. Some help.

She was pretty sure Dragović hadn't sent the message. She'd seen him read it off her phone— he'd been as confused as she was. And if he'd wanted to get hold of her, he could surely have found an easier way than sending Latin riddles to her phone.

To reach the living, navigate the dead.

The poem and the symbol—what did they mean?

The symbol on the necklace and on the stone, the poem on the stone and on the manuscript. And how did Michael ever get hold of either of them?

Michael.

Her head hurt. She thought about another coffee and decided not. Her body was starting to feel as if it might shake itself apart.

Michael. He was the missing link, the void at the centre of all her swirling thoughts. Every time she approached him, she drew back for fear of what she might find. He'd taken her to a villa owned by the most wanted man in the Balkans. Even she couldn't pretend to herself it might have been coincidence. Dragović had the poem and the symbol in stone, Michael had them in gold and papyrus.

And where did he get the necklace? She remembered what Michael had said when she asked him. *A Gypsy gave it to me.*

She had to go back. Whatever Michael was doing, it had begun in Kosovo. She put down her coffee cup and headed for the door.

At least I'm not dead, she told herself, trying to make light of it and not hear the mordant voice coming straight back at her.

Yet.

*　　　*　　　*

Pristina, Kosovo

Pristina sat on sloping foothills, with a green forested ridge above, and the constant belch of the Obelic power plant at the bottom. In between stood a fairly standard-issue Warsaw Pact town: squat apartment blocks punctuated by the occasional piece of concrete whimsy. Going back was like pulling on an old set of clothes you never much liked in the first place. Abby sat in the back of the taxi as it crawled up Avenue Bil Klinton, past the gilded statue of the former president, one arm raised to wave at the permanent traffic jam. He might have been impeached in America, but in Kosovo he remained invincible. On every corner, stern-looking NATO soldiers watched from billboards and reminded the population they were safe. Outside the parliament building, pictures of the missing flapped from a fence. Some of the pictures looked blank, so that only if you stared carefully did you see the faded traces of the photographs; others might have been put up yesterday. A row of ghosts.

And what about the people left behind? Abby wondered. The mothers and wives and children of those men (they were all men). Did their memories fade like the photographs, until all the pain had bleached to whiteness? Or did they survive, hardy and unwilting as the plastic flowers that garlanded the railings?

Is that what Michael will become? It seemed impossible.

They turned left, past the hotel with the Statue of Liberty replica on its roof, past the Palace of Youth and the Grand Hotel. If you wanted a symbol of Kosovo, that was it: forty-four storeys of socialist nostalgia, half of it wrapped in hoardings promising luxury to come, the other half untouched in fifteen years.

The taxi dropped her off at her flat. She didn't have a key, but Annukka, the pretty Finnish girl who lived opposite and worked for the OSCE mission, kept a spare. It was late Saturday afternoon; from inside the apartment, she could hear singing.

Annukka answered Abby's knock dressed with a towelled turban over her head. She must be getting ready to go out.

'Oh my God, Abby.' She threw her arms around Abby and kissed her on both cheeks. She looked genuinely pleased to see her, so much so that Abby had to check her memories. In her mind, Annukka was the sort of neighbour who watered your plants and smiled in the hallway. But perhaps it had been more than that. For all the hard work, aspects of being on mission were like summer camp. You made friends, shared intimacies, and then summer ended and most of it got forgotten in a welter of promises to write and keep in touch. That was what had made it so easy with Michael.

Except now he's gone and I'm still chasing after him.

'We've all been so worried about you,' Annukka was saying. 'We heard some crazy stuff about you and Michael. On the news, even. Some journalists came by, but I didn't say anything. Well, I didn't know. Seriously, though, are you OK?' She looked at the gash on Abby's chin where the pistol had cut it, the swelling around her mouth. 'What happened to your face?'

Abby put her hand on Annukka's shoulder. 'Can we talk about this later? I just got here and I really need to sort myself out.'

'Sure. I mean, of course, any time. Anything I can do to help, let me know, OK?'

She was so sincere, so briskly kind, Abby almost wanted to cry.

'I was hoping you still had my spare key.'

'Right.' A shadow flickered on Annukka's face.

150

'I'm really sorry, Abby, but I have to tell you I gave it to the police. Two guys from EULEX and some Kosovo Police. They wanted to search your apartment. I thought perhaps they were getting some stuff for you. I don't think they gave the key back.'

Abby stared at the wooden door, the Cyclops-eye of the peephole poking out of it.

'You're welcome to stay with me,' Annukka chattered on. She frowned. 'Except, I'm supposed to be going out with Felix tonight and I'll probably stay over. We lost the water here again and they say it won't come back until tomorrow. I can give you a key for my place, if you want?'

'Don't worry about it,' Abby assured her. 'I'll go down to the police station and get it back.'

She walked slowly down the stairs until she heard Annukka's door latch shut. Then she sat down and buried her head in her hands.

I can't even get into my own home. Of all the things that had happened since Michael drove her to the villa, that seemed the most unjust. The world had turned its back on her; she was being nudged towards the exit. The cold step was her only home, strictly temporary. Even when Annukka hugged her, she'd felt like a drowning woman slipping out of her grasp.

We lost the water here again. That was the thing with Pristina. Ten years of international government, billions of dollars in reconstruction money, and when you flipped a switch or turned a tap you still couldn't be sure what would happen. *It's lucky England got its plumbing from the Victorians*, Michael used to joke. *If we had to rely on the UN or the EU we'd still be running around with*

151

buckets picking lice off each other.

Buckets.

She stood and went downstairs. Outside, around the back of the building, there was a courtyard where the landlord kept the bins. Half a dozen satellite dishes stared down at her; the cables of illegal electrical hook-ups snaked down from a concrete pole.

The block was built in the shape of an H, but the ground-floor flat had filled in the intermediate space with a kitchen extension. Abby peered through the kitchen window and saw it was empty.

She dragged one of the bins over against the wall and clambered up on it, then hauled herself on to the kitchen roof. The wound in her chest throbbed in protest; for a second, jack-knifed over the edge of the roof, she thought she might pull the scar apart. She gritted her teeth against the pain.

I just want to get into my own home.

Anger took her over the edge and on to the gravel-covered roof, clutching her side as if she'd run a marathon. In the corner outside her bathroom window, a bucket of stagnant water sat under a sawn-off drainpipe. She'd kept it there for flushing the toilet when the water was off. It used to live inside, but somehow she always forgot to refill it. After being caught out for the third time, Michael had jury-rigged it for her so she'd never have to remember.

She'd used the bucket so often, in the end she just left the bathroom window unlocked permanently. Michael teased her it wasn't secure, but Pristina—despite Kosovo's reputation—was one of the safest cities in Europe. She worked her fingers under the lip of the window and tugged. For

152

a moment it wouldn't give—she wondered if some dutiful policeman had seen the latch and locked it. But it was only stiff from disuse. The window swung out. A few seconds later, she was standing in her own home.

*　　　*　　　*

Going back to the London flat had been disorienting for the changes: her past, rearranged. Here, it was what hadn't changed that threw her. Everything was exactly as she'd left it when she went to work that Friday morning, before the trip to Kotor Bay. The washing-up sitting in the drying rack. The cold laundry balled in the tumble drier. A jaundiced, weeks-old newspaper on the sofa. The air smelled damp and sour; dust dulled every surface. She felt like an explorer opening an Egyptian tomb.

She shivered. The flat might not have changed, but she had: she didn't belong here any more. And not everything *was* the same. The longer she looked, the more she noticed things. The drawer in the bedroom that hadn't been closed properly. The photograph on her bookcase one shelf down from where it should have been. The door to the spare room, which she always wedged open for the light, that had been allowed to close.

What were they looking for?

Suddenly, she felt very afraid. The place had dispossessed her: she didn't want to be there. She went into the bedroom and stuffed some clothes into a bag. She rummaged through the wardrobe, looking for a warm coat. Even that was painful. Interleaved on the hangers with her skirts and blouses, she found some of Michael's clothes, shirts

153

and trousers that had crept in and accumulated from all the times he'd stayed over. She found herself touching them, rubbing the cloth between finger and thumb, as if it might be possible to squeeze some small residue of Michael out of it. She knew she shouldn't, but she couldn't help it. She was crying again, but she didn't try to stop herself. It felt natural, as if something deep within her had finally managed to reach the outside.

Her hand ran over a suit jacket and stopped. Under the pin-striped cloth she felt something stiff and solid. She slipped her hand inside the pocket, and came out holding a slim red leather diary. She had to smile. Michael's diaries had been a standing joke. He'd owned at least three that she'd known about, possibly more, different shapes and sizes that lived independent existences, turning up in pockets or on desks or shelves more or less at random. Whenever Michael had to make a date, he wrote it in whichever diary came to hand. The one time Abby pointed out how inefficient this was, he'd looked mock-wounded. *I'm half-Greek and half-Irish*, he'd said. *Timekeeping's not in the genes*. Amazingly, she'd never known him miss an appointment.

She opened the diary and turned through the pages, the last weeks of Michael's life. He hadn't used it much—most of the jottings were routine meetings, minor errands. But two entries stood out. One, three weeks before he died: *Levin, OMPF*, underscored three times. The other, the following week, *Jessop, 91*.

The screech of the telephone cut through the silence. Abby almost dropped the diary. The phone rang on, penetrating every corner of the flat; Abby

154

didn't move. She felt like a burglar, caught in the act. *It's your home*, she scolded herself.

She didn't pick up. The phone kept ringing, until she was almost used to it. Then it stopped. Down on the street outside, she heard a car draw up. She ran to the window and looked down. A silver Opel 4 x 4 with EU markings had pulled up on the kerb across the road. A door opened, and she ducked back in case anyone saw her through the window. How did they know she was there? Did Annukka call them?

I'm an EU employee, standing in my own flat on a Saturday afternoon. But it wasn't really like that. She ran to the kitchen and took the spare key from the biscuit jar, just in case she needed to come back. Then she slipped into the bathroom, clambered down off the roof as quickly as the pain in her side would allow, and disappeared down the footpath that ran between the apartment buildings and chain-link fences. She didn't look back.

XVIII

Constantinople—April 337
I sit in the stern of the boat. The sun's setting over Constantinople; the palace is in shadow, while on the opposite shore the roofs of Chrysopolis burn gold. I'm in a black mood. I'm furious that I let Severus provoke me, but that's passing. It's not the first time I've lost my temper. There's something deeper, something malignant inside me that I feel but can't touch.

I force myself to think about the substance of our

155

discussion. If Constantine's son Claudius has sent his chief of staff from Trier to Constantinople, he must be worried for his father. More accurately: worried for his inheritance. As Constantine himself proved thirty years ago in York, a son's place is with his dying father. When the crown slips, he wants to be there to catch it.

It's a shock to think that Constantine might be dying. He seemed well enough when I saw him. But I'm ignorant. Constantine has physicians and doctors who examine every drop of bile or blood; he also has the slaves who attend him. If there's blood in his stool, or strange marks on his skin, or if he's up half the night coughing out his guts, someone will know. And the news will spread to those who are willing to pay for it.

So why was Severus interested in Alexander? I don't believe he had Constantine's secret will. If it was that important, Constantine would be turning the city upside down, not asking me to make discreet enquiries.

A dense web surrounds Alexander. I try to trace its spirals in my thoughts. Symacchus, unreconstructed adept of the old religion, and Eusebius, high priest of the new. Asterius the Sophist, peering into cathedrals he's forbidden from entering. Simeon the Deacon. Now Severus and Ursus.

Symacchus the persecutor who could have killed Alexander thirty years ago.

Asterius, who perjured his faith, while Alexander kept his.

Eusebius, the churchman whose promotion Alexander blocked.

Simeon, always in the wrong place at the wrong

time.

Severus the Crow, waiting for death and the future.

And Alexander, the fly in the centre of the web, jerking and twitching as the spiders stalk their threads.

A boat rowing across the Bosphorus is a good place to consider these things. The slaves strain, the oars swing; the boat seems to move, but the coast never gets any nearer.

*   *   *

I sleep badly, then wake late. I sit in my empty house and pick at Alexander's manuscripts that Simeon gave me. One's called *The Search for Truth*. I wonder if Simeon meant it ironically.

You cannot marry truth with violence, nor justice with cruelty.

Religion is to be defended not by killing but by dying; not by cruelty but by patient endurance; not by sin but by good faith.

Humanity must be defended if we want to be worth the name of human beings.

I put down the book and roll it up. I won't find the truth I'm seeking there. It makes him sound like a reasonable man—likeable, even. Nothing to suggest why someone would want to kill him.

Religion is to be defended not by killing but by dying. Who was he defending his religion from? An old enemy like Symmachus? Someone from within his own church? Or a man like Severus, for whom religion and politics are two faces of the same coin?

Alexander can't speak from beyond the grave, I realise. He isn't in it yet. He'll still be lying out for

157

the mourners to pay their respects.

A morbid curiosity overcomes me. I never knew him in life. Perhaps seeing him in death will give me knowledge.

*   *   *

In Rome, denied recognition, the Christians squeezed their churches into converted shops, warehouses, even private homes. When Constantine built his new city, he endowed it with plenty of churches—but the Christian congregation has grown so fast they've overflowed and resorted to the old expedients. The Church of Saint John fills the ground floor of a tenement block near the city walls that used to be a bathhouse. Planks cover the holes where the pools used to be; the Triton on the wall has been defaced, and the sea nymphs painted over, though they've kept a few of the fish. Whoever decided that Alexander should be laid out here didn't want to encourage his mourners.

On a Monday morning, the church is almost deserted. I'm glad there's no one to see me: I feel awkward enough trespassing in their sanctuary. Alexander's body lies on an ivory litter at the front of the church. Candles burn at the four corners; incense smokes from a brazier at his feet. He's dressed in a plain white robe, feet towards the door and a white cloth covering his face. I remember the weapon that killed him, the blood and hair matted on the bust, and hesitate. I never used to be this squeamish.

I pull back the cloth and wince. The undertaker's tried his best, but only made it worse. Bloodstains mottle the beard and the skin's floury where

158

a cosmetic's been applied. Worst of all is the forehead. It's been smashed in, a single overwhelming blow that shattered the skull and tore a bloody gash in the skin. There are small perforations where the undertaker tried to sew it shut before abandoning the effort.

I reach out two fingers and pull back the eyelids. A clear liquid oozes out like tears—a salve that the undertaker's used to hold the eyes shut. A pair of deep brown eyes gaze up at me with what looks like surprise.

And suddenly the surprise is mine. I've known him more than half my life. The tutor at the wedding chasing after the boy who'd climbed up on the bridal bed; and again, in the tent on campaign in Italy, bent over a table teaching the boy Greek, while Constantine pondered his god's intentions. I would have seen him dozens of times around Constantine's household, and never paid him the least attention. Did I know his name? I must have done.

He also tutored one of my sons, apparently.

Strange that I should have forgotten him. Like turning the house inside out for a lost coin, only to find it in your purse all along.

The smells of incense and embalming fluid have seeped into my stomach. Dark spots blot my vision; I need air. Leaving Alexander's face uncovered, I run to the door. There's a square at the end of the road with a plane tree. If I can just sit down in the shade a few minutes I'll be fine. I'll—

'Gaius Valerius?'

I can't ignore him—I've almost run into him. I step back and see a man in a formal gown, sparkling eyes and a smile too wide for the horrors inside.

159

The man I met in Symmachus's garden.

'Porfyrius?'

'I came to pay my respects to Bishop Alexander.' He sees my ashen face and breaks off. 'Are you . . . ?'

'I need to sit down.'

He steers me to his litter. I don't lie down—I'd feel I was lying on my own funeral bier. I sit awkwardly on the edge of the platform, in the shade of the canopy, while one of the slaves fetches water from a fountain.

'What are you doing here?' I ask.

'Paying my respects to Alexander.'

'You went to see him in the library.' My voice is shaky, still grappling with the memories. 'Did you know him well?'

'He helped me understand the truth of the Christian religion.'

I don't hide my surprise. 'I thought . . . as a friend of Symmachus . . .'

'Aurelius Symmachus is a Stoic.' A wry smile. 'Outward things cannot touch his soul.'

'He was less accommodating thirty years ago.'

'We all were.' His eyes lose focus for a moment, then return. 'Do you want to know the truth, Valerius? Thirty years ago I persecuted the Christians just as furiously as Symmachus. That was my first encounter with Alexander, and it wasn't pleasant.'

The web I drew around the dead bishop takes on another strand. 'What made you change your mind?'

'I saw the sign of God's truth.'

It's impossible to know if he's serious. He never stops smiling; every word he says has a subjective

160

quality, as if he's merely testing how it sounds. I try to imagine that smiling face standing over a brazier, digging his iron into the coals.

He shrugs. 'I was a former proconsul who'd slipped off the path of honour, and I was ambitious.' A quick look to see if I understand. 'There was a scandal—perhaps you heard? *Carmen et error*—a poem and a mistake, as Ovid said. The next thing I knew, I was sitting in a small house on the edge of the world, in the shadow of Trajan's Danube wall, contemplating my errors. Ten whole years I spent there.' A sigh, a shrug. 'At least I wrote a lot of poems. And I met Alexander.'

'Why was he there?'

'A religious dispute.'

He kicks at a loose stone in the road. 'You can imagine how awful it was—the persecutor and his victim, thrown together again after all those years. And yet, we became friends. Unlikely, I know, but Alexander was extraordinary. I'd tried to make a martyr of him and now he became a saint. He never mentioned what had happened. I waited and I waited—it drove me mad. I analysed every gesture, every word he said, convinced it was part of some trap. One day, I couldn't bear it any more. I asked him straight out if he remembered me.'

His voice drops. 'He forgave me everything. Not the grudging forgiveness you might get from a friend you'd done wrong, lording his generosity over you. No rebuke, no lecture. He said, "I forgive you," and that was all. He never mentioned it again.'

And a lot of good it did him, the cruel voice inside me retorts. A picture flashes in my mind of the white corpse laid out on the bier. I can smell embalming fluid on my fingers. I feel ashamed, and resent it.

Porfyrius stretches. 'Do you know what Alexander wrote in one of his books? *"In order to rule the world, we have to have the perfect virtue of one rather than the weakness of many."'*

'He was speaking about Constantine?'

'He was speaking about God. But what is true of God serves for His creation. For too long we had too many gods and too many emperors and we suffered for it. With Constantine, we have one God, one ruler, one empire united. No division, no hatred, no war. Who couldn't believe in that?'

That raises my eyebrows. 'No war? You know Constantine's massing his army for a campaign against Persia as we speak.'

I stand up from the litter, driven by a surge of anger I thought I'd mastered. 'You want to know why I didn't convert, when everyone from the Emperor to the bathhouse attendant did?'

Porfyrius waits politely. That only makes me angrier.

'The hypocrisy. You preach peace, forgiveness, eternal life—and then you end up like Alexander, laid out on a slab with your eyes glued shut.'

Porfyrius laughs and laughs. 'Do you think you won't end up like that too?'

XIX

Pristina, Kosovo—Present Day

Abby crossed the railway tracks at the bottom end of town and started climbing the hill opposite. The streets were quiet that early on a Sunday morning: no children playing, no traffic. Low cloud pressed over the valley and rendered the air milky white. She'd spent the night in a hotel, one that wasn't much used by internationals, biting her lip each time the lift next to her room made a sound. As soon as she could pretend it was decent, she'd slipped out the back entrance.

Levin, OMPF, Michael's diary had said. OMPF was the Office of Missing Persons and Forensics—or had been, until it was rebranded as the Department of Forensic Medicine a year ago. Michael had never been one to take notice of bureaucratic reshuffling. Levin, she guessed, was Shai Levin, Chief Forensic Anthropologist. Abby had met him a dozen times over the years, different encounters in different parts of the world, though she doubted she'd left much of an impression.

She'd been to a party at his house with Michael back in June. He lived in one of the freshly painted villas that climbed the slope opposite the main town, where the foreign proconsuls lived and lorded it over the city they administered. The higher you went, the nicer the houses got and the more elaborate the embassies became. At the very top of the hill, tucked behind the ridge out of sight of the diplomats, stood the ultimate authority: Camp Film City, headquarters for NATO's mission

163

keeping peace in the restive province. No one could mistake the hierarchy.

Abby walked past the diplomatic cars parked on the kerb, climbed the steps to the private villa and rang the bell. She hoped it was the right door.

'Can I help?'

Shai Levin stood in the doorway, wearing an untucked white shirt with the sleeves rolled up, cargo trousers and bare feet. He had olive skin, curly dark hair and soft dark eyes that gave no hint of the horrors he witnessed every day. His manner was mild and polite, his English faintly accented. Among international aid workers, he was something of a legend. People who didn't know better often called him a saint, to which he invariably smiled and pointed out he was Jewish.

'Abby Cormac,' she introduced herself. 'I work in Justice.'

She'd wondered how far her notoriety had spread. The look on Levin's face told her everything she needed to know.

'You were together with Michael Lascaris, from Customs, right? I'm so sorry—I heard what happened.'

What else did you hear? A grey KFOR helicopter flew low overhead, circling in to land at Film City. Abby edged closer to the door.

'I was looking through some of Michael's things. I think he met you not long before he died.'

Levin nodded. 'I guess that's right.'

'I'm trying to find out why he was killed.'

A shadow crossed Levin's face, the look of someone receiving a long-expected diagnosis. He seemed to hesitate a second, then opened the door wider.

164

'Come on in.'

He led her into the living room, modern and open-plan, with hardwood floors and full-length windows giving an uninterrupted panorama down on to the city. She admired it from a leather sofa while he made tea. Even to an uninvited guest, the room exuded calm.

He laid two cups of tea on the mahogany coffee table. 'Have you been to see the police?'

'I will.' Lying to Levin felt like swearing in church. She only really knew him by reputation, but that was plenty. Cambodia, Haiti, Bosnia, Rwanda, Iraq—wherever bodies lay buried in inconceivable numbers, Levin was the man with a shovel in the mud, piecing them together, making them human again.

'What did Michael want to see you about?'

'We were friends from Bosnia. Back in '98, there was a landowner who wouldn't give us clearance to excavate on his land, even though we were pretty sure there was a grave there. Michael turned up and made it happen. We crossed paths every so often after that, different postings, different places. It's a small world—you know how it goes.'

'And what did he want the last time you saw him?'

Levin looked uncomfortable. 'Abby, I know this must have been hell for you, but—you need to speak to the police.'

'They think I was involved. I wasn't,' she added. 'I got shot. That was about it.' A thought occurred to her. 'Did the police speak to you?'

'Just a few questions. I told them he was a good guy. I didn't know him well.'

'But he went to you just before he died.' *How*

165

many ways do I have to say this? 'All I'm doing is trying to find out the truth. I thought you might help.'

Levin had been staring out the window at the panorama below. Now he looked up, meeting her gaze with sad, sympathetic eyes.

'Michael came to see me at the lab. He had something he wanted my advice on. Professionally.'

She knew what Levin's professional interests were. 'A body?'

'I shouldn't say.'

'For God's sake,' she pleaded. 'You're supposed to be in charge of finding dead people. Giving answers. You must get widows and orphans like me every day wanting to know what happened. Just treat me like one of them.'

'There are channels,' Levin murmured, but more for his own sake than hers. He stirred his tea, then stood, as if a decision had been made.

'It's easier if I show you.'

*   *   *

He drove her down the hill and across town to the hospital. Even on a Sunday morning, traffic was heavy.

'You probably don't remember, but I was in Iraq at the same time as you. Mahaweel.' Shyly, the plain girl talking to the captain of the football team. 'We met a couple of times.'

'I remember. You were on the war crimes team—I heard good things about you. Now you're pushing papers with EULEX. What happened?'

It wasn't a new question, and she had a good stock of answers. *A new challenge, time for a change,*

166

fresh opportunities. But she knew Levin wouldn't buy it. She didn't want to insult him with platitudes.

'I gave up.'

'Iraq?'

She shook her head. 'I could deal with Iraq. It was such an epic disaster it was hard to blame anyone for what happened. Anyone who was there, I mean. Politicians, you expect to screw things up.'

He was waiting for her to say more. To her surprise, she found she wanted to. It was easy talking to him.

'It happened in Congo,' she said softly. She stared out the window at the triangular tower of Radio Kosovo, the well-dressed young Kosovars heading out for their Sunday strolls in the surrounding park. 'A village called Kibala. I was there when a Hutu militia arrived one night. It's a big mining area—lots of rare metals. The militias try to control the trade to fund themselves.'

Levin nodded.

'Anyway, this militia decided the villagers hadn't been paying them enough tribute. The UN knew there was a danger. They'd sent a battalion of Korean peacekeepers to keep an eye on things. I went to their base—I pleaded with their commander to go and secure the village. He turned me down point-blank. Then he told me to stay in the compound—said it was too dangerous to be out there.' She heard her voice rising, shaking with the emotion. 'For God's sake, those men were trained and armed to the teeth. All the militia had were machetes and cocaine. Those peacekeepers could have run them out of town in five minutes. Instead, they left the villagers to their fate. Mostly women and children—all the men were off working in the

167

mines. All I could do was listen to the screams.'

'Let me guess,' said Levin. 'No one ever heard about it.'

'Some people said it was economic. The metals from that part of the world go into a lot of mobile phones, apparently. Maybe the Koreans had orders not to disrupt the supply chain.' She shrugged. 'Maybe not. After the fact, people get so hung up on why something was allowed to happen. But there are always a million reasons not to do anything. You don't have to be corrupt, or cowardly, or inept. You just stay in bed and lock the door. When you've done that once . . .'

'. . . it's hard to ever leave again,' Levin finished. 'I know.'

He turned right. Abby glanced in the wing mirror to see if anyone had followed them.

'How do you do it?' she asked. 'Keep going. There's so much evil in the world, and whatever we do to hold it back, it just keeps coming. Doesn't it ever get to you?'

Levin stared at the road and didn't answer.

'Come on,' she pressed. 'I told you my story.'

'I haven't got a story.'

'Your secret, then.'

'No secret. I guess it's just . . .' He pulled over as an ambulance fought its way past them towards the hospital. 'If you don't bury the dead, they stick around.'

'Are we talking about ghosts?'

She'd meant it as a joke. To her surprise, Levin answered seriously.

'Not like kids on Halloween in white sheets. But if something exists in the mind, then it exists, right?'

He frowned, unsatisfied with his answer. 'If we

don't bury the dead properly, with reverence and dignity, then they haunt us. Check back through history. We're the first great civilisation that doesn't know how to deal with its dead. For us, it's just a logistical problem, making sure they don't take up too much space. Land's valuable, right? But a person doesn't just exist in his own body. There's a piece of him in everyone who knows him, that doesn't die with the body. And it's those fragments that stay to haunt you if you don't give them a proper burial.' He laughed softly. 'I sound like I've been drinking. Short answer: if you're working with the dead, you don't fool yourself the work's ever going to finish. I guess that's how I keep going.'

*   *   *

The Department of Forensic Medicine was one squat brown building among many at the sprawling hospital. Abby got out of the car and looked around. Her old office, EULEX headquarters, was just down the road, on the other side of a straggle of trees. Even on a Sunday morning she was nervous about being so close. A couple of doctors in white coats walked past, and she turned her head away. Levin saw, but didn't comment.

He led her inside and down a flight of stairs into the basement. A knot began tightening in her stomach. It was all too familiar: the blistered paint, the scuffed tiles, the smells of nicotine and disinfectant leached into the walls. Her breaths came faster as she remembered waking up in Podgorica. From somewhere in the depths of the hospital she could hear the monotone beep of a cardiac machine like a dripping tap. Or was that just her imagination?

If something exists in the mind, then it exists, right?

Levin opened a strong steel door. The swimming-pool tang of chlorine blew out at her. At least the EU had paid for a refurb here. The tiles were gloss white, the ceiling lights painfully bright after the dim corridor. On one wall a bank of metal doors like bread ovens hummed quietly.

Levin pulled on a pair of latex gloves. He spun open one of the doors and slid out a long, stainless-steel tray. Abby fixed her eyes at a point on the wall, then inched her gaze down until she could see what lay there.

It wasn't what she'd expected. A skeleton lay full length on the slab, its arms at its sides and its skull staring at the ceiling. The bones were dry, aged caramel brown. It looked more like a museum exhibit than a war crime.

'This is what Michael brought you?' A nod. 'Did he say why he had it?'

'He just wanted to know what I could tell him about it.'

'And?'

'The body belonged to an old man, probably in his sixties or seventies when he died. About six foot tall, well built. And murdered.'

A chill went through Abby. For a second she imagined Michael's skeleton laid out on a slab somewhere, a pathologist describing his murder as just another fact to be recorded.

Levin didn't notice. He leaned over the skeleton and pointed to the ribcage. 'You see here? Sharp force trauma. The fourth rib's been snapped off—you can see the break.' He poked a rubber-gloved finger through the chest cavity. 'There's a linear defect on the back of the rib where the blade cut the bone on its way out. Went right through him.'

'What does that mean?'

'Most likely that he was stabbed through the heart. From the front, based on the direction of the cut, with a big knife or a sword.'

With a shock, she realised Levin was smiling. 'Is that funny?'

'Not for him, I guess. But we're not going to open a case on him any time soon.'

She still didn't get it. 'Why not?'

'Because he died something in the order of seventeen hundred years ago.'

Levin walked over to the wall, pulled off his gloves, and washed his hands. When he turned back, the smile had gone and there were no answers in his eyes.

'Michael brought you a skeleton he'd found that was murdered over a thousand years ago?' Abby repeated.

'I got curious, so I ran some common isotope analysis on his molars and his femur. According to the chemical signatures, he grew up around here, but spent his later life somewhere around the eastern Mediterranean, near the sea. Varied diet, so probably rich.'

He pointed to greyish patches of bone on the skeleton's legs and arms, not smooth but mottled, like coral. 'That's woven bone—it grows in response to wounds or bruising. This guy lived a violent life, but always recovered. Until someone stabbed him through the heart.'

Levin crossed to a steel filing cabinet and extracted a folder. From inside came a sheaf of papers and a small brown object in a plastic bag.

171

'There was this, as well.' He slid out the object and laid it under a magnifier on the workbench. 'It's a belt buckle. Take a look.'

Abby put her eye to the glass. All she could see was a mottled brown blur, like a bed of autumn leaves. She moved the magnifier up and down until the image became clear. Letters had emerged from the background, crusted and incomplete, but still legible.

'LEG IIII FELIX.'

'It's the name of a Roman legion,' Levin translated. 'The "lucky fourth".' He caught her surprise. 'I looked it up on the Internet. Apparently, they were based in Belgrade, so not so far from here. If you look underneath the writing, you'll see the legionary crest.'

Abby squinted at it. Again, rust distorted the image, but she could make it out. A lean lion, proportioned like a greyhound, with a dreadlocked mane hanging over its shoulders.

'The NATO guys aren't the first occupying troops in this part of the world,' Levin said. 'I guess this one got unlucky.'

She remembered something he'd said. 'Why did you say murdered? If he was a soldier, and stabbed with a sword, couldn't he have been killed in battle?'

'Sure, I guess. I thought it would be unusual for a guy in his sixties to be on a battlefield, and the wound's so clean and deep he probably wasn't wearing armour. It's just a hypothesis.'

She looked up from the buckle and back at the skeleton on the table. Dead eye-sockets stared up at her. A scratch on the forehead made it look creased in thought, as if having been pulled from the darkness he was squinting to see her.

Who were you? she wondered.

Who are you? the skull seemed to reply.

'Did Michael say where he found the skeleton?'

'He said he'd been up north, near the Serbian border. Bandit country. I didn't ask why he was playing Indiana Jones there. Must have needed protection, though, because he arrived in a US Army Landcruiser. An American soldier helped bring the body in.'

'Did you get his name?'

'He left his autograph. Michael made him sign the paperwork, said it was better if his name wasn't on the docket.' Levin shuffled through the documents in the folder. 'Here—Specialist Anthony Sanchez, 957th LMT.'

'Do you know where I can find him?'

'As far as I know, all the Americans are down at Camp Bondsteel, by Ferizaj.' He could see what she was thinking. 'Have you got a yellow badge?'

Yellow badges were what admitted you to KFOR bases. They were supposed to be limited to NATO personnel, but Michael had had one, somehow. He used to drop in on the bases to buy duty-free cigarettes and alcohol at the PX's. *Is that appropriate for a customs officer?* she'd asked. Michael had just laughed.

'Did you tell the police about this? After Michael was killed?'

'I showed them the body, just in case it had anything to do with Michael. When they found out how old it was, they didn't want to know—told me to send it to the cold-case squad. I didn't mention Specialist Sanchez. I didn't think it would do him any good.'

173

The clinical smell in the enclosed basement was beginning to make Abby light-headed. She desperately needed air.

'Thanks for everything, Dr Levin. I hope I haven't got you in trouble.'

'I'll be fine. Just make sure you don't end up back here on my table. The sort of questions the police were asking when they came here . . .'

'What do you mean?'

'You might not want to know the answers.'

'I need to know.'

'I know.' Levin locked the file back in the cabinet. 'You have the look in your eyes. I see it all the time.'

'What's that?'

'The look of someone chasing ghosts.'

Two-handed, Levin pushed the drawer back into its steel mausoleum and slammed the door shut.

XX

Constantinople—April, 337

The message is waiting for me when I return home. *Come to dinner at the palace tonight.* It isn't clear if it's an invitation or an order, but I'm not going to refuse. My slaves spend the afternoon digging out the toga from the store cupboard where it's languished, and scrubbing it with chalk to obliterate the stains. It takes us an hour of folding, tucking and cursing to remember how to make it sit right. My steward murmurs that I look splendid, just like the old days. He sounds wistful.

The Hall of Nineteen Couches stands in the

palace complex in the shadow of the Hippodrome. A larger-than-life statue of Constantine with his three sons commands the entrance, staring down the length of the hall. In the apse at the opposite end, Constantine and his half-sister Constantiana lounge on the top couch like some incestuous pair of Egyptian gods. From there, the other eighteen couches run down the sides of the hall like the two straight tracks of the hippodrome. This is where the race is decided: the closer you are to the imperial couple, the nearer you are to winning. Constantine never used to like giving dinner parties: he hated having to rank the world so baldly. The sentimentalist in him couldn't bear to see his guests' disappointment when they found themselves next to the door; the pragmatist knew the value of uncertainty. You move more carefully when you don't know where you stand.

I take my allocated place—second from the end, left-hand side, sharing the couch with a gaunt chancery official, who wolfs down his food as if he hasn't eaten in a week; a senator from Bithynia; and a grain merchant who can only speak in bushels. I listen to his prattle about a blight in Egypt and whether the Nile flood will fail this year, as I scan the other guests. Eusebius is there, near the head of the room, deep in conversation with Flavius Ursus. I wonder what a bishop and a soldier have in common to talk about.

'The price is already up five denarii from last month.' The merchant tears into a skewered dormouse. Fat veined with blood dribbles down his chin. 'It's curious, you see? Usually in the spring the price drops as the seas open and the grain ships start to arrive again.' He chuckles, as if it's a riddle worthy of Daedalus. 'Augurs and conjurors read the future in dead entrails and the flight of birds. I can read it in the price of wheat.'

I humour him—it's the least painful option. 'What do you see?'

'Isn't it obvious?' He looks at me as if I'm a child. 'Trouble.'

*   *   *

At last the meal's over. Slaves clear the platters away. Guests stand and begin to mingle. The grain merchant makes his excuses and escapes to the other side of the room, as bored of me as I am of him. I push forward to the front of the room, trying to catch Constantine's eye, but the press of bodies is too thick. Instead, I stumble into a circle of men deep in a conversation. They fall silent when I intrude.

'Gaius Valerius Maximus.' It's Eusebius, in a gold-trimmed toga hardly less grand than Constantine's. Again, there's an edge of ridicule in the emphasis as he says my last name. 'Have you found the truth yet?'

'I'm waiting for someone to enlighten me.'

'One of our brothers in Christ was beaten to death with a statue of the philosopher Hierocles,' Eusebius explains for the benefit of the others. 'A notorious persecutor was sitting just behind him. The Emperor has ordered Gaius Valerius Maximus to find the killer.'

The knot of men around him nod seriously. They're strange company for a bishop to keep: the Prefect of Constantinople; the Prefect of Provisions who oversees the bread ration; two generals whose faces are more familiar than their names; and Flavius Ursus, Marshal of the Army. Nothing in his face acknowledges the conversation we had yesterday.

Eusebius glides away to talk with a pair of senators who've accosted him. He seems to know everyone here. I spend a few more minutes with Ursus and the generals, discussing arrangements for the Persian campaign, its prospects, whether they can reach Ctesiphon by autumn. *Just like the old days.*

But something's different. These are men at the peak of their powers—they should be brimming with confidence. Instead, they seem stiff and tentative. Even as they're speaking to me, their eyes dart around the hall. At first, I assume they're merely bored. But they're not looking for someone to speak to: they're watching everything. Who brushes whose arm. Who smiles, frowns, nods. Who makes a joke and who laughs.

The most powerful men in the empire, and they're rigid with fear. The Emperor's a colossus: if he falls, the carnage will be bloody and indiscriminate.

The crowd's thinning. People are slipping away, making excuses. It never used to be like this. I carry on towards the front of the room, but Constantine seems to have left already, unheralded and alone.

I think I'll do the same. I don't know why Constantine invited me here, but it's been a wasted evening. I turn to go and find my way blocked by a palace eunuch. He doesn't say anything, but beckons me towards a side door artfully hidden behind a pillar. Two dozen jealous pairs of eyes watch me go, and note it.

After the smoke, scent and heat of the hall, the night air cleanses me. The eunuch leads me across an empty courtyard, through an arch and along an arcade to a door. Lamps burn in brackets on the walls; guards from the Schola stand erect, wraithlike in their white uniforms. The eunuch knocks, hears something inaudible to me, and gestures me to go in.

Of course, I'm expecting Constantine. Instead, sitting in a wicker chair with a blanket around her shoulders like an old woman, is his sister Constantiana. It must be some sort of dressing room: there are clothes strewn over the furniture, a pair of red shoes kicked into the corner. Two slave girls kneel beside her, stripping back the layers of paste and powder on her face like workmen restoring a statue.

'I hear you have a new commission from the Augustus,' she says without preamble. Always 'the Augustus', never 'Constantine' or 'my brother'. 'I didn't think he had any use for you any more.'

She stares into a silver mirror on her dressing table without looking at me. Technically, she's Constantine's half-sister, though there's less than half a resemblance. Her face is a long oval and flat; she used to be considered beautiful, in the featureless way some men like. She wears her hair in intricate braids, piled up on her head and wrapped around an ivory headband. The style's too youthful for a woman her age.

I don't think her comment wants an answer, so I don't offer one.

'I'm told the Augustus has you investigating murders now,' she continues. 'It must make a change from committing them.'

178

I bow and focus my eyes on a painting on the wall behind her. Three Graces: Splendour, Happiness and Good Cheer. A forlorn hope, in this room.

'I obey the Augustus in all things. Always.'

Scraping off the cosmetics, one of the slave girls presses too hard. Constantiana winces; a spot of red appears on her bleached cheek. Without turning, she reaches across and plants an expert slap on the girl's face.

'I saw you at church with Eusebius of Nicomedia yesterday,' I say.

No reaction. Why should she justify herself to me?

'He had a lot to gain from Bishop Alexander's death,' I add.

'He has a lot to gain whatever happens. He's an exceptional man and he has a bright future.'

'Unless he's accused of murder.'

'You wouldn't dare.'

I think of the guards on the door. If I learned something she didn't like, would I leave alive?

'Constantine asked me to find the truth—however unlikely.'

I examine the three Graces again. The artist who painted them made some curious choices. Splendour is an elderly woman with long, silver hair and a face that looks as if a smile would break it. Happiness looks remarkably like the woman in front of me, a younger incarnation, whose proud eyes say that her greatest happiness is herself. Good Cheer is the only grace who resembles her eponym—but her face has been altered, inexpertly, so that her head's out of line with her body. As if her neck's been broken.

Constantiana catches my attention wandering.

'Are you listening to me?'

'Forgive me,' I apologise. 'I was remembering your wedding.'

*　　*　　*

Milan—February 313—Twenty-five years ago . . .
The declaration they issue begins like this:

When I, Constantine Augustus, and I, Licinius Augustus, happily met in Milan, and considered all matters pertaining to the public good . . .

Constantine and Licinius—the last two emperors. Licinius, a peasant-soldier with a homely face and a depraved imagination, has succeeded Galerius in the East, while Constantine now rules the West unopposed. They come to Milan, six months after Constantine's victory at the Milvian Bridge, to divide the world between them. To cement the partnership, Licinius is marrying Constantine's sister Constantiana. No one mentions that the last person to make a marriage alliance with Constantine's family is now a headless corpse at the bottom of the Tiber. It's a happy occasion.

And Constantiana looks radiant. At twenty-four, she must have worried that she'd be left on the shelf, a chip for a bargain never to be struck. At one stage there were rumours that Constantine might have offered her to me. Now she's sister to one Augustus and wife to the other—the most powerful woman in the world, you might think.

In fact, she's not even the most powerful woman in the room. Constantine's silver-haired mother Helena supervises the slave girls, who are combing and pinning Constantiana's hair, while Fausta, Constantine's wife, lounges on a couch and offers

180

pointed compliments. How much improved Constantiana looks with her hair up; how well her dress disguises her flat chest; how lovely it is to see a mature bride. It doesn't seem to inhibit them that Crispus and I are in the room, waiting to escort Constantiana to the wedding. They're used to talking over children and servants.

The door bangs open. There's only one man who could barge in to this gathering like that and, sure enough, it's Constantine. He takes in the three women, spies me and Crispus in the corner and fixes his gaze on us for safety.

'Gaius. I need you.'

Constantiana turns in her chair. 'Is something wrong?'

'Licinius is making trouble. He's still willing to concede toleration of Christians, but he's demanding that I offer to send Crispus back to Nicomedia as a hostage.'

'Surely it's not too much to ask,' says Constantiana.

'No.' Helena's tone allows no argument.

Constantine, who defers to no man on earth, struggles to defy his mother.

'You weren't so squeamish with me when you sent me to Galerius's court,' he complains.

'That was a necessary gamble—now you have everything. You don't need to take this risk.'

'You're speaking as if my future husband is some sort of murderer,' Constantiana complains. 'Why shouldn't my nephew come to stay with us in the east?'

She might as well not have spoken. Helena crosses to Crispus and puts a protective arm around him. He's thirteen now and growing fast, with an easy manner and a ready smile that make him the palace favourite.

'Your only son,' Helena reminds Constantine.

'Your only son *so far*.' Fausta rolls back on the couch and pats her belly, which has finally begun to swell under her dress. In my experience, there's nothing so smug and anxious as a pregnant empress.

Helena isn't interested. In her mind, her divorce was never legitimate. Constantius's children by his second wife were no children of hers: ergo, Constantine's children by his second wife will be no grandchildren of hers, whatever blood goes into them.

'I can go to Nicomedia,' says Crispus. 'If it has to be done.'

Constantine dismisses it. 'Licinius is just trying to drive a better bargain.' He thinks a moment. 'What if I offer him an extra province? Moesia, maybe.'

'If you offer him land, he'll think you're intending to take it back,' I point out. Constantine and I share a look behind Constantiana's back.

'Are the Christians so important that you want them to ruin my wedding?' says Constantiana. The slaves carry on, oblivious to our argument, pinning up her orange veil and tightening the belt on her dress.

'Do you have to name the Christians?' I suggest. 'Why not make the declaration vaguer—religious freedom to all, none specified.'

'No,' says Helena again. 'Who gave you your victories? Whose sign did you paint on your army when you defeated Maxentius?'

I cross the room and stare out of the window. 'Licinius doesn't care about the Christians. He wants reassurance.'

'So how do I reassure him?'

'Offer him nothing.'

An outraged squeal from Constantiana.

'Nothing more than you've already given,' I continue. 'Tell him it's a fair offer and that to ask more suggests bad faith.'

Constantine considers it. 'And if he says no?'

'He's staying in your palace, in your territory, guarded by your army. If he pulls out of the marriage now, he'll embarrass you badly.'

I leave the implication unspoken. I don't want to offend Constantiana so close to her wedding. But she's not obtuse. Denied armies, provinces or money to throw into this contest, she uses the only weapon she has and bursts into tears.

'For once in your life, can't you arrange a marriage without thinking what you're going to get out of it? It's almost as if you want your Christians to be there in the marriage bed with us.'

'Not at all.' Constantine rushes across and embraces her in a fraternal hug. 'It's Licinius who's complicating things. But Valerius is right. It's a fair offer and your husband's sure to see it.' Another hug. 'He won't want to let you get away from him.'

An empress isn't supposed to cry. Constantiana's tears have ruined her face. Half a dozen slave girls rush to mend the damage, dabbing and painting until the repair's invisible. By the time they lower her veil, her stormy face shows nothing but bright spring sunshine.

The marriage goes ahead and is as lavish as the bride and groom deserve. And two weeks later I head east, spying out the best ground where an invading army might forage, camp and fight.

'My wedding . . .' A tremor disturbs the remaining powder on Constantiana's face. 'I'd almost managed to forget it.'

'A happy day.'

'It bought my brother time to prepare for his next war. We both know that—now.' She gives me a pitying look. 'Did you know, the Augustus once considered marrying me to you?'

I start to make a pro-forma protest, but she talks me down. 'Some people said he'd raise you to Caesar, before Fausta started popping out sons like a breeding sow. You were handsome, then—and dangerous. More than one woman in the palace cried herself to sleep at night wondering why you didn't look at her.'

'I had no idea,' I say, truthfully.

The mask reassembles itself. The door to the past closes.

'You know the Augustus leaves on campaign next week. When he's gone, you'll report to me. Whatever you find out.'

*   *   *

I walk home, unescorted. Perhaps I should be more careful. As I approach my house, something moves by the door. Too much time in the palace has made me anxious—I pull away, pause, scan the shadows.

There's someone there.

'Are you going to rob an old man?' I call. I wish I hadn't been too proud to walk without a stick.

A figure steps into the light cast by the lamp over my door. Relief floods my body. It's Simeon.

'You could have waited inside.'

He looks surprised at the thought. Is my reputation so terrifying?

'A man walked into my church today—I didn't see him—and left a wrapped bundle on the step. There was a message inside.'

He hands over a flat wax tablet. I hold it up to the light.

Gaius Valerius Maximus—

Be at the statue of Venus at dusk tomorrow. I can give you something you want.

No name or signature. The wax is brittle and dry.

'When did this come?'

'This afternoon.'

'Did anyone see the man who left it?'

'Nothing they remembered.'

Of course they didn't. I send Simeon away and tell him to come back tomorrow. The day's gone on too long. My last thought before I go to sleep is of Constantiana, a slumped woman old before her time, with not even memories to comfort her.

My wedding. I'd almost managed to forget it.

How will I ever solve a murder in Constantinople? The city is filled with broken statues and broken people; lives smashed by everyday violence like stones under a chisel. Yet ask, and no one remembers a thing.

XXI

Pristina, Kosovo—Present Day

Abby stood in the alley across the street from her apartment building and watched. She'd been there for the last half-hour, looking for danger and screwing up her courage. All the parked cars were empty; none of the overlooking curtains twitched. Twenty minutes ago she'd seen Annukka walk out the door with her gym bag over her shoulder. That should give her an hour.

Heart in mouth, she walked briskly across the road and let herself in to the building. No sirens wailed; no cars screeched to a halt; no one shouted her name. She ran up the stairs to her flat. Just as her hand touched the handle, she noticed the corner of a sheet of paper slid under the door.

For a moment, she thought she might run down the stairs, all the way to the airport and straight back to London. *Don't be stupid*, she told herself. If someone was waiting inside, he wouldn't have left a note to announce himself. She unlocked the door and stepped in.

The flat was empty. She picked up the note and unfolded it.

Heard you're back in town. Let's meet for a drink. Jessop. A phone number with a Kosovo prefix followed.

She remembered Michael's diary, just before he died: *Jessop, 91*. She remembered an airless room in the Foreign Office, Mark fussing about while a stern man with a hard face recorded everything she said. *Jessop's from Vauxhall.* She remembered his

186

parting words to her, as she stumbled out of the room minus one gold necklace. *Be careful.*

Abby folded up the note and stuck it in her pocket. It begged fifty questions, but she wasn't going to think about them now. She went to the bedroom and found her car keys in the drawer where she'd left them a month earlier. The car was where she'd left it, too, parked around the corner outside a minimart. She went inside the shop and pretended to leaf through a rack of magazines, watching the street for the eyes that were surely looking for her, until she could almost convince herself that they weren't there.

*   *   *

On a proper highway, Ferizaj would have been fifteen minutes' drive from Pristina. On the E65 road south, it took the best part of an hour. It might have afforded Abby time to think, except that most of the time she was too busy trying to stay alive. The two-lane road was Kosovo's main corridor to the outside world, crammed every hour of the day with lorries, buses, cars and even the occasional horse-drawn cart. Traffic crawled along, and if a gap appeared it was immediately plugged by a vehicle attempting some kamikaze overtaking move. On the bridges, yellow signs gave speed restrictions for tanks, a reminder that this was still occupied territory.

Camp Bondsteel, the largest US base in the Balkans, stood in rolling hills below the pointed spire of Mount Ljuboten, better known to the soldiers as Mount Duke. Abby left her car in the parking lot and walked up a narrow path between a chain-link fence and high concrete blast barriers. To her left a high earthwork stretched around the perimeter, and it occurred to her that the basic design for a military camp hadn't changed in millennia.

The gatehouse was a windowless, corrugated-iron warehouse with red-painted walls and X-ray machines. The moment she walked in, a Hispanic man in a brown uniform accosted her. FORCE PROTECTION, said the badge on his sleeve. She wondered why the world's most powerful army needed protecting, and from whom. He asked for her badge and looked disconcerted when she couldn't produce one.

'I'm with the EULEX mission,' she said. 'I need to meet with one of your soldiers, Specialist Anthony Sanchez.'

More consternation. A tall black sergeant strode over. 'Is there a problem, ma'am?'

It was going wrong far faster than she'd expected. She found herself beginning to stutter. 'No problem—just—I need to speak to one of the soldiers here. Specialist Anthony Sanchez.'

'She's from the Justice Department,' the guard contributed.

'Is he in trouble?'

'Not at all.'

'Do you want to make a report for his commanding officer?'

'That's not—'

'Do you have security clearance?'

'I—'

'Perhaps you should come back another time, ma'am,' said the sergeant firmly. He scribbled a number on a piece of paper and gave it to her.

'Here's the number for the Public Affairs Office if you want to make a complaint.'

'Thank you.'

She trudged back down the path, among a gaggle of local cleaners and contractors finishing for the day. She couldn't face the drive back straight away: she went to the café across the road and nursed a coffee, while she watched the clouds gather in the valley. This part of the world had more than its fair share of storms.

Michael would never have let this stop him, she thought. Michael would have charmed a pass out of the guard, or talked his way in with a joke and a bottle of whisky. She replayed the conversation in her head and winced. How had she become such a wretched failure? She stared out the windows at the concrete walls and watchtowers. It wasn't the sort of place you broke into.

She finished her coffee and made her decision. The café had a payphone: she used it to dial the number on Jessop's note. He answered almost at once.

'Good to hear from you.'

'What are you doing in Kosovo?'

'I could ask you the same question.' He wasn't angry, or menacing. If anything, he sounded sympathetic. Abby fought back the urge to reciprocate.

'Is Mark here?'

'Stuck in London.' Jessop didn't sound too troubled by it.

'I need to see you.'

'Then that makes two of us.'

*   *   *

189

They met in Bar Ninety-One. Michael used to joke it was EULEX in miniature: a cross between a French café and an English pub, squatting in a Yugoslav building whose upper windows were still blown out from the war. It was warm and busy, but Abby would have preferred somewhere less obvious. This was Pristina's answer to Rick's Place in Casablanca: every diplomat, bureaucrat, journalist and spy passed through here sooner or later. She recognised three German judges, deep in conversation with the police chief; at another table the EULEX Chief of Staff laid bets on a Premier League football match with someone from the press office.

Jessop was sitting in a corner watching the football, a Peja beer and a pint of Guinness untouched in front of him. He waved when he saw her, as if their meeting was the most natural thing in the world, and pushed the beer towards her.

She remembered the entry in Michael's diary. *Jessop, 91*. 'Do you come here often?'

'When I'm in town.'

'You know, there's a rumour the CIA has bugs in the light fittings.'

He took the voice recorder out of his jacket pocket and looked at it mock-wistfully. 'I won't need this, then.'

Abby put her bag on the table and pulled it open. 'I'll save you some more trouble. Help yourself to whatever you want to steal.'

Jessop ignored it. 'You're supposed to be on sick leave. Why did you come back to Kosovo?'

'Trying to get away from people like you.'

'And how's that working out for you?' He stared

190

at her face. The wound from Dragovič's pistol cut a thin crimson ribbon down her chin; the bruising around it was in full flower.

Abby looked back defiantly and said nothing. Jessop took a long sip of his drink.

'We showed your necklace to some boffin at the British Museum. He authenticated it as genuine fourth-century Roman, the real McCoy.'

'Can I have it back, then?'

'It's in London. If you tell me the truth about how you came by it, maybe I'll ask them to FedEx it.'

She stared into his face, the hard lines and no-nonsense haircut. There wasn't much to trust there.

'I told you the truth in London. Michael gave it to me. He didn't say where he got it.'

'Did you know he was an obtainer of rare antiquities?'

But she wasn't interested in that line of conversation. 'My turn,' she countered. 'Why did you meet Michael here the week before he died?'

Jessop was too professional to look surprised. 'Did he mention it?'

'I found a note in his diary.'

He drank his Guinness and wiped foam off his upper lip. 'Nice to get a decent pint, in this part of the world.'

She didn't smile. 'Why did you meet him?'

'OK—since we seem to be getting on so well being honest with each other. I'm on the anti-trafficking taskforce. I met with Michael to discuss arms smuggling.'

'He was working with you?'

'He thought I was representing a

191

Russian businessman who wanted to import Ukrainian-made AK-47s to Italy.' He held her gaze, waiting for the penny to drop. 'He was going to help me.'

The bar erupted in cheers. Up on the TV screens the home team had grabbed an equaliser. Abby just stared at Jessop. She wished the noise could change what he'd said, sweep it back and drown it. She drank a deep gulp of beer, bitter liquid sour in her mouth. Nothing changed.

The game restarted, more urgent now.

'Do you have proof?' Abby asked. 'You were pretending, so you could trap him. Maybe he was, too.'

'We've got plenty of proof. We'd been tracking him for months.'

His face offered no hope. Abby pushed back her chair and ran to the bathroom. When she emerged five minutes later, eyes wet and skin red, Jessop was still there. He hadn't touched his drink while she was away.

'What do you want from me?' she whispered. 'Michael's dead. Who are you still chasing?'

'There's a man called Zoltán Dragović . . .'

'I've met him.'

Now it was Jessop's turn to look stunned. *A hit.* Abby took grim pleasure in it.

'He picked me up in Rome on Friday. Shouldn't you have been following me or something?'

'Jurisdictional issues,' Jessop muttered. 'Go on.'

'His men bundled me into a car and took me somewhere that looked like a museum. Like his villa in Montenegro. I thought he was going to kill me.' She touched her chin. 'He made do with this.'

'What did he want?'

192

'What does he have to do with Michael?'

Jessop sighed. 'Dragović is the biggest people-smuggler, gun-runner and drug-trafficker in the Balkans. Michael worked in Customs for the most porous country in the region. Do you need me to spell it out?'

She still couldn't believe it. She told herself she didn't believe it. But deep down, in the cold recesses of her soul, she knew it made sense. Michael's never-ending supply of easy money, the car and the holidays that were extravagant, even by Pristina expat standards. The villa. A memory flashed into her head, stripped of all the darkness and denial that had obscured it for so long.

'That night at the villa,' she said slowly. 'I woke up and went outside. Michael was by the pool with the man who killed him, but they weren't fighting. They were looking at something together. He only attacked Michael when he saw me.'

She remembered Jessop's original question. 'Dragović wanted to know why I survived.'

'They left you for dead. They were almost right.'

'No.' She pinched the skin of her forehead between finger and thumb, fighting back the headache pounding against it. 'Dragović said there was someone else there. The man he sent never came back, but there wasn't any body.' She looked up. 'Was there?'

'The police only found Michael's. I suppose the other chap could have been swept out to sea.'

'But then who killed him?' Abby looked down. She'd finished her drink and not even tasted it. 'What do you want from me?' she said again.

Jessop reached across the table and took her hands in his. She tried to pull away, but his grip was tight and he wouldn't let go.

'Look at me.' She twisted her head around like a miscreant child, refusing to meet his gaze. '*Look at me*. You think Michael's death was the end of something? Ever since that night, Dragović's been going crazy. Routine's out the window. Kidnapping you, taking you to meet him—that's not part of the plan. Some of his closest associates have never met him, so why you?'

Have you ever wondered why you're not dead?

'We're picking up chatter from Dragović's people—more than we've had in months. Whatever Michael was involved in was something huge, way beyond the low-grade smuggling stuff we had on him. And we don't have a fucking clue what it is.'

She stopped struggling and stared at him, looking for comfort in his grey eyes and finding none.

'I don't know either. I don't even know why I'm alive.'

'You've got something.'

She pointed to her bag. 'Everything I have in the world is right there.'

'Think back. Something Michael told you? Something he gave you?'

'I suppose he could have left something in my flat.'

'We went through it pretty thoroughly.' He saw her expression. 'Sorry. You weren't there to let us in.'

She pulled away from his grip, and this time he let her go. But a thought was forming in her head, a way out of the labyrinth that Jessop and Michael and Dragović had spun around her.

'Can you get me into Camp Bondsteel?'

XXII

Constantinople—April 337

Another sun is setting as the dust of another day begins to settle. The shopkeepers hang their shutters; the smiths and potters douse their fires for the night. Behind closed doors, pickpockets flex their fingers, murderers sharpen their knives, and jealous wives stir poison in their husbands' wine.

I wait on the hillside watching copper sunlight streak the sea below. I'm standing sentry duty, patrolling the frontier between day and night. I don't know who I'm looking for; I'm hoping I'll know him when I see him. I'm alone. Simeon wanted to come, but I sent him away. His story about the message left in the church hardly seems credible—but I'm curious to see where it leads.

The statue of Venus stands in a small square where five roads meet, on the southern slopes of the city overlooking the sea. Inevitably, prostitutes use it as a rendezvous, though there aren't so many about tonight. Perhaps my watching puts them off.

Like sentries the world over, my mind wanders and I remember . . .

*   *   *

. . . tumbling out of bed in the darkness, pulling on my coarse wool cloak and trying not to wake the others. The night was so cold that the waterskins have frozen solid and cracked open. It's the darkest day of the darkest month, in one of the darkest places on earth.

195

Constantine opens the door and we slip out. Across the parade ground, along behind the headquarters and past the stables. At this hour, the world exists as smells and sounds: woodsmoke from the ovens, sheep bleating in their pen as they wait for the butcher, the slurp of a horse munching hay from the byre. The main gate is locked, but there's a postern in the east tower and the sentry's asleep.

Beyond the walls, our boots crunch the frosty grass. We've crossed a frontier; we're beyond the edge of the world. We scramble over the earthen dyke, down into the valley and across the stream, up the facing hill. My head hurts with the cold but it's a good pain: clean and pure.

At the top of the hill stands a copse of three birch trees and a holly bush. There's light in the sky now, though no sun. Constantine halts, orients himself to the bluest part of the horizon, and waits. His misting breath makes a nimbus of the air around him.

'If the Tribune finds out we left camp without permission, we'll have night-time guard duty for a week,' I grumble (it must be early in our lives, this memory; I don't think we're more than sixteen). 'Or worse. What if the locals find us, two Roman soldiers on the wrong side of the wall?'

Constantine draws his sword and points it at the horizon, then swings it round behind us. 'Do you know what the difference is between here and there?'

'Better-looking women?' I guess.

He points back to the fort, dimly visible on the ridge behind us. 'That wall. Behind it, no one fears attack. In front, there's nothing worth defending.'

'Does that make you feel better about standing

here freezing to death and listening to the shadows?'

He's not paying me any attention. 'Do you know why?'

'Why what?'

'Why the empire means peace?'

'Because our armies beat the fight out of anyone who threatens us.'

'Conformity.' He's still looking at the fort behind us. 'There are fourteen thousand miles of frontier in our empire, and on every one of them there's a fort that looks like that, and the same men inside speaking the same language. Whether you're looking at the Danube, the Nile or the Tyne you taste the same food, hear the same songs, praise the same gods.'

I stamp my feet and wonder how I'll explain frostbite to the centurion. Constantine turns to me.

'Why do we pray to the gods?'

I rub my eyes; I'm too tired to be having this discussion now. The black sky above is softening to an imperial purple.

But Constantine's waiting for an answer. 'To avoid bad fortune?'

'Exactly.' It's what he wanted me to say. 'But perhaps we should expect more from our gods. They're gods, after all.'

'They're jealous, adulterous, murderous—parricidal, fratricidal, infanticidal—and have a strange taste for bestiality.'

'Old gods.' He dismisses them the same way we dismiss old men. 'You know there was a Greek philosopher, I've forgotten his name, who said the old gods were just stories—real men, whose legends got exaggerated over generations until we thought they must have been gods.'

I touch the iron amulet I wear around my neck, my lucky charm to ward off evil.

'For the last fifty years our rulers behaved like those old gods and almost lost the empire. We need to look beyond. A higher god.'

'Change begins at the top.'

'The old gods are lords of darkness. We ought to worship a god of light. A single god for a single world.' He plucks a berry from the holly tree and squeezes it between his fingers. It looks as though he's pricked himself. 'The light came into the world and the darkness could not comprehend it.'

'What's that?'

'Something I heard in the mess.' He sounds far away. 'Wherever you are in the empire, you look up and you see the sun and know that he's with you. Warming your back, ripening your crops, lighting your way. Even in the dead of winter, it returns. Unconquerable light.'

He turns to the east, arms outstretched. A dull glow glimmers on the horizon. But for the moment, the sun stays down, and the world's in darkness.

*   *   *

I wonder why I have this memory. Not because it mattered later. It doesn't say so in Alexander's *Chronicon*, but historians who are free to write after he's gone will record that Constantine's contribution to the defence of the empire was to weaken its borders. He pulled the field army back and concentrated it deep in the empire, leaving auxiliaries and local levies to patrol the frontiers. As the frontier populations mingle freely, half the people they were supposed to keep out were their own relations.

Like letting the hull of the boat rot, and hoping you've got enough buckets to bail you out, said a friend who worked in Levantine shipping.

But the memory persists. Constantine, waiting for the dawn with dewy eyes, determined to find something better over the horizon and convinced he'll get there.

*　　*　　*

I blink. Someone's coming up the street towards me, a stout old man with the hood of his cloak raised against the evening breeze. He sees me, pauses, pulls back the hood to reveal white hair tufted around a bald scalp. It's Aurelius Symmachus.

'What are you doing here?'

'Walking.' His eyes go over me. 'More than you're doing.'

'I'm waiting for someone.'

'And still waiting to find out who killed Bishop Alexander? The Augustus will be getting impatient.'

I'm only half listening to him, wondering why he's here. Is he the man I'm supposed to meet? He's certainly not acting as if he expected to run into me.

'Have you spoken with the Christians?' he demands.

'They suggested I speak to you. Your friend Porfyrius, in particular, had some very interesting stories about the persecutions.'

Symmachus rolls his eyes. 'There's nothing a Christian loves better than telling you about his

199

own past misdeeds. It lets him think he's improved himself.'

I don't disagree—but I'm surprised to hear him say it. 'I thought Porfyrius was your friend.'

'He was my guest. When you get to my age, you don't bother with the fictions of friendship.'

Again, I don't disagree.

'Do you know what I believe in?' Symmachus asks unprompted. 'Rome. Diocletian didn't persecute the Christians out of spite. He wanted to heal the empire—to end the divisions that had ruined so many emperors and let in the barbarians. He thought if he could unite Rome under a common faith, he'd save the empire. Constantine has the same agenda and a different god. That's all.'

Again, I remember that winter's morning with Constantine.

'Constantine believes in a unifying god,' I agree. 'But he doesn't try to compel piety with hot irons and the rack.'

'I suppose you think that makes him more devout.'

He swings his stick and hobbles away, surprisingly fast. Six paces on, he turns back.

'Think about Alexander,' he warns me. 'Whatever they say about love and peace, every religion needs its blood sacrifice.'

Ten paces more and he's vanished. In all the time we've been talking, I've been watching the statue behind him for anyone loitering there. Now I can hardly see it: night's falling fast.

But not so fast that I miss him. A tall, thin figure—not much more than a shadow among shadows—strides out of the gloom to the statue.

He pauses, bends as if to fix the strap of his sandal, then walks on.

A new shape's appeared in the darkness. I can see the squat outline of a box or a case sitting on the step next to the statue. I hurry down and pick it up.

It's a document case, a leather box with brass bindings. The cheeks bulge; when I lift it, I can feel the weight inside. My finger traces the Greek letters carved into the ivory handle.

ALEXANDROS.

The man who left the case has almost vanished between two tenements—but there's a cluster of lights at the end of the alley where votive lamps burn in front of a small shrine. For a moment, he's silhouetted against the dappled firelight like a monster emerging from its cave. Tall and spindly, long legs and a short tunic.

He turns left and disappears.

I hurry after him—as best I can, with old legs and the case weighing on my arm. Down to the shrine and left, up the hill. It should be dark, but it isn't: even at night, the city seems to glow with the brightness of its own existence. But if I can see him . . .

Struggling to keep up, my footsteps ring loud on the pavement. The man ahead looks back and sees me. For another few yards he tries to wish me away, or pretend he hasn't noticed. Then he checks again, sees the case in my hand and loses all doubt. He breaks into a run.

I can't go much faster, certainly not carrying the bag. Should I drop it? Even if I did, I probably couldn't catch him. He's almost at the top of the hill now, and once he crosses the main road he can disappear into the warren of streets in the old town and be lost for good.

A thin figure in a white tunic sprints past me. He looks familiar, though I can't see enough to be sure. The man ahead sees him and seems to panic. He hesitates, then ducks down a side street. It's no escape. By the time I get there, I can hear the thuds and grunts of a bare-knuckle fight in the darkness. The man's been caught and is wrestling his pursuer on the ground. He breaks free, springs up like a dog. A high wall confines the alley: he gets his arms over the top and kicks to get himself over. I try to grab his legs, but he lashes out and catches me in the face. He's over the wall and gone. My mouth's sour with blood and numb with pain, but nothing compared to the fury of letting him escape.

'Who is he?'

It's Simeon, picking himself up off the ground and rubbing his shoulder. I told him not to come, but it doesn't matter now. I need to get over the wall and I can't do it by myself. I make him crouch against the wall and cup his hands to lift me into the darkness. The bricks are cold and uneven; I half-expect I'll pull it down with my bare hands if my old arms don't give out first. I flap and flail like a fish to get myself up.

'Should I—?'

I've made it. I lie on top of the wall for a second, gasping the night air. 'Hand me the bag.' It's the one thing I've got; I'm not going to let it go.

Simeon passes it up to me.

'Now go and find the Watch.'

He nods and runs back down the alley. Clutching the bag, I drop down behind the wall. My knees jar, but nothing breaks.

I'm in a building site. One day it'll be a well-appointed villa for a court official; at the moment, it's a maze of low brick walls and shallow ditches barely visible in the darkness. I strain my eyes looking for the fugitive, but there's nothing.

As far as I can make out, the wall surrounds the entire site, but there must be a gate somewhere. I edge my way around the perimeter, scanning the darkness. The harder I look, the more my eyes adjust, the more complicated the picture becomes. In the dark, every plank or pillar or half-built wall takes on the shape of a man. But if I can get to the gate before he does, I might still catch him.

I follow the wall around a corner and on a little further. My hand trails along the brick, feels a gap, then rough wood, hinges and a hasp. The gate. I push against it, but it doesn't move. The builders probably locked it from the outside when they left.

He hasn't got out that way. He might have climbed back over the wall, but not without making a noise. That means he's still in there, trapped with me like a gladiator in the arena.

And I've still got Alexander's document case weighing me down. I move away from the gate and lay the case in a ditch behind a knee-high wall, scraping loose earth over it. Every sound plays on my imagination, distorted by fear, until I don't know what I'm hearing. Perhaps I was wrong—perhaps he's long gone, and come morning I'll still be squatting here in the mud, alone.

I can't bear the silence any longer.

'Are you there?'

No answer. The night swallows my words.

'Who are you?'

Nothing.

'Did you kill Alexander?'

I hear a clatter from my right, the noise of scattering pebbles. He must be moving again. I peer cautiously over the wall. The night breeze blows the sound to me; I think I glimpse movement.

On all fours, I crawl along behind the wall. The ground's pitted with loose stones, which dig into my palms and knees, but I can't see to avoid them. I come up against a pile of tiles and almost send them flying.

I'm nearly there. I can see the silhouette of his head just above the low parapet, swaying slightly as he glances this way and that. He doesn't know where I am.

I leap up—and stop, defeated. It's not a man; it's a bucket hanging from a rope on a tall scaffold. When the wind blows, the bucket moves; if it goes too far, the gravel inside it rattles. That's what I heard.

And he knew it. He's had me all along. Before I can move, he's there behind me. He grabs an arm and pins it behind my back; he reaches past my face and grabs the rope dangling from the scaffold, twisting it around my neck. He's going to throttle me. I struggle, but he's stronger than me. The bucket bounces against my chest, the gravel shaking like a death rattle.

And suddenly there are shouts and light. Flames light up the broken ground. Simeon's brought the Watch. Firm hands pull my antagonist off me. The rope unwinds; I collapse, gasping. By the time I've stood up, they've kicked my assailant pretty well into submission.

I walk over and stare down. Hobnailed boots pin him to the ground. He's a gaunt man with close-cropped grey hair and blood trickling out of his nose. Even now, there's a proud, superior sneer he can't shake off his face.

'Why did you leave the document case at the statue?'

'My master ordered me to.'

'Who's your master?'

He sniffs and wipes his arm across his face, smearing blood along it. Dark eyes look up at me, resist me.

The Watch sergeant puts his boot on the man's hand and slowly presses down. Something snaps; the man screams. Not an insensible, animal scream, but a name.

'Aurelius Symmachus!'

XXIII

Kosovo—Present Day

'Not long before he died, Michael turned up a seventeen-hundred-year-old Roman body. I don't know how or where. An American soldier called Sanchez helped bring it in.'

In the passenger seat, Jessop looked thoughtful. It was his car, but after three near-accidents in Monday morning traffic before they were out of Pristina, Abby had insisted on driving.

'Dragović, as you may have spotted, has the Roman bug,' Jessop said. 'He's a nut on the subject. You know he enjoys the nickname "The Emperor"? Zoltán means "emperor" in Hungarian, apparently. Dragović carries on like he's Caesar reincarnated. If Michael had connections with him—which he did—

and he found something left over from the Roman empire, Dragović would be the obvious person to call.'

If Michael had connections with him. If the man you loved was corrupt and in the pocket of the Balkans' most wanted man . . . The idea was toxic, too terrible to really understand. She had to keep it well away from her, locked in a glass box and handled with utmost care lest it shatter and poison her.

'I've been to two of Dragović's houses.' That, too, was a horrible fact. 'Dragović owns more Roman art than the British Museum. What could Michael have found that he'd want so badly?'

'According to our man, the necklace you found probably dates from the reign of Constantine the Great, around 300 AD. Heard of him?'

'Mmmm.'

He doesn't know about the Trier manuscript, she thought. She still had Gruber's transcription with her, folded in her jeans pocket, but she hadn't mentioned it. After what Jessop had done with the necklace, she wasn't going to tell him about the manuscript unless she had to.

'As you say, Dragović doesn't exactly need any more art. Or money.' Jessop stared out the window at the scrapyards and builders' yards that had sprung up along the road. 'But whatever Michael found must have been pretty special to get him so fired up.'

Abby turned on the wipers as rain began to spatter the windscreen. 'Maybe Specialist Sanchez knows what it is.'

* * *

206

The rain was falling hard and unforgiving by the time they pulled into the car park at Camp Bondsteel. They ran up the path between the blast walls and the wire. White tank traps serrated the road like teeth. By the time they reached the guard station, they were both soaked.

The guards had changed since the day before: there was no one to recognise Abby, and no fuss when Jessop presented his credentials. A captain in a high-collared jacket met them and ushered them into a green Toyota Landcruiser.

'You're here to meet with Specialist Sanchez?'

'He's not expecting us,' said Jessop.

'He's down in South Town. I'll drive you over.'

Abby got in the back and stared out the window as they drove along wide, rammed-earth roads. Everywhere she looked, the landscape's rolling hills had been forced into rigid grids: lines of cars, lines of huts, and straight roads connecting them.

Yet for all its size, there was something desolate about the base. They drove for several minutes, past long rows of brown huts, and barely saw a soul. There were no tanks or Humvees: most of the vehicles they saw were civilian Landcruisers like their own. On one stretch, a row of huge tents provided helicopter hangers, strangely impermanent in this re-engineered landscape.

'Is it true you've got a Burger King here?' Jessop asked the captain.

'And a Taco Bell. I've been here eleven months and never eaten in either of them.' He laughed. 'Just like being back home.'

'Where's home?'

'North Dakota.'

If he resented being shipped halfway round the world to police age-old feuds, in a country that was probably the size of the average farm back in his home state, he didn't show it. Abby thought of Rome, and wondered if this was how the last days of the empire had been. A few men far from home, shrinking into a fortress built for greater times. Or perhaps frontiers had always been like this: lonely, removed places where barbarians lurked and the rain fell.

The captain parked the Landcruiser at the side of the road and led them on to a veranda along the front of the densely packed SEA huts. They came to a door, knocked and entered.

Specialist Anthony Sanchez was sitting on a wooden bunk, playing an Xbox on a forty-inch TV screen perched on a steel chair. He was tall and broad-shouldered, dressed in a khaki T-shirt that left plenty of room for his gym-worked biceps. He looked around as the door opened. On screen, a racing car careered off the road and exploded in a fireball.

'I guess you're why they told me not to go out today.' The brim of his patrol cap sat low on his face, covering his eyes. His voice was husky, his features surprisingly delicate for the strong body.

'I'll wait in the car,' the captain said.

Sanchez punched the power on the television. Without its light, the room was so dim they could barely see him. He reached across to the facing bunk and swept a pizza box off it. 'Sorry we don't have crumpets or tea or none of that.'

Jessop sat. 'Tell me about Michael Lascaris.'

The patrol cap turned from Abby to Jessop, then down to the floor. 'What do you want to know?'

'You brought a body in to the Forensics department together,' Abby said. 'It's your signature on the docket.'

The cap didn't move. Rain drummed on the roof of the hut. A long, slow sibilant escaped from Sanchez's lips: maybe a drawn-out expletive, or just the air deflating from him.

'I haven't seen Mr Lascaris in a while.'

'He's dead,' Jessop told him.

'I don't really follow the news.' Sanchez fiddled with the game controller in his hand, thumbing the joystick in aimless circles.

'Tell me how you met Michael,' Abby said.

'In a bar.'

'That sounds right.'

'He came to find me here on base. He was a civilian, but I guess he knew his way around. Bought me some beers, it was all cool. Then he said he read a report I put in from one of the LMT missions.'

'LMT?' Jessop queried.

'Liaison and Monitoring Team. My unit. We go out in teams of three in an SUV and talk to the locals, feed it up the chain of command. Bridge-building, right?'

'What was your report about?'

'Up north, round about Nothing Hill. We were in this *mahallah*—'

'A what?'

'A *mahallah*. You know, like a village? Anyways, we were talking to some guys up there, and some farmer rides up on his Kosovo Harley.' He saw they didn't understand. 'You've seen them, right? They take a garden rotovator, put on some wheels instead of the blades, then bolt a handcart on the

209

back of it to make like a pick-up. We call them Kosovo Harleys.'

'I know what you mean,' said Abby. Jessop looked mystified.

'This guy says he thinks his neighbour's got a weapons stash on his land. He's an upstanding citizen and he wants us to know. Truth to tell, he probably wants the field for himself. So what, right? We go and look where he says, and sure enough there's a hole and a cave with a couple of rusted AKs and some sidearms. It's a big deal, but it's not *that* big a deal. Where it gets crazy is when we shine our flashlights around. This place—it isn't just a cave. It's like a tomb or something, old paintings on the walls and a big-ass stone coffin.'

The rain beat harder than ever. All Abby could see of Sanchez was his silhouette against the barred window.

'And that was where you found the body?'

'Not then. We had a mission. We took the guns and called the cops to arrest the landowner. The CO put a guard on the door. Then we came home. It's not really our sector—we're Battle-Group East, and that was way north. We were just up there generating some goodwill.'

Goodwill to whom? Abby wondered.

'I wrote it down in a report, and a week later Mr Lascaris showed up in the bar asking if he could see this place. I told him sure, but it ain't going to be on the clock. I only go where they tell me. And two days later, the staff sergeant calls me in and says I'm assigned to escort a civilian on a fact-finding mission. He was kind of pissed about it because it screwed up his schedule, but Michael was one of those guys, he made things happen.'

210

You can say that again.

'We went north towards Mitrovica, back to the cave. Like I said, Battle-Group North had put a guard on it, Norwegian dude, but Michael had some fancy paperwork and it was no problem. We went in there with some pry-bars and hammers. Michael points to the coffin and says, "Let's get that thing opened up."'

The rain had eased. The only sound in the room was the drip of water from the eaves outside.

'Now I did two tours in Iraq before I came here, and I saw some shit. But this was freaky. It was dark as hell in there, and I'm thinking about King Tut's curse and all that History Channel bullshit. And that lid was *heavy*. Almost bust my fingers lifting it—specially when I saw what was inside.'

'A skeleton,' said Abby. She remembered the empty sockets, the waxy bones against the steel table.

Sanchez's head flicked up at her. 'Guess you seen it, too. We wrapped that thing in a tarp and carried it out, right past the guard. Michael wanted to take the coffin lid, too, but there was no way we were carrying that thing. He took some pictures of the paintings on the walls, and the vase—'

'The what?'

'The vase.' He pronounced it the American way, to rhyme with 'haze'. 'Like a clay bottle, about the size of a forty-ounce of malt liquor. It was inside the coffin with the dead guy, all sealed up with wax or something.'

'Did Michael open it?'

'Not that I saw. We got out of there pretty fast. The Norwegian was on his radio and Michael started to get antsy. We drove off with the dead guy

211

in the trunk. Like *Goodfellas.*'

Sanchez took off his cap and twisted it between his fingers. For the first time, Abby could see his eyes, twin points of light in the darkness.

'That's how it was. I just did what he told me. I didn't think nothing would come of it.'

I feel your pain, Abby thought. *I'm in the same boat.*

'Did Michael give any sense of why he was interested?' Jessop asked.

'He talked all the time, but he didn't say much, if you know what I mean. I asked him what it was all about. He told me it was just routine procedure.'

'You didn't believe that.'

'No, but what the hell? It's not against the Geneva Convention to take a body to a morgue, especially with it being dead a few hundred years. Like I said, I just do what they tell me. Some dead Roman guy's not my problem.'

Abby looked up sharply. 'How did you know it was Roman? Did Michael say that?'

'Maybe, I guess. I don't recall. But I'm Catholic, I've been in plenty of churches. I knew the writing was Latin.'

'What writing?'

'The writing on the coffin.'

XXIV

Constantinople—April 337
Somewhere in this palace a man's being tortured. It shouldn't be happening. The law says you can't torture someone, even a slave, except in cases of

treason. Of course the law's flexible: treason's a subjective crime. You can redefine it, if you have the power, but it still takes time. Somebody had to find a lawyer in the middle of the night, draft an exemption, get the correct secretaries in the chancery to fix the correct seals—all before they can turn the first screw.

Somebody's taking this seriously.

I ought to be there making notes. Instead, I've gathered up all the lamps I can find and shut myself in a storeroom with Alexander's document case. I don't understand what's happened this evening, but I've seen rotten justice often enough to know the smell. I've also got a shrewd idea that a lot of the questions in the dungeon are going to be about the papers in my hand. Soon, someone's going to remember that I brought the case to the palace.

And it's slow work. The papers are pages of all different sizes, written in different inks and hands; mostly in Greek, though a few in Latin. I concentrate on those, though it's hard to read when you don't know what you're looking for. Some are letters or memoranda from the imperial archives; others seem to be excerpts from books. I can't find a theme.

One:

To the Emperor Constantine Augustus, from the Caesar Crispus. A heavy storm delayed our preparations and destroyed three ships, but the fleet is now ready and will sail tomorrow.

Another, a poem:

To reach the living, navigate the dead.

A third:

XII / II I'm writing with deepest condolence for the death of your grandson.

I sneeze, and curse as papers fly off my makeshift table. The room's full of dust. A dozen carved stone panels, each the weight of a horse, lean against the walls, waiting to be mounted in one of Constantine's new monuments. Marble soldiers frozen in battle knock against my legs.

I pick up another fragment. The lamps gutter and flicker; my eyes are tired, unused to so much reading. My own name leaps out of the page at me.

Granted by order of the Augustus to Gaius Valerius Maximus: put all the resources of the imperial post at his disposal and give him whatever he requests to speed his journey to Pula.

There's a date, but I don't need to check it. The world's gone dim; I think one of the lamps must have blown out. I put down the paper and lean my weight on the marble plaque.

What was Alexander doing with this?

The door flies open. The rush of air blows up the papers; one lands next to a lamp and catches fire. I flap at it, but my movements are numb and clumsy. Simeon runs in from the door, throws it on the floor and stamps it out before the whole pile goes up.

'They want to see you.'

He gathers the papers and folds them into the bag. When we met, I could have charged him with murder. Now, all I can do is follow him. Two guards from the *Schola* are in the corridor to escort us: along dark and empty halls, where painted figures

214

make shadows against the gold; past tree-filled courtyards where slaves are sweeping up the blossom that's fallen that day; back to the audience hall where four days ago Constantine ordered me to find Alexander's killer.

This time there's a proper audience. Eusebius, immaculate even at this late hour in a heavily embroidered robe. Flavius Ursus in full, burnished uniform. Ablabius, the Praetorian Prefect, and the two consuls Felicianus and Titianus. And Constantine himself on an ivory throne, dressed in so many jewels and gold you can barely glimpse the man underneath. Strands of sea pearls hang from his crown, running over his cheeks like tears.

Yet for all the raw power in the room, there's something furtive about this gathering. The great chandelier hanging over the throne makes a bright circle underneath, but the light doesn't stretch far. Beyond it, the empty hall is a dark and vast rebuke.

'Gaius Valerius Maximus.' For once, Eusebius greets me without a sneer. 'You've done excellent work. The Augustus was right to put his faith in you.'

Before I can react to this unwanted compliment, the door opens again. Four guards march Symmachus in. Since I saw him a few hours ago he's put on his toga trimmed with purple. He's dressed in a hurry: one end of the toga's come untucked and is threatening to unravel completely. His hair is a mess, like a mangy dog in the last stages of a disease.

Eusebius steps forward as prosecutor.

'Aurelius Symmachus is accused of the murder of the most holy and godly Bishop Alexander of Cyrene.'

215

No one's told Symmachus anything, though he must have suspected. He clings to his stick like a drowning man in a storm.

'You were in the library that day.'

Symmachus nods.

'You knew Alexander was there.'

He looks as if he might deny it, then thinks better of it. He doesn't want to make it easy for Eusebius.

'This evening you went for a walk near the statue of Venus. Gaius Valerius saw you there.'

No one asks me to confirm it, but Symmachus has something to say.

'I walk there every evening. Anyone who knows me would have known to find me there.'

Simeon's still holding the document case. Eusebius takes it from him and holds it up. Something changes on Symmachus's face, though I can't tell if he recognises it. Perhaps I'm being too generous. I want to believe his innocence.

'Have you seen this before?'

Symmachus tugs on his toga, which is in danger of slipping off his bony shoulder. 'No.'

'It belonged to Bishop Alexander. This evening, after you had met Valerius, your slave tried to dispose of it and was caught in the act.'

'He's lying.'

'He's testified under torture that you ordered him to do it.'

'Perhaps you shouldn't have tortured him.'

It's a rare flash of anger, but it does him no good.

'You were less scrupulous when you had Christians in your power.' Spit flecks from Eusebius's mouth. His face is alight with revenge. 'You were a notorious persecutor and hater of Christians, though when the Augustus Constantine

216

destroyed the arch-persecutors Galerius and Licinius he showed you every forgiveness. But when you saw Alexander of Cyrene in the library that day, the violence in your nature took over. You beat the life out of him, using a bust of your false ideologue Hierocles as the weapon.'

Symmachus hears out the charge in silence. No theatrical denials, no falling to his knees and clutching the Emperor's feet. He hasn't come to a secret court in the dead of night expecting to prove his innocence. When Eusebius has finished, he simply shakes his head and says a firm, 'No.'

'Perhaps it was simply because he was a Christian. Perhaps you never forgave the fact that he defied you in your own dungeon, that he defeated you. You hated him for it.'

'I respected his courage. It was the men who broke that I despised. Men like . . .' He pauses, searching for the name. 'Asterius.'

'*Enough!*' Even Eusebius seems surprised by the force of his reaction. Perhaps he's thinking of his friend's mutilated arms, the life sentence he received for betraying his faith. He draws a deep breath and turns to Constantine.

'Lord, there were no other witnesses to Alexander's tragic death. The only man who saw it was the killer.' An arm shoots out towards Symmachus. 'That man. And having killed him in the most barbaric way conceivable, he stole his papers. Who knows why? Perhaps he thought he could use Alexander's knowledge against the Church. But as the Augustus's net closed around him, as the diligent Gaius Valerius tracked down the murderer, he panicked. He worried that the bag would be found. So he ordered his slave to get rid

217

of it.'

'All lies.'

My head's spinning as I listen to my own story being rewritten in front of me. I look at Constantine. His face is as blank as glass, but he catches my glance and turns ever so fractionally to meet it.

Do you want a culprit? Or do you want me to find out who actually did it?

I don't believe any of it. If Symmachus wanted to get rid of the document case why not just throw it in the harbour or burn it? Why send a slave to hand it over exactly where he'd be taking his evening stroll? Someone is setting Symmachus up to take the blame. The only real question is who?

Constantine's still watching me. So is Symmachus. Is this my chance to save an innocent man? I've spent the last five days investigating this murder, but now that it's come to this sudden trial I can't think of anything to say. I don't have any lines in this play they're acting out. I'm a prop, a blunt instrument to be wielded by others. In that respect, I'm not much different to Symmachus.

The imperial gaze moves on. Symmachus looks away, his last hope gone. The disgust on his face condemns me.

Constantine stares down and says a single word.

'*Deportatio.*'

Exile. Symmachus will be stripped of his property, his citizenship, his family and his rights. Legally, he'll cease to exist.

Symmachus closes his eyes. His whole body is trembling; the only thing keeping him upright must be pride. I remember what Porfyrius said about him. *He's a Stoic. Outward things cannot touch his soul.* I don't think his philosophy is much help now.

'What about the bag, Augustus?' Eusebius asks.

'Burn it.'

The guards lead Symmachus away. Constantine steps down off his throne and disappears through a door. The play's over; they've no more use for me. No one tries to stop me going. As soon as I'm out of the room, I run down the palace corridors, following the tramp of the guards' boots. I catch up with them in an anteroom near the north gate.

'Have you come to celebrate your success?' Symmachus's voice is dead.

'I had nothing to do with it.'

'*I had nothing to do with it,*' he parrots back, falsetto. '*I* had nothing to do with Alexander's murder, and yet here I am.'

'I'm sorry.'

A grimace. He's got so little left, even my sympathy counts for something.

'Constantinc's a reasonable man,' I persist. 'In a few months, he'll recall you.'

'In a few months we'll all be dead. Tell yourself anything else, it's a lie. First they get rid of you; then they send the assassins.'

He wipes his forehead and gives me a look filled with hate.

'You know how it goes.'

XXV

Kosovo—Present Day

They left Camp Bondsteel and drove north, back up the highway towards Pristina. Abby was getting sick of the sight of it. Jessop had wanted Sanchez to come with them, but his commanding officer flat out refused. The best Jessop got out of him was a KFOR map, which Sanchez marked where he thought the tomb had been.

Rain sluiced over the windscreen; tarpaulined lorries veered and swayed uneasily in front of them. Abby fished a cigarette out of her pocket and fumbled under the dashboard for the cigarette lighter. All she found was an empty socket.

'They call it a power socket these days,' said Jessop, laughing at her. He took a plastic lighter out of his pocket and reached across to light the cigarette.

'Thanks.' Abby tapped the bulge in her pocket. 'Want one?'

'I quit.'

She glanced across and saw he was smiling. 'So how come you still carry the lighter?'

'In case of emergencies.'

*   *   *

Mitrovica was a shabby, low-rise town squeezed between two rivers. During the war it had seen some of the worst atrocities; even now it was a divided city. French soldiers guarded the bridges; minarets and bell towers contested the skyline. Abby had hoped to avoid it, but the main road was closed for repairs. They drove in across a causeway on a floodplain. Rusted cars littered the shoreline. Across the river a crumbling factory pumped out smoke and pollution.

While Abby drove, Jessop tapped away at his phone.

'What sort of a spy are you?' she mocked him. 'Shouldn't you at least look where we're going?'

'I'm reading about it. Apparently, the Romans were up here in a big way. Lead and silver mining. We're only about eighty miles from Niš.'

'Is that a good thing?'

'It's where the Emperor Constantine was born. Remember, I said the symbol on your necklace was his monogram?'

Abby slouched lower in her seat. She still hadn't told Jessop about the scroll in Trier. She had Gruber's translation in her pocket, a hard wad, but somehow, the moment had passed.

'So—what? Do you think this was Constantine's tomb?'

More taps on the phone. 'It says here Constantine was buried in Istanbul. The Church of the Holy Apostles, if you're interested.' He put the phone down in defeat. 'I don't know.'

Abby switched on the radio and kept her eyes on the road. She thought Jessop was watching her, and felt herself recoil. *However nice he's being, he's still a spy*, she reminded herself.

* * *

North of Mitrovica the road got quieter. Jessop put his phone away and stared out of the window. They were in a river valley, green fields on the valley floor giving way to thickly wooded hillsides and mountains beyond. Tall haystacks like beehives lined the fields at the sides of the road.

Something was puzzling Jessop. 'The signs are different,' he said. 'Serbian?'

'Up here, they almost run a parallel state. A lot

221

of them only take Serbian money, too.'

Jessop shook his head in disbelief. 'This whole so-called country's barely the size of Somerset. You'd think that would be small enough for them, without trying to subdivide it again.'

'They still think they're part of Serbia. If NATO hadn't conquered it, they would be.'

'Maybe they should have thought of that before they started massacring Albanians.'

'Maybe.'

Jessop gave her a sideways look. 'It says in your file you're supposed to be an idealist.'

From the corner of her eye, she saw a steel cross standing proud on a ridge overlooking the road. 'That was a long time ago.'

They lapsed into silence. A military lorry with a German flag on the back drove past in the opposite direction. In the rear-view mirror Abby saw bored soldiers sitting with their rifles.

'Do you think you should have brought back-up?' she asked.

'London's assessment is that the countryside up here is fairly peaceful.'

'It isn't London who'll be getting shot at if things go wrong.'

'I'm aware of that.' Jessop squinted at the map. 'I think our turn should be just around the next corner.'

They slowed to a crawl. Abby checked her mirror. There'd been a little red Opel behind them for a while, but she hadn't seen it for the last few miles. 'Is that it?'

It was a dirt track with a strip of weeds down the middle. It blended with the surrounding fields so well they might not have noticed it, if there hadn't been a white shrine standing on the corner. A bedraggled bouquet wilted at its base, testament to some too-familiar road tragedy.

Jessop stared at the map. 'Let's try it.'

The track was heavily rutted. Abby engaged the Landcruiser's four-wheel drive, wrestling to keep it moving through the mud. Jessop leaned forward and peered through the rain-spattered windscreen.

'Do those tyre-marks look fresh to you?'

Abby didn't have time to look. The track had crossed the valley and begun to climb through the trees, where the slope and protruding rocks added new complications. Rivulets streamed down the track, gouging away the soft earth. Under the tree canopy, the day was almost black.

She crested the hill, spun the car around a sharp bend—and stopped so fast she almost stalled the car. A black pick-up truck stood parked across the road, blocking it completely. Two men in dark blue camouflage fatigues and balaclavas were standing beside it, AK-47s cradled in their arms.

'KFOR are supposed to make sure this doesn't happen,' Jessop said. He had his phone out and was frantically tapping the screen. 'They're supposed to keep the roads open.'

'Looks like someone didn't get the memo.' She was surprised how steady she felt. Crazy though it was, she knew what to do in these sorts of situation—had faced them dozens of times before. The scenery changed, but the actors never did: pick-up trucks and men with guns.

She reached in her pocket for the cigarette pack, then raised her hands so that the gunmen could see. One man walked forward; the other stayed by the truck, weapon pointed at the Toyota's radiator.

223

The man drew level and gestured her to wind down the window. Dark eyes surveyed her from the balaclava's moonholes. He looked surprised to see the woman driving.

'Papers, please?' he grunted in English.

Abby fished out a cigarette with her teeth, then offered him the pack. He took it without thanks.

'Is it OK to reach in my bag?' She'd spoken in Serbian. The eyes squinted; the head nodded.

'What are you doing here?'

Abby jerked her head at the side of the Landcruiser and thanked God for the stickers on the side. 'EULEX. We're supporting the environment ministry.'

She fumbled in her bag and handed the passport to the guard. He opened to the page with the twenty-euro note slipped inside.

'And your friend?'

'Some expert from London. He wants to see the trees.'

The twenty euros disappeared into a pocket. 'Wait here.'

He walked back to the pick-up and conferred with his companion. He took out a silver mobile phone and started talking vigorously. The gun pointed at the car didn't move.

'What did you tell them?' Jessop asked.

Abby stared ahead and tried to control her breathing. 'He thinks we're looking for illegal wood.'

'Illegal wood?'

'Seventy per cent of Kosovars use log fires for heating their homes. Outside the cities life can be pretty primitive. Even in the towns, the electricity supply's mediocre at best. Illegal logging's a big

224

problem.'

'And he thinks we're hot on the trail?'

By the pick-up truck, the guard was still talking earnestly into his phone. 'Who knows what he thinks? Or who he's telling. Those uniforms are Serbian police.'

'Are they allowed—?'

'Have you still got that lighter?'

Jessop held it out, but his hands were trembling so badly he couldn't spark the flint. Abby took it from him and lit her last cigarette.

'This is the Balkans,' she said through a mouthful of smoke. 'Uniforms mean nothing. In Bosnia in the nineties, Milošević sent the Serbian army over the border, gave them new badges, and suddenly they were the Bosnian army.' She drummed her fingers on the steering wheel. 'Aren't you supposed to be some sort of expert?'

'I'm a generalist.'

In front of them, the guard finished his call and put the phone away. It flashed like a knife where the headlights caught it. He slung his gun on his shoulder, then walked slowly back to their car.

'Is everything OK?' Abby asked, reaching to take the passport back.

After that, she barely knew what happened. He dropped the passport, grabbed her wrist and pulled her forward. His other hand yanked open the door. She tumbled out of the car and landed at his feet in the mud.

A rough hand grabbed her collar and hauled her to her feet, pushing her against the side of the car. On the passenger side, Jessop was being ushered out of the car at gunpoint by the other policeman. Abby felt her hands being forced behind her back

225

and zipped together with cable ties. She didn't resist.

They dragged her to the pick-up truck and lifted her between them into the back. Jessop followed. One of the guards climbed in with them, the other got in the cab. The pick-up lurched forward: Abby slid back on the wet floor and slammed into the tailgate. The guard, hanging on to a cargo strap, followed her all the way with his AK-47. The truck bounced on the rutted track, flinging Abby and Jessop about like a pair of corpses. With her hands tied behind her, she couldn't even break the impact. The wound in her shoulder screamed in agony. She lay face down, tasting blood and rain and steel on her tongue, and waited for it to end.

The rain on her back got heavier; the air grew lighter. She twisted around and looked up. Thick forests climbed on to high mountain slopes, but the sky above was open. They must have come out into a valley.

She rolled around to face Jessop. 'Where are they taking us?'

'Serbia. It can't be more than a few miles. Once we're across the border, they—*fuck!*'

The truck stopped with a bang, so abrupt that Abby and Jessop were thrown into the air and fell hard. Even the guard banged his head. He slid open the window that connected with the cab and shouted in to the driver. Any answer was drowned by the complaint of the engine, revving and groaning, but not moving.

And suddenly it cut out. All Abby could hear now was the rain drumming on the bed of the truck, and the sweep of the wind through the trees. The guard opened the tailgate, jumped down and went forward to the cab. She heard him arguing with the driver, swearing about something broken, though she didn't know the words.

She curled in a ball, huddling against Jessop for warmth. Her sodden clothes encased her like ice; the heat had left her.

'It's OK,' Jessop whispered in her ear. 'I called it in. The cavalry are coming.'

But that required hope, and she had none. She lay there and waited for the rain to dissolve her to nothing.

*   *   *

She must have closed her eyes, because when she opened them the guard was crouched over her, shaking her awake. Her head pounded; her body shivered so hard she thought it would break apart.

Through the pain and the noise in her skull, she realised he was speaking Serbian.

'Get up. He's almost here.'

He pulled her upright and lifted her down to the ground. Jessop was already there. They'd come into a wild open meadow cupped between the mountains and the forest, a forlorn and lonely place. One track led down from the forest to the east; a second came down the valley from the north and met it at a crossroads where the pick-up had broken down. Two black Range Rovers were driving towards them, spraying mud behind the tyres. In the distance, Abby heard a roar like a waterfall.

The guard glanced nervously at the sky. He herded Abby and Jessop against the side of the truck and stood back, sweeping his gun from one to the other. The Range Rovers pulled off the track on to the grass, forming a rough triangle with the pick-up. Men in jeans and black parkas jumped out; one opened the rear door of the front car.

A slim figure in a long wool coat stepped out, daintily avoiding the mud, and walked towards them. He looked smaller in that vast landscape than he had in his office in Rome, but the aura of power that surrounded him was undiminished. Even the bodyguards seemed to keep a wary distance.

'Dragović,' Jessop mumbled beside her.

Dragović stopped a few paces in front of them. He ignored Abby, but gave Jessop a long, piercing look. He shook his head.

'It's not Lascaris.'

He pulled a pistol from under his parka and aimed it at Jessop's head. The distant noise grew louder. Abby heard Jessop shouting desperate pleas, twisting like a dog on a leash. The whole earth seemed to be trembling underneath her. The wind rose, blowing rain against her face. Dragović stepped back.

The flash from the muzzle split the world in two. The pick-up shuddered as the bullets slammed Jessop's body against it. Blood spattered her face, warmer than the rain. Dragović's gun swung towards her. He was shouting something, but through the ringing in her ears and the roar behind she couldn't understand.

This is the way it ends.

And suddenly the gun was gone. Dragović had turned, was running back to the Range Rover. Before she could wonder, a hand grabbed her throat. One of the guards had his face almost touching hers, screaming words she could barely

228

make out. 'Did you call the fucking cops? Did your friend?'

A dying memory flickered in her mind, Jessop fiddling with his phone just before they were captured. *The cavalry are coming.* She hadn't believed him.

'I don't know.'

He pulled her away from the truck, spun her around and yanked her hair so that her face pointed at the sky.

'What the fuck is that?'

A black helicopter came over the hilltop and raced up the valley towards them. It had a snub nose and a squat body; wheels poked from the undercarriage like talons. It yawed in the wind, and as it banked around Abby saw KFOR stencilled in white on the fuselage.

The men around her scattered. She saw Dragović diving into the back of his Range Rover, mud spatters up the back of his expensive trousers. Even before the door shut, the car started to move back up the valley. The second Range Rover followed.

The helicopter came right overhead. Abby felt the beat of its rotors like body blows, the draught sucking her off the ground and whipping the rain hard against her. She waited for it to pan out like the movies: for the ziplines to snake down and a platoon of hard-as-nails soldiers to land and take out the bad guys.

The helicopter flew by, following the Range Rovers. One of her captors appeared from around the pick-up and grabbed her arm, manacled behind her back. He was still wearing the blue police uniform he'd had on for the roadblock.

They saw the uniforms from the helicopter, Abby

229

realised. *They think the guards are Kosovo Police.*

The guard jammed the gun in her ribs and started screaming about killing her there if she didn't come. Leaving Jessop's corpse slumped by the truck, he dragged her across the meadow and towards the trees on the far side of the valley. The other policeman followed. The ground had looked flat from the car, but underfoot she found it much more uneven, studded with sudden hummocks and low embankments that bulged under the earth, like toys left under a carpet. With her hands tied behind her back, her wet clothes straitjacketing her and the guard hauling her on faster than she could run, she jerked and flailed like a fish on a line.

The roar, quieter now, changed to a high-pitched whine. She craned her neck around. A few hundred yards up the valley, the helicopter had overtaken Dragović's Range Rover and was coming in to land in the middle of the track. The doors slid open as it touched down with a spray of dirt. A dozen soldiers scrambled out, fanning into a rough roadblock. The two Range Rovers swerved off the track and tore across open ground to get to the forest.

She'd slowed down. The guard jerked her forward again, cracking her shin on a half-buried rock. She stumbled forward, kicked through the long wet grass and staggered into the forest. From the safety of the trees, Abby's captors turned and looked back.

The helicopter was airborne again, following the Range Rovers towards the tree line. *Why don't they shoot?* A few rounds would have stopped Dragović dead—she could see the silhouette of the heavy machine gun sticking out from the Blackhawk's side. The helicopter hovered overhead, a cat toying with a mouse, but didn't pounce.

They're not allowed to, she thought dully. She'd read the mandate; she knew the rules of engagement. Dragović in their sights, and they couldn't pull the trigger. All the troops on the ground could do was follow. Some were running after the Range Rovers; the rest were advancing down the valley towards the wrecked pick-up. Had they seen her? Would they catch her in time?

Abby felt cold steel against her wrists. The guard had pulled out his knife. Before she could feel afraid, there was a sudden jerk, and then her hands were free.

'Now you run faster,' the guard said. He jabbed his gun into the small of her back and she obeyed. She staggered through the trees, fighting the slope, the wet clothes, the mud and slick leaves—all trying to push her back into the gun.

A shot rang through the forest behind her. Instinct threw her to the ground, but she hadn't been hit. When she looked back, she saw the Serb crouched on all fours, clutching his leg where blood spilled from it. The other guard ran to his side, loosing an undirected burst of bullets into the trees.

His back was turned. Abby saw her chance and ran.

Time stopped. She was in a world of leaves and mud and lead, of shots and shouts and no horizon beyond the next tree. She ran, weaving wildly. Her legs ached from pushing against the soaked jeans, her lungs were bursting, her shoulder hurt so much she wondered if she'd even feel the bullet if it came.

The trees thinned as she came out in a small clearing where a rock face reared out of the forest floor. A low fissure opened into it, with black mounds of freshly dug earth around it and a strip of tape tied across it. Next to the entrance, a bleached ram's skull grinned at her from the stick it had been planted on. Somewhere, not far away, she heard running footsteps.

Even in her panic she felt the darkness of the place, the pull of a malevolent gravity willing her into the cave. A breeze stirred the hairs on the back of her neck; the wild part of her mind told her it was Michael's ghost trying to tell her something. A warning? A blessing? She took in the tape on the door, the cigarette butts trampled into the ground and the foil ration packs scattered among the bushes. This must be the place she'd come for. It had seemed so important. Now she hardly cared.

But the footsteps were getting closer, and she'd run out of options. She ducked into the cave.

The light from outside didn't reach far. Panicked by the darkness, she patted her pocket and felt Jessop's lighter. She flicked it on. The flame gleamed off smooth-cut walls, too straight for a cave. A passage, leading into the rock.

A few yards in, it opened into a low, rectangular chamber with a curved roof. A stone trough ran across one end, with a niche in the wall above it where a statue might once have stood. Faded paintings in ochres, greens and blues covered every inch of the walls. By the light of the flame Abby saw a boat crossing a fish-filled sea; ivy tendrils winding around painted columns; a goddess in a gauzy dress descending to a sleeping hero, flanked by lions and the moon and the sun. There was writing, too, but try as she might she couldn't make out the crumbling letters.

It's a tomb, Abby thought. The stone trough

was a sarcophagus—she could see the lid leaning against it, the white scrapes on the stone where Michael and Sanchez had prised it off.

She took her thumb off the lighter so it wouldn't give her away. She sat on the floor in darkness, her wet clothes colder than death. She was shivering, though she barely noticed. She pressed her thumb against the lighter's steel, just to feel the heat.

She thought of the skeleton ripped from his grave, and wondered if this would be her tomb, too. A life for a life, a corpse for a corpse. She remembered Shai Levin. *Most likely he was stabbed through the heart.* It was an effort to think that this chamber belonged to a man who once lived and breathed as she did. *Probably rich. Lived a violent life.* A man who had planned and commissioned his tomb for posterity, never imagining that seventeen centuries later it would be lost in an unpopulated corner of a contested country.

Noise from outside the cave. Shouts, the clatter of rocks. She lifted her head. A dull bang rolled down the passage and she knew, with the intuition of the grave, that someone else had died.

The daylight at the end of the passage went out.

She had nowhere to hide. If she was going to die, at least she'd make the bastard look at her. Soft footsteps padded down the passage, slow and cautious. She flicked on the lighter. The ghosts of gods and heroes peered down from the wasting paint and waited to claim her. The man in the passage—was it a man?—came nearer. For a moment, he existed in perfect darkness—beyond the day, before the flame. The breeze blew in his scent, dead leaves and wet soil, the smell of an open grave.

He stepped forward. His face swam in and out of the firelight. Deep shadows swallowed his cheeks, so that all she could see was the thrust of his skull, the curly grey hair matted flat by the rain.

Her head spun. She heard the gods calling her on and laughing. She must have died. She lifted the lighter, and the shadows dropped away from his face.

'Michael?'

XXVI

Constantinople—April 337
'Did you think I'd let you go without saying goodbye?'

In an empty tomb, Constantine leans across the unconsecrated altar and looks me in the eye. Last time I saw him he was dressed like a god; now all he wears is a plain white robe and a grey cloak against the evening chill. Only the weave of the cloth betrays its cost.

'I thought you'd finished with me.'

A dozen gods used to live here. Now there's only one. On the highest point of the highest hill in the city, Constantine has razed the old Temple of the Twelve Gods and built his mausoleum on its foundations. It's his second attempt—the first, in Rome, is already occupied. Outwardly, it looks no different from the monuments that his sometime co-emperors built themselves: Maxentius in Rome, Galerius in Thessalonica, Diocletian in Split. A round tower in a square courtyard, with the surrounding arcades housing all the washrooms,

234

lampstores and priestly accommodation that will be needed when the new occupant takes up permanent residence.

And he won't be alone. There are seven niches in the rotunda. One's for Constantine's sarcophagus; the other six hold effigies of the twelve apostles of Christ. It's typical of Constantine. He's taken away the twelve old gods and put twelve Christian apostles in their place—like for like, pound for pound. When his project's complete, no one will be able to see the joins.

Gods abandon the world and give way to men. That's the way of history.

But for the moment, nothing's completed. Scaffolding covers the entire eastern half of the wall. Dust sheets shroud the twelve effigies in the niches around the room. That's also typical of Constantine. Great works, still in progress. The whole structure is a giant canister filled with dust. The late sun shines through the coloured glass and makes patterns in the air.

'That night when we condemned Symmachus— you looked as if you wanted to say something.'

'It wouldn't have made any difference.'

I'm determined to resist him, to say the minimum necessary and go home to supervise the slaves packing up my household. I didn't want to come. It's only because he's the Augustus.

'You were supposed to find me the truth,' he reminds me.

'If you wanted it.'

'You think he's innocent?'

Something gives inside me. Outrage overflows my pride and spills out. 'I don't know if he's innocent—but I'm sure he's been set up. I was

235

there when his slave handed the bag over. He could hardly have arranged it to be more incrim-inating.'

'But he had the bag.'

'His slave did.'

'The slave testified under torture that his master gave it to him. We needed resolution quickly. The Christians were impatient.' He sees the look on my face and sighs. 'You never used to be squeamish, Gaius.'

Every religion needs its blood sacrifice. Symmachus saw it coming better than I did.

An awkward silence hangs in the speckled air between us. Constantine gestures around the domed hall. 'Look at this mess. If I died tomorrow, they wouldn't know what to do with me.' He laughs. 'Don't worry. I'm not going to die until the Persians are sorted out. A final victory to complete my work.'

A pause. Perhaps it's occurred to him how many final victories he's already won.

'Do you remember Chrysopolis? The day after?'

*   *   *

Chrysopolis—September 324—Thirteen years earlier
. . .

On a warm Sunday morning, Constantine and his family are taking a walk. The long, hot summer still hasn't let go: the sky is blue, the sea calm, the ground baked hard. The purple imperial boots kick up puffs of dust as they pick their way among the cypresses and pines on top of the bluffs. Constantine leads the way, with Crispus at his side pointing out details of the great fleet moored below them. I'm just behind. After me come the women

236

and children—the youngest, Constans, only a year old and still in the arms of his wet nurse. They could be any Roman family out gathering berries or looking for eggs. In fact, they're now undisputed masters of the empire. On the other side of the hill, twenty-five thousand corpses are awaiting burial.

By my count, it's only the third day since June that I haven't been in armour. We've fought our way through the summer. It's taken ten years, but the confrontation between Constantine and Licinius has finally come to a head. In June, we marched into Thrace and sent Licinius packing from the Balkans, thirty thousand men lighter. In August, when Licinius hoped to stall us at Byzantium, Constantine literally marched over the city walls by building an earth ramp against them. At the same time, Crispus led our navy from Thessalonica and defeated Licinius's fleet in the straits at Gallipolis. I was with Constantine at Byzantium, but by all accounts it was a magnificent, daring victory.

Watching them together in front of me now, father and son, it's easy to believe this is a family touched by the gods. Constantine is just past fifty but as vigorous as ever, a strong man in his late prime. Crispus is a son any man would be proud of. Tall and handsome, with Constantine's soft-featured good looks and jet-black hair, he's at an age where fresh experience meets the confidence of youth, and nothing is impossible. He laughs easily and makes others laugh, even his father. When Constantine stumbles—he's still nursing a thigh wound he sustained in the charge at Hadrianople—Crispus is quick to put out a hand and steady him. Crispus points to the fleet and tells his father stories: *this* ship grappled Licinius's flagship; *that* one, the captain fell overboard because he tripped on a chicken that had escaped its coop.

Without warning, two boys run up behind us and start attacking Crispus with pine branches. Claudius and Constantius, eight and seven years old, Constantine's elder sons by Fausta. Crispus laughs, finds a stick on the ground and chases his half-brothers shrieking back to their mother.

Constantine turns to me, eyes shining. 'Was any man ever this happy?'

Yesterday, two hundred thousand men lined up on a dusty plain between Chalcedon and Chrysopolis to contest the fate of the world. It wasn't Constantine's greatest battle as a general. No daring ruse, no clever tactics. He put his standard, the *labarum*, in the centre of his line; he massed his cavalry behind the standard and his infantry behind the cavalry, and launched them in a sledgehammer blow straight at Licinius. Perhaps the magnitude of the occasion made him conservative. Or perhaps, again, he saw what others didn't: that having been outflanked before and determined not to let it happen again, Licinius had left his centre weak. And that having marched all summer, our army was in a savage mood, ready to end the war quickly.

We've reached the end of the point. Gentle waves lap on the rocky shore below; across the sparkling sea, Byzantium rises from its promontory. At the moment it's a small ferry port: a useful staging post for travellers crossing to Asia or up to the Black Sea, but too far upwind from the Mediterranean to generate any major commerce.

At this distance, the only building of any prominence is the baths, with the low line of the hippodrome just visible beyond.

'Is this what you brought us to see?' asks Fausta. She's come up behind us with the infant Constans. Her voice is muffled under the enormous hat and veil she's wearing to keep the sun off her face. While Constantine's lived his life at the frontiers, and can walk for miles, she's a creature of the palace. She can't comprehend walking anywhere that hasn't been shaded, pruned and swept. It offends her.

'This place is the hinge of the world.' Constantine has a way of speaking sometimes which makes you believe he's seeing things you can't. 'Halfway between east and west. And now, the hinge of history.'

Claudius and Constantius seem to have conquered Crispus. He collapses to the ground, writhing theatrically and clutching an imaginary wound in his side, then goes still.

'I thought you were old enough to fight real battles now,' Fausta says.

Crispus gets to his feet and brushes dust and pine needles off his tunic. 'Not too old to play with my brothers.'

Fausta scowls. Her boys adore Crispus—the best of a brother and a father rolled into one. She can't stand it. Like Crispus, Constantine was the only son of a first marriage. Like Crispus, Constantine has three half-brothers from his father's second marriage. He treats them regally, but he's never allowed them within a hundred miles of real power. Yesterday's battle is a bitter victory for her. If there's to be only one emperor, what will her sons

239

inherit?

A shout behind us interrupts the lap of waves and the buzz of flies. When you're sole ruler of the world, you don't just go for a stroll in the countryside. The imperial guard have cordoned off the whole promontory. Now, a dozen guards are approaching, walking single file on the narrow track between the grass and bushes. A woman and a boy, both dressed in plain white tunics, walk between them. It's Constantiana and her son Licinianus.

The moment they appear, Constantine stops being a father, a husband, a friend and becomes the Augustus again. His shoulders spread; he seems to grow six inches taller.

The soldiers salute and form a line. Constantiana drops her bundle on the ground, a wad of purple cloth, and sinks to her knees in the dust. Her son kneels beside her.

'From my husband Licinius—his imperial vestments. He renounces his titles and any claim to power. All he asks is that you spare his life and his family.'

'If he'd won yesterday, would he have spared me?' Constantine makes a gesture at Fausta, Crispus and the boys. 'Them?'

'If my husband had won, I'd be kneeling in front of him this minute begging him to spare you.' Her dress is artfully torn, her hair carefully disarrayed; you might think she'd just come off the battlefield herself. But the desolation in her face is genuine. She had dreams, too.

She stares at Constantine's feet. The captain of the guard's hand drifts to the hilt of his sword. Constantine gives a small shake of his head.

He cups his sister's chin in his hand and tips her

head back. He stares into her eyes. No one sees what passes between them.

'It's my fault,' declares Constantine. 'He tricked us all—I should never have let you marry him. Go back to your husband and tell him I accept his surrender. His titles are forfeit, but he can have safe passage to Thessalonica. The palace there should make a comfortable home.' A reassuring smile. 'After all, you're still my sister.'

Constantiana stands and makes a show of embracing Constantine, so limp she can barely get her arms around him. When she's steadier, Constantine pushes her back a little and offers her his hand.

As she kisses it, I hear her say three words. *'Tu solus Dominus.'* You alone are the Lord.

*   *   *

Constantinople—April 337
'That was a good day,' Constantine says. 'Our work was done.'

'And the next day the sun came up, and you had twice as many provinces to govern, and twice as much work.'

'But we were free.' He crosses the room and pulls a sheet off one of the statues. A bearded white face stares back at him. 'Do you remember when we were children at Diocletian's court? Lying awake, listening to the floorboards, asking ourselves if this was the night the murderers would come? Every night, I prayed to God I'd live to see the morning. I was so terrified, I used to make you sleep in my bed.'

'They never did come.'

241

'I thought that when I became sole Augustus, I'd never be afraid again.' He peers into the statue's face. 'And every day since I've been terrified of losing it all.'

'What was Alexander doing for you?' I ask abruptly. Constantine frowns. He doesn't want to be dragged back from the past.

'He was writing a history. He thought if he laid out all the events of my life in order, he'd find some sort of pattern. God's will.'

'Nothing else?' Constantine has his back to me, running his fingers through the folds of the saint's marble cloak. 'I looked in his bag, I saw what was in it. It was stuffed full of papers he'd collected. Not the sort of things you'd want to go in his book. In fact, I'd say you had as much motive as anyone to want him dead.'

'Alexander was a diligent researcher. The more facts he had, the more accurately he would reveal the pattern of God's purpose. I gave him access to every archive and library in this city. Every document.'

I remember the items I found on Alexander's desk—the razor blade, the jar of glue. And suddenly it all fits.

'He wasn't writing history,' I say. 'He was rewriting it—and not in his book, but deep in the archives.' Constantine turned to listen: I can see on his face I'm right. 'Whatever shamed you, or discredited you, he could remove it for ever. Like a sculptor recutting a statue's face into a new likeness.'

When his project's complete, no one will be able to see the joins.

'A *better* likeness.' Constantine walks back to the

centre of the room. 'So many things I've achieved in my life. I found a broken world and gave it peace. The hydra of government that Diocletian left, I cut off its heads one by one until the beast was dead and all its evils gone. On the day the army acclaimed me Augustus in York, there were men dying agonising deaths, simply because they didn't want to sacrifice to old gods nobody believed in anyway. I put a stop to that. I let the people worship as they pleased—I gave the empire a God who was strong enough and merciful enough to tolerate dissent, even error, without violence.'

I think of Symmachus's slave somewhere in the palace basement. I imagine how he screamed.

'Not without violence.'

'Of course not.' He's agitated now. 'We have to live in the world we have, not the world we'd wish for. If the work was easy, or painless, there'd have been no need for me. You, more than anyone, know what it cost.'

He leans forward on the altar, as if he can't support his own weight any more. There's something that needs to be said right now—a last chance to clear away the fog between us. This is the closest we've come to being honest in years. But I can't speak.

'I should be remembered for who I was.' He's almost pleading—though not with me. He's speaking to eternity. 'The things I achieved, not the price I paid. I deserve that much.'

He wants history to love him. 'And you got Alexander to make sure of it.'

'He knew everything—*everything*—and never judged me for it. That's why I needed to know who killed him. That's why I asked you.'

243

'And then convicted the first convenient scapegoat?'

He's more human, than I've seen him in years. 'Haven't you been listening? Don't you understand?'

We're not talking about Alexander and Symmachus any more. We face each other across the room, divided by the altar. The dying sun shoots shafts of crimson light into the air above us, and his twelve apostles bear blind witness. I know what I have to say.

But the words are hard. I weigh them, and the moment I do they're like a boulder in my hand. I push, but it won't move. I'm not Alexander. I can't forgive him.

'You united the empire. That will be your legacy.'

And? He waits for more, giving me every chance. When he sees there's nothing, he gives a bitter laugh. 'Didn't you know? I've divided it between my sons. Claudius, Constantius and Constans will each inherit a third. *Mundus est omnis divisus in partes tres.*' He laughs again, so desperate it sounds like he's sobbing. 'If only things had been different.'

If only things had been different. He can rewrite the past as much as he likes, but some facts are indelible.

'Good luck against the Persians.'

His finger draws a line in the dust on the altar, then bisects it with another. 'I'll be glad to get away. Sometimes I feel this city's killing me.'

I leave him alone in his mausoleum, dwarfed by the scaffolding of his unfinished dreams. Caught in the light, dust falls but never makes a sound.

XXVII

Kosovo—Present Day

Her thumb slipped off the flint. The flame went out and the tomb went black. She flicked the lighter again, rubbing her finger raw before it relit.

Michael was still there.

What do you say to a dead man? She'd been talking to him for weeks—interrogating, begging, cursing. And now he was here, she couldn't think of a thing to say.

'I got one of the bad guys outside the cave, but there might be more. And the Americans.'

'I thought you were dead,' she whispered.

'Greatly exaggerated, like the man said.' He glanced over his shoulder. 'Still time, of course.'

All she could do was stare at him. 'How—?'

'How did I find you? Or how did I end up not dead?'

'How are we going to get out of here?'

'Always practical. That's what I loved about you.' He took her hand in his and crouched in front of her. 'God, I missed you, Abby. I'm so sorry about . . . everything.'

His hand was cold, but his breath was warm on her cheek. Through the dirt and smoke that clung to him, she caught the faintest sniff of his real scent—strong and mellow, like whisky on a winter's night. That, more than anything, convinced her he might be real.

'There's a hut in the next valley. Dragović doesn't know about it. I've been living there the last few days.'

She stared at him blankly. Joy, relief, gladness—those might all come later. For the moment, she felt hurt beyond all healing.

Michael put both hands on her cheeks and looked her in the eye.

'I've been waiting for you.'

*   *   *

They left the tomb and hiked through the forest as fast as they could—Michael leading the way, Abby struggling to keep pace. The throb of the helicopter still shook the air, though the trees made it invisible. Every so often, short bursts of automatic weapon fire echoed up the valley.

'That's the Kosovo Police,' said Michael. 'Probably shooting at shadows. If they haven't got Dragović by now, he'll be safe into Serbia.'

They crested the ridge, still in the trees, and started descending the far slope. She couldn't hear the gunfire any more, though the helicopter hadn't gone away. In fact, it seemed to be getting louder. It flew right over them, shaking water drops off the wet trees, then slowly faded away.

'At last vee are alone,' Michael said, in a mock French accent. It was a line he'd often used in Pristina, when friends had left the flat after a long evening's drinking. Hearing it here made her stomach lurch.

They didn't stop, but carried on down the valley. The sun set behind the clouds; the air grew cold. Just when Abby thought she couldn't go another step, they came out in a clearing where a small stone hut stood between two large trees. Not much to look at, but it had a chimney and a solid roof, and that was enough for Abby.

Michael didn't dare light a fire—the wood in the forest was soaked anyway. Abby huddled under a mouse-eaten blanket on a camp bed, while Michael heated a can of beans on a gas stove.

'So tell me again why you aren't dead.'

'Had you fooled, did I?' He saw the anger rising and backtracked. 'Sorry—joke. I know it isn't funny.'

If she hadn't been so exhausted, she'd have hit him. 'It's not a game.'

'No, it is not.' He pulled a cork out of a wine bottle and poured liquid into a steel cup. It came out clear as poison, with a kick she could smell from across the room.

'*Šlijvovica*. Local moonshine. It'll warm you up.'

She sipped it and wished she had a cigarette. The rough heat made her anger feel good.

'Tell me everything,' she ordered him. 'Why were we at the villa? You knew it belonged to Dragović.'

He hesitated. The only light in the room was the small blue flame on the stove, silhouetting him in the corner.

'Tell me the truth,' she warned. The *šlijvovica* burned her throat, but it couldn't touch her frozen core.

He turned towards her. 'I knew it was his villa. I'd arranged to go there to hand over some things he wanted.'

'From the tomb?'

'Yes.' He thought a moment. 'I don't know how much you found out, or figured out, but here's the background. A patrol of American KFOR troops found that cave and wrote it up. The report came up to Pristina and landed on my desk. One of life's happy coincidences.'

'You made the connection with Dragović?'

'I knew he was doolally for the Romans. I'd been trying to get close to his organisation for a while.'

'Close?'

'A sting. Infiltrate his circles and bring him down.' He held his head still. She thought he was staring at her, though his eyes were invisible in the darkness.

'You weren't working for him?'

'Is that what they told you?' He reached forward and put his hand on her arm, but she jerked it away. She wasn't ready for that. 'Christ, Abby. Is that what you thought I was?'

'I thought you were dead.'

On the stove the pan bubbled and spat.

'You know all about Dragović, I suppose. He's the most evil man in the Balkans, and that takes some doing.'

He fiddled with the knob of the stove, adjusting the heat.

'You remember Irina?'

Abby nodded. To her, Irina had been a black-and-white photograph on a bookshelf in Michael's flat—glossy hair, pale skin, dark eyes watching the room, like the missing person pictures taped to the railings of the government building in Pristina. She'd only asked Michael about the picture once, thinking she must be family. *She died in the war*, he'd said, and changed the conversation.

'Irina was one of Dragović's victims during the '99 war. I'm not going to tell you what he had done to her, but I've read the reports. You can probably use your imagination.'

And that did stall her anger. She knew all the

stories. Whatever vile, cruel or inhuman torture men could devise, it had probably happened in Kosovo during the war. There'd even been rumours of prisoners herded across the border to Albania to have their organs harvested for sale to rich buyers in the West.

'Dragović is the reason I came back to the Balkans. When this find of Roman artefacts turned up, I thought I could use it to get to him. I baited the hook—and he bit.'

'The Foreign Office thought you were corrupt.'

'I had to go vigilante. You know how it is with MMA.'

MMA was *Monitor, Mentor and Advise*— the EULEX mission's official role in post-independence Kosovo. It meant working alongside the local authorities, trying to prod and cajole them into some semblance of honest functioning. It was an uphill battle.

'Half the Kosovo government report to Dragović. MMA means they see everything. Anything that goes on paper or in an e-mail at headquarters, it's on Dragović's desk before it's reached the top floor. If I'd done this officially . . .' He sighed. 'I went off the reservation, Abby, and I took you with me, and I can't tell you how sorry I am for that.'

'Why did you get me involved?'

'I wasn't thinking straight. I knew EULEX were after me because they thought I was in bed with Dragović. Fair enough. Dragović's people were sniffing around to see if I was on the level, so actually the internal investigation made it look better. But it was tough. I didn't want EULEX bursting in on my meeting at the villa, just when I was starting to get somewhere. You know there's nothing the EU people hate more than working a weekend. I thought if you came away with me, they'd decide it was nothing and leave us alone.'

He spooned the beans out on to the plate and handed it to her. 'Only one plate. Sorry I'm not geared up for hosting.'

She pushed it away—she wasn't hungry—but he held on. 'When was the last time you ate?'

He didn't wait for an answer. 'You need food. We don't have much time.'

She took the plate. The moment the first spoonful went in, she realised she'd been ravenous.

'Things went wrong.' Michael sat back on a log, rocking back and forth. 'It was never supposed to be dangerous. Dragović was going to send his man— his name was Sloba—to pick up the artefacts, and that was it. You and I would have a nice weekend, and I'd be one step closer to Dragović.'

'It didn't work out that way.'

'Sloba was twitchy as hell from the start. He might have come with orders to kill me, I don't know. When you came out on the pool terrace, he jumped to a conclusion.'

'He threw you over the cliff,' Abby reminded him.

'Even Zoltán Dragović needs to have his pool cleaned. There's a small access gantry a few feet below the edge of the cliff. I landed on it.'

'Lucky.'

'By the time I'd got back up to the villa, Sloba had caught up with you. I . . .' He broke off, staring deep into the darkness. 'I killed him. It's a hell of a thing. In the moment . . . Afterwards . . .'

A long silence. When he spoke again, some of the colour had returned to his voice.

'I called an ambulance. Then I threw Sloba's body over the cliff and made damn sure he missed the gantry. By then, I could see the ambulance coming down the drive. So I ran. Hardest thing I ever did, Abby, leaving you. Harder than killing a man.'

'And the body? Jenny, your sister, she said it was you. Did she know?'

'I never dreamed they'd think Sloba was me. You were in a coma and surrounded by police: I called Jenny because she was the only person I could trust. She said the local police wanted her to identify a body. I told her to do it. So much easier to avoid awkward questions if everyone thinks you're dead.'

'*Easier?*' The hurt and shock and betrayal that had been smouldering inside her suddenly erupted in a flash of anger. 'Easier to leave me thinking you were dead? Easier to have me stumbling around Europe wondering why people kept trying to kill me? Is that what you call easy?'

Michael put his head in his hands. 'I'm so sorry.'

'I didn't ask for any of this.'

'I know. I owe you an apology—an explanation— so much.' He lifted his head, searching for forgiveness. 'Dragović was after you. He knew something wasn't right. The fact that Sloba's body was missing, for starters. He might have heard rumours that I'd been seen: not much happens in this part of the world that he doesn't hear about. And he guessed there was something I'd been holding back from him.'

He waited for her to respond. She knew she shouldn't—she wasn't nearly ready to give up her anger yet—but somehow she found herself saying: 'The scroll?'

251

Michael's eyes lit up. 'You found it?'

'I went to Trier. I saw Doctor Gruber.'

'Did he decode it?'

'Only a few words.' She tried to remember, then realised with a start she didn't have to. She patted her jeans pocket. The piece of paper Gruber had given her made a wad against her thigh, softened where rain had seeped into it.

She opened the paper, peeling apart the damp folds, and read the poem. *To reach the living, navigate the dead*. The words resonated strangely as she said them. She'd been navigating a world where Michael was dead; now here he was, living and breathing.

'Do you know what it means?'

'No idea,' Michael said. 'But I couldn't bear the idea of something like that being lost for ever because I'd given it to Dragović. And it was worth holding something back for a second pass. I found Doctor Gruber online and turned up on his doorstep. Even if I had to give away the scroll in the end, I wanted to make sure the information on it would survive. Whatever was in that tomb, it means something to Dragović. He thinks there's more to it.'

She passed him the plate and took another sip of the clear brandy. It burned her tongue, but at least it felt real.

'So what do you want to do?'

'I think Dragović can be had. I don't know what he wants, but he's turned half of Europe upside down looking for it. He's not thinking straight.'

That makes two of you, Abby thought.

'He's breaking his own rules on getting involved: he's left himself vulnerable. If we can get to it—

whatever *it* is—before him . . .'

'He'll crush you.'

'Not if we're careful.'

We. It was the second time he'd said it. It sounded so natural, almost inevitable.

'*You*,' she said firmly. 'You already died once—and nearly killed me, too. If you want to go off on some revenge fantasy tilting at Dragović, you're on your own.'

Michael nodded. 'Of course—I presumed—sorry. Where are you going to go?'

Such a mild question, but it stripped away the layers of shock and anger to leave nothing but raw terror. *Where am I going to go?* To a cold flat in Clapham that stank of a failed marriage? To a desk job in the Foreign Office—if they even let her back in the building after everything she'd been involved in?

She was lost. Michael read it in her face. 'You can't stay in the Balkans. Dragović has eyes on every street corner between Vienna and Istanbul. He'll eat you alive.'

'Am I supposed to live the rest of my life looking over my shoulder?'

'Who's going to protect you? You won't get a NATO helicopter flying in every time you're in trouble. The EU? The British government?'

The vision of Jessop's body lying in the mud was the only answer she could come up with.

'Why did you spend ten years of your life tramping around deserts and jungles? So you could nail people like Dragović, right?'

Abby looked at her hands. 'I gave up on saving the world.'

'You can't.' Michael leaned forward, a shadow

in the gloom. 'That Roman guy in the tomb—you know what he was doing in this God-fucking-forsaken place? Patrolling the frontiers of civilisation to keep the barbarians out. That's what we have to do, Abby. Because if you don't stamp on the barbarians, they're all over you before you know it. Look at Yugoslavia or Rwanda or Germany in the thirties. One moment you're in a nice, middle-class country washing your car on Sunday afternoon. The next, you're hacking up your neighbour with a machete or pumping him full of Zyklon B.'

'What are you saying? That this mess you're in is somehow like fighting the Nazis?'

'I'm saying *please*. Help me do this. For my sake, and Irina, and all the good people who've suffered because a shit like Dragović thinks no one will stop him. And do it for yourself. You're not going to escape until he's put away.'

Michael scoured the bowl to get the last of the sauce out. The spoon scraped the metal like a knife being sharpened.

She needed more time. Choices swirled around her head, offering infinite consequences, but no answers. In the fog, her mind went back to some of the mundane places she'd been in her life: a warehouse in Bosnia, a technical school in Rwanda. Places that the full authority of the international community had once declared safe havens. Thousands had gone there—trusting, praying, clinging to hope until it was too late. The only haven for most of them had been the silence of a mass grave.

'Where are you going to go?' she asked. Buying time.

254

'There's a man in Belgrade who knows about this kind of thing,' Michael said. 'I took some photographs of the tomb; I want to see if he has any ideas.'

And the moment he said it, she knew she would go to Belgrade—and, afterwards, wherever else this mad chase led. Not to save the world, or for love of Michael, or revenge, but because the only choice she had was to wait or to run. And she was tired of waiting.

Michael turned the knob on the stove and the flame went out.

XXVIII

Constantinople—May 337
Even in May it's cold before the sun comes up. Constantinople is a city of shadows: footsteps echo on the empty colonnades, the statues seem to come alive. A hundred feet in the air above the forum, Constantine watches me from the top of his column. Thirty feet tall and every inch the god: naked, with a radiate crown whose long spikes reach out to meet the dawn. He carries a spear in one hand, the orb of the world cupped in the other. The engineers mounted it on the column in a single night, so that when the sun came up next day Constantine had appeared above the city as if from heaven. I heard the Christians were furious.

The city feels empty. Constantine left for his war three days ago, dressed in golden armour and drawn in a gilded chariot by four white horses. In his hand was the *labarum*, the standard he forged before the Milvian Bridge. It's almost twenty-five years since he unveiled it, and there's hardly been a year since then it hasn't led the army into battle. Goths, Sarmatians, Franks, rival emperors—they've all met the unconquerable standard and been crushed. And yet it's hardly suffered a scratch. The golden wreath which frames the monogram is as bright as the day it was made; the sun shines through the nested jewels like stars.

And now it's time for another departure. Symmachus leaves today on the boat to Piraeus, with an onward journey to some anonymous rock in the Aegean. I've come to see him off. I feel I owe him that much.

I descend the steep steps between two warehouses and come out on the quay. And at one end, where a ladder leads down to a waiting skiff, four soldiers from the palace guard stand swapping dirty stories.

I approach. 'Is Aurelius Symmachus here?'

None of them recognises me, or salutes. They'd still have been children the last time I stood in front of a legion. The sergeant eyes me cautiously, just in case I make trouble.

'Who wants to know?'

'A friend of the Augustus.' I show them the ivory diptych Constantine gave me and they snap to attention.

'Not arrived yet,' the sergeant says. He glances at the sky. 'He'd better be here soon. My shift ends at dawn.'

'There's that one,' a soldier adds. He points to a figure lurking in the doorway of a grain warehouse, the hood of his cloak over his face. 'He was looking for the prisoner too.'

The figure hears our conversation and steps out of the doorway. The hood drops back: it's Porfyrius. He seems to have aged in the last week. The theatrical energy I remember from Symmachus's garden has been subdued; the spark in his eyes has dimmed. To my surprise, he embraces me like an old friend.

'We old men should stick together,' he says. 'Before the young drive us out completely.'

He steps back and gives me a searching look. 'I heard you didn't approve what they did to Symmachus.'

'The Augustus judged the case himself.'

'You'd have thought if Symmachus wanted to make it so obvious, he'd just have confessed.'

Is he trying to make me say something incriminating? I glance around at the busy wharf: a stevedore sitting on an amphora eating a wrapped pie, a shipping clerk tapping his stylus on a tablet. Wherever you go in this city, there's always an audience. Best to say nothing.

'I heard the slave's testimony was decisive,' Porfyrius persists. 'Did you interrogate him yourself?'

I wish I had. Whoever set up Symmachus, the slave was the key.

'He was tortured in the palace. By next morning, he was on his way to the silver mines in Dardania.' I open my hands. 'Sometimes Roman justice moves too quickly for an old man to keep up.'

He nods—it's as much as he'll get from me. 'But you still came to see Symmachus off. It's good of you.'

'The Augustus will want to be sure he's really gone.' I meant it as a joke, but it comes out

257

sounding cruel. Porfyrius steps back a little.

'No doubt on that score. Symmachus is a Stoic—he'll leave with dignity, if nothing else.'

But there's still no sign of him. The sun comes up; the soldiers grumble. Crates of fish get carted up the road to the market. Porfyrius starts to pace the quay, glancing up the hill expectantly.

The sergeant comes over to us. I have the Emperor's commission: suddenly, I'm an authority.

'He was supposed to be here an hour ago. Should we go to his house?'

I'm getting tired of waiting. 'I'll go.'

Porfyrius joins me without asking. It's a hard climb for two old men. By the time we reach Symmachus's house, we're both puffing like cart horses.

The door to the house is locked. We ring the bell hanging outside, but no one answers. All his possessions were forfeit: his slaves will have been confiscated and sold, but he should have been left a freedman to prepare for his departure.

'Maybe he took a different route down to the dock,' I suggest. 'We could have missed him on the way down.'

'There's a side door.' Porfyrius is already heading towards the corner of the building. I've half a mind to let him go alone, but curiosity makes me follow. There are no windows on this side of the house, just a narrow alley between Symmachus and his neighbour's mansion. And, halfway down, a wooden door in the brick wall.

Porfyrius tries the handle and it gives. We push through, into a vaulted storeroom that smells of sawdust. Splinters and bark litter the floor: even his firewood's been taken away. In the adjoining rooms, dust's already begun to settle.

Another door, another empty room, and suddenly we're in the bright light of the peristyle, overlooking the garden.

The fish sit motionless in their pond. The blind philosophers watch from their perches in the colonnade. And in the centre of the garden, Aurelius Symmachus lies propped against the side of the pool, head lolling forward.

One glance is enough to know he's not going anywhere.

XXIX

Novi Pazar, Serbia—Present Day
Novi Pazar meant 'New Bazaar'. There was a bazaar in the town and it must have been new once, though now it was derelict. The whole town was the Balkans in miniature: a southern half of minarets and winding Ottoman alleys, a northern district of monolithic concrete, and a small river dividing them. Even the refugees who thronged its streets had a symmetry to them: Muslims expelled by Serbs from Bosnia, and Serbs expelled by Muslims from Kosovo.

Abby bought some new clothes in a drab shop and changed in the toilet at the coach station. They bought two tickets from the kiosk, and took seats at the back of the bus. It was five hours to Belgrade. The countryside scrolled past the windows: river valleys and scrubby hillsides mottled green and brown, broken every so often with orchards or quarries. A primitive, lonely landscape.

Michael took a camera out of his bag and turned it on. He cupped his hand around the screen to shade it, though the bus was mostly empty. He played back pictures from the tomb, fiddling with the controls to pan and zoom for detail.

'That's the lid of the sarcophagus.' He went closer. 'You see the inscription?'

Despite their age, the letters were deep and sharp. 'C VAL MAX,' Abby read.

'Gaius Valerius Maximus,' Michael expanded. She glanced at him.

'I didn't know you read Latin.'

'Grammar school boy. Back before they all went private.' He tapped the screen. 'I did some research after I saw this. This man Valerius has a record. He was a consul in AD 314, and there are inscriptions that make him Praetorian Prefect to the emperor Constantine the Great. Sort of a chief of staff—or *consigliere,* if you like *The Godfather*. Important.'

'Until he got a sword through his heart.'

Michael thumbed on through the next pictures— the faded frescoes, their plaster falling off in scabs. He tried to zoom in on the writing, but the closer he went the more it dissolved into a pixelated blur. He put the camera down in frustration. Abby took it.

'Don't you think it's strange?' She'd pulled back out so she could see the paintings in what remained of their fullness. 'I don't see any Christian iconography. No crosses or Christograms; nothing that looks like a Bible story.'

'From what I read, Constantine's reign was a pretty confused time religiously. It's not as if everyone woke up one morning and decided they were going to be Christian.'

'Think about the necklace you gave me. You found it in the tomb, right?'

'Sealed in the vase with the scroll.'

'It's a Christian symbol. Why would the dead man, Gaius Valerius, want that right beside him in his grave, but not anywhere on the decoration?'

Michael shrugged. 'Deathbed conversion?'

She thought of the blade sliding into the man's chest, forceful enough to break the rib. She shuddered.

'Speaking of the necklace, do you still have it?'

'The Foreign Office took it.'

Michael stared out the window. 'It probably doesn't matter.'

*   *   *

Belgrade, Serbia—Present Day

The bus dropped them at the terminus at the bottom of the hill near the city centre. A black sky had brought an early twilight; relentless rain hammered the streets, and thunder rolled around the river valley. They bought an umbrella from a shop in the station concourse.

'How are we for money?' Abby asked.

'Fine,' said Michael. 'The advantage of pretending to be crooked is that a lot of cash came through my hands.'

'Then let's find somewhere to stay. There's a hotel I used to—'

'No.' Michael was firm. 'You know the drill in Serbia. Every hotel guest gets registered with the nearest police station. Even if they don't recognise our names, they'll see we don't have an entry stamp. Do you even have a passport?'

261

Abby patted her trouser pocket and felt nothing. She remembered reaching for it at the checkpoint; the hand closing around her wrist, dragging her out of the car; the passport falling unheeded into the mud.

A pang went through her. She felt herself dissolving away, a little girl lost in a foreign city. No way to get out, nothing even to prove who she was.

Michael didn't seem to have noticed. He checked his watch. 'Anyway, we've got a meeting to go to.'

She trailed after him through the bus station and out on to the busy street beyond. Michael held the umbrella low, covering their faces. Abby clung on to his arm and tried not to get soaked by the passing cars.

'Where's the meeting?'

'On a splav.'

*   *   *

Abby had never been on a splav before, though she'd seen them in the distance during her trips to Belgrade. They were a Belgrade institution—bars and nightclubs on rafts that lined the banks of the Sava and the Danube for over a mile. Some looked like houses, and others like boats: the one they'd come to had a curved steel roof and exposed girders more reminiscent of an aircraft hangar. It floated about twenty yards out in the stream, tethered to the shore by a very makeshift bridge of scaffolding poles and planks. A sign above the door said *Hazard*, though it wasn't clear if that was the name of the bar or just a general warning.

Abby looked at the rickety gangway, slick in the rain, and the grey river sweeping under it.

'We'll be in trouble if we have to leave in a hurry.'

'I didn't choose the venue.'

They wobbled and tottered across the wet planks. A security guard gave them a rudimentary pat-down—a reminder that this still wasn't a city entirely at peace with itself. A sign on the door said no guns, which didn't reassure her.

Inside, the room was vast and dark, though even the darkness couldn't disguise how empty it was. The walls were painted a burgundy so deep it looked black, broken every so often by electric pieces of neon sculpted into aggressively abstract shapes. A DJ stood in a box in the centre of the room, turning out high-wattage music, but no one was dancing. The few customers had mostly retreated into the booths at the edge of the room. One of them, an old man sitting on his own, looked up as they entered, and beckoned.

'Who is he again?' Abby asked as they crossed the floor. She was trying to be discreet, though with the music so loud she had to shout to be heard.

'Mr Giacomo. He's what, in the old days, you used to call a fence.'

There was a lot of the old days about Mr Giacomo. He had spiky white hair buzzed flat across the top of his head, tapering to a widow's peak like the bow of a boat. His face was tanned and lined, his eyebrows bushy and wild. He wore a brown tweed suit and no tie, his white shirt unbuttoned somewhere near the borders of decency. He stood as they approached and ushered them into the booth. He didn't shake hands, but beckoned a waiter over and ordered two Sidecars.

'You had a good journey?' he enquired. His

accent was unlocatable: it could have come from any one of the half-dozen countries bordering the Adriatic. He stared tactlessly at Abby's face, and she felt herself blushing. Her ordeal in the forest had added several bruises and one long scratch to the marks that Dragović had inflicted in Rome. She looked like a domestic violence poster.

'We had some problems getting here.'

He nodded, as if it were the most natural thing. 'It is your first time in Belgrade?'

His questions were aimed entirely at Abby.

'I've been before.'

'You have visited the castle? The ethnographical museum?'

'Mr Giacomo does a lot of work in museums,' Michael said. He was trying to make a joke, but Giacomo didn't smile.

'Mr Lascaris, you went to some trouble to arrange a meeting with me. I am a busy man, but I have obliged you—even though your profession and mine are often . . . antagonists.'

He spread his hands on the table and leaned forward. 'What is it you want from me?'

Michael lit a cigarette and exhaled. The neon on the wall made the smoke glow red; the strobe lights from the dance floor flickered on the edge of the cloud like distant lightning.

'I want to know what Dragović is after.'

Giacomo's eyes narrowed. 'That is not a good name to say out loud—especially in this city.' He tapped his ear. 'Even if you cannot hear yourself, always somebody else can.'

'Dragović has been turning Europe upside down for the last two months.' Michael made a point of repeating the name. The beat of the music

264

accelerated, pounding like running footsteps. 'He's looking for something.'

'A man like him is always chasing something. Guns, girls, drugs . . . Maybe even a customs inspector from the European Union.' Giacomo took out his own cigarettes and tapped the pack on the table. 'Maybe this is something you know more about than me?'

'He's after some historical artefact. Probably Roman. From the way he's going about it, he probably knows what it is. I thought you might, too.'

Giacomo considered it. 'The man you mentioned, he does not share his thoughts with me often.'

'If he's looking for a Roman artefact, surely you'd have heard about it.'

'You think I am so notorious?' He held up his drink, studying his reflection in the glass. 'Perhaps I am. What makes you think this thing he is looking for is Roman?'

The ash on the end of Michael's cigarette lengthened. 'Everyone knows he's crazy for the Romans.'

'Really?'

The question hung in the air, mingling with the smoke and noise. Giacomo stared at Michael, who turned slightly to glance at Abby. He raised his eyebrows. *What do we tell him?*

Giacomo stood. 'Excuse me.' He tapped his crotch. 'An old man's problems. Perhaps we continue this conversation in a moment.'

He slid out of the booth and edged around the dance floor to the toilets. With his brown suit and shuffling walk, he looked like a sad old man who'd got lost.

'How did you find him?' Abby asked.

Michael drained his drink. 'I've got some contacts in the art world. Smuggling stolen artworks and antiquities is big business. Mr Giacomo is one of the best—or worst, depending on your point of view.'

'And he won't betray us to Dragović?' She craned around. Deliberately or not, Giacomo had manoeuvred them so they sat with their backs to the door. With the flashing disco lights and hammer-drill bass, it more or less amounted to sensory deprivation.

'I'm not sure about anything.' Michael waved to the waiter for another drink. 'Rumour has it he competes with Dragović's organisation. For what that's worth.'

Worth our lives? Abby wondered.

Across the room she noticed a man in a leather jacket standing at the bar. He was young, hair gelled into spikes and a bad case of acne on his cheeks. He was nursing a beer, but had angled himself so that their table was in his eyeline. She nodded at him.

'Do you think he's one of Dragović's?'

'Probably a friend of Giacomo's.' Michael shook it off. 'How much do you think we should tell him?'

'Does it matter?' She couldn't take her eyes off the man at the bar.

'Dealing with someone like Giacomo is like playing poker. We don't want to show our hand too soon.'

Abby had to laugh. 'You don't think he can tell we're bluffing?'

Across the room, Giacomo emerged from the toilets. As he walked back past the bar, Abby thought she saw him swap a glance with the acne-faced man. He sat down and waited while the waiter delivered Michael's drink. His own was still more than half-full.

'So?'

Michael took a deep gulp of his drink. 'There was a tomb—in Kosovo. I found it. There were some artefacts inside, and I sold them to Dragović.'

'You should have come to me. I would give you a better price.'

'There was a poem in the tomb.' Michael took the napkin from under his drink and wrote out the first line of the poem from memory. He slid it across the table. Giacomo raised his eyebrows.

'I am not a poet. Not even a scholar.'

'I thought you might recognise it.'

'From your tomb?'

'It's a copy of a poem that's already known. It comes from a grave plaque in the Roman Forum Museum.'

'*Formerly* in the Roman Forum Museum,' Giacomo corrected him. 'It was stolen—quite recently. Though I believe it is still in Rome.'

His dark eyes flicked from Michael to Abby and back. *He knows Dragović has it*, Abby thought. *And he knows about Dragović's little museum in Rome. How does he know that?*

'Dragović stole the stone with the poem on it. He thinks it might point to something valuable.'

'If he does, he has not asked my opinion.'

'I'm asking you.'

Giacomo's gaze sidled away over Michael's shoulder, towards the door. Abby fought back the urge to look around.

'What do you know about the poem?' Giacomo

267

asked.

To her surprise, Abby found herself answering. 'It dates from around the fourth century—around the time of the Emperor Constantine.'

Giacomo sat back. 'Constantine the Great. Did you know he was born in Serbia? I think here they specialise in megalomaniacs.' He chuckled. 'Where in Kosovo did you say was this tomb?'

'In a forest,' said Michael evenly.

'When you looted it, did you leave anything behind? Anything a friend might go back and collect for you?'

'There are frescoes on the wall. Intact, pretty good condition.' Michael took the camera out of his bag and showed him on the screen. 'If you can help us, I could probably give you a more precise location.'

Abby stared at Michael. *Is he really doing this?* She imagined Giacomo's gangsters in the tomb, its walls shuddering as their drills prised out the fragile plaster. *It doesn't belong to them*, she thought—as if she could hear the protest of a seventeen-centuries-dead skeleton who had once been a man called Gaius Valerius Maximus.

Giacomo took a pen out of his jacket and added something to the napkin where Michael had written the poem.

'This is a hotel I know. Go there, make yourselves comfortable. I will ask some questions, talk to some people, and find you there when I have something to tell you.'

'Wait a minute,' Abby objected. 'If we check into a hotel, they'll ask for my passport. They'll have to register us with the police.'

Giacomo studied her. A gold tooth glinted in his

mouth. *I've shown him a weakness*, Abby thought. *He's wondering how to exploit it*. He pulled out a silver mobile phone and made a brief call. Abby wondered how anyone heard anything above the music.

'They will not ask for your passport.'

'How long do we have to wait?'

'When I have something. You know what Socrates said?'

'"I'm dying for a glass of hemlock"?' Michael suggested. It was a bad joke, and Giacomo didn't smile.

'"Knowledge lies within you."'

He got up and left without paying. The acne-faced man at the bar nodded to him as he passed, but didn't follow.

Michael spun his glass, making wet moons on the table. The permanent grin had faded. His face sagged; he looked old.

'What have you got us into?' Abby murmured. But if Michael had an answer, the music killed it.

XXX

Constantinople—May 337

Aurelius Symmachus lies slumped against the edge of the pool. His arms are flung out to balance him: his right hand's dipped in the water. His face is purple; his tunic spattered red from the blood in the vomit he coughed down his front.

I share a look with Porfyrius. Neither of us thinks this was an accident.

First they get rid of you; then they send the

269

assassins.

A white marble bust lies at Symmachus's feet. Porfyrius tries to pick it up, but it's too heavy for him. He reads the name on the base and gives a grim laugh.

'Cato the Younger. You know the story?'

'I think so.'

'He was a Stoic who chose suicide rather than exile.' He aims a flat-footed kick at the stone head, pushing it over on the gravel. 'Symmachus wasn't any stronger than I am. He didn't drag Cato here just for a piece of historical theatre.'

'Someone wanted us to think that's exactly what he did.'

'They wanted us to think it was suicide.'

A gleam in the water catches my eye. I reach in and pull out a small silver cup. One of the fish is so close I feel its scales on my skin, but it still doesn't move. None of them do.

All the fish are dead. They float belly-up on the surface, bobbing softly like feathers.

The water on my arm suddenly feels like a rash, prickling and burning my bare skin. It's probably my imagination, but there are poisons I know which can kill on contact. I rub my arm dry with the hem of my cloak, so hard I almost break the skin.

Porfyrius watches me uncertainly.

'The poison was in the cup. When Symmachus fell, he dropped it in the water. There was still enough in there to kill the fish. Probably aconite.'

'Aurelius Symmachus deserved better than this.' With a sudden burst of energy, Porfyrius seizes the bust, tugging and dragging on it until he's manhandled it over the rim of the pool. It drops in with a splash: water slops over the edge. A few fish

270

wash out onto the ground.

'We should call the Watch.'

'They'll just say it was suicide.'

'Better than accusing us of murder.'

The anger drains out of him. We're both stuck in this web now. He goes back to the colonnade and sits on a step, hunched over. I walk around the pond, resisting the compulsion to keep scrubbing my hand.

'Symmachus didn't take his own life,' I say. 'Whoever killed him probably killed Alexander, too.'

'Does that follow?'

'Let's agree Symmachus didn't murder Alexander. Can we agree that whoever did kill the Bishop then wanted to frame Symmachus?'

'We can agree they had a motive. But so did lots of other people. Even you. There are three questions here, and they don't necessarily demand the same answer. Who killed Alexander? Who framed Symmachus? And now, who poisoned him?'

He's starting to irritate me, quibbling with every word I say like a sophist in the forum. I'm not interested in his hair-splitting. 'Who else has an interest in framing Symmachus other than the man who killed Alexander? With him gone, the last loose end is tied up.'

'It was already tied up—he should have been on the boat by now. If they wanted to be sure, they could have done it at sea, or when he reached Greece. No one would have known. Or cared.'

'You're saying it was a coincidence?'

I pause, looking down at the slumped corpse on the gravel. Experience has taught me there are no coincidences in this city.

'Whoever framed Symmachus, they didn't choose him randomly. They wanted him out of the way. Exile wasn't enough—they needed him dead.'

Porfyrius says nothing, reserving judgement.

'You were his friend. Can you think of anything he knew, anyone he might have offended?'

'A lot of Christians hated him.'

'You think they waited thirty years for this?' I shake my head. 'This was urgent.'

I let the silence stretch. Even in his undoubted shock, there's a reticence about him that makes me twitch.

'We need to know who did this,' I say. 'No secrets.'

'Do you think you'll get justice?'

'I'll settle for avoiding a fate like Symmachus.'

Old habits are hard to shake. Even in this silent villa I'm talking as if someone's watching. But it's too late for caution.

A rage seizes hold of me. Suddenly, Porfyrius is a vessel for every lie and piece of treachery I've confronted in the past weeks. With a furious strength I thought I'd lost for ever, I grab Symmachus's corpse under his armpits and drag him across the gravel. Porfyrius leaps up, horrified.

I drop the body at Porfyrius's feet. 'Symmachus was your friend?'

His whole body is shaking, his head trembling like meat on a knife. I take it as a yes.

'Then for God's sake—yours or mine—tell me what you know.'

I stare at him and he can't meet it. His gaze drops to the ground. Aurelius Symmachus's poisoned eyes look up at him. He whispers something I can't quite catch. It sounds like 'secret'.

'What secret?'

'It's not mine to tell.'

'Was it Symmachus's?'

Porfyrius sinks back on to the stairs, wrapping his arms around his knees. 'It was Alexander's.'

He has my full attention.

'Alexander had been rummaging through the archives for his history. Somewhere, buried in the records office, he found a report that Symmachus wrote thirty years ago. Alexander was going to use it for blackmail.'

'How do you know?'

'You know the Patriarch of Constantinople died a few months ago?'

I remember a conversation with Simeon in the courtyard outside the church of Holy Peace. *Eusebius is one of the obvious men to replace him. Alexander opposed his election.*

'The Patriarch of Constantinople is the most powerful churchman in the empire. Eusebius wants that job with all his soul. Alexander was equally determined to stop him.'

A lot of things are falling into place. 'He found a secret? A secret about Eusebius?'

'Have you heard of a man called Asterius the Sophist?'

I remember the withered old man, his mutilated arms pulled back in his sleeves, staring into a church he was forbidden from entering. 'He was in the library that day, too.'

Porfyrius looks around the peristyle garden. His only audience is a dead man, some dead fish, some long-dead philosophers—and me. Even so, it isn't easy to voice a secret that's been kept so long. His words are barely audible.

273

'During the persecutions, Symmachus had Asterius and Eusebius in his dungeon. Both men were rising talents with reputations for integrity: a lot of Christians looked up to them. The Emperor Diocletian thought that if he could break those two, many others would follow.'

Simeon: *There were a dozen Christians—families, with children—hiding in the cistern below Asterius's house. He betrayed them to the Emperor, who crucified them all.*

'I've heard this story,' I say. 'Asterius broke. Eusebius didn't.'

Porfyrius shakes his head. His chin rests on his collar, as if he's peering into the depths of his soul.

'Eusebius broke. Asterius didn't.'

He mumbles it; at first I think he's just repeated what I said. Then I realise.

'*Eusebius* betrayed those Christians?' He nods. 'Then how—?'

'How did Eusebius end up a bishop, and Asterius forbidden from even entering a church?' He combs his fingers through his hair, leaving a smear of dust. 'They made a bargain with Symmachus that Asterius would take the blame.'

I'm struggling to digest the implications. 'How do you know this?'

'Because Symmachus told me at the time. It amused him—the hypocrisy of it.

'And why didn't he say anything afterwards?'

'Because he was honest, true to his word. And because he thought it didn't matter. The persecution ended not long afterwards, so there was nothing to gain by bringing down Eusebius. And when Constantine took power, attacking Eusebius became a dangerous proposition.'

I think through the implications, trying to draw the thread that connects Porfyrius's story to the corpse at my feet.

'Why did Alexander hate Eusebius so much? You said he didn't want to be Patriarch himself.'

Porfyrius gives me a pitying look. 'You really don't know anything about Christians, do you?'

'I never claimed to.'

'There are two factions. They have various names for each other, but the easiest way to describe them is as Arians and Orthodox. The Arians follow the doctrine of a priest called Arius, that Christ the Son of God was created out of nothing by the Father. The Orthodox maintain that to be fully God, Christ must be the same eternal substance as his Father.

My gaze drifts on to Symmachus's outstretched corpse. Rigor mortis has begun to set in, the body arching back as if in untold agonies. I wonder what difference these impenetrable theological quibbles make where he is now.

'I've heard all this before. I thought the argument was settled at Constantine's conference in Nicaea twelve years ago.'

Eusebius: *You were at Nicaea. Standing in the shadows, listening to what we said with one hand on your sword. We used to call you Brutus. Did you know that?*

Porfyrius plucks a rose and starts pulling the petals off it. 'The argument was never settled. Constantine brokered a compromise, but almost before they'd left Nicaea they were at each other's throats again. Eusebius was exiled, for a time.' He sighs. 'It's not about theology any more. I doubt half the people who claim to be Arian or Orthodox could explain the intricacies of the godhead. People took sides, and what matters now is whether they're winning.'

'Eusebius is an Arian?' I think I know this, but it's been twelve years. Porfyrius confirms it.

'*The* Arian. He adopted it as his cause, and Asterius the Sophist became his key lieutenant. Poor Arius the priest had to play second fiddle in his own heresy. Alexander, meanwhile, was one of the leading thinkers of the Orthodox party. The contest to fill the Patriarchy of Constantinople was the latest battle in their war.'

I think back to that night in the palace. Eusebius, the chief prosecutor—and his rage when Symmachus mentioned Asterius. No wonder, if he thought Symmachus might reveal the truth.

I try to form a narrative.

'Alexander found the evidence that Eusebius betrayed the Church in the persecutions. He summoned Eusebius to the library to confront him, to force him to withdraw from the election to the Patriarchate. He brought Symmachus to the library, too, to confirm the story. Eusebius had every reason for wanting them both dead—the two men who could prove he betrayed the Church.'

They murdered their own god—what wouldn't they do to keep their privileges?

'Eusebius wasn't in the library that day,' Porfyrius points out. 'He didn't make it.'

'Asterius did.'

But even saying it, I know that can't be right. Asterius didn't crush Alexander's skull with no hands.

A hammering on the gate erupts into the silent garden; impatient voices shout from the street. I think I recognise the sergeant's voice from the docks. It's long past the end of his shift now. Porfyrius leaps up in panic.

'Stay,' I tell him. 'Let them in.'

'And Symmachus? What shall I tell them about him?'

'Tell them it was suicide.' I hurry across to the side door. 'It's all they're going to want to hear anyway.'

XXXI

Belgrade, Serbia—Present Day

The hotel was on the top floor of an apartment block in the old town, south of the main boulevard Knez Mihailova. The streets were tangled and characterful, the apartment block—imposed on it by Tito's planners—square and concrete. Drop cloths shrouded the front hall like cobwebs, though there was no evidence in the peeling paint that the workmen had done anything.

A clanking lift took them up to a brown corridor on the sixth floor. Reception was a small cubbyhole in the wall halfway along, where a mustachioed man sat behind an iron grille watching TV. He gave them a key and pointed further down the corridor.

'Last room.'

The best that could be said was that it had a view—across the river, through the rain, where the high-rise towers of Novi Belgrad made dappled pillars of light. It looked like another world. Michael locked the door and put a chair against it; Abby threw herself down on the bed and burrowed her head into the pillow.

Michael sat down on the bed beside her. He moved to stroke her shoulder, then thought better of it.

'I'm sorry,' he murmured.

'What are we going to do?'

'What can we do?'

'I don't trust Giacomo.'

'I don't trust him either. But—he's the best we've got.' He rolled on to his back and lit a cigarette. 'This world we're in, we have to deal with people like him. You're not in the Hague any more.'

'You think I don't know that?' She lifted herself on her elbows so he could see her anger. 'I've dealt with some of the worst murderers on the planet—men who make Giacomo and even Dragović look like wallflowers.'

'I know—'

'You *don't* know.' All the anger, all the terror of the last few days, was rushing out of her in a torrent. 'You know why it was possible? Why a nobody like me could stand face to face with these monsters—no gun, no guards—and walk away alive?'

'Because you've got guts.'

'Because we have rules and institutions and laws to deal with these people. Now we're no better than they are.'

Michael jerked his hand out the window. 'Look where we are—*and this also has been one of the dark places of the Earth.* You think rules and institutions and laws made any difference here, when Milošević was waging war against all and sundry?'

'Milošević ended up in a jail cell in the Hague.'

'After he'd killed 140,000 people. And after NATO finally grew some balls and bombed him to hell. And what happened back in that valley in Kosovo? The Americans had Dragović right in their sights, and all they could do was watch him drive over the border, because that's what the rules say. Is that good enough?'

'It has to be,' Abby insisted. 'Remember what you said about barbarians? About patrolling the frontiers of civilisation so that good people can sleep safely? Following the rules is what lets us draw the line.'

Michael reached out to touch her, but she jerked away. Tears threatened; she didn't want to give him the satisfaction.

Michael swung himself off the bed. He stared into the mirror, as if looking for someone.

'So what are we going to do?' she asked again. Her voice sounded dead.

'Knowledge lies within you,' Michael murmured. 'The only clue we've got is the poem. Dragović thinks so, too—otherwise he wouldn't have stolen the copy from the Forum Museum.'

Abby thought about it. It didn't make her wounds go away, but at least it took her mind off the pain.

'The version on the gravestone in Rome only had two lines. The one Gruber deciphered from the scroll had four.'

She took out the paper Gruber had given her, wrinkled and creased from too long in a damp pocket. Michael studied it. 'Still not much to go on.'

Behind the flimsy curtains, rain drummed on the windows. Abby thought back to another wet day in another city on the fringe of the old Roman empire. *I have analysed the first few lines.*

'What if there's more?' she said. 'Gruber hadn't

279

finished analysing the scroll—he'd barely begun. There might be more of the poem.'

A light went on in Michael's eyes. He spun around.

'Wait here.'

He pulled on his coat and headed to the door.

'Where are you going?'

'To make a phone call.' He wagged his finger at her. 'Don't open the door to strangers.'

She was alone for twelve minutes, and each one felt like a year. The room was heated by a cast-iron radiator that banged and popped as if it were haunted. Every noise it made shocked her like a gunshot. She found herself staring at the door, her heart racing, breath held in anticipation. She waited for a knock, for the handle to turn. When Michael came back, she almost fainted in relief.

His face was triumphant.

'Dr Gruber will be flying to Belgrade first thing tomorrow. He'll bring us his copy of the scroll, and the words he's managed to decipher so far.'

'Did he say there was more? Of the poem?'

'He hinted.'

'Couldn't he just have read it over the phone?'

Michael gave a wolfish grin. 'He could. But then he wouldn't have been sure to collect the hundred thousand euros he thinks are coming his way.'

*　　*　　*

It felt like the longest night of Abby's life. She lay under the covers, too frightened even to undress. The whole city seemed to be made of endlessly colliding parts: the heating pipes and radiator, the lift mechanism, the cars and trams on the street

280

below. Once, she heard what sounded like shots in the distance, though it might have been an engine backfiring. She wasted half an hour waiting to hear it again—in her career, she'd got pretty good at knowing the sound of gunfire—but it didn't come back.

It didn't seem to bother Michael. He slept through, snoring quietly. In the end, she unplugged the clock radio from the bedside table and took it into the bathroom, trying to drown out the night with soft rock. Red numbers flashed the time at her, taunting her efforts to get to sleep. Eventually, slumped in the bathtub with a pillow behind her head and a rough blanket thrown over her, she slept.

*　　　*　　　*

She woke with a cricked neck and a headache. Michael stood in the bathroom door wearing nothing but his boxer shorts.

'I thought you'd gone.' Perhaps he hadn't slept as well as she'd thought. His eyes were bloodshot, the hair on his cheeks too long to be stubble and too thin for a beard. The lines around his eyes didn't look wise, but tired.

'I couldn't sleep.'

'Sign of a guilty conscience.' He forced a smile, so she'd know it was a joke. 'I'm starving.'

Giacomo's room rate didn't include breakfast. They went to a café across the road and ordered omelettes and coffee. The legacy of the Ottoman Empire meant that at least they brewed it strong.

'Do you actually have a hundred thousand euros?'

Michael sliced apart his omelette. 'We'll cross that bridge.'

'What time is Gruber due in?'

'Lunchtime. I said we'd meet him at the castle.'

'How Kafkaesque.'

She chewed her food in silence. Michael signalled the waiter for more coffee.

'There might be something more,' she tried at last. 'When Giacomo said the answer was within us, he didn't know there was any more of the poem. What if there's a clue in the text we have?'

Michael took the crumpled paper and smoothed it on the table. He read the English translation first, then tried the Latin, mouthing words under his breath.

'All Greek to me,' he said at last.

'It's Latin,' she reminded him. 'I thought you said you could read it.'

'I failed my O level.'

'Then let's find someone who can.'

*   *   *

Studentski Trg—Student Square—stood at the end of Belgrade's main promontory, near the citadel, a football pitch's worth of grass and trees, surrounded by the usual local mix of neoclassical and paleo-socialist buildings that made up Belgrade University. Statues dotted the park—once devoted to heroes of Communism, now torn down and replaced with safer figures from a less contested past. At one stage there had been plans to make it part of a green artery of parks through the heart of the city. Now it mostly served as a bus terminus.

They found the Faculty of Classics and

282

Philosophy in a handsome pink and grey building on the south side of the square. Five minutes in an Internet café had given them a name; that, plus Michael's charm and Abby's Serbo-Croat talked them past the porter, up a flight of stairs and into a small office. Files bursting with papers were crammed on to a row of steel shelves; on a facing wall, a tattered map showed the Roman Empire at its height. A green terracotta bust poked out from the pot plants on the windowsill: a round-faced man with a turned-out chin and flat cheeks, and eyes that seemed to be staring at a point just above your head. There was a tension in the face, every muscle clenched in the exercise of power.

The owner of the office—Dr Adrian Nikolić—was an altogether milder proposition: medium build, with a brown beard and brown curly hair and brown eyes that seemed inclined to smile. He wore a Pringle sweater over a check shirt, and brown corduroy trousers with lace-up boots.

'Thank you for agreeing to see us,' Abby said, in Serbian.

He nodded, pleased she spoke the language. In a small country with a bad reputation, it made a difference. She saw him take in the bruises on her face, but he didn't comment.

'I did not know I had such international fame. Perhaps I should ask for a rise.' He spun slowly in his chair, gesturing them to sit on the threadbare couch opposite. 'I have a class in fifteen minutes. Until then, how can I help?'

Abby handed him the battered paper with the poem and the translation. 'We found this, um, unexpectedly.'

'Found it?'

'It's complicated.'

He nodded. 'This is the Balkans. Things are found, things go missing. We learn not to ask questions.'

He took a pair of tortoiseshell glasses from his desk drawer and read through the poem.

'Obviously you have translated it. What else do you want for me to tell you?'

'Anything you can think of.'

A dry laugh. 'Anything?'

'The context we found it in, there were suggestions it dated from the reign of Constantine the Great.'

'So you thought of me.' He nodded to the bust on the window. 'You know he was born in Niš? My home town.'

Abby took a deep breath. 'This probably sounds crazy—but we think the poem might point to a lost treasure or artefact. Maybe to do with the reign of Constantine.'

Nikolić looked her dead in the eye, his expression unfathomable.

'You're absolutely right.'

'I am?'

'It does sound crazy. You think this happens in real life, that someone walks into your office with a piece of paper or a map that leads to long lost buried treasure?' He stood. 'I cannot help you.'

Abby and Michael stayed seated.

'The poem's genuine, if that's what you're worried about,' said Michael.

'You have the original?' Michael nodded. 'Maybe if you let me see I can decide myself. And from which institution do you come from, by the way?'

284

'We work for the EU.' Michael flashed his EULEX ID from his wallet. 'I'm with the Customs directorate. We're investigating a ring of art smugglers and this was one of the antiquities we intercepted.'

'We think there might be other treasures,' Abby added. 'All we want to know is if this poem gives any hint of what they might be.'

Still standing, Nikolić picked up the paper and studied it.

'This word—*signum*. Do you know what it means?'

'Sign,' said Michael. ' "The saving sign that lights the path ahead." '

'So. It is an important word in the life of Constantine. Before his great battle at Milvian Bridge, he saw a cross of light in the sky and heard the words *"In hoc signo vinces"*—"In this sign you will conquer." You know what this sign was?'

'The X-P symbol,' said Abby.

'Chi-rho,' Nikolić corrected her. 'The first two letters of the name of Christ in Greek. And, if you think ideogrammatically, the X is the shape of a cross and the P superimposed on it is the man.'

Abby remembered the necklace, now locked in a safe in Whitehall.

'Though, actually, this is not a true Christogram. This one is called a staurogram. From the Greek word *stavros*, meaning "cross".'

'OK.'

'But the original account of this battle of Milvian Bridge was written in Greek. You know the Greek equivalent of *signum*?' They shook their heads. '*Tropaion*. Now this has many meanings, too. It can be a trophy or a war memorial, or the standard that

285

the army carries into battle.'

Another searching glance.

'You know about Constantine's battle standard?'

'The *labarum*,' Abby said. She remembered something Dr Gruber had said at the Landesmuseum in Trier. 'The chi-rho symbol that he saw in his vision. He turned it into a golden standard surrounded by jewels.'

She waited for him to reply. But Nikolić had folded his arms and was staring at her, as if he expected something.

'You wanted to know something from the age of Constantine that is extremely valuable? A treasure of the first historical significance which has been lost for centuries?'

The penny dropped. 'You're saying the poem could refer to the actual *labarum*. The trophy that Constantine's army carried?'

He shrugged. 'Why not?'

'But what happened to it?' Michael asked. 'A treasure like that can't just have got lost—I mean, the Byzantine Empire lasted until almost five hundred years ago. Isn't it in a museum somewhere?'

'You think because something is important people look after it? Even Constantine's tomb, in Istanbul, has not survived. When the Turks conquered Constantinople they destroyed his mausoleum, which was the Church of the Holy Apostles, and built their own mosque on the site.'

He turned to the map on the wall and drew a line with his finger across the Balkans, from the Adriatic to the Black Sea.

'This region has been the frontier for more than two thousand years. Alexander the Great?

286

To the east and south, his empire stretched as far as India and Egypt. But to north and west, it went through Kosovo. The Roman diocese of Moesia—modern Serbia—was tossed back and forth between the eastern and western emperors; when the western empire fell in 476, this city Singidunum—Belgrade—was a fortress looking down on the barbarians across the Danube. Then the Ottomans, the Austro-Hungarians through to the Soviet Union and Yugoslavia. You know one of the reasons we fought Croatia in the nineties? Because they were western Catholics, and we were eastern Orthodox—a legacy of the division of the Byzantine Empire in the eleventh century. A frontier means wars. So yes—things get lost.'

He pulled a book off one of the shelves and flipped through it. 'This is a Byzantine account of Constantine's life, written in the ninth century. After describing the *labarum* and its use at the Milvian Bridge, the author says, "It still exists today, and is kept as the greatest treasure in the imperial palace, for if any enemy or evil force threatens the city, its power will destroy them."'

'So that was'—Michael did the sums—'twelve hundred years ago. Nothing since?'

'Constantinople was sacked in 1204 by the army of the Fourth Crusade. Many of its treasures were lost or hidden; some were brought back to Venice by the crusaders. The Byzantines reconquered the city, but it fell to the Turks for good in 1453. They would have taken whatever was left.'

'So it could be in Venice . . . or Istanbul . . . or hidden somewhere else completely?'

'Venice was looted by Napoleon, Paris by the Nazis, Berlin by the Soviets, and Moscow by anyone with money.' Nikolić gave a sad smile. '*Sic transit gloria mundi*. Or, if you like me to translate as a professional historian: shit happens.'

A bell-tree chime sounded from his computer. 'It is time for my class. I am sorry I cannot help you more.'

They let themselves out on to the street. Trolley buses sat by the kerb, their drivers clustered round the doors smoking. Michael checked his watch.

'Perhaps Gruber can tell us more.'

XXXII

Constantinople—May 337

I hurry down the alley, then up an avenue lined with plane trees. They're only saplings now, but one day they'll shade the whole street. If the city lasts that long. The empire is littered with half-finished cities built to flatter different emperors' vanity. I've seen them all: Thessalonica, Nicomedia, Milan, Aquileia, Sirmium—even Rome is ringed with hippodromes that never staged a race, mausoleums whose occupants were waylaid elsewhere. Will another emperor stand to live in a city named after his predecessor?

My footsteps quicken, driven by the pace of my thoughts. I remember what Constantine told me, the day he dragged me to the palace. *The Christians spit and scratch, but they don't bite.* And I remember Flavius Ursus's parting shot from the far shore of the Bosphorus, waiting for Constantine to die. *Have you wondered why Constantine asked someone who knows nothing about the Christians to investigate the death of a bishop?*

Was Constantine playing me for a fool? Did Eusebius put him up to it? Even if I was going to find out anything, they must have been sure I'd bury it. I've been burying Constantine's problems all my life.

There are two factions. They have various names for each other, but the easiest way to describe them is as Arians and Orthodox. The Arians follow the doctrine of a priest called Arius, that Christ the Son of God was created out of nothing by the Father. The Orthodox maintain that to be fully God, Christ must be the same eternal substance as his Father.

I've heard all this before.

*   *   *

Nicaea—June 325—Twelve years earlier . . .
I never understood the arguments. So far as I know, no one ever asked if Apollo was co-eternal with Diana, or whether Hercules was of the same substance as Jupiter. My brothers and I never sat in our cave enquiring into the nature and persons of Mithra. We made the sacrifices, we performed the rituals the way we were taught. We trusted the gods to know their own business.

But the Christians are different: a nitpicking, hair-splitting, prying bunch who spend endless hours asking unanswerable questions—purely, I think, for those moments of joyous insight when they discover they have something else to argue about. It drives Constantine to distraction. He needs the Christians praying for his continued success, not squabbling over technicalities like lawyers.

'A united empire needs a united religion,' he complains to me one day. 'A divided church is an affront to the One God.'

And an affronted God might decide to look for a new champion.

The Christians can agree that their God has three parts—a father, who is like Jupiter; the son, Christ, he fathered by a mortal woman to do his work on Earth, like Hercules; and a spirit messenger, who I think must be like Mercury. Why these have to be one God, and not three, no one ever explains. But they spend endless hours debating the relationship between them, in the same way that senators speculate about the changing fortunes of the court favourites.

One of these intellectual busybodies is a priest called Arius, from Alexandria. Trying to describe his god, he's said something so outrageous that half the Christians will have no truck with him; the other half have leapt to his defence, and suddenly the Church is at war.

'I've spent twenty years uniting the empire so the Christians can live in peace,' Constantine laments. 'And within a year of my victory, they're trying to tear it apart again.'

What did you expect? I want to say.

In war, Constantine always looks for the decisive battle. So he applies the same logic to the Church: he summons all the contestants to his palace at Nicaea to do battle and declare a winner that everyone will recognise.

'The question is so trivial, it doesn't merit this controversy,' he says hopefully. 'I'm sure we can settle it without fuss.'

*   *   *

The palace stands on the shore of a lake, looking west. Nicaea's a modest town among fertile hills: the great profusion of Christians who've descended from across the empire can barely squeeze inside its walls. There are two hundred and fifty bishops, twice as many priests and presbyters, plus all the servants, attendants, hangers-on and baggage they bring. The only room big enough to hold the council session is the great hall of the palace, where carpenters have erected twin banks of tiered seating. On the opening morning of the council, the bishops take their seats, ranked on either side of the hall like spectators in the hippodrome.

For most of them—especially the eastern bishops who've just come under his rule—it's the first time they've set eyes on Constantine. He dazzles them. When they're all standing, he enters alone wearing a bright purple robe. The silk shimmers like water in the sunlight, while the precious stones sewn into the fabric paint the floor with colour. He walks solemnly down the aisle, head bowed, hands clasped. He mounts the dais at the end, where a gold curule chair, like judges use, is waiting. He turns to face the bishops and motions to the stool.

'With your permission?'

They're so shocked, they almost forget to murmur their assent. An emperor's never asked them for anything. Constantine sits. The bishops sit. Eusebius, who's seated closest to Constantine's right hand, makes a speech thanking God for Constantine's benevolent wisdom. Constantine makes a speech in reply. 'Free yourselves from the shackles of dispute,' he tells them, 'and live in the

291

freedom of the laws of peace. This is what pleases God—and me.'

His eyes sweep the room to make sure they understand. Two hundred and fifty heads humbly bow.

*   *   *

But two weeks later, they still haven't bent. To Constantine's surprise, it turns out that Christians are just as devious as anyone else. Bringing them together in the palace hasn't concentrated their minds on divine unity: it's concentrated their poison and their scheming. Nothing's achieved.

We meet in Constantine's bedchamber at sunset. Outside the window, lake waves lap against the foot of the wall. The bishops are at one of their interminable services—the only time we can be sure no one's listening. Even the palace slaves have been dismissed. It's just Crispus and me—the only two men he can trust.

Constantine bursts through the door. He always pushes too hard, I've noticed—he's not used to having to open a door himself. A secretary scurries in behind him, carrying a pile of scrolls stacked up like firewood in his arms.

'Put them there.' Constantine points to a bed next to me. The secretary dumps them, bows and retreats. Constantine unrolls one, moving his lips as he tries to read it. I wonder if the Christians write in Greek deliberately, a delicate humiliation.

'"From the church at Alexandria, to the Lord Constantine, Augustus, Caesar, etc., etc. Whereas it is alleged that Eustathius, Bishop of Antioch, consorts with prostitutes and immoral women,

292

we earnestly implore you to nullify his election so that a righteous and godly man may be appointed . . ."' He tosses the paper back on to the pile. 'And somewhere in here, you can be sure there'll be a petition from the Bishop of Antioch's friends, urging me to disregard the lies being spread about him and punish his oppressors.'

He pushes them across the bed towards me. Some slide on to the floor.

'Take them, Gaius.'

'What shall I do?'

'Burn the lot of them.'

I move to pick them up, but Constantine waves me back. 'Not now. Wait until the bishops are out of church—and do it somewhere you'll be seen. I want them to know they're wasting their time.'

He throws himself down on the bed. 'What do I have to do to get these bishops to agree?'

I keep quiet. None of my ideas are what Constantine would call constructive, and he's in a foul mood. In a couple of weeks, it'll be the launch of his *vicennalia*—the twentieth year of his reign. There'll be feasts, parades, celebrations. Later in the year, we'll go to Rome for the first time since we defeated Maxentius. He's desperate to finish the council by then.

Crispus crosses to the window and peers out at the lake. Sunset's amber light streams in, bathing his face like flame. He's twenty-five now and at the height of his powers: a more measured, confident version of his father. At the same age, Constantine still lived at a despot's whim, going to bed every night not knowing if he'd wake up. Like a man who's survived a famine, in his heart he can't let go of the fear he'll go hungry again one day. By

293

contrast, all Crispus has ever known is success.

'It's Eusebius,' he says. 'He won't challenge you openly, but he's totally opposed to any compromise. And he knows every way there is to string out the debate so that nothing gets decided.'

'He's always very supportive when I speak to him.'

'He survived as Bishop of Nicomedia—Licinius's capital—for seven years while Licinius reigned. He's a snake who can worm his way into any hole to keep warm.'

It's a dangerous throw for Crispus—dangerous to mention Licinius just now. After his defeat at Chrysopolis, Licinius went into exile at Thessalonica with his wife Constantiana and their nine-year-old son. Two months ago rumours reached us that Licinius was conspiring with certain senators to escape to Rome, declare himself Emperor and launch a general massacre of all Christians in the empire. Repeating it now, it sounds far-fetched—but even rumours can become self-fulfilling. And Licinius had exhausted his credit with Constantine.

I was sent to Thessalonica to take care of it. Breathless gossip says that I slit Licinius's throat, then butchered the son while his mother watched. It's only half-true—the garrison commander killed the son after I'd gone, and paid for his over-zealousness later—but half-truths have a knack of spreading that the truth would envy.

'Eusebius is the one you need to win round,' Crispus insists. 'If he breaks, enough of his faction will follow that you can declare victory. Think of your battles,' he urges his father. 'Sometimes you can win the war by outmanoeuvring your opponent.

But other times, like at Chrysopolis, a direct charge is the best tactic.'

'You lose fewer casualties in a war of manoeuvre,' I murmur.

'But your enemy lives to fight another day.'

Constantine silences him. 'I didn't summon the bishops here for a war. I came to make peace. *Peace.*' He springs off the bed, takes three strides across the room and turns. 'Am I the only man in the world who wants that?'

'We all want it.'

'Then don't talk as if we're fighting a war. *Manoeuvres, attacks, battles*—they're metaphors. No one's dying. At the end of this all the combatants will get up and go about their business as they did before. That doesn't happen on a battlefield.'

He slams his fist on an ivory side table. An oil lamp is laid too close to the edge: it shakes loose and smashes. Oil leaks across the floor.

'What do you want me to do?' he asks Crispus. 'Call out the cavalry to trample the bishops under their hooves? Put out the Christians' eyes and burn them with hot irons until they agree to my way of thinking, like my predecessors did? Shall I march my army around the world and raze every village that believes differently to me?'

'I didn't mean—'

'Because that would be so easy. Anyone can wield a sword.' He stares down Crispus with a father's authority. 'Valerius and I were knocking sticks together when we were five years old, and all that's changed since then is that the blades have got sharper. But if we rely on that, the empire will never be at peace.'

He rubs his foot in the pool of oil, swirling

295

patterns across the floor.

'Why did Diocletian divide the empire? Because he needed more commanders to fight his wars. And do you know what? The more men he set to fighting, the more fighting there was. We've ended that. One man, one peace, one God. But unless we find new ways of settling our quarrels, of binding this empire together without swords, it'll all fall apart. That's what the Christian God offers.'

'That's what you offer,' I say.

'It's the work of generations.' He turns in front of the window and spreads his arms wide. 'I am what I am—imperfect, hard to change. I haven't touched my sword since the day we beat Licinius, almost nine months now, but by God it's difficult. You know the Christian story of the prophet Moses?'

'He led his people out of slavery in Egypt,' says Crispus, for my benefit.

'But he never reached the Promised Land. That was left to his successor . . .' Constantine pinches his brow, trying to remember.

'Joshua.' Crispus supplies the name, but he's not really thinking about it. He's staring at his father. Something profound has just happened—a flash of truth, a shift in understanding. One day, historians will say that Crispus succeeded Constantine as sole Augustus of the empire: their words were written in this moment.

That was left to his successor.

Successor—not *successors*. Constantine's never mentioned succession before. Fausta's pestered him for years, desperate to find out what's in store for her three sons, but even she's learned not to raise the subject. From the shocked, delighted look on his face, it's obvious Crispus was just as hungry

296

to know. And now he does.

Constantine smiles at his son—a complicit smile full of promise. A burden's lifted from both of them. I feel as if I'm intruding.

'We'll remake the empire in God's image,' Constantine says. 'A new world of peace. But nothing will change if we don't *persuade* men to change.'

Crispus nods, still dazed.

'And if the Church can't agree, what hope is there for anyone else?'

No hope at all, I think. My mind's back in Thessalonica, watching blood flow across the red marble, while Constantiana's screams shake the palace. That's how you keep the peace. I wish they'd spared the boy.

Constantine sits down on the edge of the bed. Crispus perches next to him.

'Now—how do we persuade the Arians to moderate their views?'

Crispus shakes his head. 'You'll never persuade Arius. If it were just him, maybe—but now his ideas have been endorsed by powerful patrons, he can't back down. He'd humiliate Eusebius.'

'These questions about the Trinity are so obscure, so trivial, they should never even be asked.' Constantine looks genuinely vexed. 'And if they were, everyone should have the good sense not to answer.'

'You can't unask the question. So you need to provide an answer.' Crispus reaches in the folds of his tunic and pulls out a small, scrolled piece of paper. Constantine groans.

'Another petition?'

'Alexander of Cyrene—my old tutor—you

remember him? He's composed a creed.'

A creed is the sort of document that Christians love: an inventory of the attributes of their God. Finding one that all the bishops can put their names to has become the chief goal of the council.

Constantine reads it through. Even high in the etherea of Christian doctrine, he has an extraordinary ability to extract the crucial point.

'This phrase—"Christ is begotten of God, not made"—that's what Arius will object to?'

'If God made Christ, then Christ would be something other than God. But if He's begotten from his father, then they exist from the same substance, so Christ must have existed for as long as God has.'

'So the father and the son are the same substance.' I can see the idea taking root in Constantine's mind. A certain amount of discussion follows, which I take no notice of. All that matters is the conclusion.

'You have to give them a lead.' Crispus points to the pile of forgotten petitions still scattered on the bed. 'Why do you think they give you those?'

'To frustrate me?'

'Because they need a judge.'

*   *   *

Next morning Constantine summons a full session of the council in the great hall of the palace. The bishops line up in their long, white rows, standing until Constantine's taken his golden seat. A dozen hands wave in the air to be noticed. Constantine looks them over, then points to Crispus's old tutor.

'The council recognises Alexander of Cyrene.'

298

The old man—stout, stern-faced, his dark beard halfway to white—stands and begins to speak. The words mean nothing to me, but I still remember how it begins.

'We believe in one God . . .'

Eusebius is on his feet the moment Alexander finishes, but Constantine doesn't call on him. He surveys the assembled bishops with a mild gaze.

'This sounds very reasonable to me,' he remarks. 'Nearly identical to my own beliefs. In fact, if you added something to be clear that the Son is made of the same substance as the Father . . .'

'*Homoousios*'—his translator supplies the Greek word.

'. . . then who could possibly argue with it?'

His eyes sweep the room, and come to rest on Eusebius, still standing, waiting to be recognised.

'Bishop?'

Eusebius licks his lips and clears his throat. His hand tugs at a stray thread in his robe, winding it around his fat finger until the tip goes red.

'I—'

He's defeated. He can call Constantine a heretic, or he can accept the compromise. Suicide or surrender.

He spreads his arms wide. 'Who could possibly argue with this?'

Constantine smiles, delighted. The rest of the bishops—most of them—stamp their feet and applaud. Eusebius's smile lasts exactly as long as it takes for Constantine's gaze to move off him.

Looking back now, I'm surprised I remember it so clearly. I haven't thought about it often since. What happened so soon afterwards drove it out of my mind and changed everything. This is the broken stub of a story that never happened. It doesn't fit.

You can say that fathers and sons are the same substance. You can write it in a creed subscribed by two hundred and forty-seven eminent Christians (Arius and two other zealots refused and went into exile). That doesn't make it true.

The father creates the son. They're not the same.

XXXIII

Belgrade, Serbia—Present Day
This city Singidunum—Belgrade—was a fortress looking down on the barbarians across the Danube, Nikolić had said. The fortress was still there, now called the Kalemegdan Citadel. Over time the Roman foundations had been built on by medieval Serbs, Ottoman Turks and Austro-Hungarians: almost two thousand years of fortification. A reproduction red banner hung from a lamp post, emblazoned with a golden lion and the words *Leg IIII Flavia Felix*, in honour of the 'lucky' fourth legion who'd originally built the fort. Seeing it there was a shock. Abby remembered peering through the magnifier in Shai Levin's lab, seeing the same lion and the same inscription on the dead man's belt buckle.

Was he here? Am I following him?

Now the castle was a park, a leafy enclave where paths wound through the old fortifications, sprawled over the end of the promontory where the Sava and the Danube met. In summer it was a popular destination for tourists and locals alike.

300

This late in the autumn it was usually reserved for a few dog-walkers and joggers—but today seemed to be an exception. Metal barriers cordoned off a route along one of the lower paths; athletic men with numbers pinned to their chests milled about, waiting for some kind of race to begin. A few hardy spectators lined the barricades. A lone ice-cream vendor stood by his cart near the entrance, reading a magazine.

A plastic panel gave a map of the citadel, and a brief history. 'Kalemegdan means "Battleground Fortress",' Michael read. 'Looks peaceful enough today.' He studied the map. 'Gruber said he'd meet us by the Victory Monument.'

They followed a stony path around the edge of the summit to the very tip of the promontory, where a brick terrace thrust out high above the Sava. A white column stood on it, supporting a copper-green god striding forward into the air: twenty feet tall, naked, with absurdly sculpted muscles and a laurel crown circling his head. Below the terrace, steep bluffs dropped towards the river. A black sign in Serbian and English warned: *Walking in this area you risk your life.*

Gruber hadn't arrived.

'I'll wait by the monument,' Michael told Abby. 'You keep out of sight. Just in case anything goes wrong.'

She stood by the parapet and stared down at the two rivers. Even in this city of a million and half inhabitants, she could feel the wilderness. Look one way and you saw the concrete high-rises of Novi Belgrad, the traffic crossing the bridges and the rusting derricks of the docks. But look the other way, up the river, and you saw an overwhelming forest, seeming to stretch unbroken eastwards to the horizon. It was easy to imagine a Roman sentry standing there at the end of the world—the river the colour of lead, the sky the colour of smoke—scanning the forest and wondering what might stir from within it.

She shook herself free of the illusion: this wasn't the time for daydreaming. She glanced back at the monument. Michael was standing there, but not alone: he was chatting to a young blonde woman with a pushchair, talking easily and laughing about something. In the distance, the race announcer barked instructions through a loudspeaker.

She shook her head again and tried to keep down the jealousy. Michael was the sort of person others warmed to: in a foreign country, a language he barely spoke, he could still strike up a conversation. Particularly if the other person was young, attractive and female.

Michael leaned over the pushchair and ruffled the child's hair. He said something to the woman; she laughed and pulled back, flapping her arm at him in a mock-scolding gesture. Still laughing, she waved goodbye and started wheeling the pushchair back along the path. Michael looked across the terrace and caught Abby's eye. He shrugged his shoulders and smiled. *Nothing to worry about.*

But someone was coming from around the wall behind him—a tall, thin man in a long black coat, with walnut-brown skin and a bristling black moustache. Gruber. He had a briefcase in one hand and an umbrella in the other. He walked stiffly, ill at ease; he saw Michael and crossed straight to him, not noticing Abby loitering by the parapet.

She watched it in dumbshow. Michael reached

to shake Gruber's hand, smiling broadly; Gruber's hands stayed sunk in his coat pockets. He said something terse. Michael nodded, still smiling. He lifted up the blue zip-up bag they'd bought from a sports shop and patted it, as you would a horse.

Gruber won't dare count that much money in public, Michael had predicted. *He'll have a quick look, see what he's expecting—and find out it's ninety thousand short when it's too late.*

Gruber unzipped the bag and peered inside. The frown on his face deepened. On the far side of the terrace, the ice-cream seller wandered past, looking for customers.

Gruber pointed at the parapet. For a moment, Abby thought he'd seen her. Michael seemed to argue, then put up his hands in a have-it-your-way gesture and followed Gruber across. They stopped a few yards away. Michael rested the bag on the low wall.

A cold wind blew across the Sava, carrying their conversation to Abby.

'It's all there,' Michael said.

'I would like to be sure.'

'And I'd like to be sure you've brought what you promised.' Michael kept his hand on the bag.

Gruber unbuttoned his coat and reached inside. Abby turned and leaned against the parapet, her back to the river, as if studying the citadel walls. By the gate, the child in the pushchair had unbuckled herself and run across to the ice-cream seller. Her mother hurried after her. In the distance, Abby heard shouts and the blast of air-horns. The race must have started.

Gruber pulled out a plastic wallet with a few sheets of paper inside. 'I would not have come if I did not have it. A reconstruction of the text, and my own transcription.'

'Anything interesting?'

'I would say so.' He put a hand on the bag. '*If everything is in order.*'

Michael stepped back. 'Be my guest.'

He glanced along the wall and met Abby's gaze. He gave a small nod.

They hadn't planned for this. *Was he expecting her to mug Gruber in broad daylight?* She began moving towards them. Concentrating on trying to peel apart the wad of euros in the bag without being noticed, Gruber didn't see her. The folder had disappeared back inside his coat.

Gruber's head snapped up. 'You said a hundred thousand euros. This is not enough.'

'You'll get the rest when we've verified the document.' Michael was speaking quickly, improvising. 'We have to know that what's in there is worth it.' His eyes darted over Gruber's shoulder and motioned Abby forward. *Come on.* She took another step.

A child's scream cut the chilly air. Abby, Gruber and Michael all whipped around. The ice-cream seller had stopped halfway across the terrace, the steel lid of his cart raised as if to serve the girl from the pushchair. A long-nosed black pistol had appeared in his hand.

Instinct took over; Abby threw herself to the ground, just before the shot rang out. The terrace became a cauldron of frantic screams and chaotic footsteps. She peered up, and saw the ice-cream man running towards the bag on the parapet.

Michael and Gruber had vanished.

The gunman ran to the wall and ripped open the

bag. He glanced inside, then threw it on the ground and peered down over the edge. He raised his pistol, aiming for something at the foot of the wall.

That's where Michael went. There was nowhere else. Without thinking, Abby lifted herself up and launched herself at the gunman. He had one eye closed and the other trained on his target: he didn't see her. Not knowing what else to do, she put out her arms and barged into him.

Agony exploded through the wound in her shoulder, worse than being shot because this time she felt every shred of pain. The man buckled under the impact, but didn't go down. Abby wrapped her arms around his legs and clung on, rolling and writhing as he tried to shake her off. Then something struck her hard on the head. Pain flashed through her skull and she let go.

The ice-cream man kicked her away and looked back over the wall. He raised his gun again—but didn't fire. From down below, she could hear shouts and motion.

Trying to keep low, crying with the pain in her side, she hauled herself just high enough to peer over the parapet. Thirty-odd men in singlets and shorts were running along the path at the foot of the wall, egged on by a handful of spectators. One or two glanced up at the commotion on the terrace above; most kept their eyes on the ground.

The wall was too high for Michael to have jumped—but there was scaffolding against it where masons had been repairing the ancient brickwork. Plastic sheeting flapped from the poles, sheltering anyone working inside.

The leading racers had just passed the bottom of the scaffolding. As the rest came level, a flap of plastic billowed out. Michael and Gruber ran out from the scaffold tower and plunged in among the athletes. There were shouts, a couple of angry shoves, but Michael and Gruber sprinted along, staying within the pack. The gunman followed them with his pistol, but two moving targets in a sea of people, jostling and overtaking all the time, were too difficult. He didn't risk it.

The terrace had emptied—Abby and the gunman were the only ones left. He glanced down at her; she rolled herself in a ball and prayed he didn't know who she was.

He hesitated. More shouts echoed across the terrace, and these were different: not panicked or confused, but threatening and authoritative. Abby peered through her fingers.

A soldier in combat fatigues was standing on the wall of the citadel, aiming a rifle at the ice-cream seller. A second soldier had come out of the gate and was advancing, rifle at his shoulder. For a confused second, Abby wondered if another war had begun; or if the ancient legionaries who'd guarded this spot had been reincarnated in modern dress. Then she remembered the military museum inside the citadel. The guards must have heard the shots.

The gunman threw his pistol over the wall and raised his arms. He looked calm, almost resigned—a man for whom this had happened before, would probably happen again. He stood still. But his mouth was moving, rapid-fire muttering apparently to himself. Looking closer, Abby saw a silver earpiece with a small microphone clipped on his ear.

He's on the phone. He could have been talking to

anyone around the world, but Abby guessed it was a whole lot closer than that. She began to crawl away. She had to find Michael and warn him.

The soldiers saw her moving and paused. 'Stay down!' they shouted, first in Serbian and then, in English, '*Down!*' She didn't listen to them. She didn't think they'd shoot a civilian, particularly one who might be a tourist. She scrambled to her feet and started to move. Every step sent more jolts of pain into her shoulder; she wanted to run, but could only stagger like a drunk. Shouts rang after her, but nothing more. The guards were too preoccupied with the gunman.

She came around the corner of a brick defile and left the terrace behind. Police sirens wailed in the distance. She limped along a paved road through the trees, searching for Michael and Gruber. The shots had sparked chaos. Dozens of people were running through the woods, strung out like peasants fleeing an advancing army.

She'd barely gone a hundred yards when she heard fresh shouts behind her. Two more soldiers had appeared. Were they looking for her? They must have opened the bag, seen the money inside and decided maybe she wasn't as much a victim as she'd seemed. She pulled off her coat and stuffed it in a bin by a tree, hoping the colour change would be enough. *Where was Michael?*

The shouts suddenly changed, became more urgent: not looking for someone, but finding them. She risked a glance back. One of the soldiers was standing up against a tree, gun held against his body like something out of a war movie. The other had dropped to one knee and was squinting down the rifle sight.

307

Abby followed the line of the gun. Fifty yards away a dark-haired woman in a red windcheater was facing the soldier, arms raised, face white with terror. She looked about Abby's age.

They've got the wrong girl.

She felt sorry for her double—but the soldiers would find out their mistake soon enough. She turned her back and walked away, passing through the old Ottoman gate, jostling with the panicked crowds. Ahead, she thought she saw two men— one in a green anorak, the other in a long black coat. She forced herself to lengthen her stride, swallowing the pain that twisted like a knife in her shoulder.

'Michael!' she called.

Michael and Gruber stopped and turned. Michael gave an unobtrusive nod; Gruber looked as if he was going to be sick.

Ten paces ahead of her, a man in a New York Mets baseball cap stopped as well. He had a fat camera bag around his neck, unzipped as if he'd been interrupted in the middle of taking a photograph.

Too late, Abby noticed the silver Bluetooth headset clipped on his ear.

The man pulled a small pistol from the camera bag. He raised it, aimed towards Michael and fired.

XXXIV

Constantinople—May 337

I've arrived at the Church of Holy Peace. Constantine's words at Nicaea are still echoing in my ears.

Am I the only man in the world who wants peace?

You were, I think, *and the world didn't want it.* Last week a thousand soldiers marched past this church on their way to the Persian war. There hasn't been a year in the last decade when Constantine hasn't led his army on campaign, accumulating victory titles faster than the masons can recut the inscriptions on his monuments. If I were a younger man, with clearer views, I'd despise him for the hypocrisy. But all I feel is pity.

Even early in the morning, the church is busy. Paupers queue at a side door, where two women are doling out bread and milk. Serious young men with new-grown beards walk in twos and threes across the courtyard, clutching sheaves of paper. A group of children sit under a plane tree with writing tablets, taking instruction from a stern priest. It's like its own village.

A priest is standing by the church door, greeting people as they enter. He sees me approach and offers a warm smile.

'Peace be with you.'

All I can think of is Symmachus, slumped by his fishpond. 'I want to see Eusebius.'

The smile doesn't falter. 'The Bishop left this morning for his home in Nicomedia. His work here was finished.'

'Of course.'

'You look tired, brother. Will you come and break bread with us?'

He's still smiling, still solicitous.

'Is it true,' I ask him, 'that part of your ritual is drinking blood?'

'We share in the blood of Christ.'

'I hope you drown in it.'

I wait just long enough to enjoy the look on his face, then spin on my heel and walk away. I'm halfway across the courtyard when I hear a voice calling my name.

'Gaius Valerius?'

It's Simeon the deacon, hurrying across the square. He looks well rested, pleased to see me. Not as if he murdered someone last night.

'I've been meaning to find you,' he says.

'I could say the same.'

'I'd like to get Alexander's books back. Someone should finish his history.'

The *Chronicon*—the true compendium of all the history of the world, illuminating the pattern of God's purpose. Except it was a myth, a benevolent past that never existed.

'I went to the docks this morning to see Aurelius Symmachus on to his ship,' I say. 'He didn't come.'

Simeon's surprise seems entirely natural. 'Did something happen?'

I'm still waiting for him to betray himself. But there's nothing—only a mirror reflecting my curiosity back at me.

'Don't you know?'

Exasperation hardens his face. If he does know, he won't give it away.

'Aurelius Symmachus died last night.'

His reaction is exactly what you'd expect. Eyes wide, mouth open—a picture of surprise. Maybe a hint of satisfaction—but perhaps I'm looking for it.

'I'm sorry,' he says.

'I thought you'd want him dead.'

'I prayed for him. Christ came into the world to save sinners.'

It's a strange thing to say. I'd dismiss it completely, if I didn't remember Porfyrius saying something similar about Alexander—how he never bore a grudge for Porfyrius's role in the persecutions.

But I don't have time for his pieties. If he's saying prayers for Symmachus, he's more likely giving thanks that the old man took the blame for Alexander's murder. I look up at the high church behind him. Scaffolding sticks out of the roof like birds' nests; workmen crawl over the dome, applying gold leaf. I remember the crowds who gathered herc whcn Eusebius came to preach the day after Alexander's murder.

'Are you working here now?'

A nod. 'Bishop Eusebius found me a position here before he left for Nicomedia.'

'A promotion?'

Another guess—and right again. Simeon can see the drift of my questions and is starting to look uncomfortable.

'You've done well out of Alexander's death.'

'If you want to be malicious.'

'Didn't it feel wrong?' I push him. 'Taking the patronage of your dead master's enemy?'

'Alexander and Eusebius had a quarrel that went back to Nicaea. It was none of my business.'

'Alexander was going to stop Eusebius becoming

Patriarch of Constantinople.'

'It's a free vote among the clergy, and he was one voice.' Simeon shakes his head in frustration, wanting me to understand. 'It's not like your world. We argue and debate, but with humility. We don't have to obliterate our opponents to win. God is the only judge we recognise.'

We don't have to obliterate our opponents. Was that aimed at me? He's so young, so earnest, I could almost believe he doesn't know my past.

I stick to my line. 'Alexander did get obliterated,' I point out. 'It could hardly have been more convenient for Eusebius—the last obstacle removed from his path. He won.'

'You're seeing patterns where they don't exist.'

'Am I? Researching his history, Alexander dug deep. There was plenty of scandalous material in that document case. Some of it concerned Eusebius.'

'He never let me see what was in it.'

I step closer. 'You were at the library with Alexander—probably the last man to see him alive. Then I found you at his ransacked apartment, looking through his papers. You brought the message from Symmachus's slave that set up the meeting where he handed over the case, and you were there to make sure he was caught.'

He isn't afraid—I'll give him that. He's looking at me as if I'm mad: as if the only person I'm condemning by carrying on is myself.

'Symmachus had the documents,' he reminds me.

'You were spying for Eusebius all along. When he realised what Alexander knew, he had you kill the old man in the library. You used the bust of Hierocles to make it look as if Symmachus had done it, and when that wasn't enough, you gave his slave the document case and arranged the meeting to set him up. And when even that wouldn't do, you broke into his house and faked his suicide.'

There's a strange look on his face, but it isn't guilt or fear or even anger. He's preternaturally calm. I think he's pitying me.

'I had the key to Alexander's apartment,' he points out. 'If—as you say—Eusebius wanted me to get rid of Alexander, why would I do it so violently in a public place? Why would I go to such elaborate lengths to provide a scapegoat? Why not just go into his room one night and kill him there? Especially if I'm so adept at faking a suicide?'

Give the Christians credit: they know how to argue. Was he always like this? He seems different from before—stronger, more confident. I remember the first time I saw him, glowing with anger, dripping sparks at every prod. Now the steel's been quenched cold.

His answers are so ready it's easy to believe he's prepared them in advance. Or maybe the story I'm trying to weave is so threadbare it's easy to poke holes.

And then there's Porfyrius's question. Why draw attention to Symmachus by killing him? Why not just let the old man go into exile?

A great weariness overwhelms me. I feel faint; I start to sway. Simeon grabs my arm and tries to guide me to a bench, but I shake him off. He stands back, eyes shining.

'The Augustus knew that a Christian couldn't have done it. That's why he asked you to investigate. He knew it was an adept of the old religion who had done this.'

313

Sharp anger cuts through the daze. 'I'm sick of being told a Christian couldn't have done it. All you ever do is fight each other.'

'You don't know anything about Christians.'

'Do you remember the Council of Nicaea?'

He shrugs. 'I was twelve years old.'

'I was there. Two hundred and fifty bishops brought together, and all they could do was quarrel.'

'Of course they argued. We argue all the time; we can't help ourselves. But only because it matters so much to us.' He starts two sentences, breaks off, recomposes himself and tries again.

'Have you ever loved someone?'

It's the last thing I expect him to say. But he wasn't trying to be cruel. His face is open: he meant it honestly, trying to tap a common root we must both share. At his age, he can't imagine it's possible to live without passion.

What do I say? Do I tell him about the women I've had? That I married late, badly and briefly, when it became clear I'd never marry into the imperial family? That's not what he's asking about. The true answer is: *yes, I've loved.* And look what it's done to me.

'I've loved.'

He nods, pleased. 'And when you love someone, you want to find out every detail of their existence. You want to know every thought, every feeling, because the more you know them the more you love them.'

I don't understand. 'Are you talking about your God?'

'We argue because we want to know Him. Because we love Him.'

314

'How can you love a god?' Gods are terrible and dangerous, capricious as fire. Constantine's enjoyed their favour more than any man, but even he's never shaken off the terror of losing it.

Simeon leans forward. 'All your life you've been walking in darkness—and in the dark, the world is a frightening place. But Christ came to bring light. He tore down the curtain and let us see the light of God's love. Do you know what Saint John says? "God so loved the world that he gave us his only son, so that we could believe and have eternal life." Not your gods, who break men like playthings. Our God sacrificed his only son out of love for His creation. Can you imagine it?'

I can't stand it any more. I turn and start walking away, as fast as I can.

'I'll pray for you!' he calls after me.

I look back over my shoulder, but don't break stride. 'You can pray I find out who really killed Alexander.'

*　　　*　　　*

I need a bath. I've been up since before dawn and I feel filthy. Dust's got in my hair, on my cheeks, even on my tongue. Every time I look at my forearm I shudder at the thought of Symmachus's poisoned pool.

It's a private bathhouse, quite large, but I'm well known there. Most of the men who frequent it work in the government. In the main courtyard, young men box and wrestle and strut, as young men do, while their friends look on in knots. In the shadows of the arcade, hawkers drift around with their boxes of oils, combs and foreign potions that will make us

315

stronger or more handsome.

I undress in the changing rooms, and make my way to the *tepidarium*. Some days I find the shock of the cold pool invigorates my old body; today, I need warmth. I tip the attendant to make sure the pedlars and masseurs don't bother me, and slide into the warm water. I close my eyes.

My thoughts drift in the water. Is Simeon guilty—of Alexander's murder, or Symmachus's, or both? I still can't decide. Simeon was so sincere, he's almost persuaded me to believe him.

But then, I know it's possible for a murderer to live with his crime as if it never happened.

In my mind, I see poor Symmachus slumped in his garden. Maybe it *was* a suicide. Other Stoics have chosen that route. Cato, whose marble head is now sunk in Symmachus's fishpond; Seneca, the great philosopher and statesman who plotted to assassinate Nero. He died in a bath, opening his veins so that the heat would draw the blood out of him. Though I've heard another version: that he didn't die of his wounds, but actually suffocated from the steam.

I think I'll avoid the hot room today. Seneca wasn't the last person to die in a hot bath.

Aurelius Symmachus is a Stoic. Outward things cannot touch his soul.

What is it about these Stoics? They claim to have mastered the world, to be beyond its reach. And then they kill themselves. Is it the effort—the vast will required to hold down their emotions in the face of life's provocations that finally wears them out?

To be out of reach of the world is to become a god. Stoics think they can do it by intellect and force of will; Christians by faith. Perhaps they aren't so different after all. They're trying to escape human nature.

No wonder so many commit suicide.

I don't like where these thoughts are going. I open my eyes and sluice water over my back. 'It's too cold!' I shout at the bath attendant. 'Throw more wood on the fire!' And someone says my name.

I tip my head back and look up. It takes me a moment to place him: a man called Bassus, a functionary at the palace. He served on my staff years ago when I was consul. Now he's naked, floury skin damp with sweat and his hair plastered to his skull. He looks terrible, but I greet him as cheerfully as I can. He clambers in beside me.

'Did you hear about Aurelius Symmachus?'

Sitting beside me, he can't see the surprise on my face. I should have expected it. An ancient family, a murder and now a suicide: the scandal will consume the city for days, until something better comes along.

'I heard he killed himself,' I say.

'Poison.' He splashes the water with his hand. 'Lucky he didn't come here to do it, like Seneca. Imagine the mess.'

'Imagine.'

Bassus leans back and scratches his armpit. 'The strange thing is, I saw him last night. He came to the palace.'

Some of the other men in the pool drift closer. I half-close my eyes.

'Did he think he'd get a pardon?' someone asks.

'He was very agitated. He said he had to see the Prefect.'

317

'He'd probably realised what the Greeks do to old men,' says a stocky guards captain. There's laughter, a few obscene gestures. Bassus waits for them to die down.

'He said he'd found out something about a Christian bishop. A scandal.'

Did the attendant follow my instructions? The water's so cold I'm starting to shiver. In the general conversation which has broken out, I sidle closer to Bassus and whisper in his ear. 'Did he tell anyone his secret?'

'No one would speak to him. He hung around for a few hours, then gave up.'

'Did he say which bishop?'

Bassus slides around the pool so he can give me a long, searching stare. *How much scandal do you want to rake?* his eyes ask.

'He didn't say.' And then, because he can't resist an easy joke. 'He wasn't *that* suicidal.'

XXXV

Belgrade, Serbia—Present Day
The man in the baseball cap fired twice.

Ten yards away, Gruber lurched backwards, as if he'd tripped on something.

The gun moved towards Michael. Panic greased the air: a lot of the people who'd fled the citadel had gathered here, torn between fear and curiosity. Now fear had free rein. They poured towards the park exit, blocking the police cars which were trying to nose their way in. Screams and sirens battled for supremacy.

The man in the baseball cap shouted something at Michael. By Michael's feet, Gruber lay still. Blood seeped into the gravel. The man's finger tightened on the trigger.

Abby was too far away to help. She wanted to move, but her legs were frozen. All she could see was the gun, Michael, and the short space between them.

A man in shorts and a black tracksuit top barrelled out of the crowd and flung himself at the gunman. Unlike Abby, he made no mistake. He drove his shoulder into the man's side, whipped his legs from under him and dropped him heavily to the ground. The gunman struggled; the baseball cap came off, but the man in the tracksuit pinned him down. He wrenched the gun out of his hand and hurled it into a thicket of bushes.

Michael was kneeling beside Gruber, pulling something from inside his pocket. Blood smeared his hands.

'*Come on!*' he shouted.

Abby still couldn't move. Michael ran over, grabbed her hand and pulled her along. It felt as though he'd tugged open her bullet scar; it was all she could do not to scream. When she looked back, two policemen had converged on the gunman and were pointing machine pistols at him. The man in the tracksuit was speaking quickly, looking around and waving his arms.

'We need to get out of sight,' said Michael. 'As soon as the police start interviewing witnesses, they'll know pretty quick they want to speak to us.'

'What about Gruber?'

Michael shook his head. 'No chance.' He held up the plastic wallet he'd taken off the corpse. A

319

neat hole the size of a five-pence piece had been punched clean through.

They hurried out of the park and crossed the main road. A tram rumbled past, briefly blocking them from sight.

'Where to now?' Abby asked.

'Who do we know in Belgrade?'

*   *   *

Studentski Trg was busier than when they'd been there that morning. Classes had just finished; the students gathered in knots in the square, wondering what was happening at the citadel. They were close enough that they'd heard the shots and sirens. Fortunately, no one seemed to connect Michael and Abby with the chaos.

The porter recognised them from before and waved them through upstairs. They were just in time. They found Dr Nikolić outside his office door, a leather jacket pulled on over his sweater and a bunch of keys in his hand. He saw them and gave a polite, resigned smile.

'You forgot something?'

Michael took out Gruber's plastic wallet and handed it across. Abby had barely looked at it herself—a quick glance on their way over, huddled in a doorway, hoping no one noticed. Just enough to see a dark printout with blurry characters dim against it, and to wipe Gruber's blood off the plastic.

But it meant something to Nikolić. He extracted the top sheet of paper and scanned it intently. He didn't comment on the bullet hole.

'This is a micro-CT scan of an ancient papyrus?'

320

'It's the original source for the poem we showed you earlier,' Abby said. 'If there's any more of it, it'll be in here.'

Nikolić looked surprised. 'You have not checked yourself?'

'We're in a bit of a hurry,' Michael explained.

'And we need someone who can read Latin,' Abby added.

Nikolić slid the papers back in the wallet. Though they'd done their best to wipe off the blood, some of the residue still streaked the plastic. Police sirens pulsed through the building, so loud they might have been in the square outside.

Michael turned to Nikolić. 'Do you have a car? Can you get us out of Belgrade?'

Nikolić stared at him. Michael pre-empted anything he might say.

'This printout comes from a scroll that belonged to one of Constantine's top generals. It's been lost until five minutes ago, never published, and right now it's looking for a new owner.'

To Abby's astonishment, Nikolić didn't laugh them out of the building, or call security. He stood there for a long moment, looking between her, Michael and the wallet. He looked neither shocked nor offended—just bemused.

He shrugged, reached into the pocket of his jacket and pulled out a car key on a rabbit's-foot charm.

'My car is parked around the corner.'

He led them down the stairs.

'I can't believe he's doing this,' Abby muttered to Michael. Ahead, Nikolić heard her and turned.

'This is Serbia. You think actually this is the weirdest thing that has happened in my life?'

*　　*　　*

Nikolić's car was a small red Fiat. Abby sat in the front, her hair down and pulled forward so that it shielded her face; Michael squeezed in the back and pretended to be asleep, lolling his head away from the window. Traffic was at a standstill: police cars had blocked several major intersections, though there didn't seem to be any method to it. Abby kept waiting for a roadblock to appear, for someone to tap on the window and demand their papers, but it never came. They followed a series of switchback streets down through the old town, then came out on the main road. They crossed the Sava and accelerated on to the highway that cut through the grid of Novi Belgrad. Within minutes they were out of the city and driving through rolling farmland. It always surprised Abby how abruptly the city ended.

Nikolić kept his eyes on the road.

'You wanted to be out of Belgrade? Now you are here. What next?'

Abby looked at the plastic wallet sitting on her lap. 'Is there somewhere we can go to talk?'

Nikolić pulled the car into a Lukoil station just past the airport turning. There was a small café attached to the minimart: they sat at a plastic table and sipped oily coffee from plastic cups. Paper placemats advertised fast food and offered puzzles to distract children.

'I don't want for you to tell me what you are doing,' Nikolić announced. 'If the police ask me, I will say you forced me to drive you at gunpoint.'

'Fair enough,' Abby agreed. If the police caught them, that was going to be the least of their worries.

'Let me see the document.'

Abby handed him the wallet. He spread the papers on the table—four sheets of blurred images, and two of Gruber's typed transcription.

> To reach the living, navigate the dead,
> Beyond the shadow burns the sun,
> The saving sign that lights the path ahead,
> Unconquered brilliance of a life begun.

Abby could see the Latin text in neat lines on the typescript. But there was more. Nikolić studied it for some minutes, then began, hesitantly:

> From the garden to the cave,
> The grieving father gave his son,
> And buried in the hollow grave,
> The trophy of his victory won.

They looked at each other with something like awe, aware they were hearing words that hadn't been read in seventeen centuries.

'"The trophy of his victory won,"' Michael repeated. 'You said trophy was another word for the *labarum*—the battle standard.'

'It can be.'

Michael made Nikolić read the translation again, slowly, while he copied it out on the paper. He frowned at it. 'Other than the "trophy", it doesn't seem to take us much further.'

'Can you tell us anything more about the poem?' Abby asked.

Nikolić looked up. 'I can maybe tell you the name of the poet.'

He enjoyed their astonishment. Even under the

circumstances, he couldn't keep from smiling.

'It was written by a Roman politician and poet called Publilius Optatianus Porfyrius.'

'How do you know?'

'Further up the scroll, there is a list of names.' He showed them on Gruber's transcription. 'By itself, that would make this a significant find. Eusebius of Nicomedia, the most notorious bishop of Constantine's reign. Aurelius Symmachus, a noted pagan and minor philosopher. Asterius Sophistes, a controversial Christian theorist. And Porfyrius—a poet who specialised in highly technical, unconventional poetry.'

It was like reading a Russian novel—a deluge of unfamiliar, unpronounceable names. But Abby got the drift.

'You've heard of all these people?'

'For a scholar of Constantine, it is impossible not to.'

'And Porfyrius wrote poetry?' Michael repeated.

'His poems are called *technopaegnia*. Riddles for amusing the Emperor. All his surviving poems contain secret messages.'

The smile had turned into a sheepish grin.

'Is this for real?' Michael asked at last. 'This morning, you laughed us out of your office when we thought the poem had a clue to a treasure. Now you're saying the chap who wrote it is famous for putting secret messages in poems?'

The smile faded. Under Nikolić's calm good humour, the strain had begun to tell.

'I don't know, OK? There's a poem and the name of a poet. You say the poem has a secret message and his poems are famous for secret messages. I made a connection. Maybe it means nothing.' He brushed a hand across the table, pushing the papers away. 'Maybe your German friend invented everything, and said what he thought you wanted to be true.'

They sat there in silence for a moment. Abby sipped at her coffee and realised she'd finished it. Trucks thundered past on the motorway.

'Let's assume the poem's genuine, and written by who you say it is,' Michael said at last. 'How do we decode the secret message?'

'It is like . . . I don't know the English word.'

He said something in Serbian, but Abby drew blank. Nikolić stared at the table in frustration, trying to find a translation. Suddenly, his face lit up. He took the paper placemat that had been laid in front of him and spun it around. It was designed for children: a collage of bright pictures of fast food, dancing cartoon animals and puzzle games. There was a maze, a tangle of lines, a join-the-dots picture—and a word search.

Nikolić tapped his finger on the word search. 'Exactly like this. You have the text of the poem, and then you read up or down or diagonally to find other words hidden inside it, yes?'

Abby and Michael both nodded. Underneath the grid of letters, the mat listed a dozen words for the children to find. Abby pointed to them.

'In a word search, you know what you're looking for.'

'On Porfyrius's poems, that is not the case.' Nikolić sat back, doodling on the mat. 'For the original manuscripts, the letters would have been picked out in red ink, or underlined. Some scholars think they might even have been presented to the Emperor inscribed on gold tablets, with gemstones underneath the key letters—though no such tablet is surviving.'

'That would have been nice to find,' said Michael.

Nikolić ignored him. Absent-mindedly, he drew bubbles around a couple of words in the puzzle on the mat.

'Porfyrius's poems are much more intricate, actually. The hidden words spell out messages, but they also make pictures.'

'What do you mean?'

Nikolić circled some more letters in the grid, apparently at random. When he'd finished, the marks outlined the shape of a stick man. 'Like so. Porfyrius was very clever. Sometimes the pictures themselves were of letters that spelled out short words, or numbers. For Constantine's *vicennalia*, when he celebrated twenty years of his rule, Porfyrius wrote a poem where the hidden message made the form XX, the Roman numerals for twenty. One famous poem, the message makes the shape of a ship. In others, the Emperor's titles or his monogram.'

Abby stared at him. 'His monogram?'

'The chi-rho. Like on the *labarum*.'

'The *labarum* again,' Michael said. 'That's got to be it.'

But Abby was thinking further and faster. She pulled Gruber's printout from the pile—not the typed transcription, but the raw image reconstructed from the scroll.

'Show me where the poem is here.'

Nikolić pointed to it. The whole page was dim and blurred, the letters dark shapes like twigs floating in muddy water. But she could see the

326

place. A dark block of text, eight lines long.

She made a square with her forefingers and thumbs and framed the text between them. Keeping the shape, she lifted her hands against her collarbone.

Some scholars think they might even have been presented to the Emperor inscribed on gold tablets, with gemstones underneath the key letters.

'There was a gold necklace,' she said. Michael shot her a warning look—*not in front of* Nikolić—but she carried on regardless. 'We found it with the scroll—a square pattern with the chi-rho in the middle. I think it would have fitted perfectly on top of the poem.' She thought back, remembering the feel of the cold metal against her skin and the way the inset glass caught the light. 'It had beads set into it. What if they show which letters you need to read to get the hidden message?'

Nikolić stared at her, as if he couldn't decide whether to trust her or to dismiss her as a lunatic.

'And where, please, is this necklace now?'

Abby shot Michael a *what-do-we-have-to-lose* look.

'The British Secret Intelligence Service have it.'

XXXVI

Constantinople—May 337

The day's hot, but the bath has left me chilled to the bone. A new idea grips me like a fever. Perhaps Symmachus was spinning lies in a last attempt to avoid exile, but I don't think so.

Simeon, baffled that I was accusing him when

the evidence was so obvious: *Symmachus had the documents.* I convinced myself the old man was set up. But what if he had the documents all along? He killed Alexander in the library, took his document case and found all Constantine's dirty secrets locked inside it. No wonder he wanted to be rid of it.

I don't care who killed Alexander any more. All I want to know is what Symmachus found out—and why he died for it.

*   *   *

Constantine wasn't the first emperor to build his palace on the promontory. As ever, he demolished the past and rebuilt on its foundations, to a scale beyond his predecessors' imaginations. When his engineers started excavating, they found a vast empty cistern underneath the site. Constantine himself came down to inspect it.

'A shame to waste all this space,' was his verdict. 'Use it for the paperwork.'

And so it was allocated to the *Scrinia Memoriae*, the Chamber of Records. In a way, it's appropriate it sits in the old cistern. It's the run-off of the empire, the well of memory. And the records stacked on its winding shelves are so deep they're unfathomable.

You enter the Chamber of Records through a reading room, seldom used, in the palace. An archivist sits at a desk, annotating a manuscript. I lean over and put Constantine's commission under his nose.

'There was a bishop called Alexander. He came here, probably often, researching a history for the

Augustus.'

'I remember him.' He sucks the end of his reed pen. 'He hasn't been here in a couple of weeks.'

'He died. I need to see the papers he was looking at.'

'Do you know what they were?'

'I was hoping you'd remember.'

His eyes flick back to the commission lying open on the desk. 'Those papers have been stored, untouched, under the Augustus's private seal for ten years. I had to check with the palace three times before I could believe the Bishop was really allowed access.' He squints up at me: small, boring eyes. 'You said he died?'

'Just show them to me.'

He shuffles across to the high door, takes the large key off his neck and slots it in the lock. He snaps the key with a practised movement, like a farmwife wringing a chicken's neck.

'After you.'

*   *   *

It's like entering a mine, or a dungeon. The shadows seem to stretch to infinity. The columns that support the roof rise every few yards, lifeless ranks of a petrified forest. Dusty shelves wall up the spaces between, lined with wicker baskets full of scrolled papers. You could believe that all the knowledge in the world was stored here somewhere—if you only knew where to look.

Each of the columns has a Greek letter and a Roman number chiselled into it. As long as we go straight, the letters change, but the numbers stay the same. When we turn, the numbers start to change, but the letter stays constant. The whole room is arranged as a giant grid. I start counting off the pillars we pass. XV / Φ. XV / X. XV / Ψ. I try to remember the Greek alphabet in order, counting back so I can find my way out if I get lost.

XV / Ω. The archivist stops. We've reached Omega, the last letter, though the corridor continues into still deeper darkness beyond. I wonder what comes after. He picks up a bronze lamp from a hollow cut into the column, and lights it from his own.

'Is it safe, the fire?' I wonder aloud. My voice sounds faint against the vast darkness.

'What else can you do?' He hands me the new lamp and turns. 'Bring what you want back to the reading room.'

He retreats down the long corridor. The lamp trembles in my hand; for a second, I imagine dropping it in a basket of papyri and the wave of flame that would sweep the chamber clean. I tighten my grip.

I work my way along the aisle. Every time my shoulder brushes one of the baskets, rivulets of dust trickle down from the shelves over me. Here, all the baskets have lids, each tied shut with a ribbon and the knot sealed with wax. Most of the seals have started to crumble—but one, I notice, is supple and glossy, the imprint still sharp. A dark stain next to it shows where a previous seal sat. A clay tag tied on with twine labels it as diplomatic correspondence from the twentieth year of Constantine's reign.

I check the rest of the aisle and find five baskets whose seals have been removed and replaced. All of them date from year twenty or the year before.

I know what happened that year, the *vicennalia*

year. I lift down the first basket and set it on the floor next to the lamp. There's no point taking it back to the reading room. Once I leave this dark labyrinth, I know I'll never come back.

I sit on the floor and start to read. Alexander's handiwork is evident on almost every page. Some of it's been done subtly, a whole column excised and the remainder pasted together, so that the only telltale is a faint ridge in the papyrus; other interventions are more obvious. Paragraphs, sentences, sometimes individual words have been cut out of the text, so that when I hold the scroll up to the light it's riddled with holes, as though a worm's been through it.

But I can fill in the blanks.

*　　　*　　　*

Aquileia, Italy—April 326—Eleven years ago . . .
Everything starts to go wrong from the moment we reach Aquileia.

It should be a joyful moment, springtime in the empire. We're travelling to Rome, where Constantine's *vicennalia* celebrations will culminate. Everybody understands that it's more than just a celebration of his rule. The last emperor to achieve twenty years' reign was Diocletian, who marked the occasion by announcing his retirement and promoting his successors. Constantine's older now than his father was when he died; Crispus is in his prime. Constantine hasn't said anything, even to me, but I was there in Nicaea. *We'll remake the empire in God's image.* One God, one emperor, one peace—and he's been as good as his word. Since Chrysopolis, his armies have been confined to their

331

barracks.

Crispus has come to Aquileia to join us for the final stages to Rome. Black clouds have been massing all day: the storm breaks just as we arrive at the outskirts. The driving rain tears away the flowers that garland the tombs along the road and soak the waiting dignitaries. Crispus, who arrived two days earlier, has come out to meet us: he tries to deliver his prepared speech, but thunder drowns his words.

'Just shut up and stop blocking the road!' Constantine barks at him, loud enough that the watching audience can hear. Crispus flushes crimson. By the time we reach the palace, the baggage is sodden and tempers are short.

'What sort of son keeps his father standing out in the cold?' says Fausta, wrapped in a heavy fur mantle. In the dim light she prowls around the room like a wolf in its cave. 'And at your age. Poor Claudius'—her eldest son—'hasn't stopped sneezing since we arrived. His tutor says he might have a fever.'

'Then perhaps I'll send him to Britain,' snaps Constantine. 'A winter in York would get him used to being wet.'

'Just like it did for your father.'

Constantine crosses the floor so fast I think he'll knock her into the next room. He puts up his arms, as if he's going to grab her cloak and lift her off her feet. Fausta just smirks at him, a cruel pleasure in her eyes. She's got a reaction. At her age, it's the most she can hope for.

Constantine's hands stop a hair's breadth from her cloak. Perhaps he can't bear to touch her. Perhaps he doesn't dare. Fausta is the daughter, brother and wife of emperors: she's a woman who carries an aura about her, like Constantine. But while Constantine's is golden, hers is cancerous black.

Constantine turns abruptly. 'Don't blame me if your snivelling son can't stand the damp!' he shouts back at her as he storms out of the room.

The smirk vanishes.

'*Our* son!' she screams. 'My boys are your sons, just as much as Crispus.'

'At least Crispus doesn't melt in the rain.'

Fausta stares after him, blazing. She's been like this ever since we left Constantinople, a burr under the saddle. Nothing is ever good enough. The beds are too hard, the wine too sour, the slaves too insolent.

It's obvious why. If Constantine proclaims Crispus Augustus when we get to Rome, her own sons will be out of the running. She's spent twenty years married to the man who killed her father and her brother, in the expectation that one day she'll be mother to a dynasty. She's thirty-five and carried five children: it takes four oxen to pull the cart with all her creams and cosmetics, but they can't disguise the extra weight she's carrying, or the lines starting to crease her face. She and Constantine almost never sleep in the same room any more. In a rare moment of pity, I think: she's losing everything.

I'm still there in the room. Fausta's blocking the door; there's no discreet way to slip out. She hears me move and snaps around.

'His faithful hunting dog. Run along and go and lick his arse.'

*   *   *

I wake in the depths of the night and don't know where I am. There have been so many new beds and new rooms on this trip that it's become almost routine. The room spins slowly around me until it comes to rest in its proper orientation. The door, the window, the dagger under my pillow. It's shared my bed since I was nine years old, more constant than any lover.

And a slave standing over me, tugging my sleeve. I didn't hear him come in. Palace slaves move like cats in the dark. Or perhaps I'm getting old.

'What is it?'

'The Augustus.'

I'm out of bed in a trice, pulling on my old military cloak, hurrying after the slave. In the corridor outside my room, all the lamps are lit. Men from the Schola guard every door.

'What's happened?'

The slave shrugs. 'Whatever it is, it's still happening.'

It isn't far to Constantine's room, but the slave doesn't take me there. Instead, we go down a flight of stairs to where Fausta's children sleep. The door's open, and the guards outside have drawn swords. I glance at them as I enter, and though I've stood on more battlefields than I can count, I shiver. *Is this about me?*

One look at the room says it's much worse than that. Constantine, Crispus and Fausta are all there, together with Fausta's three sons, a dozen guards and various slaves. Claudius, the eldest son, has a blanket around his shoulders. It hangs open, revealing blood that's run down his neck and drenched his tunic. He looks as though he

334

had his throat slit a second before I walked in and hasn't realised it yet: he's still standing up, pale but unassisted, a walking corpse. Fausta stands next to him, ready to catch him if he falls. Her nightdress is smeared with blood, though I think it must be her son's. The two other boys cower behind her, wrapped in their bedclothes. Constantine stands opposite, flanked by guards, while Crispus waits in between. There's blood on his hands.

Constantine looks at me. With all the confusion and blood, it's the weariness in his face that makes me realise how serious this is.

'Can I rely on you?'

'Always.'

'Search Crispus's apartments. Anything you find, bring it to me here.'

Fausta's face is hard, her dark eyes alive with passion. 'How do you know Valerius wasn't part of this?'

'I trust him.'

'I don't. Send Junius with him.'

Junius is a smug, heavy-lipped courtier who never smiles except in a mirror. One of Fausta's favourites. He accompanies me back up the stairs to Crispus's room. I still don't know what's happening, but I'm starting to put the pieces together. A boy with a wound and a man with bloody hands. We haven't come to look for proof of Crispus's innocence.

Crispus's room is neat and spare; it doesn't take long to search. The bed's been slept in, with the covers still thrown back from when he got up. Yesterday's clothes have been folded and put away; tomorrow's are set out on a chest. A sheaf of papers sits on a desk where he was working before he went

335

to bed. He's always been diligent.

Junius makes straight for the papers. I get down on my knees and look under the bed. The lamplight doesn't reach: I flap my arm about in the darkness. There's a pair of boots, a few rags that have fallen out of the mattress—and a slim tube that feels like cold lead when I put my hand on it.

Junius sees me slide it out and pounces. '*Let me have that.*' I fend him off with one arm, like two hounds scrapping over a bone. I remember what Fausta called me yesterday: *Constantine's faithful hunting dog*. This is what happens when terror gets loose in the palace.

It's a thinly beaten sheet of lead that's been rolled into a scroll, like papyrus. A gold pin has been hammered through the soft metal to fasten it. The moment I see it, I recognise it for the terrible thing it is.

Despair makes me falter. Junius snatches the lead from of my hands, pulls out the pin and reads greedily. He licks his lips.

'Wait until the Augustus sees this.' He can't hide his glee; he's already imagining the promotion he'll get. I'd like to hit him, hard enough to break his neck, but that would be a mistake. There's blood in the palace and the wolves are hunting. The only way to survive is to keep perfectly still.

Downstairs in the boys' bedroom, nothing's changed. Junius presents the scroll to Constantine, who shies away from it like poison. He beckons a slave to hold it up so he can read it.

'We found it under the Caesar's bed,' Junius says.

'There was nothing under my bed except my boots.' Crispus stares at me, imploring me to support him. There's nothing I can say. Except—in the pause while Constantine mumbles the tablet to himself—'What happened?'

Fausta answers. 'I'd come down to check on my children when the Caesar'—she points to Crispus—'burst in. He had a knife in his hand; he was wild. When he saw me, he told me that the army had deserted the Augustus, that my husband would be dead before dawn. I could join him, or my children and I would die.'

Half the men in the room—those who owe their position to Fausta—let loose with shock, outrage. The other half stay silent.

'It's a lie,' says Crispus. He's looking at his father, but Constantine won't meet his gaze. Neither will I. I'm staring at his bare feet, wondering what sort of conspirator tries to seize the empire and leaves his boots under the bed.

'Of course, I could see he was lying.' Fausta bores on with remorseless intensity. 'He didn't expect me to be there. He'd come to kill his brothers, so there would be no rivals when he killed the Augustus. I told him so; he flew at Claudius in a rage and tried to cut his throat. Thank God the guards came in time.'

Crispus shakes his head slowly, like a man trapped under a heavy yoke. 'She came to my room and told me my brother Claudius had hurt himself. I went with her straight away and saw his ear was bleeding. Before I could do anything, her guards had wrestled me to the floor.'

He stares around the room, defying us to disbelieve him. There must be two dozen people, and not one of us will meet his gaze. No one except Fausta, who eyes him with the clear-eyed venom of

337

a serpent.

Constantine looks up at me. 'Have you read it?'

The slave turns, so I can see the words scratched on to the black metal.

To the great god Nemesis, I Crispus Caesar curse my father Constantine Augustus and give him into your power. Drive him to his death, allow him neither health nor sleep nor happiness until the empire is mine.

It's a curse tablet—the sort of thing jilted lovers and burgled shopkeepers throw down wells to invoke the gods against their enemies. Junius shows Constantine the pin that was stabbed through it. It's gold, a hook-shaped clasp in the form of a pouncing lion. I've seen it often enough gleaming from the shoulder of Constantine's cloak.

'Your fibula,' says Fausta. 'He must have stolen it, to work his black magic on you.'

'I never touched this piece of evil.' Contempt wins out over fear in Crispus's voice—for the moment.

The expression on Constantine's face haunts me to this day. He's aged ten years in a night. For the first time in his life, he looks lost.

'What is the truth?' he murmurs. 'That my own son wanted to overthrow me, when I would willingly have given him all the power and glory he could want? Or that my wife is spreading the most terrible and false lies?'

'How can you ignore what's in front of you?' There's a hysterical edge to Fausta's voice. 'Do you want to wait until all our children are dead before you'll believe it?'

'And believe my heir's a murderer?'

Fausta spreads her arms around her children.

'I'm taking our sons back to Constantinople. They won't spend one more hour under the same roof as this monster.' She advances across the room, eyes blazing. She's a head shorter than Constantine, but just at the moment she seems to have grown to an equal size. And he's shrinking; he doesn't know what to do. This was supposed to be his triumph, his moment of mastery, and it's all disintegrating.

Junius steps forward. 'If I may . . . ?'

Constantine nods.

'There's a villa at Pula, three days ride from here. The governor's a loyal man. Send Crispus there, out of the way, until the facts can be established.'

'*No.*' Desperation makes Crispus's voice unnaturally high. 'If you want to establish the truth, keep me here so I can prove it.'

'If he stays, I go,' says Fausta.

They both look to Constantine, whose gaze is fixed at a point on the wall midway between them. His face is as hard as marble, unreadable. The whole room—the whole world—hangs on his decision.

Something Crispus said about the bishops at Nicaea comes back to me. *They need a judge.* He never guessed it would be him in the dock.

Constantine decides. The merest twitch of the head—that's all it takes. Fausta bows. Four guards in white surround Crispus and lead him out of the room. He doesn't resist.

'I'll send someone,' Constantine says, but it's so faint I doubt Crispus hears him.

*   *   *

Constantinople—May 337

In the Chamber of Records the lamp's burning low.
I sit cross-legged on the floor, ringed by a circle
of scattered papers. I've pulled out so many, they
spill beyond the light and into the infinite darkness
beyond. Alexander did his work too well. I've read
for an hour, maybe more, and I haven't seen the
least hint that Crispus and Fausta were there in
Aquileia. Or that they even existed at all.

I'm defeated. I sweep up the papers and jam
them back into their files, cramming them in like
rubbish. I struggle to my feet. A wash of dizziness
rocks me; I sway, clinging on to the lamp for dear
life. If I lose that, I'll be lost in this darkness for
ever. I try to anchor my gaze on a distant point, but
there's nothing to latch on to. The shelves stretch
for ever. The harder I look, the further they retreat.

I feel as if I'm floating, my physical self dissolved
in the air. I've been reduced to my soul. Or perhaps
this whole room *is* my soul, my own personal
Chamber of Records. I inhabit it; I walk its dark
passages, plucking memories from the shelves
without regard for space or time. *The mind is a
strange land—many walls but no distance.*

I can't blame Alexander for what he did to
the records. I've done the same thing in my own
memory, editing it and cleansing it to make it
bearable. It isn't painless: each cut leaves a hole, so
many that in the end I'm little more than a paper
cut-out of a man. But how else could I live with
myself?

I put out an arm and feel something solid. One
of the pillars. It's cold against my palm and the

cold feels real. My fingers claw into the stone, feeling the grooves where the characters have been chiselled. XV / Ω. I press my skin against the sharp edges.

A thought comes to me. All the files have the same designation—XV / Ω—as you'd expect. But when I was looking through the scraps in Alexander's case, that night in the palace, there were other marks.

XII / Π I'm writing with deepest condolence for the death of your grandson.

The thought gives me purpose. Purpose makes me real again. I lift the lamp and hurry down the passages between the shelves, counting off the columns until I find the right place.

Simeon's voice drifts back to me through the paper walls. *All your life, you've been walking in darkness.*

Alexander definitely came here—the seals give him away. I pull out anything where the wax is fresh. After a few pages it's clear that most of these papers have come from the court of the Dowager Empress Helena. She never settled in Constantinople; she lived in Rome and died nine years ago. Constantine must have had her papers shipped here for safekeeping.

A lot of the boxes have been opened, and a lot of the pages have been mutilated. Helena doted on her eldest grandson and wrote to him often. Unlike the imperial chancery, she kept her records bound up in codices like the Christians use. I can follow Alexander's path through them by the holes left in the pages like footprints in snow. The only sound in the vast chamber is the murmur of my own voice as I read aloud.

The lamp's starting to flicker; the oil must be almost dry. I know I have to get out, but I still sit there, turning the pages compulsively.

To reach the living, navigate the dead.

My sight's so blurred from the thousands of words I've read, I almost don't notice it. I've already started to turn the page. But something registers. I turn back.

It's a letter to the empress. It must be a duplicate, copied into the correspondence book by a secretary. There's a tear in the corner of the page, as if Alexander began to rip it out and then thought better of it. Instead, he contented himself with excising the first paragraph. It means the sender and the date have gone. The text picks up halfway down the page.

> To reach the living, navigate the dead,
> Beyond the shadow burns the sun,
> The saving sign that lights the path ahead,
> Unconquered brilliance of a life begun.
>
> From the garden to the cave,
> The grieving father gave his son,
> And buried in the hollow grave,
> The trophy of his victory won.

I stare at the page, trying to tease out some meaning. I wonder why Alexander removed the version that he had in his case, but not this one. Perhaps I understand his ambivalence. Everything in the poem screams Crispus, but there's nothing explicit that mentions him. Is it a riddle? Who wrote it?

I've stayed too long. The lamp flickers, spits—

and goes out. A shudder passes through me. I cry out like a child. My old hands aren't so firm as they used to be. The lamp drops and shatters on the floor. I'm trapped in total darkness.

Far away in the labyrinth, I hear a voice calling my name.

XXXVII

Near Belgrade, Serbia—Present Day
'Good evening, the Foreign Office. How may I direct your call?'

'I need to speak to the Office of Balkan Liaison.'

'One moment, please.'

The telephone played Bach—an ethereal sound among the diesel engines and squeaking brakes of the service station. Standing outside the café, Abby pressed thc phone tighter to her ear.

'Duty Officer.' A woman's voice, young and weary.

'I need to speak to Mark Wilson.'

'I'm afraid he's out of the office at the moment. Can I—?'

'Get hold of him.' The ferocity in her voice surprised her. 'Tell him Abby Cormac wants to speak to him.'

'Do you have a number he can reach you on?'

Was it her paranoia, or had the voice changed? *Do I know you?* Abby wondered. *Did we exchange e-mails, or sit opposite each other in the canteen?* She tried to put a face to the voice, but found she lacked the imagination.

'I'll call back in an hour. Make sure he's there.'

She rung off and went back inside. Michael and Nikolić were still at the table, staring at their coffee cups.

'Well?' Michael asked.

'He wasn't there. I said I'd call back in an hour.'

Michael pushed back his chair. 'We need to keep moving.' He turned to Nikolić. 'Can you get us to the Croatian border? We'll make it worth your time.'

Nikolić checked his watch. 'I have two sons with no mother. My sister fetches them from school, but they already must be wondering where I am. I can drive you to Sremska Mitrovica. From there, you get a bus.'

*   *   *

They carried on down the dark highway.

'What else do you know about Porfyrius?' Abby asked.

'A little. He was exiled for some time—nobody knows why or how long. We think he wrote most of his poems in exile, to persuade Constantine to let him come home.'

'Did it work?'

Nikolić nodded. 'Around 326 he was pardoned and came home. He must have done something so that the Emperor liked him: he was made Prefect of the City of Rome. Like the mayor. This is all we know.'

He lapsed into silence. 'It is strange . . .'

He broke off as he changed lanes to overtake a petrol tanker lumbering towards the border.

'What's strange?' Abby asked, when they were past.

'The poem—this line: *The grieving father gave his son.*'

'Isn't that just some Christian stuff?' Michael put in from the back seat.

Nikolić frowned. 'The whole poem is very full of Christian Neoplatonist thought. But here there is a historical parallel also. The Emperor Constantine had a son named Crispus—a successful general, a loyal deputy and his presumed heir.'

'I've never heard of him,' Abby said.

'In 326 Constantine had him murdered. Not only murdered, but erased also from history. The Roman state had a policy called *damnatio memoriae*—the damnation of the memory— for disgraced senior officials. They become an unperson, if you like George Orwell. The statues are torn down or defaced, the inscriptions removed, the histories edited. Constantine's official biographer, Eusebius, rewrote his book to exclude any mention that Crispus ever existed. We only know because copies of both editions have survived.'

'What did Crispus do to piss him off?' Michael asked.

'No one knows. The earliest reference to the killing comes nearly two hundred years later, in the work of a pagan historian who wants to discredit Constantine. He says Crispus was poisoned for allegedly having an affair with Constantine's second wife, Fausta, who died as well that year.'

'This family sounds like *The Sopranos*.'

'You said it was strange that the poem references the death,' Abby said. 'Strange because it should have been edited out?'

'Several of Porfyrius's other surviving poems

345

praise Crispus. Historians assume this means he wrote them before 326, when Crispus was still favoured. But to write a poem that mentions Crispus after his death—even more, one that seems to refer to his murder—doesn't help the poet. In fact, he risks his own execution.'

'And where does all this get us?' Michael asked. Impatience was never far away.

By way of answer, Nikolić flipped the indicator and pulled off the motorway. He nodded to the road sign.

'Sremska Mitrovica,' he announced.

*   *   *

Night had fallen; a light rain had begun again, glossing the streets and dappling the windscreen. Abby looked out through the reflected neon smeared on the windows, taking in the puddles and empty doorways as they drove through the deserted town. It felt like the last place on earth, a film noir set that had fallen through a wormhole.

'In Roman times this was a great city of the empire,' Nikolić said. 'Sirmium, it was called—capital of the Emperor Galerius. In fact, it is here that Constantine's son Crispus was proclaimed Caesar.'

'It's gone downhill,' Michael observed.

Nikolić pulled up against the kerb opposite the bus station.

'Last stop,' he announced. 'From here, you can go to Zagreb, Budapest, Vienna—wherever you want. Me, I go home to my boys.'

Abby looked at the photograph tucked behind the gearstick, two boys in their cowboy hats and the

346

sheriffs' stars. She imagined Nikolić parking outside his flat, the screams of delight as his children heard him coming up the stairs. A warm home and dinner on the table, and the concern in his sister's eyes, asking *Where have you been?*

On impulse, she leaned across and planted an awkward kiss on his cheek. 'Thank you for everything.'

He looked embarrassed. 'Be careful, OK?'

'You too. Don't publish that poem until it's safe.'

'How will I know?'

'We'll be in touch.'

'Unless you see us on the news first,' Michael added.

Abby got out. The rain was harder than it had looked from inside the car, wetting her face almost at once. She slammed the door and ran across the pavement into the shelter of a doorway. Nikolić waved, then pulled away.

'What now?'

As if he'd heard the loneliness in her voice, Michael put his arms around her and hugged her close. He nodded towards the bus station. 'We have to get out of Serbia. Dragović has the whole country covered.'

'Do you think it was his people in the park this afternoon?' Had it only been that afternoon? Her memories had begun to collapse in on themselves again, a house of cards falling flat and shuffled out of order.

'Maybe Dragović's people. Or Giacomo's. Or both. Giacomo wouldn't hesitate to sell us out if he saw a profit.' He glanced at the bus station. 'All the more reason to be on our way.'

'Aren't you forgetting something?' She pulled

347

away, looking up into his face. 'I don't have a passport.'

'I work for the customs service.' He pushed back a damp lock of hair from her face and smiled. 'The fact that you don't have an umbrella—*that's* something to worry about.'

He took her arm. Down a side street, littered with junk food wrappers, they found a travel agent. Faded posters taped to the window showed Air Yugo planes soaring against a blue sky; socialist families smiling on socialist beaches in Dalmatia or the Crimea. More recent signs advertised discount international calls, foreign currency, SIM cards. And in the bottom corner, framed by flashing Christmas lights, a cardboard sign in red felt-tipped letters offered visas.

A woman in a black dress with dusty grey hair sat behind a trestle table, reading a gossip webpage on a black laptop.

'I'd like a passport for my sister,' Michael said in Serbian, gesturing to Abby. 'Her aunt in Zagreb is very ill and she must go at once.'

The woman frowned. 'The passport office is shut.'

A fifty-euro note appeared in Michael's hand. The woman gave it a disapproving look.

'You are police? You think you can bribe me?' She shook her head vigorously. 'This is honest shop.'

'I'm not police. I need a passport for my sister. Her aunt is very ill.' Two hundred-euro notes came out.

The woman studied Abby's face, taking in the bruises staining her cheek, the cut above her forehead. She gave Michael a knowing look, her tongue stuck in the corner of her lips.

She thinks he's trafficking me, Abby realised. Her skin crawled as if she'd been smeared with filth; she felt naked.

'Maybe you come back in a week. Maybe your aunt gets better. This is honest shop,' the woman said again. But she was smiling as she said it.

Michael laid the money on the table. 'Perhaps you could just see what you have in the back room,' he encouraged her.

*   *   *

They walked out of the travel agent a thousand euros poorer, though that wasn't what made Abby feel cheap. But they had the passport. She studied the photograph under a streetlight, sucking in her cheeks to try and mimic the pinched face of the woman it had once belonged to.

'It doesn't have to be perfect,' Michael told her. 'Just credible enough for the border guards to accept the bribe.'

She checked her watch, eager to have something else to think about. 'It's been over an hour. I should call London.'

She found a payphone in the main square and dialled the number from memory. Michael waited outside the booth. The same routine with the Foreign Office front desk took her through to the Office of Balkan Liaison. This time, Mark answered straight away.

'Where are you?'

'In the Balkans.' They'd probably trace the number, but she wasn't going to make it easy for them.

'What the hell's going on? Jessop's dead; you're missing. I'm hearing barmy things about a shooting war in Kosovo and a Roman tomb.'

'It's crazy,' Abby agreed. 'Remind me to tell you about it some time.'

Mark's tone altered. 'You have to come in Abby. You haven't done anything wrong. We just need to speak to you.'

'You remember the necklace you and Jessop took off me?'

'What about it?'

'I want you to bring it to me.' She felt the stiff new passport in her pocket and prayed it would do the job. 'You know the town of Split, in Croatia? Meet me at the cathedral there at two o'clock tomorrow.'

'You're expecting me to drop everything and fly out, just to give you a piece of jewellery? You've got to give me more than that.'

She put her hand over the receiver and looked around. Michael didn't fit in the phone box; he'd wandered across the square and was buying some cigarettes from a Gypsy woman. He had his back to her.

'Michael's alive,' she said.

'Michael Lascaris?'

'He didn't die that night in the villa. He's with me now.'

Across the square, Michael was sauntering back towards her.

'Two o'clock, the cathedral in Split,' she repeated. 'Bring the necklace.'

'Wait—'

She hung up. Michael had opened the door and was peering in.

'Did they bite?'

'He'll come,' she said. She took out the passport again and stared at the unfamiliar face. 'The question is, will we get there?'

XXXVIII

Constantinople—May 337

The darkness in the Chamber of Records is immense. I've wandered so far, I don't know where the door is. I can barely tell which way is up.

But still there's a voice calling my name. I open my eyes. The darkness recedes. A light approaches, flickering through the gaps in the shelves.

'Gaius Valerius?'

It's the archivist.

'I told you to come out if you wanted to read,' he reproves me. 'The atmosphere down here, it can overwhelm you.'

I'm too exhausted for pride. 'Thank you for coming to rescue me.'

'Rescue you?' He sounds amused. 'I came to fetch you. The Augustus wants to see you.'

I don't understand. 'Constantine? Has he returned from the war so soon?'

'He's at Nicomedia.'

And there's a finality in those words that tells me he won't be coming back.

*   *   *

Villa Achyron, near Nicomedia—May 337

It's seventy miles to Nicomedia. In my youth, I'd

351

have flogged every post horse on the road to get there in a day. Now, it takes me the best part of two. It isn't just my age. The road's busier than I've ever seen it; at every waystation, there are long queues for fresh horses. The messengers are tight-lipped, but the grooms know the gossip. From them, I gather that Constantine's final campaign ended before it really began. He didn't even get as far as Nicaea before he started complaining of a pain in his stomach. He diverted to the hot baths at Pythia Therma, hoping for a quick cure, but it only made the symptoms worse. His doctors said he was too ill to make the journey back to Constantinople; instead, they decamped to an imperial villa, one of Diocletian's old estates near Nicomedia: the Villa Achyron. *Achyron* means 'threshing floor', where the grain and the chaff are separated. I don't suppose Constantine finds that comforting.

The villa stands five miles outside Nicomedia, on terraces cut into the slopes above the coast. Fields of corn surround it, though the threshing floor that gave the villa its name is long gone. The corn should be ripening gold in the May sunshine, but there'll be no harvest this year. The crop's been trampled back into the earth by the boots and tents of two thousand soldiers camped around it. It's hard to tell if they're guarding the villa or besieging it. I trudge up the hill along an avenue of poplars, and announce myself to the clerk, who has set up an administrative headquarters in the vestibule. Not a secretary or a palace functionary, but an officer of the *Protectores*.

'How's the Augustus? Is he . . . ?' *Dying?* I can't say it—can barely think it.

An unforgiving stare. 'His doctors prescribed

352

rest.'

'He sent a message—he summoned me here from Constantinople.'

'Your name?'

The question spins me off balance like a slap in the face. Is he making a point? Deliberately putting me in my place? People never ask my name: they *know* it.

He taps his pen on the desk. He's a busy man; an ambitious young officer in a thankless job. And he has no idea who I am.

I tell him; the eyes don't blink. All I am is a name to be compared against a list. And found absent.

'Is Flavius Ursus here? The chief of staff?' That earns me a few seconds more of his time. 'Tell him Gaius Valerius Maximus is here to see the Augustus.'

'I'll tell him.'

They leave me to wait in an anteroom near the heart of the villa. Priests, officials and soldiers pass in and out and through the chamber: Schola guards in their white uniforms, but also field commanders in red battledress. This is still a campaign headquarters, after all.

Hours stretch by, and my mind reaches back to a different villa on a different sea.

*　　　*　　　*

Pula, Adriatic Coast—July 326—Eleven years ago
. . .
Pula's a small port near the head of the Adriatic. It's a quiet, well-maintained town, full of merchants who've made modest fortunes in regional trade. I imagine it's the sort of place Constantine has in

mind when he rhapsodises about the delights of his peaceful empire: neat, prosperous and dull. A backwater. A good place for a man to disappear.

I reach the governor's villa near sunset. It's taken me almost a week to complete the three-day journey here: I've slept badly, started late, found infinite faults with the horses, the food, the lodgings. I don't want to be here. I pleaded with Constantine to send someone else. For the first time in our lives, he wouldn't meet my eye.

'It has to be a man I can trust,' he told me. 'You're the only one.' He handed me the leather bag with its knotted string, the glass vial heavy inside. 'I don't want . . .' He trailed off with something that sounded like a sob. The things he doesn't want are so terrible he can't give voice to them.

'Do it quickly.'

*   *   *

I find Crispus on a pebble beach on a promontory south of the town. Grass grows between the stones; fish flit among the rocks in the clear water. Two guards, armed, watch from the pines that fringe the cove, while their prisoner sits by the water's edge, barefoot and bareheaded, letting the waves ripple over his toes.

The guards see me coming and call a wary challenge, their hands on their swords. They're anxious. Even when they recognise me, they don't relax. They're worried I'm going to make them do it.

I send them away. 'Make sure no one disturbs us,' I tell them. They're so grateful to be gone, they

354

don't look back once.

Now Crispus and I are alone. I scramble down the rocky bank and cross the beach towards him. He turns, smiles, and gets up.

'I hoped it would be you.'

A clumsy embrace. An over-zealous wave races up the beach and breaks over my boots. I take a step back and stare into his face. There are bags under his eyes, a grey cast to his skin. The smile which once came so naturally is now forced, an act of defiance.

I start to say something, but he interrupts, 'How's my father?'

'Lost without you.'

'I'm sorry I ruined his celebrations.' He scoops up some pebbles and tosses them one by one into the sea. 'It's funny. Three weeks ago, I was watching everything, imagining how it would be for my own *vicennalia*. Now . . .'

The last pebble drops into the water and barely makes a splash.

'Your father—' I begin. Again, Crispus cuts me short.

'Did he get to the root of the conspiracy?'

'Which conspiracy?'

'The conspiracy against me.' He swings away, as if he knows that looking at me will rob him of something valuable. 'The whole thing was ridiculous. You know I never tried to kill my brothers. I love them like . . .' He pauses, laughs. 'Like brothers.'

'Constantine conducted a thorough investigation.'

In fact, he almost tore the palace apart looking for evidence to clear Crispus. All he did was damn him more. Letters from Crispus emerged boasting

When I am sole Augustus . . . Chests of coins struck with his insignia were found in his baggage. Two commanders of the imperial bodyguard came forward and testified that Crispus had ordered them to have their men ready to secure the palace. No one explained why the first act of Crispus's supposed coup was the botched murder of his adolescent brothers, rather than striking at Constantine himself.

'The tablet you found under my bed—I never saw it. Never knew it existed.'

'It doesn't matter.'

'Doesn't it?' He stares out to sea, to the flaming sun slowly being eclipsed by the horizon. 'I suppose not.'

'You broke your father's heart,' I say.

At last he listens to me. He spins around, anger animating his face. 'I didn't do anything. Nothing. If my father wants to believe their lies, instead of his own son, then he can break his own heart.'

I try to block out the bitterness. '*Their* lies—*whose* lies?'

'Can't you guess?' A husk of a crab shell is lying on the beach, long since picked clean by the gulls. He pokes it with his toe. 'Who accused me? Who benefits? If I'm gone, Fausta's children will inherit the empire.'

'Probably.'

He stamps on the crab shell, shattering its thin carapace. 'Am I the only one who can see the truth staring him in the face? Can't you recognise it? Don't you care?'

I shrug. 'What is truth, after all?'

Crispus drifts away from me. He wanders close to the water, flinching a little as the waves nibble

356

his feet.

'I loved him,' he declares, speaking to the sea. 'More than any son ever loved his father. I'd have died for him.' He pauses, lets his breathing slow. 'Now I suppose I will.'

I loosen the string that binds the leather bag and pull out the bottle. 'Your father told me to give you this.'

There were tears in Constantine's eyes then, and they're here in mine now. *Please*, I beg silently, *don't make this any harder for me*.

But it's his life. He looks at the little bottle, doesn't touch it.

'Don't make me do this.'

'Do you think you could escape? That you wouldn't be recognised? Your statue's in every forum from York to Alexandria. You wouldn't last a week.'

I step forward, press the vial into his fist and clasp my hand around it. Like a suitor trying to get his beloved to accept his token. Crispus tries to pull away, but I keep my grip tight. I only brought one bottle.

'It's an honourable death.' The lie tastes like dirt in my mouth. Neither of us believes it. Maybe opening your veins because you've defended the republic and lost, a final victory over your enemies, is honourable. Drinking aconite on a deserted beach, merely for the convenience of your murderers, is rather different.

'If I kill myself, I sin against God,' says Crispus.

'That's God's business.'

But he won't accept it. The tired face turns up to me, taut with desperation.

'You're an old friend, Gaius. Are you going to

take away my last consolation?'

'I can't.'

'I don't want to die a guilty man,' he pleads. 'Leave me my innocence. It's all I've got now.' I shake my head, but it doesn't stop him. 'Why do you think my father sent you, instead of some thug from the legions? He knew you'd do the right thing.'

Because he knew how hard it would be, I think. *Because he couldn't bear to be alone in his pain. He wanted to make someone else hurt as much as he did. To take the weight of his guilt.*

With a sudden movement, Crispus pulls his hand free of my grip. I'm not expecting it; before I can react, he's leapt away from me, arm poised to throw the poison into the sea.

I don't move. 'If you make me do this, you're no better than your father.'

'And if you force me to do it? What does that make you?'

We stand there for long moments, nothing between us except the light. More than ever before, I see his father as he was twenty years ago: tousled hair, handsome face, eyes brimming, even now, with life.

He holds out his arm to offer me the bottle. 'You choose.'

I take it from him. With a sudden rush of purpose, I dash it onto the beach. It shatters, very loud in the still evening air. The aconite leaches into the stones.

'Thank you.'

The gratitude on his face is too painful to bear. I reach into my tunic and take out the dagger strapped inside. Crispus laughs, though it's a small and lonely sound.

'Always ready for anything, Gaius Valerius.'

I can't look at his face. 'Turn around,' I order him.

He obeys, staring at the western horizon, eye to eye with the setting sun. The last of the daylight burns up his face, as if his translation to the next world has already begun. For a moment, the whole beach is aglow. Every pore in my body is open to the world, every sound and scent magnified a thousandfold. The splash of fish rising to the surface; a cock crowing in a distant field; the warm smell of pine. Perhaps this is how it feels to be in love.

The knife goes through his back and straight into his heart. The horizon swallows the sun; the world goes grey. Crispus drops into the surf without a sound. The incoming waves pick up pebbles and fling them against his corpse. Foaming water streams down the beach like tears.

*   *   *

Villa Achyron, near Nicomedia—May 337
There are tears on my face again. The memory's been buried deep inside me for ten years. Yet at the same time, it feels as if I've never escaped that beach. The empty plinths, the defaced monuments, the deleted inscriptions: every one of them shouted my guilt. So many times I've wished I'd pulled the knife out of Crispus and turned it on myself that day, or licked the spilled poison off the stones until I'd tasted enough to kill me.

Crispus got his last wish: he died an innocent man. Constantine, for all the terrible burden he

359

had to bear, never had to confront the reality of his decision. He's devoted his last ten years to erasing every trace of it. The burden of the crime's been left to me.

Perhaps that's why he wants to see me now.

I get to my feet. Pain cramps my old joints—too much riding—but I hobble across to the bronze door.

'Can I see him?'

The sentry doesn't move. 'I've had no orders.'

'He asked to see me. He called me here from Constantinople.' I'm desperate; I don't know how long I've got.

There's a noise on the other side of the door. Suddenly, it swings open. A flock of priests emerge, swarming around the gold-robed figure in their midst. For a second, I think it might be Constantine.

It's Eusebius. Whatever tragedies are unfolding in this house, they haven't touched him. His face is tipped back in triumph, a beatific smile stretching his fat cheeks. His gaze sweeps imperiously around the room—and stops on me.

'Gaius Valerius *Maximus*. How fortunate. The Augustus wants to see you.' He pushes me through the door. 'Be quick. You haven't got long.'

The room's far too big, a dining hall that's been cleared of all its couches except one. I don't understand why they've put him here. The solitary couch stands in the centre of the room, draped with white sheets, an island adrift in a vast ocean of space. Constantine is lying back, his eyes closed, his mouth slightly open. The colour's drained from his face, leaving only a sallow hint of the old vitality. The only other furniture is a gold basin filled with

360

water, on a wooden plinth beside the bed. Ripples shimmer the surface as I walk by.

My heart races. Am I too late? 'Augustus,' I call out. 'Constantine. It's Gaius.'

The eyes flick open. 'I told them to send for you. I've been counting the hours.'

'They wouldn't let me in.'

That stirs him. He tries to prop himself up, but his arms are so feeble they won't hold him. 'Doesn't my word carry weight any more? In my own house?'

'Why did they leave you unattended?'

'So I could prepare myself. Eusebius is going to baptise me.'

He sees the look on my face, something between disgust and anguish.

'It's time, Gaius. I've put it off long enough. I've spent my whole life trying to compass the breadth of this empire, to be a ruler for all my people, whatever god they might worship. I've never preached to them—or to you.'

He's misread me. I don't care about some arcane piece of Christian mystery, if it'll make him comfortable on the way out of this life. I hate the fact that here, on his deathbed, Eusebius has a claim on him.

The eyes close again. 'I wish my son was here.'

I go cold. Perhaps I knew this was coming. Perhaps, sitting in the anteroom, I was sharing Constantine's fevered dreams.

Deliberately, I misinterpret him. 'Constantius will be here soon from Antioch. And Claudius and Constans will come as fast as they can.' Too late, I imagine. The last I heard, Claudius, the eldest of Fausta's sons, was in Trier, ruling from Crispus's old palace. Constans, the youngest, is in Milan.

361

'They're good boys.' Perhaps it's his sickness, but there's not a lot of conviction in the words. 'They'll protect the empire.'

They're Fausta's sons, grandsons of the old warhorse Maximian. Scheming, murder and usurpation is their birthright. I give it three years before there's open war.

'And you'll make sure my daughters are protected?'

'I'll do what I can.' Even in the height of the moment, there's a voice at the back of my mind thinking clearly. When Constantine goes, I won't be in a position to guarantee anybody's safety—least of all my own. I'm a relic of a past that's vanishing before my eyes.

Constantine's breathing is fast and ragged. 'I need to prepare. I have to confess my sins.'

'You don't need to confess anything to me.'

'I do.' A hand shoots out from under the sheet. Bony fingers clasp my wrist. When did he get so thin? 'Eusebius says I need to confess my sins before I can receive baptism. I told him I could only confess to you.'

I doubt Eusebius liked that. No wonder he kept me waiting.

'You know what I did.'

'Then there's no need to say it.' I pull the sheet back over his chin. 'Keep warm.'

'*Please*. The door to heaven is closing on me, Gaius. The things I've done . . . Not just this. Every death warrant I signed, every child I failed to protect, every innocent man I condemned because the empire demanded it . . .'

I wonder if he's thinking about Symmachus.

'I still see him, you know,' says Constantine,

suddenly. 'Only a month ago, at dusk as I was riding through the Augusteum. I was so happy I almost jumped off my horse to embrace him. I thought of all the things I would say to him, and every drop of bile seemed to flow out of my soul.'

A fleck of spit has dribbled down his cheek. I wipe it away with the corner of the sheet.

'Of course he was gone when I got there.' He rolls over—a jerky movement, like a man being tossed on a wave. 'So many times I prayed you'd disobeyed me. That it was all a lie, that you'd let him escape. Remember, the joke we used to have, when we were trapped at Galerius's court? That we'd run to the mountains, leave our fame and troubles behind and live as shepherds in Dalmatia. That was what I hoped had happened to him.'

Is this a confession? I doubt it would satisfy Eusebius. I can't blame Constantine for skirting around the issue, but there isn't much time. The bronze doors at the far end of the room keep making noises, thuds and groans as if there's a boxed animal behind them. Eusebius must be coming soon. This is his moment of triumph: he doesn't want death to snatch away his prize convert too soon.

Constantine's speaking again, but his voice is so low I can barely hear it. I slip off the stool and kneel on the marble floor. My eyes are inches from his. I can see the web of red lines surrounding the irises; the puffy, bruised skin around them. Eyes that surveyed the world.

'Why do you think I sent you to Pula?' he whispers. 'I thought if anyone would show mercy, you would. You should have known better.'

His words are like a jagged knife sawing open

my heart. Does he mean it? Was it *my* mistake all along? Or is he rewriting history again to suit his conscience? I stare into those eyes, hardly able to breathe.

What is truth, after all? Philosophers say that the gods know, and perhaps they're right. For the rest of us, it's just an accumulation of faded memories and lies.

'I did what you sent me to do.'

His eyes seem to lose their focus. 'Do you remember Aurelius Symmachus?' he whispers.

Is this another part of his confession?

'The day before I left Constantinople, he wrote to me at the palace. He wanted to see me. He said he knew the truth about my son. Should I have seen him, do you think?'

'The truth about your son?' Surely he means about Alexander, about Eusebius and the persecutions.

'I didn't want to know. I sent him to my sister.'

My head's starting to spin. 'You sent Symmachus to see your sister?'

But this conversation isn't about Symmachus. 'I thought perhaps the truth . . .' He trails off. 'I saw him, you know. In the Augusteum, among the statues. He should have been there.'

'You'll be reunited soon,' I say.

'Will we?' Suddenly, the eyes are wide open, the voice firm. 'This life I've lived, do you think I've earned it? Eusebius says he can wash away the deepest stain.' He shakes his head. 'Do you believe that?'

'You lived a good life. You brought peace to the world.'

'I brought no peace but the sword,' he says,

364

inscrutably. 'I've campaigned every summer for the last ten years. I'll die here with more soldiers around me than priests. Do you think the titles I've accumulated will count for anything when Christ meets me at the gates of heaven? Unconquered Constantine, four times victor over the Germans, twice over the Sarmatians, twice the Goths, twice the Dacians . . . Is that how he'll call me?'

At the far end of the room, the bronze doors creak open. A worried priest's face appears.

'Eusebius . . .'

'Tell him to wait!' I shout. But Constantine is running out of patience—and time. He clasps his bony fingers on to the front of my tunic and hauls himself up. I can feel the fever burning off his face.

'Do you forgive me?'

Do I? I can hardly draw breath. For eleven years I've waited for him to ask me. It's been the void between us, the death of our friendship and the hollowing out of our selves. And now that he's asked, the reply sticks in my throat. I don't know what to say.

I remember something Porfyrius told me about Alexander: *He forgave me everything. No rebuke, no lecture.*

I lean across to embrace Constantine. I put my head against his shoulder, feeling the powdery skin against my cheek, and wrap my arms around his head. I whisper in his ear.

'Goodbye.'

His body tenses. A scream of strangled rage or despair rasps in his throat until he chokes on it. It takes all my strength to prise his fingers off me so I can push him back down on the bed. Even then, he struggles and flails, throwing back the sheets.

365

I blunder towards the door. It's already open: guards are rushing in, with a mass of priests and soldiers pressing behind them. I struggle against the tide and find myself face to face with Eusebius.

'You can have your prize,' I tell him.

I don't think he hears me. The crowd carries him forward to Constantine's bedside, while I slink out of the hall.

The moment I'm alone, remorse overwhelms me. Whatever's happened between us, who am I to deny an old friend his last comfort. I turn to go back, to tell him I forgive him. That I love him.

But the throng of courtiers blocking the way is so thick I'll never get through. They make a circle around the bed, where Eusebius is standing next to the bowl of water. A snatch of what he's saying reaches back to me.

'Die and rise to new life, so that you may live for ever.'

The doors close in my face, and Constantine is gone.

XXXIX

Split, Croatia—Present Day
There weren't many places in the world where you could inhabit a Roman emperor's palace. Split might be the only one. When the Emperor Diocletian defied all precedent and expectation by quitting his office at the peak of his powers, he built himself a retirement home on an imperial scale: a seafront palace on a quiet bay overlooking the Dalmatian coast, based on the plan of a

366

military camp the area of eight football pitches, with walls ten storeys high. Inside the walls were gardens, where the peasant emperor could tend his vegetable patch; opulent living quarters and ceremonial halls (even a retired emperor expects a certain grandeur); several temples to the old gods, whom Diocletian had defended with cruel vigour against the depredations of the Christians; a garrison, because even though he'd pacified the empire, his successors were jealous, violent men; and his own mausoleum, so he would never need to leave.

But the Christians had survived his persecution, flourished, and eventually thrown out the old gods and their champion. Five hundred years after his death, Diocletian had suffered the ultimate indignity. His porphyry sarcophagus had been torn out of his mausoleum, his bones thrown into a ditch and replaced with those of a man he'd martyred. The church he'd tried to destroy had appropriated his final monument, turning his mausoleum into a cathedral.

And the palace remained. When barbarians came, the local citizens retreated inside Diocletian's walls and squatted in the ruins. Over time, houses grew up like weeds, weaving through the remains and making them their own. New walls absorbed columns and arches; old walls sprouted new roofs. Bit by bit, the palace turned into a town. Roman *Spalato* became Croatian Split.

*   *   *

Abby had been there with Michael a few months ago, another stolen weekend away from Kosovo.

She'd instantly decided it was one of her favourite places in the world. They stayed in a boutique hotel with bits of Diocletian's wall jutting into the bedrooms; wandered down narrow alleys that suddenly opened up on intact Roman temples; ate Dalmatian ham on freshly baked bread, and drank red wine late into the night.

That had been June; this was October. The tourists had gone home, the pavement cafés retreated indoors, the hotels emptied. She'd thought her memories of the summer might bring back some warmth: instead, they only mocked her with echoes of happiness. It reminded her of the dying days of her marriage, when she and Hector had gone back to Venice, scene of their honeymoon, hoping a spark of the old feeling might rekindle something. That was when she'd realised there was no way back.

At least she and Michael had reached Split. After all her worries, getting out of Serbia had been the easiest part of the journey. At the border, the bus driver had collected passports and handed the stack to the guard, who took them in to his hut. Ten heart-stopping minutes later, the guard came back and returned them to the driver, who redistributed them among the sleepy passengers.

The bus rolled on, the border receded. Across the aisle and three rows forward, Michael glanced back and winked.

*   *   *

They checked into the Hotel Marjan, another hulk of Soviet-era luxury squatting on the waterfront half a mile from the old town centre. They registered under their own names—Michael spun the bored clerk a story about how a pickpocket had stolen their passports, until the man surrendered the keys to room 213. Abby went up, washed her face, and got ready to go straight back out. It was already almost one thirty.

Do it as quickly as possible, Michael had said. *Don't give them time to prepare.*

Michael flopped down on the bed.

'Are you sure you're all right doing this on your own?'

'We've got to assume Mark will have people watching. It won't work if they see you.'

He leaned over on his side and stared across the room at her. 'Be careful, OK?'

'I'll see you later.'

*   *   *

She walked along a palm-lined esplanade, past the mostly empty marina and the few ferries tied up at the dock. At the far end, the pillars of the palace façade rose above the shops that had been tucked into the wall. Just past a jeweller's she turned left through an arch into an underground arcade that had once been a water gate, but now housed stalls selling trinkets and art. Ahead, a flight of stairs led up towards daylight.

Unlike most people living in the West, Abby actually knew what it was like to be followed by secret police. She'd experienced it countless times: a blacked-out car trailing her from the airport in Belgrade; a window cleaner in Khartoum who'd spent an hour outside the meeting room making smudges in the dust; a telephone that clicked all

369

through her conversations and cut out unexpectedly in Kinshasa. She'd once asked her boss if she should have some sort of counter-espionage training to deal with it. *Bad idea*, she'd been told. *If you look like an amateur, they just watch. It's when you look like you know what you're doing that it gets dangerous.*

This time, they picked her up the moment she entered the palace. It was the obvious move— seventeen hundred years on, Diocletian's walls still held good, allowing only five ways in to the old town. She could feel eyes on her as she walked along the arcade. A man in a green anorak who'd been browsing through a rack of art prints peeled off and started walking ahead of her. Just after she'd passed a woman in a red skirt at a coffee stall, she heard a second set of footsteps fall in behind her. She forced herself not to look back.

She climbed the stairs and crossed a courtyard boxed in by high blank walls. The footsteps behind kept pace, following her through a door into a high round chamber that had once been the entrance vestibule of the imperial apartments. A pair of Japanese tourists stood in its centre, aiming their cameras at the doughnut hole of the *oculus* in the domed roof. Off to the right, another man in a black fleece stared at his guidebook. Was it her imagination, or did he glance up at her as she swerved around the two tourists and crossed to the doorway in the far wall?

Beyond the vestibule was the peristyle—the formal courtyard at the heart of any Roman dwelling. A row of columns soared above it, free-standing and intact; the facing columns were also intact, though now built into the façade of a

370

Venetian palazzo that had become a coffee-house. Behind the arches stood the stone octagon of Diocletian's mausoleum, now the cathedral. A high belltower rose next to it, overlooking the city; at its foot, a black Egyptian sphinx crouched beside the door and riddled passers-by.

The man in the green anorak diverted to the coffee shop and took a seat in the window. The woman in the red skirt walked briskly past and climbed the steps to the mausoleum. Abby turned, admiring the architecture, and saw the man in the black fleece lounging against the vestibule doorway taking a photograph.

'Abby?' Mark wasn't giving her any time for second thoughts. He'd emerged from behind the sphinx, was hurrying down the well-worn steps. He was wearing a navy blue wool coat, the sort of sensible thing his mother might have bought him, and a striped college scarf. He stuck out his hand, and pumped hers too enthusiastically.

'Do you want to get a coffee?'

So that's how he wants to play it. She nodded.

'Do you know anywhere good?'

Was that a test? She shrugged, noncommittal. 'This town used to be colonised by the Italians. Pretty much everywhere has good coffee.'

'Might as well stay here, then.' He led her across the peristyle courtyard, to the coffee shop opposite the cathedral. He offered her a seat with her back to the door, and seated himself facing her and the window. She tried to see the street in the gilded mirror behind him, but it was too high.

They were the only customers there, except for the green-anoraked man at the table by the window. Presumably that would help with whatever

371

devices Mark had recording the conversation. A white-aproned waiter came and took their order: black coffee for Abby, tea for Mark.

He looked at her face. 'You look as if you've been in the wars.'

'Where's the necklace?'

To her surprise, he didn't stall. He reached in his pocket and pulled out a slim black jewellery box with an Asprey logo on the top. He pressed the catch and flipped open the lid. There was the necklace, laid on a ruffle of black silk. To the waiter, polishing the coffee machine and peering over the bar, she must look like an exceptionally expensive, hard-to-please girlfriend. She shuddered at the thought.

'Are you going to tell me why you want this?'

'You wouldn't believe me.'

Mark snapped the box shut. 'We took it to a nice man at the British Museum. He said it's antique—fourth-century Roman. About the same vintage as the tomb in Kosovo where we found Jessop's body.'

The waiter brought the drinks. Abby looked at her hands. 'I'm sorry about Jessop.'

'He was a good man.' Mark said it stiffly, as though he'd learned the line from a film. 'He filed a report just before he died, saying he suspected Michael Lascaris had been supplying Dragović with stolen antiquities looted from this tomb.'

'That's what it looked like.'

'Did Michael tell you differently?'

'You can ask him yourself.'

Mark looked around, as if he expected Michael to materialise out of the Roman stones. 'You didn't bring him here.'

She put her elbows on the table and leaned

forward over her coffee. Her heart was racing.

'Michael's at the Hotel Marjan on the waterfront. Room 213.'

'Alone?'

'When I left him.'

Mark produced a mobile phone and tapped out a text message. She assumed that was for show, that hidden microphones had already radioed the details to whatever accomplices Mark had waiting. They probably had a car. Even on foot, it wouldn't take more than ten minutes to get there.

She took the necklace out of the jewellery box and clasped it around her neck, cold metal on cold skin. Mark opened his mouth as if he wanted to stop her, but didn't.

'What do you want with Michael?' she asked.

Mark smoothed back his hair. 'Michael isn't the target. Dragović is. All we want Michael for is to lead us to him.'

'What's going to happen to Michael?'

'Maybe a prison sentence. Maybe not, if he cooperates and it comes to something. And if he gets a good lawyer.'

'He wants the same thing you do,' Abby protested. She stared into Mark's young eyes and didn't hide her contempt. 'He was getting close to Dragović to bring him down.'

'Then why are you selling him out?'

Abruptly, Abby stood. Mark jumped up, knocking the table and rattling the coffee cups. The green-coated man in the window looked around.

'Relax,' Abby said to the room. 'I just need a wee.'

Before anyone could stop her, she pushed through the wooden door into the toilet and

373

locked it. She listened for footsteps, for banging on the door, but they didn't come. The toilet was at the back of the café, a windowless dead end. They didn't have to worry about her escaping that way.

She checked her watch and got to work.

First, she closed the toilet seat and took a piece of paper out of her coat. It was Gruber's scan of the papyrus, but traced out on clean paper so that the letters were clear and legible. She laid it flat on the toilet seat, then unlatched the necklace and laid it over the text.

The gold fitted exactly—the square outline of the necklace and the square layout of the writing. Abby peered closer, and swore in quiet amazement. Each of the glass beads that studded the gold lined up perfectly with a letter underneath.

She checked the time. A minute gone.

Hands trembling, she took out a magnifying glass she'd bought in Zadar and read off all the letters she could see through the beads. She circled them in pencil on a copy of the text, then traced the outline of the gold over it in case that was important too.

Three minutes gone.

She took a slim digital camera out of her coat and photographed the necklace in place over the writing, holding the camera as close and as still as she could. Then she ejected the memory card, wrapped it in the small square of paper, and tucked it into her bra. She picked up the necklace and clasped it back on. Finally, she lifted the lid of the cistern and dropped in the camera and the magnifying glass, then tore up the extra copy of the papyrus and flushed it down the toilet.

If they don't find a camera, they won't look for pictures.

The whole business had taken five and a half minutes. She washed her hands, just in case anyone was going to sniff them, and went back out. Mark was sitting indecisively in his chair, half-poised to get up. The green-coated man had gone.

'Michael's not at the Hotel Marjan,' Mark said. He sounded angry. 'The receptionist said he checked in an hour ago, but the room's empty.'

That didn't take long. She tried to look apologetic. 'He probably went for a walk. We've been on the road for most of the last fourteen hours.'

'Why didn't you bring him here?'

'Because he knows better than to walk into a walled town that's crawling with SIS.'

'Did you tell him we were here?'

'Of course not.'

'Does he trust you?'

'Maybe. Probably not.' She let exasperation show. 'Michael convinced the world he was dead, and then covered his tracks so well that neither you nor Dragović could find him. Do you think he's just going to sit in a bedroom watching TV, while I go and meet with the people who want to arrest him? If I was him, I'd be sitting in the café next door to the hotel, watching to see if any flat-footed thugs came charging in looking for Michael Lascaris.'

Mark's eyes narrowed. 'How did you get here?'

'By car.'

'Make? Model?'

'It's blue.'

Mark started to say something patronising and stereotypical, then realised she was playing with

375

him.

'It's a Skoda Fabia—the hatchback. I don't remember the registration.'

This time, he didn't bother to pretend with his phone. He pushed back his chair and stood. Outside the window, Abby saw the flash of a red skirt between the columns across the street.

'Where are you going?'

'*We*. You're staying with me until we get our hands on Michael.'

'Bollocks to that. If he's seen your people, he'll know I've turned him in.' She got up and pulled on her coat. 'I'll take care of myself.'

'Come with me,' he said. Not an order, more a plea. For a moment she could almost believe he cared about her. 'I've got a car waiting on the promenade. A clean passport, too. In three hours you can be back home and safe. You can have your life back.'

And why not? No more running. No more drifting around these concrete cities at the end of civilisation, waking up every morning not knowing if she'd live or die. Out of the cold, into the warmth.

But what was her life, after all? An empty flat, a failed marriage and a lost faith. She'd come too far down this road.

She put a twenty-kuna note on the table. 'That's for the coffee.'

Mark didn't try to stop her.

'Aren't you forgetting something?' He waggled a finger in the direction of her neck; she gave him an *I'm-sorry* grimace, unhooked the necklace and laid it back in the box.

'I bet you do that to all your ex-girlfriends.'

She left the warmth of the café and stepped out

into the courtyard. The lady in the red skirt had moved along to the far end and was examining a shop window; the man in the black fleece was enthusiastically photographing the sphinx. The day was so dark the flash kept going off.

She turned right, then immediately right again down a narrow alley barely wider than she was. Footsteps followed—the snare-drum tap of a woman's boots.

That's why they let you go. They think you'll lead them to Michael.

She came out into a small square. Ahead loomed the stark front of a grey Roman temple, squeezed tight between the red-roofed houses. She skirted around its monumental base, past a shuttered café and along an even narrower alley. The tight walls echoed the footsteps back at her like the chatter of crows.

The alley intersected with a wider street, the old Roman *Cardo*, running through the heart of the palace. East was the mausoleum and the peristyle; west, the double arches of Diocletian's Iron Gate, leading out to the rest of the city. She looked both ways. To her right, the man in the black fleece was ambling along the street from the peristyle. On her left, a man was reading a tourist plaque mounted next to the gate. He looked like the green-anoraked man from the café, though he'd changed into a long fawn-coloured trenchcoat, a newspaper tucked under his arm.

She went left. The man half-turned, as if studying some detail of the architecture, but didn't try to block her way. The gate was actually two gateways with a tower connecting them: it would be easy to hide someone inside, invisible until you'd stepped through.

Two sets of feet joined step behind her as Red Skirt and Black Fleece met. Ahead, she could see Trenchcoat looking past her. He moved the folded newspaper from his left arm to his right. Was that some sort of signal?

At the last moment, she veered right up another narrow lane. Stone arches soared overhead, connecting the buildings on both sides; all the houses had squat doors and shuttered windows cut into the dressed stone. Some were homes, but a few were shops. She quickened her pace.

Halfway down, one of the buildings housed a fashion boutique. Abby had been there when they'd visited in June. Michael had bought her a dress with bright orange flowers: she'd fussed about the cost, but worn it all through the summer. She reached the door and turned suddenly in. A bell chimed. There were no other customers. Behind the counter, a well-dressed woman was folding and smoothing a pile of cashmere sweaters. She smiled at Abby.

'Can I help you?'

Abby smiled and shook her head. She flicked through the rails, one eye on the sizes and one on the door. No one came in; no one came past. Mark's people had her trapped: they didn't need to barge in and make a scene.

She picked off a pair of black trousers and a black V-neck sweater.

'Could I try these on?'

'Of course.' The shopkeeper indicated a doorway next to the counter, where a dim stone staircase curved upwards. 'The dressing room is at the top.'

Abby went upstairs. The walls on each side

seemed so massive she had to presume she was climbing through the original fortifications. At the top of the stairs a wooden door led into a small white cubicle with a mirror on the wall, a stool, and an old-fashioned hatstand in the corner. A curtained window overlooked the house behind.

Abby went in and bolted the door. She pulled back the curtain and looked down on a red-tiled rooftop. The shop was built right into the wall: the roof she could see was on the outside of the old town. It led down to a courtyard between two buildings and there, dressed in motorcycle leathers and looking up expectantly, was Michael. He saw her face in the window and beckoned urgently.

A bell chimed downstairs. Someone had come into the shop. They must be getting impatient. How long would they give her—maybe two minutes? She put her hands against the wooden sash and lifted.

It rose three inches—and stopped. Adrenaline kicked in; she heaved and cursed, but it still wouldn't move. Looking up, she saw two silver cylinders screwed into the window frame. Window locks.

The window wouldn't open any further. From outside the door, she heard footsteps mounting the stairs.

'Come on!' she heard Michael shout. She tried harder, rattling the window in its casing, thumping it against the locks. They didn't give.

The person outside stopped at the door and knocked.

'Is everything OK? You need another size?'

It sounded like the saleswoman, though she couldn't be sure through the door. 'I'm fine,' she called. 'Just trying to make up my mind.'

'You say if you need something.'

The footsteps didn't go away.

Down in the courtyard, Michael had realised what had happened. 'Did you get the pictures? Throw me the card.'

Abby took a deep breath. *Time to decide.* She'd seen some bad situations in her old line of work, in some of the worst places in the world. She knew the temptation of waiting just a little longer, maybe only a few seconds, to see if things turned out better than she feared. She knew you could stretch those seconds for minutes, maybe even hours if you got the chance. Hope could always justify doing nothing—right up until the moment it killed you.

She picked up the stool, held it by the legs and swung it against the window. Almost at once, an alarm went off—she hadn't thought of that. The door rattled as someone tried the handle, then shuddered as they started banging.

The window was still intact. And her shoulder hurt like hell from the impact.

She stared at the stool impotently. It felt like a toothpick in her hand. The banging on the door had turned into an all-out onslaught. More than one person, it sounded like. The dinky bolt wouldn't hold more than a few seconds.

Even Michael must have been able to hear. 'Throw me the card!' he said again.

She fished out the memory card from inside her bra, snaked her wrist through the opening in the window and threw. For a heartstopping moment she thought she hadn't thrown hard enough, that it would skip down the roof and lodge in the guttering. It just dropped clear. Michael stretched and caught it one-handed. He raised his arm—half

380

a salute, half a farewell.

The bolt snapped; the door crashed open. The man in the black fleece strode in and grabbed her arms, while Mark watched from the corridor and the shopowner screamed complaints from the stairwell.

Abby took a last glance out the window, but the courtyard was empty.

XL

Nicomedia—22 May 337
The world changed two hours ago. Flavius Ursus, Flavius the Bear, Flavius the son-of-a-barbarian who is now the commander of the armies, came out of Constantine's room to confirm the news everyone expected. The Augustus is dead. The body has been sent to the cellars, the coolest place, while the undertakers do their work. There aren't many men alive who can remember the last time an Augustus died a natural death. It's like waking up one morning and discovering that the sun hasn't risen. What do you do?

I know what I want to do: run to the stables, commandeer the fastest horse I can find and keep riding until I reach my villa in the Balkans. But that would be impossible—and unwise. The army have locked down the whole estate. Guards are watching every door and window. Anyone who moves too quickly; anyone who looks too happy, or too ostentatiously sad; anyone who tries to leave: all suspect.

In the febrile heat of the villa, rumours breed

and swarm like flies. Constantine was sixty-five years old, but until ten days ago he seemed in good health. Perhaps, after all, his death wasn't natural.

A door swings open. Flavius Ursus walks in. He's a busy man today.

'I thought I'd find you here,' he says.

'If there's anything I can do—'

'Wait there. We may need you to smooth things over with the old guard.'

He leaves me and goes into the great hall, where the army's high command have gathered. Notwithstanding what Constantine wrote in his will, these are the men who'll decide the inheritance. For generations, the empire's practised a savage sort of meritocracy where any man who's bold and ruthless enough can rise to the top of the army. From there, he's within striking distance of the throne. Diocletian was commander of the imperial bodyguard until the man he was guarding unaccountably took a dagger in the back; far from harming his career, it put Diocletian on the throne. Constantine's own father had risen from a humble legionary to become Diocletian's chief of staff, when Diocletian picked him to be his successor.

I remember something Constantiana said, that night in the palace. *Some people said Constantine would raise you to Caesar, before Fausta started popping out sons like a breeding sow.* Would he have? Would it be me lying in the cellars having my entrails drawn out on a hook, while my generals and courtiers tried to comprehend a world without me?

A vision comes to me: the empire as a walled town built on the back of a ravenous beast. Constantine cut off so many of its heads and tamed it; he chained it down in pasture and made it eat grass. But now that he's gone, other heads will grow back. Slowly at first, testing their teeth and claws, rediscovering their old power. It won't take long. They'll start with murders and end in war.

High clouds cover the sky, as if the sun itself is veiled in mourning. There aren't words to describe how I feel. Not wretched, not angry, just—empty.

My thoughts turn back to another palace, and the aftermath of another death.

*　　*　　*

Milan—July 326—Eleven years earlier . . .
By the time I get back from Pula, the court has left Aquileia and hurried on to Milan. I join them there—I have to make my report—though I'd rather be anywhere else. The weight of my guilt is like a millstone suffocating the life out of me. I don't eat; I barely speak. It takes me hours to get to sleep at night, only to wake up screaming from my bloody dreams. And it's about to get worse.

For the first time in my life, Constantine keeps me waiting. I pace in a mournful room, high above the main courtyard. A piece of plaster falls off the ceiling and lands in my hair. Half the rooms in the palace are unusable; most of the rest are covered in sheeting, hiding damage or pictures that might upset the imperial eye. The whole building is rotten with history. It was built by old Maximian, an overblown outgrowth of his twisted mind. This is where Constantine came to meet with Licinius— *When I, Constantine Augustus, and I, Licinius Augustus, happily met in Milan, and considered all matters pertaining to the public good*; where he made

383

his famous pronouncement of religious support for the Christians, and where he married his sister Constantiana to the man he'd later execute.

So many people, so many memories—and not one that doesn't end in blood.

'The Augusta wants to see you.' I almost jump with fright: the slave seems to have materialised out of the dust in the air. He keeps his eyes down—does he know what I've done? Has he heard? He leads me through endless connections of empty rooms, down a broad staircase with no windows, and into another wing of the palace. The air moistens: we must be near the bath complex.

They're all waiting for me in a square room with blood-red walls: Constantine, a ghost of himself; Fausta, her proud face livid with anger; the Dowager Empress Helena, Constantine's mother, her eyes hooded and her mouth set like concrete. Fausta's three sons stand in a row near the back of the room and fidget.

Nobody asks what I've done. Nobody thanks me, commiserates, accuses. Helena hands me a scrolled piece of paper.

'Read it.'

'"To the great god Nemesis, I curse my enemy and give him into your power. Drive him to his death . . ."'

I don't need to go on. 'This is the curse I found under Crispus's bed in Aquileia.'

Helena fixes her pitiless gaze on me. 'But?'

'Without the names.'

'And do you know—?' She's addressing me, but I'm just the sounding board. The words are aimed elsewhere in the room. 'Do you know where I found this?'

No one dares to answer.

'In Fausta's room.'

I'm seized by a violent, uncontrollable shaking; so hard I think I might faint. No one notices—or, if they do, they don't care. My mouth's dry and my head hurts; I'm desperate for a drink.

Fausta tries to shrug it off. 'I copied it off the tablet. I wanted a record of Crispus's treachery.'

'I took this paper to the temple of Nemesis in Aquileia.' Helena continues as if Fausta hadn't spoken. 'I showed it to the priestess. She told me that she wrote it out for a woman who wanted to know the correct form of words. A noblewoman, too well bred to know how soldiers and fishwives curse.'

'I suppose you would know,' Fausta snaps, 'being a brothel-keeper's daughter.'

Helena ignores the insult and looks at Constantine. 'The noblewoman was your wife. She wrote out the curse on the lead tablet, stole your pin and hid it under Crispus's bed.'

Colour rises in Fausta's cheeks. 'You'd believe this priestess? She's probably just a prostitute. And what about the guard captains who said Crispus bribed them to turn against my husband?'

'I've spoken to them, too.' Helena's tone is sharp, like hooks in a dungeon. 'They retracted their claim.'

Her eyes shoot daggers at Fausta, who stares back in furious defiance. If they had armies to command, these two women, the whole world would tremble.

They both turn to Constantine, who's listened to the exchange in silence. The only sign he's heard anything is the way he flinches each time they say

Crispus's name.

The whole room holds its breath.

'What about Claudius?' I ask. I'm as surprised as anyone to hear my own voice. Through the pain and dizziness burning in my skull, I've lost all sense of what's appropriate. 'Fausta said Crispus tried to murder him.'

All eyes turn to the three boys. They're still children: even Claudius, the eldest, isn't yet ten years old. They carry themselves proudly—their mother's made them aware of their rank since the day they were born—but they're out of their depth here. Constans, the youngest, is trying to blink back tears; Claudius looks at his mother, silently begging her to speak for him. He won't look at Constantine.

'She made us do it.'

It isn't Claudius who says it; it's the middle brother, Constantius. He steps forward, head held high. 'Our mother cut Claudius's ear and then told us to blame Crispus when he came.' He glances at his father, falters. 'We didn't want to.'

A sickened silence grips the room. Fausta's face has crumpled in like a pillow; Constantine is so still I wonder if his heart has stopped. Only Helena takes it in her stride. She expected it.

'How old are you?' she asks Constantius. He's Helena's grandson, but you wouldn't know it from the contempt in her voice.

'Nearly nine.'

'Old enough to know it was a murderous lie.'

He wilts. 'Our mother told us.'

'And if she'd told you to stab your father while he slept, would you have done that too?'

'No.' It's the first word Constantine's spoken, and even that's been wrenched out of him. 'Not the

386

children.'

'They were accomplices.'

'They're your children,' Fausta pleads to Constantine.

So was Crispus, I think.

'Crispus was worth the three of them put together.' Helena's hated that family since Constantine's father jilted her for one of old Maximian's daughters. Now, at the end of her life, they've robbed her again. She'd like them obliterated from the face of the earth.

'Show mercy,' Fausta begs. She must know her life is over, but she's fighting like a lioness for her cubs. She throws herself to the floor, grabs Constantine's purple shoes and starts kissing them wildly, which turns into a scream as Helena steps forward and kicks her in the face. She was born a stable girl, and even at eighty she still has that strength. Fausta reels away, blood trickling from her lip. And Constantine still can't move. For a long moment they look between each other, chained to each other like slaves on a sinking ship. Fausta, whimpering on the floor; Helena, breathing hard; Constantine like a statue.

Unexpectedly, it's Constans—the youngest son— who breaks the moment. He's only six, with a head of blond curls and soft pale skin like a barbarian. He runs forward and wraps his arms around Constantine's legs.

'When is Uncle Crispus coming home, Father?'

A tear runs down Constantine's face. He crouches and hugs his son, closing his eyes in agony.

Undeniably, it's a tender moment—and after what's just happened, everyone in the room is susceptible. We're desperate to believe in reconciliation. But I can't help wondering. This family gobble each other like primordial gods. Fausta betrayed old Maximian when he plotted against Constantine; now Constantius and Constans have condemned their mother and probably saved themselves.

Constantine rises, keeping his hand on his son's shoulder.

'You destroyed Crispus,' he says to Fausta.

Blood's still running from her cut lip. She rubs it with the back of her hand, smearing a ghastly rictus across her cheek. Her eyes dart around the room like a cornered animal, and finally come to rest on Constantine.

'I did,' she whispers.

'Why?' He turns away. 'No, don't tell me.' He glances at Helena. 'You can take care of this? Discreetly?'

'And the children?' Helena presses.

'Find them a tutor.'

She wants to argue, but Constantine isn't listening. He turns his back and walks to the door, his shoulders slumped in defeat. I want to run to him, to put my arm around him and console him. With a great pang of loss, I realise that I can never comfort him again. Not after what I've done.

Helena grips Fausta's arm so hard she gasps. 'I think it's time that you and I visited the baths.'

Memories collapse; my own voice comes back to me out of the recent past.

Cato the Stoic died in a bath, opening his veins so that the heat would draw the blood out of him. Though I've heard another version, that he didn't die of his wounds but actually suffocated from the steam.

It doesn't matter which version you hear. They

388

all end the same way.

*   *   *

Villa Achyron—22 May 337
Whatever happened today, Constantine effectively
died over those four weeks during his *vicennalia*.
For eleven years the empire's been living in that
shadow. We have an emperor with three sons,
but no wife; history books full of victories, but no
victor. We've kept our eyes down, our voices low,
and never dared to contradict the lie. Some days I
think the effort of the charade has driven the whole
empire to the brink of madness.

Did it cost Alexander his life? A week ago, I
was convinced he must have been killed because
of what he knew about Eusebius. Symmachus, too.
Now, I'm not so sure.

Constantine: *Symmachus said he knew the truth
about my son.*

But Bassus, sweating in the baths: *He said he'd
found out something about a Christian bishop. A
scandal.*

Which was it?

Alexander burrowed deep in the Chamber
of Records, stripping out every last reference
to Crispus. I know he was looking at the papers
from Aquileia, and from Helena's household. Did
he find something that got him killed—and that
Symmachus saw when he took the document case?

Does it matter? What are one or two deaths
against the death of an emperor? I remember
something Eusebius said: *Leave the dead to bury the
dead*. It sounds like good advice.

But if there is a truth behind Crispus's death—a

truth that's worth killing for—then . . .

Heavy boots echo down the corridor. The generals have emerged from their meeting. They knot around the courtyard in twos and threes, grim-faced and urgent. Flavius Ursus comes across to me, flanked by four guards. His position is the most powerful—but also the most precarious.

'Is everything decided?'

'The Emperor's sons will divide the empire between them.' He's holding a piece of paper; I imagine a map on it, the fates of millions described in a room in this villa.

'Does everyone accept that?'

'The army's content.' No doubt Claudius, Constantius and Constans will reward them handsomely for their support—and there's the war with Persia, which promises rich pickings for the army and its sycophants. 'This is a time for unity.'

I think of old Constantius, left on his deathbed for two days after he died until Constantine got there. It's lucky York's so cold.

'When will you announce the death?'

'Constantius is coming from Antioch. We'll wait for him.'

That'll be two weeks—maybe three or four depending on the roads and the mountain passes. 'Can you keep the secret that long?'

'It's safest. The army is united, but there are other factions that might try to take advantage. Already, there are rumours . . .'

'There are always rumours.'

'And they need to be investigated. So we have a job for you.'

He hands me the piece of paper—not a map, but a list. I scan down it: eminent senators, retired officials. The old guard, men who might object to the new settlement. Among them, I notice Porfyrius's name.

'Find these men. Tell them that if or when the Augustus's sons take power, they've got nothing to fear.'

'*Have* they got anything to fear?'

He gives me a crooked look. 'Just tell them.' He sees my reluctance and growls. 'I'm doing you a favour, Gaius—for old times' sake. I'm giving you a chance to prove your loyalty.'

He jerks his head over his shoulder, at the generals and tribunes congregated in the courtyard. 'Not everyone would give you that. There are rumours, and with your history . . .'

He pats me on the shoulder.

'Now get out, while you have the chance.'

XLI

Split, Croatia—Present Day

Abby sat in the hotel room. It was the nicest place she'd been in a week—Egyptian cotton on the bed, Swiss chocolates under the pillows and Welsh mineral water in the fridge. She barely noticed. She sat hunched on the bed, her knees pulled up against her chest and her arms wrapped around her legs.

Across the room, a woman in a red skirt and a cream jumper sat in a wingback chair. She must have been about the same age as Abby, though far more robust: a strong, big-limbed body; an athletic rosiness on her cheeks and long, honey-coloured hair worn loose. She said her name was Connie.

She didn't try to make conversation, but sat there watching Abby, occasionally looking down to fiddle with the BlackBerry in her hand.

In the corner, a man in a black fleece leaned against the door, arms folded. The curtains were drawn, the lights tastefully low, but he still wore a pair of sunglasses. Something bulged under the fleece, brutish like a tumour. Connie called him Barry.

The remnants of a chicken salad lay on a plate beside her. At least her captors had let her order room service. She'd eaten their food and told them everything. The tomb, the scroll, the poem and Gruber. A Roman soldier who'd been stabbed seventeen hundred years ago; and Michael, who jumped off a cliff and came back again. She'd told them about the *labarum*, Constantine's unconquerable standard, how Dragović wanted it and how the poem and the necklace might lead to it. The only person she left out was Dr Nikolvić, whose one crime had been helping them. By the time she'd finished, she felt as though there was nothing left in her.

Someone knocked discreetly at the door and murmured something. Barry raised his sunglasses and put his eye to the peephole. Satisfied, he dropped the safety bolt and took three steps back.

Mark entered, holding a piece of paper.

'The good Germans in Trier just faxed this through. A printout from Dr Gruber's computer. Apparently, they were quite upset to find out he'd been moonlighting for wanted criminals.'

The jewellery box sat on a chest of drawers next to the television. Mark took out the necklace and laid it on the bed with the fax. He took a pen from his jacket.

'Show me how it works.'

She leaned forward and aligned the necklace with the poem. The original had been blurred; the fax was muddier still. But she'd spent so long staring at it on the bus from Serbia, puzzling out the letters one by one, she found they came more easily now. She traced the outline of the necklace on the paper, boxing in the letters, then lifted off the necklace. This time, she could see what she'd connected. Starting from the top of the monogram, she read:

'CONSTANTINUS INVICTUS IMP AUG XXI.'

Mark made her read it again, then wrote it out on a blank sheet of paper.

'I've got a classicist from Oxford waiting on the line—someone who's worked for us before. We'll see what he makes of it.'

Abby looked up. It would have taken a lot to make her laugh just then, but she managed a bleak smile.

'I can save you the phone bill. "Constantine the Unconquered Emperor Augustus, twenty-one."'

'What else?'

'That's it.'

'But that's just his name.' He brushed back a lock of hair that had fallen in front of his eyes. 'And what does twenty-one mean?'

She slumped back. 'Ask your expert.'

Mark disappeared into the bathroom. The noise of the extractor fan drowned anything Abby might have heard—not that it mattered. When Mark came out, he looked baffled and angry.

'He gave the same translation. Twenty-one probably means the twenty-first year of

393

Constantine's reign, which would date the poem to 326 or 327. For what that's worth.'

It jogged something in Abby's memory—something Nikolić had said.

'The *labarum* was still around in the ninth century. A Byzantine historian wrote about it.'

'Is there a point to this history lesson?'

'So even if this poem is about the *labarum*, it's not going to tell you where it's hidden. The Byzantine emperors had it on open display for another five hundred years.'

Mark stared at her blankly. 'It doesn't tell us anything—that's the *point*.' He kicked the leg of the bed. 'This whole thing's bonkers.'

In the armchair, Connie looked up from her BlackBerry. 'It doesn't matter. If Dragović thinks it leads somewhere, he'll go there. We just have to plant the idea in his mind.'

Mark shook his head. 'It's got to be watertight. If he's going to show up, he has to be convinced 100 per cent it's genuine. He has to see it for himself.'

He went back into the bathroom. Abby leaned forward again and studied the poem. Whether as a child with a riddle, or a UN investigator wading through witness testimony by the light of a wind-up torch, she'd never been able to leave a puzzle.

She tried to clear her mind of everything that had happened in the last two days and focus on what was relevant.

All his surviving poems contain secret messages.

OK. If you traced the shape of the monogram over the letters, it gave you Constantine's name and titles. That was pretty clever—she could only imagine the patience it must have taken to arrange the words to make that happen.

But for a man with that kind of mind, why stop there? Why go to all that effort just to spell out a name?

Around 326 Porfyrius was pardoned and came home.

So maybe he was grateful. But then there was the awkward question of the substance of the poem. *The grieving father gave his son*. If Constantine had just had his son Crispus murdered, you wouldn't write a poem pointing it out, however clever you were. Not if you'd just come back from exile and didn't want to go back.

There had to be something else.

She picked up the necklace and examined it. Connie looked up, but didn't say anything. Barry watched from behind his dark glasses. Mark stayed locked in the bathroom.

Though, actually, this is not a true Christogram. This one is called a staurogram. From the Greek word stavros, *meaning 'cross'.*

Now that he'd said it, she could see it clearly. A simple cross, with the extra loop connecting the top point and the right arm. And at each of the four points of the cross, and in its centre, a red glass bead that showed the letter underneath.

Some scholars think the poems might even have been presented to the Emperor inscribed on gold tablets, with gemstones underneath the key letters.

Five beads, five letters. She'd marked them on the piece of paper in the café toilet, but she'd been so rushed she hadn't even had time to think, let alone read them. She laid the necklace over the poem and squinted through the cloudy red glass.

S S S S S.

The same letter under each of the beads.

It couldn't be a coincidence—but then what did it mean?

She lifted the necklace off and studied the placement of the letters in the poem. Unsurprisingly, they made the same shape as they did on the necklace: a cross.

Gemstones underneath the key letters. But the letters were all the same. She frowned; she felt her headache coming back.

And then an idea. *What if it isn't the key letters, but the key words?* She picked out the five words that contained the S's and wrote them out, then swung herself off the bed and knocked on the bathroom door. Barry followed the movement with his head; his hand moved closer to his jacket pocket.

Mark unlocked the door and jerked it open, his phone pressed to his ear. He scowled when he saw her.

'What is it?'

'Is your Oxford professor still on the line?'

'Why?'

'Ask him what this means.' She handed him the paper with five words written on it. SIGNUM INVICTUS SEPELIVIT SUB SEPULCHRO.

Mark's eyes widened. 'I'll call you back,' he said to whoever was on the other end of the phone. He pressed some buttons and put it back against his ear. Abby waited while he read out the phrase, then spelled it letter by letter. Jamming the phone against his shoulder, he leaned over the bathroom counter top so he could write down the reply.

'Thanks.' He rung off and stared in the bathroom mirror for a moment. Over his shoulder, Abby could see total confusion wrapping his face.

'A basic translation is, "The unconquered one buried the sign under the grave." My man Nigel says that it's not too much of stretch to say, *"The unconquered one—i.e., the Emperor Constantine—buried the standard—i.e., the labarum—beneath his tomb."'*

'Do we know where his tomb is?' It was Connie, who had come up behind Abby and was staring past her at Mark.

But Abby knew the answer. She remembered Nikolić telling her.

When the Turks conquered Constantinople, they destroyed Constantine's mausoleum, which was the Church of the Holy Apostles, and built their own mosque on the site.

'It's in Constantinople.'

'Istanbul,' said Connie. 'Constantinople got the works.'

'Under a mosque.'

'A mosque?' Mark looked worried. Connie tapped something into her BlackBerry and had an answer in less than thirty seconds.

'The Fatih Mosque.'

Mark was already halfway to the door. 'Let's go.'

'What about Michael?' Abby asked. She remembered his face in the courtyard, the anguish as he turned and vanished out the gate. To lose him again so soon hurt her worse than the bullet.

But Mark wasn't interested. 'Dragović is the target here. We'll bring Michael in sooner or later.'

'And what about me.' She remembered what he'd said in the café—three hours to be home, safe and out of this insane rat run. All she wanted to do was sleep.

'You're coming with us.' He saw her face

397

collapse and gave a mean smile. 'We need you. You're the bait.'

XLII

Constantinople—June 337
There's nothing like the threat of death to slow a man down. The last month is the slowest I've ever lived. Each day since I returned from Nicomedia I've followed the same unimpeachable routine. I rise late and go to bed early. I work my way through Ursus's list, using the lie that Constantine has asked me to canvass their support for his sons. I visit the public baths, but avoid conversation; I never go to the forum. I've dismissed all my slaves except my steward, and even he isn't taxed with my simple demands.

Sometimes I wonder if this was how Crispus spent the last week of his exile in Pula. And I wonder who's coming for me.

The last name on my list is Porfyrius. I've saved him to the end—he represents things I don't want to think about. When you're living under a suspended death sentence, you need to keep a tight grip on your imagination.

The day I go to see him is hot and stifling: the naked sun beats down on the city, enraged by the loss of his favourite son. I spend a long time on the doorstep; I'm almost resigned to going home when at last the door opens.

'I'm not receiving many visitors these days,' Porfyrius apologises. 'It's safer.'

Through an open door I can see a table set out

in the atrium, loaded with cups and plates. I don't comment.

'You don't mind if we speak in the study? I'm having the atrium redecorated.'

I glance back towards the atrium—I hadn't noticed any sign of workmen. All I see is the door, silently shut by an unseen hand.

He leads me into his study. The desk is littered with papers, plans and drawings for what looks like a temple. A slave brings us wine. I take a cup, but don't drink.

'Constantine asked me to come.' The line's so well rehearsed by now, I've almost forgotten it's a lie. Porfyrius isn't so naïve.

'I heard the Augustus had . . .' A delicate pause. 'Taken sick.'

'He was alive the last time I saw him.' That much is true. 'But—he's an old man. He's concerned for the future of the empire.'

'Does he have a list of troublemakers he's worried about?' He holds up a hand to stop me answering, and rattles off the names of half a dozen of the men I've been to visit in the last fortnight.

'If you know who I've seen, you probably know what I've said to them.'

'Probably.'

'This is no time for factions. Whoever Constantine names as his successor, or successors, they'll need a peaceful, united empire. People who support them will have nothing to fear.'

A shrewd look. 'Are you making me an offer?'

'I'm passing on a message.' I open my hands in innocence—or impotence. *No guarantees.*

'Consider it delivered.' He picks up a pen from the desktop and spins it in his fingers. 'You forget—I spent ten years in exile because I wrote a poem that offended Constantine. I'm not keen to go back.'

He puts the pen down. His hand's shaking; it knocks against a brass lamp which is weighing down the end of a scroll. The lamp falls on the floor; the scroll ravels up, pulling back like a curtain to reveal the drawings underneath. I peer forward.

It's an elevation of the pediment of a temple or a mausoleum, a triangular face with a wreath in the centre. And inside the wreath, a monogram: a slanted X with its top looped around.

'The plans for my tomb,' says Porfyrius. 'I have an architect working on it.'

'Are you expecting to need it soon?'

'I'm prepared. Our generation—you, me, the Augustus himself—our time is running out. You should think about your own.'

'Mine's already built.' Dug into the slopes of the valley behind my villa in Moesia, surrounded by cypresses and laurels. A lonely place. I wonder if I'll live to see it.

I make a show of examining the plans. 'It's an interesting choice of decoration.'

His face—usually so animated—is very still. 'Everybody has Constantine's monogram on their tombs these days. I wanted something different— but still to proclaim my faith. I remembered it from the necklace you showed me. And a way to remember my old friend Alexander.'

He rolls up the plans and slots them into a rack on the wall. 'Thank you for coming.'

I'm about to go when shouts intrude from the street, piercing through a high window in the back wall. It sounds like a riot. A moment later a slave

400

runs in, flustered and jabbering.

'They're saying the Augustus is dead.'

Porfyrius takes the news calmly. He doesn't look any more surprised than I do.

'Things are going to start changing.'

'Be careful,' I remind him. 'It would be a shame to need your tomb before it's ready.'

*   *   *

The next day, Constantine's body is laid out in the great hall of the palace. The line of mourners stretches a full mile down the main avenue, under the shadow of Constantine's column. Senators queue with tavern-keepers, actresses with priests— every face a fragment in a mosaic of united grief. It's moving: they genuinely loved their Augustus, I think. He built their city. He kept the granaries full, the markets stocked and the barbarians back beyond the frontiers. He let them worship in temples or churches as they chose, whichever gods spoke to them. And now the world trembles.

The queue passes not far from my house: I can hear them through my windows, sitting in my garden or lying on my bed through the hot nights. For two days, I lock myself in and wait for the crowds to subside. On the third day, I can't resist any longer. I put on my toga, brush my hair and join the mourners. It takes hours to inch my way up the avenue, through the Augusteum, where the statues of deified emperors wait to greet their new companion. Long before I get there, my legs ache and my back feels as though hot coals have been poured inside it. My body's drenched with sweat. More than once I'm within an inch of breaking away and running back home. Even when I reach the palace gate, it's still another two hours' wait.

At last I'm there. There must be two thousand people in the hall, but they hardly make a sound. They shuffle slowly in a long loop. At the side of the hall, there's a space where people have left offerings: amulets and pieces of jewellery, coins and medallions, pieces of tile or stone with prayers scratched on to them. A lot show the X-P monogram. Are they funeral offerings—or offerings to a god?

The last few yards are the slowest of all. The heat in the hall, all those bodies on a hot summer evening, numbs me: I have to fight against it. This is the last time I'll see him. I want to hold the moment.

The line inches forward. And suddenly, there he is, lying in state on a golden bier atop a three-stepped plinth. Cypress boughs deck the floor around him; braziers smoke with incense and candles flicker on golden stands. The white robes he had on for his baptism are gone, banished by the full imperial regalia. The purple robe trimmed with jewels and gold, that used to rattle like armour when he walked; the gold diadem set with pearls; the red boots with toecaps buffed smooth where men have knelt to kiss them. The shroud underneath him is emblazoned with his monogram, but woven all around it are scenes from legend. And above it all, the golden *labarum* on its pole, the all-conquering standard.

I stare into his face. The embalmed skin is grey and artificial; somehow the undertakers seem to have subtly altered his face, so that he doesn't quite resemble the man he was. The man I loved to

402

destruction; the man whose dying wish I couldn't grant.

A fly buzzes down and lands on Constantine's nose. A slave sitting on a stool beside the bier flaps an ostrich feather to shoo it away. It draws my eye, changes my focus. Suddenly, I see the corpse for what it really is.

It's a waxwork.

The tears that were beading in my eye are gone. I feel a fool. Of course, they wouldn't lay out the real corpse. He died a month ago: even the best undertaker would struggle to keep him looking fresh. And in this heat . . . Now that I see, I'm embarrassed I was ever taken in. The sun's softened one of the cheeks, making it subside as if he had a stroke. The wig they've used for the hair is slightly crooked.

This is how he is now. The man who lived and breathed—the man I knew—is gone. All people will remember now is a statue.

The crowd swells behind me, nudging me on. I whisper a prayer for Constantine—my friend, not this bloodless effigy—and let others take my place. I'm desperate to be outside. I hurry to the door, towards the long arcade that leads out of the city. Mourners mill around, talking quietly; the palace officials are distributing hot food to those who've been waiting.

But through the crowd, there's something else. A flash, an intuition, the weight of a gaze. Someone's watching me.

Our eyes meet. He turns away, pretending he hasn't seen me. But I'm not going to let him escape. I push through the crowd. They squeeze tighter as I approach the gate—I almost lose sight of him—but then I'm through and there's space to move. He's hobbling without a stick, a hunched figure in a blue cloak, the hood pulled up despite the heat. It takes me twenty paces to catch him. He knows he can't beat me. He hears me coming, stops and turns.

The hood slides back. It's Asterius the Sophist.

'What are you doing?'

'Paying my respects to the Augustus.' It's getting dark; the crevices of his face are black as ink, etching each bitter line. 'He was the greatest Christian since Christ.'

'It must be hard for you, now that it's over.'

'For you, it's over. For us, this is just the beginning.'

Urgency overwhelms me. 'Tell me about Symmachus. Tell me about Alexander.'

'They're all dead.'

'Then tell me about Eusebius. What happened in that dungeon, during the persecutions? Did it hurt, taking the blame for his betrayal? Watching him rise through the ranks of your religion, the Emperor's favourite, while you were forbidden from setting foot in a church?'

I've scored a hit. Pain flashes across his face.

'Alexander knew,' I continue. 'Symmachus knew. But they weren't the only ones. Someone else knows, is willing to testify.'

'You have no idea what you're talking about.'

'Haven't I?'

He hesitates, then decides. A cruel light comes on in his eyes.

'Walk with me.'

The procession of mourners is as long as ever. We force our way past them, down the street, and slip into the gardens beside the hippodrome. Above us, the last sunlight gleams on the four-horsed chariot that crowns the north end.

Asterius gives me a sly glance. 'I was never worried about the persecutions. Eusebius was, but Eusebius is prone to fits of panic. That was how they got to him in the first place.'

'*Got to him?*'

'In prison.'

His honesty takes me aback. 'So it's true?'

'That Eusebius betrayed a family of Christians and I took the blame to protect him?' He shrugs, careless of the impact of his words. 'Alexander could never have proved it. A doddering bishop relying on the evidence of a notorious persecutor? He'd only have sacrificed what little credibility he had left. Can you imagine if he'd turned up to the episcopal election with Symmachus in tow? Eusebius would have won without a vote.'

For the last month, I've been living in a coffin. Asterius's casual honesty is like a storm wind blowing the lid off my carefully constrained existence. A dangerous elation rushes through me.

'But Eusebius still killed Alexander. And then Symmachus, who could have corroborated the story.'

Asterius gives me a scornful look. 'Do you want to know why we killed Symmachus? I can tell you. The week before he died, Symmachus went to the palace twice. He wanted to speak to the Augustus, and when he was refused, he got agitated. He said some things that he'd have been safer keeping to himself.'

'About Eusebius?' But I know that's not true. 'That he knew the truth about Crispus's death.'

'I'd be careful saying that name aloud.' Asterius

405

glances around the gardens. Families wander among the trees, speaking in hushed voices. 'Constantine may be a waxwork now, but his sons don't care to be reminded of it any more than he did.'

Asterius stops at the base of a statue, the great Olympic charioteer Scorpus standing with his legs apart, a whip dangling from his shoulder. He turns. His eyes glow with malicious pleasure.

'In Alexander's box of secrets, Symmachus uncovered something that had been kept hidden for ten years. Something even the Augustus didn't know.'

He's baiting me. And I don't have the strength to fight. 'What?'

'You know what happened to Crispus?' He puts an arm on my shoulder in mock sympathy. The touch makes me shudder. 'Of course you do. And afterwards, poor Fausta in her bath. But did you ever wonder, while you were overseeing the decimation of the Emperor's household, why she did it?'

I can feel a tightness in my chest, as though a strap's being buckled around it. 'She wanted her sons to inherit the throne,' I say.

'Of course she did. But who put the idea into Fausta's head? Who helped her forge the documents? Who found Christians in the bodyguard who were willing to pretend they'd been enlisted in Crispus's alleged plot, and be martyred for it?'

'Who?' I can't breathe; it comes out a whisper.

Perhaps it's because of his abbreviated reach, but Asterius has a habit of standing closer than is comfortable. I can almost feel the anger boiling off him. His head's tipped back like a bird, staring up at me, waiting for me to realise—

'*You?*'

A ghastly smile spreads across his face. 'Crispus couldn't stand Eusebius. Three months after Nicaea, Crispus arranged to have Eusebius exiled to Trier. We knew Eusebius would never be allowed back while Crispus was alive—and that if Constantine went ahead and elevated Crispus as Augustus, that might be for ever.'

'We?'

'Eusebius and I. Well, mostly me. Eusebius was a thousand miles away. But I had an ally at the palace.'

Fausta? I don't think so—from what he's said, there was someone else. I wrestle with the question; I don't want to let Asterius dictate the terms of the conversation. And it comes to me. I remember the litter I saw leaving Eusebius's church service, the proud peacocks embroidered on the purple curtains. *He's an exceptional man and he has a bright future.* I remember the powder streaked across her lined face, silver hairs on a golden brush late at night. *Did you know, the Augustus once considered marrying me to you?*

'Constantine's sister. Constantiana.'

The smile gets wider. He's patronising me.

'She was always a better Christian than her brother. She struggled so hard to love Constantine. She might have forgiven him for executing her husband Licinius, but killing her little boy was too much. She needed revenge: a spouse for a spouse, a child for a child.'

'And you encouraged her?'

'Eusebius was her chaplain. Her spiritual guide.

When Crispus exiled him, Constantiana turned to me. I saw how we could all achieve our aims.'

'I thought your God preached peace and mercy.'

'Sometimes, we have to do terrible things to achieve God's will.'

It sounds glib, a throwaway justification. But the pain behind those words is immense, a deep wound that's scarred to the bone. His arms are trembling in his sleeves. For the briefest instant, I have a glimpse—not even a thought, more a feeling— of how he might deserve sympathy for what he's suffered.

But not for what he's done.

'You killed Crispus to bring back Eusebius?'

'*You* killed Crispus,' he retorts. 'You and Constantine. I just'—he lifts up his arms, baring the scarred stumps—'pulled some strings.'

'Why are you telling me this?'

'Because I want you to know. It's your own story, and you never knew it.'

I can see why he's brought me to this public place. If we were alone, I'd have killed him by now.

'And if I expose you?'

'It won't matter. Fausta's sons have just inherited the empire. If you go to them, do you think they'll punish the people who lifted them on to the throne?' He cocks his head, as if an idea's just come to him. 'If they want justice, they can always execute the man who murdered Crispus.'

'Why? Because of what happened at Nicaea? Because Crispus made you prefer one form of words over another?'

'*One form of words*?' he echoes. 'We were describing *God*. Do you think we could afford to get it wrong?' He starts walking again, past the dark gates of the hippodrome. 'It was Constantine's fault. Ten or twenty years ago, Arius would have been one voice among many. He could have written whatever he liked, and all his enemies could have done is write against it. But Constantine wanted something definite, something as absolute as his rule. To pin down God. He forced us to choose.'

He pauses, looks at me. For once, there's no craft in his face: he wants me to understand him.

'What else could we do?'

I'm desperate to be away, to slink into my cave and lick the wounds that Asterius has opened on every inch of my being. But I have to see this through.

'You said Symmachus died because he learned the truth about Crispus. Who killed Symmachus?'

'Constantiana sent one of her men. She told him to make it look like suicide.'

No evasion, not even a blush of guilt. This is the problem with men who spend too long thinking about God. In the end, they forget what a mortal life is worth. Perhaps that's what happened to Constantine.

'And Alexander? That must have been twice as sweet. Revenge on your enemy from Nicaea, as well as hiding the evidence of your murder.'

He actually laughs. 'You know the funniest thing?' He leans so close to me that his tunic rubs against mine. 'I have no idea who killed Alexander.'

He relishes my surprise.

'Eusebius didn't do it—though he might have, if he'd been given the chance. I didn't. At first I thought Constantine might have ordered it, to bury what Alexander had found, but I don't think that's likely.' He shrugs. 'It must have been Aurelius

Symmachus—he had the document case, after all. Ironic, don't you think? At least you can console yourself that justice was done.'

I stare at him with dead eyes—his withered body stuffed so full of bitterness and hate. How could he ever preach a religion of love and peace?

'Why did you do it?' I ask. 'In the persecutions— taking the blame for Eusebius's betrayal of those Christian families?'

He puts the two stumps of his arms together, caressing them against each other. 'This is what Symmachus did to me. Then he was going to kill me. Eusebius betrayed the Christians to save my life.' A desperate edge comes into his voice, a man on the brink of losing control. 'He sacrificed himself to save me.'

'And you sacrificed me.'

XLIII

Istanbul, Turkey—Present Day
'You go in alone. Look around, take some photos, then come back.'

Abby sat in the back seat of the taxi in a busy shopping street in a north-western district of Istanbul. The taxi was genuine; the driver was Barry, still in his dark glasses, but now with a leather jacket and a gold chain around his neck. Mark sat in the passenger seat opposite and pointed down the road, where the myriad domes of the Fatih Mosque bubbled down on each other until they vanished behind a large stone gate.

'Don't try anything like escaping,' Barry said

from the front seat. 'You're not really alone.'

They'd touched down in Istanbul twelve hours ago. She was done with buses, borrowed cars and stolen passports: with Mark in charge, an unmarked plane had flown them out of Split and straight to Ataturk Airport. A delegation of hard-faced men in rigid suits had met them and escorted them through a private channel past customs and immigration.

'The government here can't wait to get their hands on Dragović,' Mark had explained during the drive from the airport. 'They had him in prison three years ago and he escaped—that was a big embarrassment. They don't appreciate what he did to Muslims in Bosnia either, for that matter. They're giving us everything they can.'

'How do they know Dragović will come? If he was in prison here once before, won't he be shy of risking it again?'

'He'll come,' Mark had said confidently. 'All our networks are telling us he's absolutely obsessed with this thing. Won't trust it to anyone else.'

*   *   *

Abby got out of the car, made a show of sticking a ten-lira note through the window to Barry, and walked down to the mosque. She'd been to Istanbul once before, for an ICC conference, but that had been high summer when the city groaned with tourists and dust clogged the hot air. Now, in late autumn, the city seemed to have shrunk as it cooled. There was more air; the spaces between the buildings felt wider. The noise of the ships in the Bosphorus sounded unnaturally loud.

The tourists had gone home, but the street

was still busy with locals shopping or visiting the mosque for their devotions. A white police van sat on the corner; two more policemen with automatic weapons wandered down the street, chatting to each other. Abby wondered if that was normal.

Mark had given her a guidebook as part of her cover. She opened it to the right page, and read the brief entry on the Fatih Mosque. *Fatih* meant *conqueror*, she learned. On the highest point of the highest hill in the city, the Ottomon sultan Mehmet the Conquerer had razed the old Church of the Twelve Holy Apostles and built his mausoleum on its foundations, when he captured Constantinople in 1453. Three hundred years later, an earthquake had destroyed his mosque; his successors had rebuilt it in what the guidebook called Ottoman Baroque style.

She went through the gate, into a wide open park of square lawns and leafless trees. The mosque stood in the centre, as if in a state of siege. Steel hoardings surrounded its base; scaffolding climbed its outer walls. Abby looked for any sign of the Roman building that had once stood there, but couldn't see anything. She wondered, not for the first time, how a treasure like the *labarum* could have remained hidden through all the centuries of renovations, excavations, demolitions and rebuildings. Surely someone would have noticed something. Or perhaps it lay buried under a thousand years of rubble.

Mark had given her a camera. She took some pictures—a few general tourist views, some of less obvious features like doors, culverts and drainpipes. *Make it look as if you're scoping it out*, Mark had told her. *Look furtive*. That part was easy enough.

412

She didn't go into the mosque, but skirted around the outside to the back. This part was a cemetery: flat graves surrounded by wrought-iron fences; pillars that had once supported canopies now chopped off at the knees. And beyond them, far grander than the others though still dwarfed by the mosque, an octagonal mausoleum topped by a dome.

Abby's heart beat a little faster. The octagonal shape was exactly like Diocletian's mausoleum in Split. Could this be Constantine's? She opened the guidebook again.

'Behind the main mosque stands the türbe *or tomb of Mehmet the Conqueror, reconstructed in the Baroque style after the earthquake . . .'*

She should have known. And yet she still found the parallel intriguing. Mehmet the Conqueror and Constantine the Unconquered. Two men separated by religion and geography and a thousand years, but both wanting the world to know they had *dominated*. Two men who, for all their differences, had chosen to be buried in the same place. Was it Mehmet's way of conquering the past—burying Constantine beneath him the same way the mosque buried the church? Abby didn't think so. It was affinity, not rivalry, that had brought him here. He wanted the company.

Gruber: *There are certain places where power abides*. This was one of them—she could feel it. She thought of the dead man in Kosovo, Gaius Valerius Maximus, and wondered if he'd walked through this same courtyard, in the service of the Emperor who first built it.

She snapped a few more pictures, finished her circuit of the mosque and went back out on to the

413

street. A taxi rolled by, the same number as before. She pretended to hail it and got in.

'Well?' Mark said.

She clipped on her seatbelt as the car started moving. 'I didn't see Dragović, if that's what you were expecting. There's a lot of building work going on, though. It looks as if they've excavated down near the foundations. That might give him a way in.'

'We'll get on to the Culture Ministry. Perhaps we can slip a couple of people into the crews to look out for anything dubious.'

His phone buzzed. He tapped the screen, read the message and grunted.

'No sign of Dragović moving yet. We're watching the airports in all his known haunts. We've also put out the word to our networks. Nothing yet.'

Abby remembered the man in the black room in Rome, his silver gun against her head. She shivered.

'Will he suspect anything?'

'We gave the necklace and the text to a man called Giacomo in Belgrade.'

'I've met him.'

Mark's head flicked up; he gave her a suspicious stare. 'You've got some interesting connections. When we get you back to London, we'll have to sit down and have a conversation about all the people you've met.'

'Can't wait.'

They drove past a vast brick aqueduct, so huge that buses could easily drive through its arches. Just beyond it, Barry stopped the taxi on the kerb by a park. Mark ushered Abby out.

'Go back and keep an eye on the mosque,' he told Barry. 'Call if anything happens. And no guns,' he added. 'If we start shooting up a mosque, we'll have another fatwa on our hands before we know it. Starting from Whitehall.'

The taxi roared away and carved an aggressive U-turn across seven lanes of traffic. If Barry was trying to impersonate a Turkish taxi driver, he had the cover perfect. Almost as soon as he'd gone, an unmarked blue hatchback pulled up in its place. Mark and Abby climbed in; Abby wondered how many SIS agents—she assumed they were SIS— were swarming around Istanbul.

'Where now?'

'You wait at the hotel with Connie. I need to go to the consulate to talk to some people.'

The thought of sitting in another hotel room, watching canned TV and waiting for other people to decide her fate made her ill.

'Isn't there something I can do?'

'Leave it to the professionals.' He was so condescending she wanted to slap him. 'Even if we did trust you—which we don't—there's nothing you can do.'

Thanks for spelling that out.

'So what was that business at the mosque for? If Dragović's people are watching me, you think they're going to believe I just turn up, take a few photos and go back to the hotel? Don't you think you can make it a little more convincing?'

'What did you have in mind?' Mark was looking out of the window, not really listening. Abby thought quickly.

'There must be some kind of historical library in Istanbul. Somewhere that would have books about the Fatih Mosque, Constantine's mausoleum and so on. Someone must have done some archaeological work on it in the last five hundred years.'

'Are you a historian?'

'I'm a lawyer. You get pretty good digging through a mountain of old documents looking for evidence. And as far as Dragović knows, I'm supposed to be looking for ways to sneak in underneath the mosque. Maybe I'll even find something.'

Mark tapped away at the screen of his phone. Abby wondered if it substituted for thought.

'OK.'

*   *   *

The palace stood at the eastern end of the peninsula, bordered by nothing but the sea. Not a palace in the monolithic western style, like Blenheim or Versailles—solid monuments to power. This was an eastern palace: a complex organism that grew and sprawled over centuries, a place of shady courtyards and quiet corners where lovers and plotters could listen and conspire.

Most of the site was a park: broad paths winding between oaks and elms, with the sea sparkling through the trees. Abby let herself in through a gate, trying to ignore the Connie-shaped shadow that followed twenty yards back. She walked past Hagia Eirene—the Church of Holy Peace, one of the oldest in Istanbul—and around to the one courtyard where classical columns and porticoes still held their own against the surrounding minarets and domes. Somehow, after two thousand years, there was still nothing that said 'museum' quite like Graeco-Roman architecture.

She'd called ahead. The receptionist showed her

through to the library at the back of the building, a long room whose high windows looked out across the grounds to the pointed towers of the main palace gate. The librarian had perfect English and a perfect smile: in no time, a small pile of books and journals had appeared on the oak table beside her. Abby started reading.

From the *Oxford Dictionary of Byzantium*, she learned that the first construction on the mosque site had been a circular mausoleum built by Constantine for himself. His son Constantius had added a cruciform church; emperors had been buried there until 1028, when they ran out of room.

The article listed references for further reading, including a contemporary description of the mausoleum by the Bishop Eusebius, Constantine's biographer.

The building stood impossibly high, every inch glinting with gemstones of every colour. The roof was gilded, reflecting back the sun's rays to dazzle watchers for miles around.

It sounded like the sort of place you might keep your most valuable treasure. Abby read on through later, less evocative historians, skimming through pages of argument and counter-argument, speculation and guesswork. It seemed that no one had managed to add much definite about Constantine's mausoleum since Eusebius—and with the mosque now planted on top of it, no one was likely to either.

At the bottom of the pile was a dog-eared archaeology journal. It mentioned an excavation done in the 1940s, which had found traces of Byzantine stonework, and a colonnaded cistern under the mosque courtyard. It observed that the

417

mihrab inside the mosque—the holy niche that directed worshippers towards Mecca—wasn't centred on the mosque walls. Anomalies and asymmetries in architecture often happened if a new building was built on old foundations, the authors said: by looking at what didn't line up, you could infer what lay underneath.

That jogged something in Abby's mind, an uneasy asymmetry in her own thoughts. It niggled, but she couldn't place it. She read on.

'During the excavations in the 1950s, the Director of Tombs reported the discovery of a Byzantine chamber under the mihrab of the modern mosque, accessible via a tunnel from the cellar of Mehmet the Conqueror's mausoleum.'

She stared: her head spun. She felt herself trembling as she read the final sentence of the conclusion.

'Perhaps the original Roman structure, last resting place of the emperor Constantine, has at last been found.'

She went over to the librarian and flashed her most beguiling smile.

'Is there still a Director of Tombs in Istanbul?'

He nodded. 'This office is part of the General Directorate of Monuments and Museums.'

'Where can I find him?'

He looked surprised. 'Here in this building. The office is upstairs. I can call for you if you want.' Abby hesitated, then nodded. The librarian picked up the phone and spoke briefly. 'One moment.'

A minute later, Abby heard high heels clacking on the wooden floor. The door opened and in walked a tall, strikingly beautiful woman with long black hair and an elegant dark dress. Her lips, her nails and her shoes were all bright red; her eyes were shadowed a shimmering aquamarine. Abby had rarely felt so drab—a disgrace to every ideal of femininity.

'Dr Yasemin Ipek,' the woman introduced herself. And then, seeing the doubt in Abby's face, 'I am the Director of Tombs.'

It was hard to imagine her scrambling around in dank, ancient holes underground.

'I understand you are interested in the tomb of Constantine the Great?' She smiled. 'I have many tombs in my directorate. Sadly, his has been lost for centuries.'

Abby pointed to the article and quoted the last line. 'It says here there's a Byzantine chamber right underneath the holiest point of the mosque.'

Dr Ipek nodded. 'I have read about this excavation. One of the directors of this museum, Professor Fıratlı, conducted it after the war. In fact, if you go into the crypt underneath Mehmet's mausoleum, you can still see the wooden boards they put up to close the passage.'

'Have you ever opened it?'

'Never.'

'How about in the 1940s? Do you know if they found anything down there? Any kind of relic or artefact?'

Dr Ipek narrowed her eyes. 'There is nothing in the records.'

'Is it possible to open the chamber?'

Abby could see the warmth fading from Dr Ipek's face; a discreet glance at the silver wristwatch.

'It is closed for structural reasons. The chamber is directly under the wall of the mosque, and we have many earthquakes here. You would have to apply for a permit from the minister directly.'

She saw Abby's disappointment and relented a little. 'You were thinking perhaps you will find Constantine's lost sarcophagus under there?'

'Something like that.'

'Sometimes I wonder the same. But Professor Firatlı was a scholar. If he had discovered something, he would have reported it.' She smiled to herself. 'Poor Constantine. He should have kept to his original plan and been buried in Rome. Then his tomb would have survived, and today he would be safe in the Vatican Museum.'

Abby blinked.

'What do you mean?'

'Constantine did not always intend to be buried in Constantinople, not until very late in his life. He built a mausoleum in Rome, which still stands at Tor Pignattara. When he changed his plan, he had his mother, the Dowager Empress Helena, buried there instead. You can still see her sarcophagus in the Vatican Museum.'

She carried on speaking, but Abby didn't hear it. Her mind was racing, trying to compute all the names and dates she'd heard in the last few days.

CONSTANTINUS INVICTUS IMP AUG XXI.

XXI. Twenty-one probably means the twenty-first year of Constantine's reign, which would date the poem to 326 or 327. For what that's worth.

'When did Constantine change his mind about where he wanted to be buried?' she asked.

'His mother died in 328. So far as we can tell, he did not start building the mausoleum in Constantinople until near his death. Nine years later.'

420

Abby's mouth was dry. She knew she had to get this right.

'So if someone was writing about Constantine's tomb in the year 326 . . .'

Yasemin Ipek, Director of Tombs, finished the sentence for her.

'. . . almost certainly, he meant the mausoleum in Rome.'

'And you said it still survives.'

'On the outskirts of Rome. It is just a ruin now.' She smiled. 'If you are interested in underground passages, I think this is the place for you. It stands above the catacomb of Saints Marcellus and Peter.'

'Excuse me.'

Abby ran out of the library. Connie was waiting in the corridor, pretending to examine some Ottoman vases. She saw Abby coming and moved to cut her off, but Abby wasn't trying to get past her.

'We're in the wrong place.'

XLIV

Constantinople—June 337

I sit alone in my study, scratching at a roll of parchment. I woke before dawn and couldn't get back to sleep; there's a tightness in my chest that makes it hard to breathe, as if something is fighting to get out from inside my heart. Just when I started to drift off, the family of swallows who've made their home under the tiles of my colonnade started feeding their young and woke me all over again.

I'm trapped in a nightmare and there's only one

way it can end. In half an hour last night, Asterius tore up so many things I believed. Now I'm buried in the ruins of my own Chamber of Records, snatching at scraps that disintegrate in my hands.

The whole city's in a daze. Baths and markets are shut, the hippodrome gates chained and locked. From my study I can hear people wandering through the streets, wailing and crying as if they've lost their own children. It's been going on for two weeks, though tonight it will be over. By then, Constantine's body will have been laid in the great porphyry sarcophagus that's waiting for him in his mausoleum, taking his place among the twelve apostles of Christ. What they'll say when they find out who their new companion in eternity is, I can't imagine.

Today it ends. I'm sitting here in my white toga, my hair washed and my boots polished, dressed for the funeral. Constantius, Constantine's second son, has made it back from Antioch. With the speed he arrived, they're probably eating horsemeat all the way across Asia Minor. The dissent that worried Flavius Ursus hasn't crystallised into any public demonstration. I'd like to think I've played my part, but mostly I think it's because there's no alternative.

It doesn't matter. Today, I'll process behind the coffin like a captive barbarian. Tomorrow morning, if Ursus keeps his bargain, I'll be on a wagon heading home to Moesia.

I've almost reached the end of my scroll—the one I began two months ago at the library. I read down the list of names I made that day: Eusebius of Nicomedia, Aurelius Symmachus, Asterius the Sophist, Porfyrius. Any one of them might have killed Alexander, or ordered it, though in the balance of everything else they've done I suppose it would barely twitch the scales.

In this city, not all murders are crimes. And not all criminals are guilty.

In the last few inches of papyrus, I copy out the poem I found in the Chamber of Records. Perhaps it has nothing to do with Alexander's death, but its elusive meaning haunts me.

To reach the living, navigate the dead ...

I've been navigating the dead these last ten years, eyes downcast, trying not to see the ghosts that surround me. I haven't reached the living.

But copying out the poem, I notice something new. Every line is the same length—not almost or approximately, but exactly—and the eight lines are spaced so that the whole text forms a perfect square block.

I don't know why I didn't notice it before. I puzzle over it, wondering what it means. Whoever wrote it certainly took great care to make it so. Just writing the lines to be the same length must have needed an immense creative effort.

I stare at it. One moment I don't see it, the next moment it's there, as if a god had whispered it in my ear. I run over to my drawer and pull out the necklace they found in the library by Alexander's body. A golden square, with the monogram in the centre. So similar to Constantine's, but subtly different.

I lay it over the poem on the piece of paper I found in the Scrinia Memoriae. It fits perfectly— the square of text and the square of gold, exactly the same size.

Porfyrius was a poet. When I asked him why he

was exiled, he told me, 'a poem and a mistake'.

Porfyrius had the same unusual monogram on the design for his tomb.

Porfyrius was in the library that day.

*　　　*　　　*

The toga's a stately garment, not made for running. Several times, it threatens to trip me up; once, it almost unravels completely. It's hard pushing my way through the crowds that have already gathered to watch the funeral. It's going to be the greatest piece of theatre in the whole brief history of the city. The few hundred yards to Porfyrius's villa take almost half an hour. At the palace, the procession will already be forming up.

Porfyrius has gone. He hasn't even bothered to lock the door—perhaps he isn't expecting to come back. A neglected silence hangs over the house, as though its owner died unexpectedly and hasn't been found yet. The whole house is empty, not even a single slave, though nothing's been packed or put away. The long table that I saw before is still standing in the atrium, stacked with plates and bowls ready for serving.

I go to his study and rummage on the shelves for the plans to his mausoleum. *It would be a shame to need your tomb before it's ready.* I unroll them on the desk. The word *Roma* is scribbled on the top left-hand corner—presumably he wants to be buried in Rome. I doubt he'll get there.

There are three drawings. The first shows the front, with its strange *labarum*-like monogram filling the pediment. The second illustrates the paintings intended for the wall. The third shows the niche at the back of the tomb where the remains will be buried. A stone plaque's been drawn on the wall, and written on it—clearly, so the masons make no mistake—are two lines of poetry.

To reach the living navigate the dead,
Beyond the shadow burns the sun.

The story's clear enough. Porfyrius found out that Alexander had uncovered his poem and attacked him in the library. In the struggle, Alexander ripped the gold necklace off Porfyrius: it slid under the bookshelf, and Porfyrius didn't have time to retrieve it. Perhaps Symmachus was there, too. That would explain how he ended up with Alexander's document case. He kept it, but then he got cold feet. He tried to arrange to hand it back, but did it so clumsily he got caught instead.

So why was Porfyrius concerned about the poem? Was he worried about the allusions to Crispus? It hardly seems worth killing a man for. But Porfyrius had been exiled once before: he might well have had a horror of suffering it again.

I take out the poem and align it with the necklace, hoping I'll see something I missed before.

There are five red beads set into the gold, making the points and centre of a cross. Through the glass you can see fragments of words underneath. I press my thumbnail into the papyrus to underline them, then lift the necklace away to see what I've found.

SIGNUM INVICTUS SEPELIVIT SUB SEPULCHRO. *The unconquered man hid the sign under his tomb.*

I don't know what it means, but I need to get to the funeral.

425

*　　*　　*

The procession will have set out by now. If Flavius
Ursus is watching, he'll have noticed I haven't
taken my place, perhaps mentioned it to one of his
assistants. It's too late for me. But from the palace
to the mausoleum is almost two miles: it'll take at
least an hour to get there. I duck down a side alley,
away from the ceremonial route, and join a wide
and empty boulevard heading west. In the distance
I can hear the shouts of the crowds, a roar like
the sea that's strangely stifled by the windless day.
Every man, woman and child in the city must be
there. I walk a full mile, and the only living thing I
see is a cat curled up on a doorstep. Windows are
shuttered, shops barred. I might be the last man left
alive in the world.

The illusion fades as I approach the mausoleum.
I can see its copper dome flashing above the
surrounding rooftops; the gold trelliswork in the
arches underneath. Nervous soldiers guard the
street corners in twos and threes. It'll be some time
before the funeral gets here, but the mourners have
already gathered twelve deep behind the wooden
barricades that line the route.

The road ends at a wall. Twenty guards from the
Schola make a human gate, ready to admit their
emperor one last time. I show them my commission
from Constantine, the ivory diptych he gave me
the day Alexander died. They don't question the
fact that the portrait on the lid is of a corpse. Even
in death, Constantine hasn't surrendered his grip
on the throne. New laws are issued every day in
his name; his coins still pour out of the mints. The

426

bureaucracy's given him eternal life.

'Has Publilius Porfyrius arrived yet?' I ask the guard.

'Here since this morning.' He nods towards the mausoleum. 'It's been a bit of a rush job. The clerk of works wanted him to inspect the foundations, just to be sure. Embarrassing if it fell with all the city watching.'

'How about Flavius Ursus?'

'He'll be in the procession.'

'I need you to get a message to him. As quickly as possible, even if it means running in front of the Emperor's coffin.' I repeat the five words of Porfyrius's hidden message. 'Tell him it comes from Gaius Valerius.' I push my commission under his face. '*Do it!*'

He looks surprised—doubly so when I step past him through the gate. 'Where are you going?'

'To find Porfyrius.'

*   *   *

The wall makes a compound, broad and square, covering the hilltop. One day this will all be gardens: at the moment, it's a builders' yard. Squares of earth show where the stacks of bricks and timber have hurriedly been moved around the back. Even now, Constantine's legacy is a work in progress. Ahead, the mausoleum stands surrounded on three sides by arcades. Eventually, the fourth side will be closed off to make a courtyard. Today, it stands open, framing the immense rotunda rising in its centre. The gold facing ripples in the sun.

In front of the tomb stands a huge pyre, half as high as the building behind. It's almost a building in its own right: stripped tree trunks make columns around its base, painted to look like fluted marble; planks form storeys inside. Gold banners hang over the sides, and at the very summit a live eagle preens itself in a gilded cage. Wooden stands have been erected on the open ground either side, so that the assembled senators and generals have box seats.

I skirt around the pyre and climb the steps to the courtyard. Huge crimson banners woven with portraits of Constantine's three sons hang from the unconnected pillars; guards in gilded ceremonial armour stand at every column.

I find their centurion. 'Has Publilius Porfyrius come this way?'

'In the tomb.'

Again, Constantine's pass lets me through—into the courtyard, into the presence of the mausoleum. The open side faces south, so that the golden wall catches the midday sun face on, bending its rays around the courtyard like a mirror. It dazzles me; from ten feet away I can feel the heat coming off it.

Suddenly, I need to sit down. I'm an old man who's walked too far on a hot day. I'm parched. My mouth is dry, my limbs are like sand. I feel as if I'm drowning in a shimmering sea of heat and light.

'Gaius Valerius?'

I spin around, unsure where the voice came from. The sun's burned out my senses, I can't locate anything. The dark figure stands in the glare like a spot in front of my eyes.

'Porfyrius?' I guess.

'What are you doing here?'

'I read your poem.'

'I wondered if you'd work it out.' I can't see his face, but he doesn't sound angry. 'I hoped the

Emperor had destroyed it when he burned the papers from Alexander's bag.'

'There was another copy. In the Chamber of Records, the Scrinia Memoriae.'

'Memory's a funny thing.'

'Did you kill Alexander?'

He laughs. 'Poor Valerius. You've been stumbling around, chasing shadows and ghosts. You have no idea what this is really about.'

I'm sick of hearing that. 'Why don't you tell me?'

'Come and see.'

He takes my hand and leads me around the rotunda. The tomb eclipses the sun; I can see again. Even the mausoleum isn't what it seems. The gold panelling only comes halfway round, and a roofer's scaffold is still erected against its north side, where no one will see it. Next to it, a small flight of steps descends to a little door in the tomb's basement. Porfyrius knocks—a precise rhythm that sends a message.

The door swings open. To my aching eyes, the interior is perfect darkness. Porfyrius pushes me forward.

'We won't hurt you. You've waited ten years for this moment.'

The moment I step through the door, strong hands pin my arms to my side. I'd cry out, but another hand is clamped over my mouth.

The door closes and I'm plunged in darkness.

XLV

Rome—Present Day

Three miles from the centre of Rome, Via Casilina was an unlovely artery: four lanes of traffic split down the middle by a light rail line. Behind the San Marcellino metro station, a pink plastered church stood dedicated to the early Christian martyrs Saint Peter and Saint Marcellinus. Next door was a brick school that looked like a warehouse, and in between ran a concrete wall with two gates, one large and one small. The large gate opened on to an asphalt car park that doubled as a playground for the school; the small one, which was barely high enough for an adult, led on to a narrow passage between two walls. A metal gate barred the way.

Mark studied it through a pair of binoculars. They were parked in the forecourt of the petrol station across the road—Mark and Abby, Barry and Connie. Abby was getting sick of the sight of them.

'It doesn't look like much,' Barry said. About fifty metres back from the road, the broken curve of a brick rotunda poked above the line of the wall. It had no roof, and more than half its wall was missing. It was a poor cousin to the grandeur of the Fatih Mosque, or even Diocletian's mausoleum in Split.

'It belongs to the Vatican,' said Connie from the back seat. 'I suppose they can't look after everything.'

Mark swore. 'First it was a mosque, now it's the Pope. Can't we go somewhere that doesn't belong to a touchy religion that's famous for starting

430

holy wars?'

'Why don't you bring in the police?' Abby asked.

'And piss off another country?' Mark shook his head. 'Our ambassador in Ankara is currently grovelling in front of Turkish intelligence explaining why we mobilised five hundred policemen, almost invaded one of their holiest mosques, then skipped town without so much as a thank you. From now on, we act on the basis of credible intelligence.'

'I'm sure that'll make a pleasant change for you.'

A white Fiat pulled in to the petrol station and stopped alongside them. Mark rolled down his window and gestured the driver to do likewise. Barry cradled a black semi-automatic pistol on his lap.

'Dr Lusetti?' Mark enquired.

The Fiat driver nodded. They all got out and shook hands, like travelling salesmen carpooling to a conference. Dr Mario Lusetti from the Pontifical Commission for Sacred Archaeology was a middle-aged man with a severe buzz cut and rimless spectacles. He wore jeans, a white shirt and a black blazer. He didn't look as if he smiled very often; just then, he looked particularly unhappy.

'You want to see the catacombs?'

'We think one of Europe's most wanted men—a dangerous criminal—will try to break in to steal a priceless artefact,' Mark said. He spoke loudly, an Englishman abroad; it made him sound ridiculously melodramatic.

Lusetti pursed his lips and blew out a puff of air. 'The catacomb has a footprint of thirty thousand square metres. There are four and a half kilometres of passages and galleries spread over three levels,

431

with twenty or twenty-five thousand burials inside. Even maybe there are more places that nobody has ever excavated. And, by the way, the catacombs have been discovered since the sixteenth century: every grave robber and thief in Rome has been down there. If your criminals are looking for something, probably they are four hundred years too late. If not, for sure it will take them another four hundred years to find it.'

'I don't care what they find. As long as we find them.'

Connie stayed in the car to watch. Lusetti led the others across the road and unlocked the little gate, then shepherded them down the narrow alley. At the end, a second gate led them through a steel fence topped with razor wire, into the circular enclosure that surrounded the old rotunda. Close to, Abby could see how vast it must have been: so big, in fact, that a two-storey house had been built inside the ruin. There were a few signs of restoration work—a couple of concrete buttresses, some broken-ended walls that had been squared off—but no evidence of recent activity.

'You know the story here?' Lusetti asked. 'It was the tomb of Saint Helena. The Emperor Constantine decided he did not want to be buried in Rome, so he gave it to his mother instead. Before, it had been the cemetery of the Imperial Cavalry Guard—but they fought against Constantine at the battle of Milvian Bridge. He disbanded the legion and pissed on their bones.'

He unlocked the door to the house and led them in to a marble-floored hall. Shutters shaded the rooms, and Abby could taste dust and damp in the air.

432

'This whole area had been an imperial estate called AD Duas Lauros for centuries. After the Dowager Empress Helena was buried here, Constantine gave it to the papacy. We have it still.'

Two owners in two thousand years. In that moment, Abby began to understand the timescales that popes and emperors thought in.

Lusetti took hard hats, head torches and fluorescent workmen's vests off wooden pegs and handed them round. Barry stared at the reflective stripes on the vests and frowned.

'Do we want to be highly visible if we're chasing a dangerous criminal?'

'In the catacomb is very dark. If we lose you, maybe we never see you again.'

They pulled on the protective clothing. Lusetti opened a side door and flicked a light switch. The naked bulb illuminated a stone staircase going down.

'Is that it?' Mark asked. It looked like nothing, the sort of entrance any Victorian house might have going down to its cellar.

'This is the way down.'

'Is there any other way in?'

'Officially, no.'

'Unofficially?'

'It is an ancient city.' Lusetti shrugged. 'If anyone digs under his basement, he will find caves, old quarries, lost tunnels. Not so long ago, they found a completely unknown catacomb under Via Latina.'

With Lusetti leading the way, they went down into the darkness.

*   *   *

433

'Let me tell you some things about the dark places of this world.'

In the chamber beneath Constantine's mausoleum, the darkness is absolute. My captors have pushed me down on to a stone bench against the wall—not so as to hurt me, but not gently either. They've let go my hands, though I can sense them hovering just out of reach, ready to pounce if I try to escape.

Where would I go? What would I say?

The only sense I have in that room is my ears. I listen to Porfyrius's story.

'Thirty years ago, during the persecutions, Symmachus sent me on a mission to Caesarea Palaestina. For a zealot like me, it was a career-making assignment: the heartland of the Christian religion.

'I knew what to do. I commandeered a basement, not unlike this, and turned it into a dungeon. I was scrupulous in chasing down every rumour of a magistrate who refused to sacrifice, or a wife who didn't emerge from her house on a Sunday.

'One day, in winter, my agents heard rumours of a Christian hiding in a certain merchant's house. They searched it and found nothing; then they noticed he didn't have the heating on. They stoked up the fire and waited. Soon enough, they heard noises from the *hippocaust* under the floor where the Christian was hiding. What they hadn't realised was that he had no intention of coming out. When they opened the hatch, they found him trying to burn a manuscript on the very fire they'd set. Naturally, they were curious. They seized the man and the manuscript and brought them both to me.

434

'The man told me nothing. I tried every tool in my arsenal and just played into his hands. All he wanted was martyrdom. But the manuscript . . .' Porfyrius sighs, the sound of a great weight settling. 'The manuscript told an extraordinary tale. You know that the Christian god Jesus Christ was crucified during the reign of Tiberius Augustus?'

I do. One of Constantine's early reforms was to outlaw crucifixion as a punishment, because it offended him.

'When Christ came down from the Cross, his followers kept the wood, because they couldn't bear to let him go. When he rose again from the dead, they realised it had a power beyond any man—the weapon that killed a god. They kept it in a secret place that only a tiny circle knew, down eleven generations. The manuscript listed them all. Read carefully, it was easy to guess where they'd hidden it.'

'You found it?'

'Not then. My efforts hadn't gone unnoticed, and Symmachus brought me back to Nicomedia. With Christians purged from every imperial office, there were plenty of opportunities for promotion. But I never forgot. Years later, in exile, I wondered if it might be true—if I could use it to negotiate my return to Rome. I sent a batch of poems to Constantine, hoping to impress him, but he rebuffed me. Then I heard what had happened to Crispus.'

Out in the darkness something stirs, like a monster from the old world chained up in its cave.

'The manuscript told a legend that the early Christians attached to the Cross—that on the day when Christ was crucified the blood he shed seeped into the wood and transformed it. From then on, they said, it had the power to raise men from the dead.'

It's such an absurd thing to say I actually burst out laughing. A stony silence reproaches me from the shadows. Porfyrius is deadly serious.

'I guessed that the Dowager Empress Helena would have taken the death of her grandson badly. I wrote to her, hinting at what I knew. She was a pious woman, shattered by grief: she was ready enough to believe. She recalled me, heard what I had to say and set out at once for Palestine.'

This bit I know. The streets of Rome had barely been swept clean from the *vicennalia* celebrations before Helena took her trip to Jerusalem. At the time, we all assumed she was undertaking some sort of ritual purification for what had happened to Crispus, or that she wanted to get as far away from Constantine as possible. She returned a year later and died soon after.

'She found it,' Porfyrius says abruptly. 'She followed the clues I gave her, and she found the old Cross. She brought it back to Rome. By then, thanks to her patronage, I was a *praetor* of the city—soon to be Prefect. I oversaw the estate at Duas Lauros.' A touch of his old, crooked humour surfaces in his voice. 'I think you might have been there, once.'

Once. June, that doomed *vicennalia* year. Constantine going through the motions of the *vicennalia* ritual like a statue, while a hundred thousand blank-faced Romans watched and cheered and pretended they'd never heard of Crispus. And late one night, when Constantine was drunk, I remember riding three miles out of

Rome down the Via Casilina, to the old cemetery where Constantine had built his mausoleum. With me came two trusted guards from the Schola, and a long coffin we'd carried all the way from Pula. I remember the shadow of that vast rotunda over the old gravestones; the squeak of the lock and the slap of our feet as we went down the stairs. I remember the lamps like eyes in the walls, the deep shadows they cast down the endless tunnels. I remember the slam of the lid as we closed the sarcophagus in the deepest, furthest part of the catacomb; the noise echoing around the small chamber, knocking loose grit off the ceiling, and the flash of terror that I would be buried alive with the man I murdered. I remember the tears, wet on my face as I kissed his coffin and murmured my final farewell.

'Why are you telling me all this?' The memories are throttling me. My voice barely comes out as a croak.

'So you'll understand.'

A light flares in the darkness. One of the men around me has touched a glow-worm to a lamp. For a moment, my eyes can't see anything. As they adapt, I see brick vaults above my head; a circle of men standing around me. And a little distance away, hanging back as if ashamed of something, the face that's haunted my nightmares for ten years.

I stare. My heart shatters at the impossibility of it.

I'm looking at a dead man.

*　　　*　　　*

Rome—Present Day
She'd never been claustrophobic, but this was

something else. All Abby could think of was being surrounded by the dead. The passage was so narrow her shoulders almost rubbed the walls—a waxy grey rock that still carried the scars of the chisels that had carved it. Abby tried to imagine the gravediggers who'd quarried out the catacombs by hand, trapped below ground without light or air. How did they survive?

Dr Lusetti put a hand on the wall. 'You know this rock? It is called *tufa*. In a natural state, it is soft and easy to quarry, but when you expose it to the air, it becomes hard like concrete. It is why the catacombs were so easy to dig—and why they have survived so well.'

The walls weren't solid. From floor to ceiling, with minimal gaps in between, shelves had been cut into them. Some lay open; others were walled up with pieces of tile or marble. The whole effect was to make the walls seem like giant filing cabinets.

'*Cubicula*,' Lusetti said. 'This is where they buried the people.'

He pointed his head torch at a marble plaque. Scratched into the striated surface was a crude X-P Christogram. 'They decorated the tombs so they knew where to find their ancestors.'

It made Abby think of something. 'Do you know a symbol called the staurogram?'

'Of course.'

'Are there any instances of it down here?'

Lusetti frowned. 'This catacomb has been closed for many years—it is a long time ago I have been down myself. And most of the inscribed pieces have been stolen by the thieves.'

For the first few hundred yards, a string of electric bulbs lit their way. Then they gave out. The

438

lamps on their helmets were the only light now, four narrow beams nodding and swivelling as they advanced deeper into the tunnel.

'How did people find their way down here?' Mark asked. Abby thought he only said it to hear the sound of a human voice.

Lusetti's torch beam moved to a small niche, about waist high. 'This shelf is for an oil lamp. We find them everywhere we dig in the catacombs. In Roman times, you saw hundreds, maybe thousands of lamps lighting the way.'

They carried on, past countless rows of *cubiculae*. After another twenty yards, the tunnel split into three. They halted.

'Which way now?' Barry asked.

'There's no sign of Dragović's people.' Mark's torch beam inscribed an arc across the walls as he looked around, back the way they'd come. 'If he's coming, he hasn't arrived yet. We should get back upstairs and set up the surveillance.'

He hates this even more than me, Abby thought. She wondered if the catacomb had tapped some dark terror—or if it was just the discomfort of youth suddenly faced with the bare bones of mortality. She forced herself to breathe slowly. *It's not an evil place*, she told herself. On the wall, her torch beam settled on a small piece of marble lodged in the opening of a cubicula. IN PACE, said the inscription, and even Abby knew what it meant. *In Peace*. Next to it was a Christogram, and above it a crudely drawn dove with an olive branch in its mouth.

Peace and hope. For a moment, Abby glimpsed the humanity of the people who'd been buried here, row upon row of them patiently waiting. The tombs

439

no longer seemed so macabre. They felt almost companionable.

Her beam moved along—and as it moved, it caught something. A shadow in the stone, a pattern flitting into the light like a moth. She turned her head back slowly, trying to pin it down.

There. The design was thin and shallow, angled slightly so that lit from below it cast almost no shadow. It was only because the lamp was mounted on her helmet that she'd caught it. Even then, she had to keep the beam slightly oblique: if she pointed it straight, the incisions melted back into the rock. The shape that had governed her life since Michael gave her a jewellery box in Pristina two months ago. The staurogram. It sat above the door of the left-hand passage, inviting her on.

She squeezed past Lusetti and padded down the passage. She heard a plaintive 'Hey' from Mark behind her, but ignored him. Ten yards further along, the passage ended at a T-junction. She looked left and right, and there it was again: the same symbol carved above the left doorway.

The saving sign that lights the path ahead.

*   *   *

Lusetti led the way, with Barry and Mark behind him. Abby brought up the rear. Sometimes she imagined she could hear soft footsteps behind her, though each time she pointed her torch back down the tunnel she saw nothing but the graves.

It was like walking through fog—timeless and placeless. The rows of tombs, sometimes interrupted by doorways that led into small chambers where richer or grander families had

440

been buried; the dark passages that forked and crossed, weaving a web deep underground. If the staurograms had led them in a circle, they might have followed it round and round for ever.

They went down a staircase, then another. The air grew colder. The ground underfoot was damp and clammy, like wet sand. The ceiling got lower, pressed down by the weight of the world above them. Abby lost count of the number of turns they'd made. Without the staurograms, she was pretty certain they'd never find their way out.

They stopped—so abruptly she bumped into Mark. The tunnel had reached a T-junction. Lusetti, in the lead, shone his torch right and left, and right again.

'There is no mark here.'

'There must be,' said Mark. Tension told in his voice. 'They can't have brought us all this way to drop us now.'

'*They*?' echoed Lusetti. 'You think *they* are leading you where you want to go?'

Four torch beams crisscrossed the grainy rock. All they illuminated was the scrapes and gouges of the hand tools that had cut the passage. And, ahead, a dirty brick wall filling a niche in the rock from floor to ceiling.

'Is this recent?' Mark asked. Lusetti shook his head.

'This is Roman brickwork.'

'Maybe we're supposed to go straight on,' Abby said. She edged past Mark and Barry and tapped the brickwork. Even after so many centuries, it felt solid.

'I think maybe—'

The bullet caught Mark clean in the chest. The

441

gunshot roared down the catacomb. Barry dropped to one knee, turned and squeezed off three shots of his own. Abby hurled herself to the floor of the passage and started to crawl.

More shots echoed behind her; lights flashed. In the tight space, it sounded like an artillery battle. She picked herself up and ran down the tunnel, looking for a side passage that might help lose her in the labyrinth.

The tunnel ended in a rough-finished wall. No bricks, no turnings—just a piece of rock where the diggers' patience or will had run out, where they'd shouldered their tools and turned for the surface.

The sound of gunfire settled in the tunnel like dust. The silence was even more unnerving, though it didn't last long. From behind—not far—Abby heard slow footsteps coming after her.

Metal snapped on metal as the slide of a gun slid back.

XLVI

Constantinople—June 337
Someone must have died. At this moment, I don't know if it's him or me. The man I'm looking at died on a beach eleven years ago. I put the knife in his back myself; I carried his corpse halfway across the empire and buried it in the deepest hole I could find.

And now he's standing in front of me—living, breathing, dark eyes watching me.

I close my eyes, squeezing them until all I see is spots. When I reopen them, he's still there.

442

It's all I can do to stop my stomach emptying itself on the floor. My head feels as if it's about to break open. This isn't possible.

I concentrate on the eyes. Are they really his? They've lost their clarity, as though a veil's been drawn over them. They don't seem to focus. He looks bewildered, as though he doesn't know what he's doing here.

I don't either.

'Crispus?' I stammer.

Something like terror creases his face. He steps away, sinking into the shadows. I'm glad. Having to look at him is like staring at the sun: too stark, too painful to endure.

I turn to Porfyrius.

'How have you done this?'

'I told you.'

'It's impossible.'

'Nothing is impossible through God,' he answers calmly. 'Do you want to stick your fingers into the scar you made in his back?'

How does he know I stabbed Crispus in the back? Everyone believes he was poisoned.

'Impossible,' I whisper again.

'Once, I thought the same as you.'

'And why . . . ?'

From outside, rendered distant by the thick walls, I hear the blare of trumpets. Constantine's funeral procession must be coming near. And with the sound, a resonance. At long last, too late, I know what Porfyrius is going to do.

'You're going to present . . . *him* . . . as Constantine's successor.'

'When the flames go up and the eagle flies out of the fire, the people will see Constantine's true heir.

443

A miracle. What chance will Constantius and his brothers have against that?' A chuckle. 'Of course, we've bribed some of the guards as well. They'll cut Constantius to pieces, and Crispus will rally the empire.'

'With you behind the throne telling him what to do?'

'This isn't about me,' he snaps. 'This is for the empire, and for God.'

I've heard too many people telling me they've done things for God recently. 'Is this all because of the Arians? Because of Eusebius and Alexander?' Compared with the enormity of what I've just witnessed, their jealousies and hair-splitting seem irrelevant.

'I couldn't give two obols for Eusebius, or his enemies.' There's genuine frustration in Porfyrius's voice. 'Do you think Christ returned from the dead so that men would kill each other debating whether he was co-eternal or consubstantial with the Father? Eusebius and his kind are like men who inherit a book of wisdom and simply use it as kindling for a cooking fire.'

I'm lost. 'What then?'

'I'm doing this for Constantine. Because he was right—that unity is the only way to save the empire from tearing itself apart. One God, one church, one emperor. The moment you divide it, the divisions multiply on themselves until they consume the world in chaos. Constantine knew that—but in the end, he wasn't strong enough to defeat the forces of chaos. By this miracle, we have a second chance.'

I try to digest it. So much of what he's saying makes such perfect sense, it's easy to forget it's built on the most ludicrous foundation.

444

In order to rule the world, we have to have the perfect virtue of one rather than the weakness of many.

Crispus—the new Crispus—is still obscured in the shadows. Out of sight, the shock receding, reason reasserts itself.

'Do you really think the people will accept this imposter you've dug up?'

'They'll accept it because it's the truth.' A grunt. 'And because they're desperate to believe.'

A knock sounds from the door, the same intricate pattern that Porfyrius used. One of his men cracks it open.

'It's time.'

*   *   *

Rome—Present Day

There was nowhere to hide—not even a niche. The gravediggers hadn't cut any *cubicula* here. With a flash of despair, she realised even the darkness didn't hide her. The lamp on her helmet was still on, shining its futile light on the rock wall and drawing her pursuers like a beacon.

She thought of what Mark had said—almost his last words, it turned out. *They can't have brought us all this way to drop us now.* It reminded her of a line from an old gospel record her parents used to play when she was a child.

Nobody told me that the road would be easy.

'Abby?'

It was the last voice she expected to hear—warm and reassuring in the darkest place imaginable.

'Michael?'

'You can come out now.'

She didn't ask why or how; she didn't stop to think. She turned back and walked slowly around the bend in the tunnel. There was Michael, caught in the head torch like a deer in headlights. And there, behind him, two men with raised guns.

There was no fight left in her. All she could do was stare.

Michael gave a sad, tight smile. 'I'm sorry, Abby. I had no choice.'

A fourth man appeared in the shadows beyond them, a dark silhouette against a light whose source she couldn't see. He was smaller than the others, a slight man with close-cropped hair, maybe a small beard. He seemed to absorb light: the only part of him that reflected anything was the chrome-handled pistol tucked in his waistband.

'Abigail Cormac. Again, I have to ask you: why are you not dead?'

Dragović. Abby had no answer. He laughed, then shrugged.

'It does not matter. Now that I have you, you will wish you were dead. Many times, before I let you die.'

One of his men came down the passage and pinned her arms. She didn't resist. He dragged her back to the junction. Her feet kicked against something soft and recently human on the ground; she didn't look down.

Dragović's men all had head torches, though no helmets. They trained their beams on the brick wall.

'This is the place you came to,' said Dragović. 'Left is nothing; right is nothing. I think we must go straight on.'

One of his men—Abby counted four, plus

446

Dragović and Michael—stepped forward and unslung the backpack he carried. From inside, he took out a nail gun and a coil of plastic tube that looked like a fat clothesline. He fired three nails into the brickwork, then wrapped the tube around them like wool, making a rough triangle against the bricks. Two metal plugs and a length of electrical cable came out of the bag. He stuck the plugs into the tube, then unspooled the cable. The hands that gripped Abby pulled her back down the tunnel; the others followed. Round a corner, they paused.

'You're going to be OK,' Michael whispered in her ear.

They all crouched down. Her guard released her, though only so he could put his hands over his ears. Abby did the same. The man at the front connected the wires to a small, remote-control box.

Abby didn't see him press the button. All she felt was the blast, pulsing through her hands and into her ears; and a punch of air against her chest. Fine grit rained down from the ceiling; Abby braced herself for worse, for the whole catacomb to shake itself apart and bury her. It didn't happen.

The man with the detonator ran forward, shouted something. They all advanced down the tunnel. Now the wall was just a heap of bricks, wreathed in a cloud of dust that was still settling. The dust blocked the torch beams, but as it swirled small holes appeared in the cloud, letting the light through. Not on to brick or stone, but into dark space beyond.

One by one they ducked through the hole. For a moment, all Abby could feel was the dust, coating her tongue, choking her lungs. She gagged. Then she was through.

447

In the deepest part of the catacomb, seven torch beams played over a chamber that hadn't been seen in seventeen centuries. It reminded Abby of the tomb in Kosovo: larger, though not much— perhaps three metres long and almost square, with a barrel ceiling just high enough for them all to stand upright. Every surface was painted: an eclectic mix of doves and fish, ranked soldiers standing to attention, a clean-shaven Jesus peering out from behind a huge Bible, and bearded saints or prophets leaning on their staffs. A curved niche filled one end, flanked on the walls by two enormous painted symbols, the Christogram and the staurogram.

☧   ☧

Between them, filling the niche, stood a coffin. Not a plain stone affair, as had served for Gaius Valerius Maximus: Abby could tell at once that this was different. It was made from a lustrous purple marble, intricately carved. Two rows of cavalry trotted towards each other on its face; on its pitched lid, a flotilla of boats seemed to be engaged in a naval battle. Even in the torchlight, the detail leapt out at Abby: every oar and rower, every link of armour and twist of rope.

'How did they ever get that down here?' Michael wondered aloud.

Dragović walked across the chamber. He bent over the sarcophagus, put his cheek against the surface and stretched out his arms to embrace it, communing with the cold stone.

'Porphyry,' he said. 'The right and prerogative of emperors.'

'Is that . . . Constantine's?' Abby asked.

'Constantine was buried in Istanbul.' Dragović straightened and turned to Michael. 'This, I think, is for Constantine's son Crispus.'

There was something in the way that he spoke to Michael that chilled Abby. Not cruelty or malice—familiarity.

She looked at Michael. 'How did you get here?'

'They caught me just outside Split. I didn't have a chance.'

Dragović heard him and laughed.

'Don't lie to your little girlfriend. You still think she loves you? You came to *me,* just like in Kosovo. And for the same reason. Because you wanted money.'

Abby felt a pit opening inside her. 'What about Irina?'

'Irina?' Dragović asked. 'Who is Irina, please?'

Michael's shoulders slumped. 'There was no Irina.'

'But—the photo? In your apartment.'

'Her name's Cathy. My ex-wife. She's never been to the Balkans. So far as I know, she's living with her second husband back in Donegal.'

Abby felt another part of her world collapsing in on her. Dragović sensed her pain and chuckled.

'You thought he was one of the angels? The good sheriff in the white hat?' He jerked his head dismissively. 'He wanted money. Like everyone.'

Abby stared at Michael, willing it not to be true. '*Why?* What happened to doing the right thing? Fighting the barbarians?'

Michael tried to force a grin, a ghost of his old

449

insouciance. He couldn't quite make it. His face simply looked broken.

'If you can't beat them . . .'

Dragović had lost interest. He barked an order: his men surrounded the sarcophagus, one on each point. Stubby crowbars came out of a backpack. They levered them under the lid, cursing and sweating.

'How did they get that down here?' Michael said again. He'd turned so that he had his back to Abby.

Dragović pointed to a thin crack down the corner. 'They bring it in as panels and cement it together. Like IKEA.'

The four men leaned on their crowbars. They were large men, built like weightlifters, but they struggled to make an impact on the purple stone.

'Maybe we use some detcord?' grunted one.

'No.' Dragović was watching them intently, his whole body tensed. In that moment, Abby almost thought she could have slipped away without being noticed. She didn't dare try.

'We do nothing to damage the *labarum*.'

The men heaved again. The bars strained, the stone resisted. Nothing gave. Abby felt the tension taut in the air, the quiver of something about to snap.

The bars moved—first one corner, then spreading to all four. A deep rumble rolled around the room.

The lid lifted and slid back. Dragović walked forward and peered into the open coffin.

*   *   *

450

Constantinople—June 337

The sun from the open door is a blinding, brilliant white. Porfyrius turns to me.

'It's time. Are you with us, or against us?'

I'm alone, I want to say.

'We can tie you up, leave you here until it's over. Or you can join us.'

There's no choice. I have to see how this ends. 'I'll come.'

I follow them up the stairs. In daylight, I can see that there are about twenty of them, mostly with the close-cropped hair and straight shoulders of military men. They're dressed in white Schola uniforms, though that doesn't mean anything. The *man*—I still can't bring myself to call him Crispus—is near the front; all I can see is his back. His hair is curly, almost touching his collar—longer than he wore it eleven years ago, but still jet black. Is there a hunch to his left shoulder, a stiffness when he moves? Does he remember what I said to him on that beach? If only I could have five minutes alone with him, I could be sure one way or the other.

The scaffolding's still standing at the rear of the mausoleum, screened from the crowds who have gathered on the ground outside. I can hear their quiet roar as we climb the ladders, criss-crossing back and forth up the platforms. No one tries to stop us.

Just below the copper dome, there's a walkway around the outside of the rotunda. A stone balustrade guards it, with latticed metalwork in between the pillars. The outside is painted gold, though from behind all you see is iron.

We crouch beneath the balustrade and wait. Peering through the lattice, I can see the audience

451

settling. The senators and generals have taken their seats on the banked stands facing the pyre; the legions have drawn up in scarlet squares around them, with the great mass of people behind straining for a view.

How many of them will be alive at sunset if Porfyrius has his way? He says he wants to unite the empire—but even Constantine needed twenty years of fighting to achieve it. Not everyone will accept Porfyrius's miraculous proposition on faith.

I try to get a glimpse of Crispus, but the walkway's narrow and jammed with Porfyrius's men. Crispus is out of sight, further around the curve of the building.

Down in the city below, the funeral bier is still making its slow progress up the hill. I turn to Porfyrius, crouched beside me.

'Did Alexander discover *him*? Your secret? Is that why you killed him in the library?'

Porfyrius wipes sweat from his eyes. 'He discovered it in the worst way possible. Crispus had come to meet me in the library that day—there were papers he needed to see. Alexander saw him and recognised him. Crispus panicked; he grabbed the first thing that came to hand and lashed out. He's strong. One blow was all it took.'

'He bludgeoned his old tutor to death?' I shake my head. 'The Crispus I knew would never have done that.'

'Death changes a man. And these are desperate times.'

Porfyrius turns away and studies the landscape below. The tail end of the procession has finally made it into the mausoleum compound. The crowds slow its path as it winds its way to the pyre—hundreds of arms reach across the barriers just to touch the hem of the shroud. The priests who accompanied the bier from the palace have suddenly melted away, even Eusebius. None of them wants to witness this ancient rite, the way Romans have buried their rulers since the time of the kings. Afterwards, when the ashes are cold and the army dispersed, they'll perform their own Christian ritual in the sanitised presence of the holy apostles. Though by then, things might be very different.

The bier reaches the pyre. Six guards lift the body off and carry it up a flight of stairs to the first floor of the wooden tower. From here, I can't tell if it's the wax effigy or the real man—not that it matters. A solitary figure in a golden robe mounts the dais in front of it. He's got his back to me: I can only see the top of his head, sparkling from the pearls in his crown. I guess it's Constantius.

Shouts ring out—not from below, but from up on the rooftop behind us. A hidden door's opened; palace guards are pouring out of it on to the walkway. Swords clash as Porfyrius's men wake up to the danger and try to beat them back.

The last battle for Constantine begins.

*　　　*　　　*

Rome—Present Day
Dragović stared into the open coffin. The beam from his head torch shone down like a lance. Standing in the back corner of the chamber, Abby couldn't see his face, but she saw the change in his body. He seemed to sag; he gripped the rim and swung his head from side to side as if drunk.

He turned back. All the venom had drained from his face.

'It's empty.'

His men peered in. Michael stepped forward and joined them. He reached in his hand, shoulder deep, and felt around. It came out closed in a fist, but when he opened it, there was nothing there but dust. It trickled through his fingers.

'All for nothing,' he murmured. 'No *labarum*. Not even a body.'

Dragović rubbed his hand along the top edge of the sarcophagus. By his light, Abby saw chips and gouges chewed out of the lip.

'Someone has been here before.' He swung back towards Michael. Suddenly, the silver pistol was in his hand and aimed at Michael's heart. 'Maybe you thought you could cheat Zoltán Dragović?'

Michael stepped back against the wall. Behind him, a forlorn Jonah disappeared into the mouth of a giant blue whale.

'For Christ's sake, it was bricked up hundreds of years ago.'

'It's true,' Abby said desperately. 'Dr Lusetti— the archaeologist who was with us—he said those bricks were Roman. If grave robbers were here, they were Roman grave robbers.'

Michael held out his arms in innocence. Dragović looked at his gun. From the cave floor, an electric buzz sounded from one of the backpacks that had been laid beside the sarcophagus.

The man beside it lifted the flap of the pack and pulled out a small handset, linked by a wire to an unseen antenna in the backpack. He read something off the display and swore.

'That was Darko,' he said in Serbian. 'He says

454

carabinieri have entered the catacomb.'

Dragović nodded. Far from worrying him, the threat seemed to restore his energy.

'Rig the explosives,' he ordered.

'What about the coffin?'

'Leave it. It's empty.'

More of the plastic tubing came out. Working briskly, the men began punching nails into the roof of the chamber and attaching the explosives. Dragović turned to Michael.

'You know the good thing about catacombs?'

'What?'

'It's no problem to dispose of the body.'

Abby saw what he was going to do a split second before it happened. She launched herself at Dragović, but his finger was already on the trigger. The gun fired; the bullet tore open Michael's chest. He slammed back against the wall.

Abby screamed. Her momentum carried her on towards Dragović, but his men were faster. An outstretched arm blocked her progress; two hands wrapped around her waist and almost lifted her off the ground. Dragović spun around. His face glowed with savage delight as he raised the gun and put it against her forehead. The heat of the barrel scalded her. She struggled, but couldn't move.

By the wall, Michael slumped to the ground and lay still.

'Are you going to kill me too?' The words sounded sluggish, drowned in noise. Her ears were still ringing from the gunshot. Dragović couldn't have been much better, but he understood the sense. He thumbed back the hammer. Anticipation lit up his eyes.

Across the room, one of his men tapped his

watch, muttering something about carabinieri. Dragović nodded and lowered the gun.

'Later. Maybe for now we need a hostage to get out of here.'

The men gathered their packs. The last of the explosives were rigged to the ceiling—heavy bricks, as well as the thin tube connecting them. It looked like enough to bring down the whole catacomb.

'Why are you doing this?' Abby asked. A bleak numbness had settled over her, a fatalism that knew no fear because it knew no hope. She didn't look at Michael's body in the corner.

'Sometimes it is useful for people to believe you are dead. Michael Lascaris should have obeyed that rule.'

One by one, they crossed the brick rubble back into the main catacomb. On the threshold, Abby turned back. For a second, she saw the two symbols on the wall, the purple sarcophagus cracked open, and Michael's corpse curled on the floor. Then it vanished.

*   *   *

Constantinople—June 337
This is the war Constantine wanted to avoid, played out in miniature sixty feet above his tomb. Roman against Roman, soldiers in identical uniforms, except the badges on their shields. It's a small battle, more of a wrestling match—the narrow walkway makes it hard for the soldiers to wield their swords—but no less savage for that. That close, you can smell every drop of blood or oil on the blade that stabs you.

Most extraordinary, the crowds on the ground

456

have no idea it's happening. We're hidden behind the lattice; they can't see through its dazzling mesh from the outside. Down below, Constantius is still giving his oration to his father; the senators and generals are listening in their seats; the captain of the guard is holding a burning brand, ready to light the pyre. They don't know that the corpses are already piling up in Constantine's mausoleum.

Blood spatters the white stone. The battle slows as bodies choke the walkway. We're being attacked from both sides, but we're still moving. Flavius Ursus's men—I assume they're Ursus's men—are edging us round to the back of the building where they can finish us off. Some of the guards have blocked the door; others are keeping us back from the scaffolding so we can't escape.

Porfyrius's men make a human bulwark either side of us, but they're slowly being whittled back. It occurs to me, quite calmly, that I'll die here: a blood sacrifice at Constantine's tomb. I can't see Crispus. Is he dead already?

Porfyrius is shouting something in my ear, pointing up. A roofer's ladder leans against the rotunda, leading up to the dome. Ursus's guards are hemming us ever closer. I start to climb. The ladder wobbles and sways under the press of men at its base. A sword flashes so close it almost severs my ankle. Hands try to pull me down, but I kick them off. From the corner of my eye, I see Porfyrius go down.

I come over the lip of the roof and cry out in agony. The copper tiles are blinding, and when I touch them I feel my skin shrivel. I swallow the pain and haul myself up. Ahead, through the glare, I can see a crouched figure staggering up the pitched

457

copper tiles to the top of the dome. I crawl after him, using the folds of my toga to try and stop the metal burning me. I think it might catch fire, but I don't care. All I want with what's left of my life is to ask him one question.

Are you really him?

Below, the spectators have begun to realise something is happening. A murmur sweeps the crowd, loud enough that I can hear it on the rooftop. Senators crane around in their seats to look up. Constantius, on the dais, seems to falter and look back.

This is the moment.

At the top of the dome, the roof flattens around an open circular hole: the *oculus*, the eye for the sun to peer in to the mausoleum. Crispus scrambles to the edge, turns and stands. He faces the crowd arms spread apart in divine embrace.

On the dais, next to Constantius, Flavius Ursus grabs the burning torch from a guard's hand and hurls it on to the pyre. It's well primed with oil and pitch: the flames catch straight away, racing up the columns of the wooden tower. Inexorably, the fire draws the crowd's attention away from the action on the roof.

Crouched on my hands and knees, I stare up at Crispus. He looms over me like a god; like a god, I doubt he even sees me.

'Are you him?' My throat's parched, my voice a burned-out whisper. But somehow, above the crackle of the pyre and the roar of the crowd, he seems to hear me. He looks down; he smiles at me, warm with forgiveness.

A shadow darkens the blazing air. Crispus cries out and clutches his side. Blood blooms in his tunic; an arrow hangs from his ribs. Archers have appeared on the roof of the eastern portico surrounding the courtyard. Another arrow hits him in the shoulder. He staggers back.

He hangs on the edge of the *oculus*. The copper tiles shimmer under his feet, creating the illusion that he's hovering in the air. For a moment, I can almost believe he'll rise above it, lifted by angels away from danger.

Without a sound, he falls back through the hole. The arrows are still falling, clattering on the roof, but they don't hit me. I crawl to the edge and peer down.

Far below, in an alcove against the back wall, I can see the huge porphyry sarcophagus waiting to receive Constantine's body. In front of it, sprawled in the very heart of the starburst sun laid into the floor, lies a corpse. The marble rays splay out around him; through the *oculus*, the sun makes an almost perfect circle of light around him.

A fragment of shadow breaks the circle. After a moment, I realise it's my own.

*   *   *

Rome—Present Day
They hurried along the passages, following the footsteps they'd left in the soft mud floor. The detonator wire unspooled behind them. They hadn't quite reached the first staircase when the man at the back called a halt.

'No more wire,' he said.

For the first time, Abby saw a hint of concern cross Dragović's face. 'Are we far enough?'

The man pursed his lips. 'This place is old—and

459

we put a lot of plastic in there.'

'You stay here,' Dragović told him. 'Give us two minutes.'

The man pulled out the control box and plugged in the wires. Abby wondered if she could get at him, if she might detonate the explosives too soon and bring the roof down on Dragović. But there was another man between them, and the tunnel was too narrow to get past.

'Maybe five minutes is safer?'

'Two. The carabinieri must be close.'

Dragović led them on. They all felt the urgency now. Heavy boots kicked at Abby's heels; several times, a hand on her back pushed her forward when she started to falter. She tried to count off seconds in her head, but the remorseless pace disrupted any rhythm. *How long was two minutes?* Long enough? Perhaps she wasn't ready to die after all.

They reached the stairs and hurried up to the second level. Here there was a wider chamber, a sort of crossroads where four tunnels intersected. The floor was rocky, the footprints harder to make out. Dragović studied it for a second.

He doesn't know the way, Abby thought.

'What's that?'

The man beside Dragović pointed down one of the tunnels. Abby followed his gaze. Around a bend, a dim light glowed, getting steadily brighter.

'Carabinieri.'

'Split up,' Dragović ordered. 'We can lose them in the tunnels.'

They moved apart. Abby made to follow the guard behind her, but Dragović grabbed her collar and pushed her in front of him.

'You come with me. In case I need—'

460

A muted roar rose out of the depths of the catacomb. *Two minutes.* The first thing Abby noticed was the air racing past her—not out of the catacomb but back, sucked in by the explosion. A moment later it came rushing back with interest, a pressure wave sharpened with a million pieces of grit and sand that stripped her skin raw. The earth shook so hard she thought it would split open the rock.

She didn't look; she didn't wait. She turned her back—on the explosion, on Dragović, on the pieces of rock that were shaking loose from the roof—and ran. Down the nearest tunnel, without thought for where it led, just so long as it was *away*.

But she wouldn't escape that easily. Someone else had the same idea. Among the rumbling echoes of the explosion and shifting rubble, she heard the quickfire beat of footsteps chasing after her.

She couldn't outrun him. All she could think of was to hide. The walls here were lined with *cubiculae*, the narrow shelves where the dead had once been laid to rest. *If it's big enough for a corpse, it ought to be big enough for me.* She turned off the lamp on her head torch, lay down on the ground and squeezed her way in.

The rock pressed her like a vice. She turned her head ninety degrees, one cheek against the roof and the other against the floor. She pulled her arm as tight to her body as she could. She tried to breathe, but the rock beat down on her chest and forced the air out.

The footsteps came closer. A beam of light, dulled by dust or dying batteries, played along the stone corridor. Abby prayed he wouldn't look down.

'Abigail?' Dust slurred Dragovic's voice. 'You think you can escape? You think Zoltán Dragović ever forgets his enemies?'

He gave a cough that turned into a snarling laugh.

'Let me give you a piece of advice, Abigail, from a man who has seen many dark places in this world. If you want to hide in the dark, you should not wear a reflective coat.'

Squeezed between the rock, she saw Dragovic's boots stop six inches from her face. Even if she'd wanted to, she couldn't have moved. She closed her eyes and listened for her own death.

More footsteps—what was he doing? A choked shout; a cry of surprise. A single gunshot, and a heavy thud that she felt rather than heard. Then nothing.

In that ancient catacomb, time became a river flowing through her. She didn't know how long she lay there in the grave. It could have been an hour, or a day or three. Her only companion was stone. Its smell filled her nose; it pressed against her ears until the blood pumping through them felt like the pulse of the rock. It embraced her, so that she no longer knew where flesh ended and rock began. With nowhere to flow, her tears pooled in her eyes. She wondered if, given a few millennia, they might bore a channel to the surface and well up as a spring.

But, by degrees, feeling returned. She felt pins and needles prickling her legs; an ache in her shoulder where a knob of rock dug into it. She reached out into the passage. The space felt good.

Tentatively, tugging with her free arm, she wriggled herself out of the niche into the tunnel.

462

She felt the smooth plastic dome of her helmet, and when she flicked the switch on the lamp it came on.

Dragović lay a few feet away, dead, a single bullet punched through his skull. Abby looked at him for a moment, just to be sure. Then she turned and headed for the light.

XLVII

Constantinople—July 337

The palace is still unfinished, but renovations have already started. Murals have been whitewashed over, ready to take new paint; inscriptions filled in with cement. A whole mosaic floor showing the labours of ancient heroes has been lifted out, to be replaced with salutary scenes from the life of Christ. Through a doorway, I glimpse a room crowded with statucs: a marble host stoically awaiting their fate. Soon they'll be sold off, or recut into something more fashionable. I can empathise.

An age has passed. Constantine is sealed in his porphyry sarcophagus, surrounded by the Christian apostles. Porfyrius's corpse, rescued from the rooftop, is embalmed and on a boat to Rome, in accordance with his last wishes. I don't know what happened to Crispus. The body was gone by the time I came down from the rooftop.

I'm the last one left. An old man, standing in a corridor, waiting to hear his fate.

The door opens. A slave beckons me in. Flavius Ursus stands behind a desk, arms folded. Two secretaries sit in front of him with tablets and styli. A breeze blows through the open window from one of the inner courtyards, chattering with the sound of a fountain.

He dismisses the secretaries and studies me. His face is unreadable.

'You've had an extraordinary life, Gaius Valerius.'

I note the past tense.

'There's been a lot of discussion of what you've done. Some men think you should be executed for your part in the plot against the Emperor. Others say you saved the empire.'

I stay silent. Whatever they've said, the judgement's already been made.

'Some people are saying that they saw Constantine that day, his spirit rising above the pyre to heaven. The new Bishop of Constantinople hasn't contradicted them.'

The new Bishop of Constantinople is Eusebius. Constantius confirmed him in the post last week.

'As for what you were doing on the roof, with known enemies of the state . . .' He shakes his head. 'If you hadn't sent me that message, things might have been different. As it is, everything is settled as it should be.'

Everything is settled. Constantine's three sons—Constantius, Claudius and Constans—will divide their inheritance equally. Each with his own court, each with his own army needing conquests, battle and spoils. *I give it three years before there's open war.*

'You did the right thing,' he says. 'You've earned your rest. Go back to your villa in Moesia and enjoy your retirement.'

There's something else he wants to say. He stares out the window into the courtyard, trying to find

464

the words. He picks up a marble paperweight, a bird, and plays with it absent-mindedly.

'You of all men ought to know. Up on the roof—was it really . . . ?'

'No,' I say firmly.

'I didn't think so.' He puts down the bird. His hand reaches for a piece of paper, another piece of work. Instinctively, he starts to read it. When he looks up, he's surprised to see I'm still there.

'My secretary will give you the necessary permissions on your way out. Go home to Moesia and rest.'

A reassuring smile, one old soldier to another.

'If anything comes up, I'll send someone.'

*   *   *

Belgrade, Serbia—June
It felt like the first day of summer. On Knez Mihailova, you could barely move for all the tables and chairs jamming the pavement outside the cafés. Geraniums spilled out from the concrete planters. Abby, dressed for work in a cream suit, sat bare-legged in the sun and picked away at an ice cream, letting it melt on her tongue. Behind her, a big-screen television showed a tennis match from Wimbledon.

She saw Nikolić, scanning the café tables with a newspaper under his arm, and waved him over.

'You look well,' she said.

'You too.'

He ordered a coffee and angled his chair so as not to be distracted by the TV. He looked anxious, Abby thought. *Fair enough, given that last time we ended up making him our getaway driver.*

'Thanks for agreeing to see me.'

'A pleasure. You are in Belgrade on business?'

'Different business to last time. I'm back in my old job with the International Criminal Tribunal. We're here for some meetings.'

'On the side of the sheriff. Last time, I was not so sure.'

'Neither was I.' It was the first time she'd been back to Belgrade since she'd fled that day in Nikolić's car. She'd been nervous about returning; she'd avoided the Kalemegdan Citadel. But the seasons had changed—she'd changed.

As unemotionally as she could, she told him what had happened: the message hidden in the poem, how they'd gone to Istanbul—

'But in 326, Constantine intended he would be buried in Rome,' Nikolić interrupted.

'If you'd been with us, you could have saved us a trip. We worked it out in the end.'

She carried on: the catacomb, the staurograms, and the sarcophagus that had been walled up for centuries. Nikolić heard her out in silence, letting his coffee go cold.

When she'd finished, he sat for a long time in silence.

'Every time I see you, your story is more remarkable.'

Her ice cream had melted into a pool at the bottom of the dish. She scooped it up with her spoon.

'Everything except the ending. The coffin was empty—it was all for nothing.'

'Dragović died,' he reminded her. 'I saw it on television—his body pulled out of the ground. They had to show it here so we would believe he was

466

dead.' He thought a moment longer.

'Of course, there is another possibility.'

'What?'

'There is another legend associated with Constantine. His mother Helena made a pilgrimage to the Holy Land just before she died. There, it is said, the Christians showed her the place where the True Cross had been kept secret since the Crucifixion of Christ. One report says that she proved it was the right one by bringing an old peasant woman back from the dead.'

Behind her, on the grass at Wimbledon, the Serbian player had won a set. People at the surrounding tables applauded and shouted encouragement.

'You think—?'

'Your poem—this word which is *signum* in Latin, *tropaion* in Greek. I said it has many meanings. It can be a battle standard or a military insignia—but it is also used by religious writers to refer to the Cross.'

'The saving sign that lights the path ahead.'

'And the symbol you found—the staurogram. I told you comes from the Greek word *stavros*, meaning "cross". Many people think it is a variant of Constantine's Christogram, but in fact it has a different origin. In very early manuscripts, scribes used it as an abbreviation, a shorthand symbol for writing "cross".'

Abby considered it. 'You're saying we might have found the True Cross—the one Jesus was actually crucified on—and not even known it?'

Nikolić thought for a moment, then smiled in defeat. 'Who knows? You said there was nothing in the coffin except dust. All history turns to dust

467

eventually.'

He waved to the waiter for another coffee. 'Maybe you can go down one time and have another look?'

She shivered at the thought. 'It's impossible. When Dragović blew up the tomb, he didn't just take out that bit of the catacomb. There was an apartment block sitting on top of it: the whole thing came down. The landlord poured about a million tons of concrete over it so he could rebuild quickly. It wasn't Vatican land so there was nothing they could do.'

'Maybe it is for the best.' He laughed, though only to cover something more genuine. 'The power to raise someone from the dead would be a terrible thing, much though we might wish it sometimes.'

Abby closed her eyes. The sun had moved, pushing back the shade of the umbrella so that her face was now fully exposed. The glare blinded her.

'In the catacomb . . .' She paused—this was something she hadn't told anyone. But she found she wanted Nikolić to know. 'At the end, when Dragović got shot. There were carabinieri in the tunnels, but they hadn't reached that part yet. And the bullet that killed him—they said they couldn't match it to any of the guns they use. You don't think . . .'

She slid her chair around, back into the shade, and shook her head decisively. 'Of course not. No one comes back from the dead. Not really.'

'Only in the Balkans.' Nikolić unfolded his newspaper. On the front page, a hard-faced man with spiky white hair stared at the camera with a malevolence that hadn't dimmed in the eighteen years since his exploits in Bosnia made him one of the world's most notorious men.

'Two years ago, this man's family had a court declare him legally dead. Yesterday, police found him alive and well in a flat across the river in Zemun.'

Abby knew the ending to this one. 'Tomorrow he'll be on a plane to the Hague to stand trial for crimes against humanity. I'm on the same flight.'

Nikolić looked satisfied. 'Was this something because of what happened to Dragović?'

'That's classified.' She grinned. 'But yes. Whenever there's a power shift, things open up. If we're lucky, a few of the bad guys fall through the cracks into our hands.' She took the bill out of the shotglass where the waiter had left it, and put some dinars on the table. 'There'll be someone else, a new Zoltán Dragović, picking up where he left off soon enough. It never goes away.'

'But if there are people like you pushing back, they cannot win either.'

Abby blushed at the compliment. They both stood and shook hands.

'I'll probably be in Belgrade quite a lot in the next few months. Perhaps we could have dinner some time.'

'I would like that.'

She leaned over and kissed him on the cheek. 'Thank you for saving me.'

'Go well, as the Romans used to say.'

*   *   *

Moesia—August 337
The fire's burned low; the slaves have gone to bed. Cold steam beads on the vault of my bathhouse and

drips in puddles on the floor. My tunic's soaked. Perhaps the murderers won't come tonight.

They'll come soon, though. For all Flavius Ursus's smiles, I know he won't let me live. I know too much, not just from the last three months but the last thirty years. I'm the past. As long as I'm alive they'll see me as a threat.

First they get rid of you, then they send the assassins.

I stare at my reflection in the bottom of the empty pool, a blurry likeness drifting above the nymphs and gods in the tiles. This is me. I've spent my life among men who stood like gods; when I'm gone, their names and faces will survive in stone and mine will wash away from history.

Unless . . .

Did Crispus rise from the dead? Was Porfyrius's story true, or just a vast lie to justify his coup? I've asked myself this question every hour of every day in the last two months. I still don't know. Sometimes I think of the glazed eyes and say it couldn't have been, but then I remember his last, forgiving smile and can't imagine it was anyone else.

Have I spent my whole life worshipping the wrong gods? I feel like a traveller who's nearing the end of a long journey, only to discover he's been facing the wrong way all that time. I've gone too far from where I started. But how can I continue on this path, even one more step, if I know it's the wrong direction?

Does it matter? If Crispus did rise, it was surely a miracle—but no different to the miracle the Christians profess, that a man was murdered and God brought him back. If this is God's gift, we hardly deserve it. Men like Eusebius and Asterius take their faith and use it as a weapon, dividing the world into those who are for them and against them. Constantine, for all his faults, tried harder than most to give the empire peace. He thought his new religion would achieve it. His mistake, I suppose, was to rely on the Christians rather than their god.

Symmachus: *The Christians are a confused and vicious sect.* I can't deny it. For what Asterius and Eusebius did, his verdict sounds too kind.

But should there be nothing good or true in the world because bad men might turn it to evil? Should we surrender the field to the persecutors and torturers, men like Maxentius and Galerius and old Maximian?

I remember a sentence I read in Alexander's book. *Humanity must be defended if we want to be worthy of the name of human beings.*

A knock at the door. A shiver of dread shakes through me, but it's just a reflex. I'm prepared. My tomb is dug, out in the woods beyond the house; a sealed jar with a few keepsakes—the scroll with my notes, Porfyrius's necklace—is waiting in my coffin. I'll take my secrets to the grave. If anyone ever finds me, let them puzzle out what it means. I've reached the end of my life and I don't know anything.

The knock sounds again, loud and impatient. No doubt Flavius Ursus keeps them busy these days, tying up loose ends. I shouldn't make them wait.

I get to my feet, but I don't look round. My gaze fixes at the bottom of the pool, a tiny piece of decoration I've never noticed before, where two tendrils of seaweed tangle over each other in white

471

space, making the sign of the Cross. Such a simple shape—you see it everywhere.

I'm ready. I'm not afraid of dying, or of what comes after. My voice, when I speak, is clear and strong.

'Come in.'

Historical Note

My first major encounter with Constantine the Great was an undergraduate essay titled 'Did Constantine feel he had a divine mission, and, if so, was it Christian?' This book is, in a way, an extended attempt to engage with that same question.

Paul Stephenson's recent biography of Constantine warns us how hard it is to be sure about the details of his life. 'The written sources do not exist or are partial; they have not been preserved or have been preserved by design; they have been altered or miscopied; they cannot simply be mined for data.' The best contemporary source, Eusebius's *Life of Constantine*, was written by a churchman with a very particular agenda and focus. Constantine's selective editing of his own history, described in this novel, was a real process. With that caveat, I've tried to be as accurate as possible regarding what the sources say about the history behind this book.

Most of the main characters in the historical narrative really existed. Publilius Optatianus Porfyrius was a poet, exile, and twice Prefect of Rome, who did actually write poems with secret messages which survive in many copies. Eusebius of Nicomedia was one of the principal churchmen of Constantine's reign, ringleader of the Arian faction during the Arian controversy, and later Bishop of Constantinople. You get some idea of the way he played power politics from the fact that within ten years of the Council of Nicaea (which was, after all, a defeat for him) all his leading opponents had ended up dead or in exile. Asterius the Sophist was a Christian who lapsed during the persecutions, was excommunicated, but remained active in church circles as an *éminence grise* of the Arian faction. Aurelius Symmachus was a Neoplatonist philosopher and politician from an eminent family of pagans. Flavius Ursus became Consul the year after Constantine's death, and is presumed to have been high up in the military command. Biographical details for all of them are incomplete, and I've used a novelist's licence to fill in the gaps.

The members of Constantine's family featured in the novel also all existed, and met more or less the fates described. Constantine's campaign of *damnatio memoriae* was so effective that the truth of what happened to Crispus and Fausta will always remain a mystery: my account follows the most widely circulated version of events.

One minor change I've made from the standard historical usage is the way I refer to Constantine's second son. He's more commonly known as Constantine II, but in a novel which already features one Constantine, two Constantiuses, a Constans and a Constantiana, it seemed less confusing to call him by his first name, Claudius.

Bishop Alexander is a fictional creation, composited from aspects of Eusebius of Caesarea and the Christian writer Lactantius, who tutored Crispus. The 'quotes' from Alexander's book in chapter eighteen are borrowed from Lactantius's *Divine Institutes*. Gaius Valerius is also fictional, though you can trace his career path in the lives of other men.

As for Constantine, he remains one of the most

474

significant, elusive and challenging figures in all history. His success in uniting the Roman Empire, almost for the last time, was extraordinary, though fleeting. His founding of Constantinople created a city that remained an imperial capital into the twentieth century. But his achievement in taking Christianity from a suspect cult to a world religion is as relevant today as in his lifetime. Almost seventeen hundred years after the battle of the Milvian Bridge, the faith he adopted remains the world's biggest religion. And wherever there's a church, chances are you'll hear the creed he called into being at Nicaea being recited, still the great unifier of Christianity.

The question posed in my undergraduate essay— did Constantine have a Christian mission?— is unanswerable. The imagery and narrative of Christianity, imperial Rome, Hercules, Apollo, the Unconquered Sun and other contemporary cults overlap so much that it's impossible to draw clear lines; I don't imagine Constantine did.

In the end, Constantine infuriates us for the same reason that Christianity angers its detractors: the painful gap between noble ideals and compromised reality. Constantine lived his life in that gap. How we judge him depends, ultimately, on how we judge ourselves.

Acknowledgements

A lot of people gave me a lot of help in researching and writing this book.

Jelena Mirkovi ć introduced me to Belgrade, and gave me three chapters I didn't expect. In Kosovo, Nick Hawton and his colleagues in the EULEX Press Office, especially Irina Gudeljevi ć, gave me invaluable insights into international life in Pristina. Captain Daniel Murphy showed me around Camp Bondsteel and gave me one of the most memorable days of any research trip; he was also unflagging in answering my questions when I tracked him down to North Dakota. I'm very grateful to Lieutenant Colonel Jerry Anderson, Major Robert Fugere and 1st Sergeant Rick Marschner, all of the North Dakota National Guard, for taking so much time to tcll mc about their work in Kosovo; also to Colonel Patrick Moran of the Irish Army, Major Hagen Messer of the German Army, and Lieutenant Toufik Bablah of the Moroccan Army for my visit to Camp Film City in Pristina.

A novel like this always trades in bad news and bad people. It's worth saying that my overwhelming impression of the EU and NATO personnel I met in Kosovo was of thoughtful professionals doing a difficult and essential job in a small corner of the world a long way from home. I left with huge admiration for them and the work they do.

Back in England, my sister Iona told me about the Foreign Office; Emma Davies told me about war crimes; Kevin Anderson told me about gunshot wounds; Sue and David Hawkins told me about

Istanbul; and Dr Tim Thompson told me about bones. Dr Linda Jones Hall steered me in the right direction for Porfyrius.

For every novel, there are a couple of books which become indispensable references. On this project, they were Paul Stephenson's superb biography *Constantine* (Quercus), and Timothy D. Barnes's meticulously detailed *The New Empire of Diocletian and Constantine* (Harvard University Press).

My colleagues in the Crime Writers' Association, especially Michael Ridpath, made my year as Chair hugely enjoyable, and played their part in making sure I escaped the traditional 'lost book' curse of the CWA. My agent Jane Conway-Gordon kept my blood sugar up. My editors Kate Elton and Kate Burke, and all their talented colleagues at Random House, did a wonderful job improving, producing and promoting the book.

My son Owen crawled through catacombs with me and took a memorable train ride to Ostia. His brother Matthew arrived bang on time, and made the months writing this book a delight when he could easily have sabotaged it beyond repair. And my wife Emma, as usual, made everything better.

Hoc 2/13
woodpath 12/15
O/L 4/17
DEK 8/18
OL 10/19
WP 3/20